SLIGHTLY MARRIED

Center Point
Large Print

**This Large Print Book carries the
Seal of Approval of N.A.V.H.**

SLIGHTLY MARRIED

MARY BALOGH

CENTER POINT PUBLISHING
THORNDIKE, MAINE

This Center Point Large Print edition
is published in the year 2003 by arrangement with
The Bantam Dell Publishing Group, a division of
Random House, Inc.

The text of this Large Print edition is unabridged. In other
aspects, this book may vary from the original edition. Printed in
Thailand. Set in 16-point Times New Roman type by
Bill Coskrey and Gary Socquet.

ISBN 1-58547-338-3

Cataloging-in-Publication data is available from the Library of Congress.

PROLOGUE

The scene was all too familiar to the man surveying it. There was not a great deal of difference between one battlefield and another, he had discovered through long experience—not, at least, when the battle was over.

The smoke of the heavy artillery and of the myriad muskets and rifles of two armies was beginning to clear sufficiently to reveal the victorious British and Allied troops establishing their newly won positions along the Calvinet Ridge to the east of the city and turning the big guns on Toulouse itself, into which the French forces under Soult's command had recently retreated. But the acrid smell lingered and mingled with the odors of dust and mud and horse and blood. Despite an ever-present noise—voices bellowing out commands, horses whinnying, swords clanging, wheels rumbling—there was the usual impression of an unnatural, fuzzy-eared silence now that the thunderous pounding of the guns had ceased. The ground was carpeted with the dead and wounded.

It was a sight against which the sensibilities of Colonel Lord Aidan Bedwyn never became totally hardened. Tall and solidly built, dark-complexioned, hook-nosed, and granite-faced, the colonel was feared by many. But he always took the time after battle to roam the battlefield, gazing at the dead of his own battalion, offering comfort to the wounded wherever he could.

He gazed downward with dark, inscrutable eyes and grimly set lips at one particular bundle of scarlet, his hands clasped behind him, his great cavalry sword, uncleaned after battle, sheathed at his side.

"An officer," he said, indicating the red sash with a curt nod. The man who wore it lay facedown on the ground, spread-eagled and twisted from his fall off his horse. "Who is he?"

His aide-de-camp stooped down and turned the dead officer over onto his back.

The dead man opened his eyes.

"Captain Morris," Colonel Bedwyn said, "you have taken a hit. Call for a stretcher, Rawlings. Without delay."

"No," the captain said faintly. "I am done for, sir."

His commanding officer did not argue the point. He made a slight staying gesture to his aide and continued to gaze down at the dying man, whose red coat was soaked with a deeper red. There could be no more than a few minutes of life remaining to him.

"What may I do for you?" the colonel asked. "Bring you a drink of water?"

"A favor. A promise." Captain Morris closed parchment-pale eyelids over fading eyes, and for a moment the colonel thought he was already gone. He sank down onto one knee beside him, pushing his sword out of the way as he did so. But the eyelids fluttered and half lifted again. "The debt, sir. I said I would never call it in." His voice was very faint now, his eyes unfocused.

"But I swore I would repay it nonetheless." Colonel

Bedwyn leaned over him, the better to hear. "Tell me what I can do."

Captain Morris, then a lieutenant, had saved his life two years before at the Battle of Salamanca, when the colonel's horse had been shot out from under him and he had been about to be cut down from behind while engaging a mounted opponent in a ferocious frontal fight. The lieutenant had killed the second assailant and had then dismounted and insisted that his superior officer take his horse. He had been severely wounded in the ensuing fight. But he had been awarded his captaincy as a result, a promotion he could not afford to purchase. He had insisted at the time that Colonel Bedwyn owed him nothing, that in a battle it was a soldier's duty to watch the backs of his comrades, particularly those of his superior officers. He was right, of course, but his colonel had never forgotten the obligation.

"My sister," the captain said now, his eyes closed again. "Take the news to her."

"I'll do it in person," the colonel assured him. "I'll inform her that your last thoughts were of her."

"Don't let her mourn." The man's breath was being drawn in on slow, audible heaves. "She has had too much of that. Tell her she must not wear black. My dying wish."

"I'll tell her."

"Promise me . . ." The voice trailed away. But death had still not quite claimed him. Suddenly he opened his eyes wide, somehow found the strength to move one arm until he could touch the colonel's hand with limp, deathly cold fingers, and spoke with an urgency that only imminent death could provoke.

"Promise me you will protect her," he said. His fingers plucked feebly at the colonel's hand. "Promise me! No matter what!"

"I promise." The colonel bent his head closer in the hope that his eyes and his voice would penetrate the fog of death engulfing the agitated man. "I give you my solemn vow."

The last breath sighed out of the captain's lungs even as the words were being spoken. The colonel reached out a hand to close Morris's eyes and remained on one knee for a minute or two longer as if in prayer, though in reality he was considering the promise he had made Captain Morris. He had promised to take the news of her brother's death to Miss Morris in person though he did not even know who she was or where she lived. He had promised to inform her of Morris's dying wish that she not wear mourning for him.

And he had sworn on his most sacred honor to protect her. From what—or from whom—he had no idea.

No matter what!

The echo of those last three words of the dying man rang in his ears. What could they possibly mean? What exactly had he sworn to?

No matter what!

CHAPTER I

England ~ 1814

There was a shady dell slicing through the woods on the western side of the park at Ringwood Manor in Oxfordshire. The water of the brook gurgling over its rocky bed joined up eventually with a larger river that formed the boundary of the park and flowed through the nearby village of Heybridge. The dell was always secluded and lovely. However, on this particular morning in May it was breathtakingly beautiful. The bluebells, which did not usually bloom until June, had been seduced by a mild spring into making an early appearance. The azaleas were in flower too, so that the sloping banks were carpeted in blue and pink. Bright sunbeams slanted through the dark-leafed branches of tall cypress trees and dappled the ground with brightness and shadow while sparkling off the bubbling water of the brook.

Eve Morris was knee-deep in bluebells. She had decided that it was too glorious a morning to be spent in any of the usual activities about the house and farm or in the village. The bluebells were in bloom for such a short time, and picking them for the house had always been one of her favorite springtime activities. She was not alone. She had persuaded Thelma Rice, the governess, to cancel classes for a few hours and bring her two pupils and her infant son out flower picking. Even Aunt Mari had come despite her arthritic knees and frequent shortness of breath. Indeed, it had been her idea to turn the occasion into an impromptu picnic. She was sitting now on the sturdy chair Charlie had carried down for her, her knitting needles clicking steadily, a large basket of food and drink at her side.

Eve straightened up to stretch her back. A pile of long-stemmed flowers lay along the basket over her arm. With her free hand she pressed her ancient, floppy straw hat more firmly onto her head, even though the wide gray ribbon attached to its crown and brim was securely fastened beneath her chin. The ribbon matched her dress, a simply styled, high-waisted, short-sleeved cotton garment ideal for a morning in the country when no company was expected. She savored a conscious feeling of well-being. All of the summer stretched ahead, a summer unmarred by anxiety for the first time in many years. Well, *almost* unmarred. There was, of course, the continuing question of what was keeping John away. He had expected to be home by March, or April at the latest. But he would come as soon as he was able. Of that she was certain. In the meantime, she viewed her surroundings and her companions with placid contentment.

Aunt Mari was not watching her busy hands. Instead she watched the children, an affectionate smile on her lined and wrinkled face. Eve felt a rush of tenderness for her. She had spent forty years hauling carts of coal along passageways deep in a coal mine until Papa had granted her a small pension after the death of her husband, Papa's uncle. Eve had persuaded her to come to Ringwood to live a little over a year ago, when Papa was very ill.

Seven-year-old Davy was picking earnestly, a frown on his thin face, as if he had been set a task of grave importance. Close behind him, as usual, five-year-old Becky, his sister, picked with more obvious enjoyment and less concentration, humming tunelessly as she did so. She looked like a child who felt secure in her surroundings. If only Davy could learn to relax like that, to lose the strained, serious look that made him appear too old for his years. But it would come, Eve told herself, if she would just be patient. Neither child was her own, though they had lived with her for the past seven months. They had no one else.

Muffin was down by the brook, three of his paws braced precariously on three different rocks, the fourth tucked under his belly, his nose half an inch above the shallow water. He was not drinking. He fancied himself as a prize fisher-dog though he had never caught even as much as a tadpole. Silly dog!

Young Benjamin Rice toddled up to his mother, a cluster of azalea and bluebell heads clutched tightly in one outstretched fist. Thelma bent to take them in her cupped hands as if they were some rare and precious treasure—as of course they were.

Eve felt a moment's envy of that mother love, but she shook it off as unworthy of her. She was one of the most fortunate of mortals. She lived in this idyllic place, and she was surrounded by people with whom she shared a reciprocal love, the loneliness of her girlhood a thing of the distant past. In a week's time she would be able to leave off her half-mourning on the first anniversary of Papa's death and wear *colors* again. She could scarcely wait. Soon—any day now—John would be back, and she could admit to the world at long last that she was in love, love, love. She could have twirled about at the thought, like an exuberant girl, but she contented herself with a smile instead.

And then there was the other prospect to complete her happiness. Percy would be coming home. He had written in his last letter that he would take leave as soon as he was able, and now surely he must be able. A little over a week ago she had heard the glorious news that Napoléon Bonaparte had surrendered to the Allied forces in France and that the long wars were over at last. James Robson, Eve's neighbor, had come in person to Ringwood as soon as he heard himself, knowing what the news would mean to her—the end to years of anxiety for Percy's safety.

Eve stooped to pick more bluebells. She wanted to be able to set a filled vase in every room of the house. They would all celebrate springtime and victory and security and an end to mourning with color and fragrance. If only John would come.

"Who's ready for something to eat, then?" Aunt Mari called a few minutes later in her thick Welsh accent. "I'm exhausted just watching all of you."

"I am," Becky cried, skipping happily toward the basket and setting her flowers down at Aunt Mari's side. "I am starved."

Davy straightened up but stood uncertainly where he was, as if he half suspected that the offer would be snatched away if he moved.

Muffin came bobbing up from the brook, his one and a half ears cocked, woofing as he came.

"You must be famished too, Davy." Eve strode toward him, set her free arm about his thin shoulders, and swept him along with her. "What an excellent worker you are. You have picked more than anyone else."

"Thank you, Aunt Eve," he said gravely. He still spoke her name awkwardly as if he thought it an impertinence to use so familiar a form of address. He and Becky were not related to her, except by a very tenuous link through marriage, but how could she have two young children growing up in her home and addressing her as *Miss Morris?* Or Aunt Mari as *Mrs. Pritchard?*

Thelma was laughing. Flowers along one arm, Benjamin on the other, she was unable to prevent him from pushing her bonnet backward off her head.

Aunt Mari had the basket open and was taking out freshly baked bread rolls, which had been carefully wrapped in a tea towel. The yeasty smell of them and of fried chicken made Eve realize how hungry she was. She knelt on the blanket Davy and Becky had spread on the grass and took charge of the large bottle of lemonade.

The ten minutes or so of near silence that followed were testament to both their hard work and the culinary skills of Mrs. Rowe, Eve's cook. Why did food always taste so much more appetizing out-of-doors? Eve wondered, wiping her greasy fingertips on a linen napkin after devouring a second piece of chicken.

"I suppose," Aunt Mari said, "we'd better pack up

and take all these flowers back to the house before they wilt. If someone would just hand me my cane as soon as I have my wool and needles in this bag, I could haul these old bones upright."

"Oh, must we?" Eve asked with a sigh as Davy scrambled to offer the cane.

But at that moment someone called her name.

"Miss Morris," the voice called with breathless urgency. "Miss Morris."

"We are still here, Charlie." She swiveled around to watch a large, fresh-faced young man come lumbering over the top of the bank from the direction of the house and crash downward toward them in his usual ungainly manner. "Take your time or you will slip and hurt yourself." She had hired him several months ago, even though Ringwood had not needed any more servants, to do odd jobs about the house and stable and park. No one else had wanted to offer Charlie employment after the death of his father, the village blacksmith, because he was generally described as a half-wit. Even his father had constantly berated him as a useless lump. Eve had never known anyone more eager to work and to please.

"Miss Morris." He was gasping and ruddy-cheeked by the time he came close enough to deliver his message. Whenever Charlie was sent on an errand, he behaved as if he had been sent to announce the end of the world or something of similarly dire import. "I am sent. By Mrs. Fuller. To fetch you back to the house." He fought for air between each short sentence.

"Did she say why, Charlie?" Eve got unhurriedly to

her feet and shook out her skirt. "We are all on our way home anyway."

"Someone's come," Charlie said. He stood very still then, his large feet planted wide, his brow creased in deep furrows of concentration, and tried to bring something else to mind. "I can't remember his name."

Eve felt a lurching of excitement in the pit of her stomach. *John?* But she had been disappointed so many times in the last two months that it was best not to consider the possibility. Indeed, she was even beginning to wonder if he was coming at all, if he had ever intended to come. But she was not yet prepared to draw such a drastic conclusion—she pushed it firmly away.

"Well, never mind," she said cheerfully. "I daresay I will find it out soon enough. Thank you for bringing the message so promptly, Charlie. Would you carry the chair back to the house for Mrs. Pritchard and then return for the basket?"

He beamed at the prospect of being able to make himself useful and stood poised to scoop up the chair the moment Aunt Mari got to her feet. Then he turned back to Eve with a beaming smile of triumph.

"He is a military feller," he said. "I seen him before Mrs. Fuller sent me to fetch you and he was wearing one of them red uniform things."

A military man.

"Oh, Eve, my love," Aunt Mari said, but Eve did not even hear her.

"Percy!" she cried in a burst of exuberance. Basket and flowers and companions were forgotten. She gathered up her skirts with both hands and began to run up

the bank, leaving her aunt and Thelma and Charlie to gather up the children and the bluebells.

It was not a long way back to the house, but most of the distance was uphill. Eve scarcely noticed. Nor did she notice that Muffin ran panting at her heels every step of the way. She was up to the top of the dell in a few moments and then through the trees and around the lily pond and up over the sloping lawn to the stables, along in front of the buildings and across the cobbled terrace to the front doors of the house. By the time she burst into the entrance hall, she was flushed and panting and probably looking alarmingly disheveled, even grubby. She did not care one iota. Percy would not care.

The rogue! He had sent no word that he was coming. But that did not matter now. And surprises were wonderful things—at least *happy* surprises were. He was home!

"Where is he?" she asked Agnes Fuller, her housekeeper, who awaited her in the hall, large and solid and hatchet-faced. How like Percy to keep her in suspense, not simply to rush out to meet her and sweep her off her feet and into a bear hug.

"In the parlor," Agnes said, jerking a thumb to her right. "Out you get, dog, until you have had your paws washed! You'd better go upstairs first, my lamb, and wash your—"

But Eve did not even hear her. She dashed across the checkered floor of the hall, flung open the door of the visitors' parlor, and hurried inside.

"You wretch!" she cried, pulling undone the ribbon

16

of her hat. And then she stopped dead in her tracks, feeling intense mortification. He was not Percy. He was a stranger.

He was standing before the empty hearth, his back to it, facing the door. He seemed to half fill the room. He looked seven feet tall, dressed as he was in full regimentals, his scarlet coat and its gold facings immaculate, his white pantaloons spotless, his knee-high black cavalry boots polished to a high gloss, his sheathed sword gleaming at his side. He looked broad and solid and powerful and menacing. He had a harsh, weathered face, its darkness accentuated by black hair and eyebrows. It was a grim face, with hard, nearly black eyes, a great hooked nose, and thin, cruel-looking lips.

"Oh, I do beg your pardon," she said, suddenly, horribly aware of her bedraggled appearance. She pulled off her hat—her old, shapeless hat—and held it at her side. Her hair must be flattened and untidy. She surely had grass and flower bits all over her. She probably had streaks of dirt all over her face. *Why* had she not stopped to ask Agnes the identity of the military man who had come calling? And *why* was he here? "I thought you were someone else."

He stared at her for a long moment before bowing. "Miss Morris, I presume?" he said.

She inclined her head to him. "You have the advantage of me, I am afraid, sir," she said. "The servant who came for me had forgotten your name."

"Colonel Bedwyn at your service, ma'am," he said.

She recognized the name instantly. She could even supply the rest of it. He was Colonel Lord Aidan

Bedwyn and Percy's commanding officer. If she had felt deep mortification before, now she wished a black hole would open beneath her feet and swallow her up.

But it did not take her longer than a moment to realize that embarrassment was the least of her concerns. He was *Percy's commanding officer*. And he was standing in the visitors' parlor at Ringwood in full, formal dress uniform. There was no need to ask why. In that instant she *knew*. Her head turned cold, as if all the blood had gushed downward out of it. Even the air in her nostrils felt icy. Unconsciously she let her hat fall to the floor and with both hands closed the door at her back, sought out the handle, and clung on tightly.

"What can I do for you, Colonel?" She heard her voice now as if it came from a long way off.

He looked hard at her, his face devoid of expression. "I am the bearer of unhappy tidings," he said. "Is there someone you would wish to summon?"

"Percy?" His name came out as a whisper. She could well imagine this man wielding the cold, heavy steel at his side, a detached part of her mind thought. Killing with it. "But the wars are at an end. Napoléon Bonaparte has been defeated. He has surrendered."

"Captain Percival Morris fell in action at Toulouse in the south of France on April the tenth," he said. "He died a hero's death, ma'am. I am deeply regretful of the pain it will cause you."

Percy. Her only brother, her only sibling, whom she had worshipped during childhood, adored fiercely through her girlhood, when he had been restless and rebellious and constantly at odds with Papa, and loved unwaveringly during the long years after he had gone away and then used the unexpected legacy left him by their maternal great-uncle to purchase a commission in a cavalry regiment. He had loved her cheerfully, generously, in return. She had received a letter from him—from France—just two weeks ago.

Captain Morris fell in action . . .

"Will you sit down?" The colonel had moved closer, though he did not touch her. He loomed over her, huge and dark and menacing. "You are very pale. *May* I have someone fetched to you, ma'am?"

"He is dead?" He had been dead for almost a month and she had not known. She had not even sensed it. He had been two weeks dead when she read his letter, more than two weeks dead when James brought the news of victory and she had felt such enormous relief. "Did he suffer?" Foolish question.

"I think not, ma'am," the colonel said. He had not stepped back away from her and she felt suffocated, deprived of air and space. Seated on horseback, sword in hand, he must be truly terrifying. "There is often a merciful shock that keeps dying men from feeling the pain of their wounds. I believe Captain Morris was one of them. He did not look to be in pain and did not speak of it."

"Speak?" She looked sharply up at him. "He spoke? To you?"

"His final thoughts and words were of you," he said, inclining his head. "He begged me to bring you the news myself."

"It was extremely kind of you to honor such a

request," she said, realizing suddenly how strange it was that Percy's commanding officer should come in person all the way from the south of France to inform her of his death.

"I owe Captain Morris my life," he explained. "He saved it in an act of extraordinary courage and at the risk of considerable personal danger two years ago at the Battle of Salamanca."

"Did he say anything else?"

"He asked that you not wear black for him," the colonel told her. "I believe he added that you have had too much of that."

His eyes swept downward over her gray dress, which she was so looking forward to discarding for something more colorful, more in tune with the season in a week's time. But it no longer mattered.

Her brother was gone. Forever.

She was engulfed in pain, blinded, deafened by it, by the unbearable agony of loss.

"Ma'am?" The colonel took another half-step forward and reached out a hand as if to take her by the arm.

She recoiled. "Anything else?"

"He asked me to protect you," he said.

"To *protect* me?" Her eyes flew to his face again. It was like granite, she thought. Without warmth, without expression, without sentiment. If there was a person behind the hard military facade, there was no sign of him. Though perhaps that was unfair. He had come close as if to aid her and had reached out a steadying hand. And he *had* come all the way from the south of

France to repay a debt to Percy.

"I have taken a room at the Three Feathers Inn in Heybridge," he said. "I will remain there until tomorrow, ma'am. The next time I call here you will inform me how I may be of service to you. But at the moment you need the assistance of people who are familiar to you. You are in shock."

He stepped to one side and pulled on the bell rope beside the door. *Was* she in shock? She felt perfectly in command of herself. She even wondered if that bell still worked since she could not recall the last time it had been used. She also realized that if it *did* work and if Agnes *did* answer it, she was going to have to move. She was still standing against the door, her hands clinging to the handle as if for very life. She did not believe she would be able to move if she tried. The universe would shatter into a billion fragments. Perhaps she really was not quite herself.

Percy was dead.

Agnes answered the summons almost immediately. The colonel grasped Eve firmly by the upper arm just in time to move her to one side as the door opened.

"Is there someone you can summon to Miss Morris's assistance?" he asked, though in truth his words sounded far more like a crisp command than a courteous request. "If so, do it immediately."

Agnes, in true Agnes fashion, merely turned her head and bellowed. "Charlie? Char-*lie,* do you hear me? Set down that chair and run back for Mrs. Pritchard. Tell her to hurry. Miss Morris needs her. *Now!*"

"You must sit before you faint," the colonel said.

"Even your lips are colorless."

Eve sank obediently onto the closest chair and sat there, very upright, her spine not quite touching the back, her hands clasped tightly, painfully, in her lap. Poor Aunt Mari, she thought—*tell her to hurry*. Then she heard the echo of something the colonel had said a minute or two ago.

. . . you will inform me how I may be of service to you.

"There is nothing you can do for me, Colonel," she said. "There is little point in subjecting yourself to the discomforts of a country inn. But I do thank you for your offer. And for coming all this way. You are very kind."

How was it possible, she wondered, watching Agnes pick up her hat from the floor and hold it against her chest, frowning ferociously the while, to mouth mundane courtesies when *Percy was dead?* She felt the sharp pain of her fingernails digging into her palms.

"The amenities of even the humblest of country inns seem like the lap of luxury to a man newly returned from a military campaign, ma'am," he said. "You need not concern yourself about my comfort."

She had not offered him refreshments, she thought in the minute or two of silence that followed while Agnes stared at her and Colonel Bedwyn did not. He had taken up his stand before the hearth again, his back to it. She had not even offered him a seat.

Aunt Mari, still wearing her hat, came hobbling into the room before any conversation could resume, her cane tapping out an urgent tattoo on the floor, her eyes wide with dismay, as if she already understood what

22

this was all about. Charlie must have outdone himself in conveying a sense of doom. Eve swayed to her feet.

"Miss Morris has need of you, ma'am," Colonel Bedwyn said without waiting for any introductions to be made. "I have been the bearer of sad tidings concerning Captain Percival Morris, her brother, I am afraid."

"Oh, my poor love." Aunt Mari came straight toward her and gathered her into her arms. Her cane clattered to the floor. Eve rested her forehead on her aunt's bony shoulder for a weary spell, drawing comfort from the human touch of someone familiar, someone who loved her, someone who would make all better if she possibly could. But no one could make this better. No one could bring Percy back. Wretchedness enveloped her like a dark cloud.

When she lifted her head again, her aunt's eyes were filled with tears and her lips were wobbling in an effort to control her emotions. Muffin was standing at her feet, wagging his bit of a tail, looking soulful. Agnes still hovered just inside the room, clutching Eve's hat and looking as if she would gladly fight a dragon or two if someone would only point her in the right direction. Thelma, her eyes wide with dismay, was there too, though there was no sign of the children. Nanny Johnson must have taken them upstairs.

Colonel Lord Aidan Bedwyn had gone.

CHAPTER II

His bed at the Three Feathers was hard, the pillow lumpy, the ale insipid, the food ill-prepared, the service less than prompt, the taproom noisy, and the whole place lacking something in spruceness even though it was passably clean. If he had been anywhere else but England, where his mind almost unconsciously reverted to old standards of quality, Aidan might indeed have considered that he was in the lap of luxury. As it was, he was sorely displeased and wished heartily that he could go straight home to Lindsey Hall in Hampshire, country seat of his elder brother, the Duke of Bewcastle, and be pampered there for the remainder of his leave.

But first he must complete his business with Captain Morris's sister, and he still had no idea how long that would take or what it would involve beyond offering her what comfort he could in another visit or two. She had told him there was nothing he could do for her, but of course by the time she had said that she was deeply in shock. *He* still felt some shock over the change a couple of minutes had wrought in her—one minute a vibrant, flushed, bright-eyed, rather pretty young woman despite the plainness, even shabbiness, of her clothes and the generally disheveled look of someone who had been busy at some outdoor activity, and the next minute a pale, listless ghost of herself. And he was the one who had done it to her. Ah, the power of words, with which he had never been adept.

When he returned to Ringwood Manor on the second morning, on foot rather than on horseback this time since he had discovered the distance from inn to house to be not much farther than a mile, he felt more at leisure to notice his surroundings since he was no longer preoccupied with the most unpleasant part of his mission. Breaking the news of a death must be one of the most wretched tasks anyone could be called upon to undertake. He had done it by letter on numerous occasions, but he had never before been compelled to do it in person.

Ringwood was an attractive place, the manor old and mellow, the park sizable and nicely set out. It looked prosperous enough, though looks might be deceiving. Captain Morris, without any obviously expensive vices, such as drinking or gambling, had been unable to buy promotions as most of his peers did. Ringwood might be mortgaged to its figurative eyebrows. Was *that* the sister's problem?

But would it be hers anyway? To whom did Ringwood now belong? The father was dead. Aidan had discovered that yesterday. Had it been Captain Morris's, then? Was it entailed?

There were people out on the lawn before the house, Aidan could see as he walked up the long driveway, his boots crunching on the gravel. Three of them were women, two standing, one seated on a chair. There were also three children, all sitting on the grass. The seated woman held an open book in her hands. She was either reading to the children or giving a lesson. She must be a governess, he concluded. He had passed her in the entrance hall yesterday as he left, he recalled. The two women standing and observing were Miss Morris and the elderly lady who had come to comfort her yesterday—she was supporting herself on a cane as she had been then. One of the children looked up and pointed in his direction, and both ladies turned to look.

For a moment it seemed that Miss Morris did not recognize him. Today he wore civilian clothes. He stepped off the gravel to make his way diagonally across the grass, and the two ladies came to meet him. Miss Morris, he could see, was as pale as parchment, her eyes shadowed from lack of sleep, but she was composed.

"Colonel?" She smiled wanly. She was tall, willowy, long-limbed, brown-haired, gray-eyed. Today she looked fragile and rather plain. "Good morning. How kind of you to call again. I am not sure I thanked you properly yesterday for your kindness in coming in person to break the news to me. It would have been worse to have had to read it in a letter."

She spoke with a slight lilt, which made her words sound musical.

"Good morning, ma'am." Aidan bowed to her. "I am pleased to discover you up and about and taking the air." She held a shawl about her shoulders with both hands even though it was a warm day.

"May I beg the honor of presenting my great-aunt?" she asked him. "Mrs. Pritchard, Colonel. This is Colonel Lord Aidan Bedwyn, Aunt Mari."

Ah, so she knew his full identity, did she? He bowed again.

"I am delighted to meet you, Colonel," the aunt said. "I just wish the reason behind it was not such a sad one." She spoke with such a thick Welsh accent that he had to concentrate in order to understand her.

"As do I, ma'am," he said.

"May I offer you refreshments?" Miss Morris asked, gesturing toward the house. "I am afraid I neglected my duty yesterday."

"I would rather stroll with you out here," he said.

"I need to go inside to rest my legs, my love," Mrs. Pritchard said.

Miss Morris nodded and Aidan turned to walk with her across the grass, away from the house and driveway toward a picturesque lily pond with woods beyond it. But they had taken no more than a dozen steps before she stopped and turned at the sound of barking. A brown dog of indeterminate breed, perhaps partly terrier, came streaking from the place where the children sat, barking excitedly as it came and moving with a strange, bobbing gait. It was running mainly on three legs, Aidan saw as it approached, the fourth curled up beneath it. It was a scruffy mutt with tufty hair interspersed with bald patches, one eye, and one and a half ears. It scrambled to a halt when it came up to them and paid homage to Miss Morris by snuffling at her hand and then lifting its head to expose its throat. It panted with ecstasy when she stooped and scratched it beneath its chin.

"Did you almost miss the chance for a walk, Muffin?" she asked. She looked up, half apologetically, at Aidan. "He would not win any prizes at a dog show, would he? But he is very precious nonetheless."

Aidan made no comment. The dog looked as if it had engaged in a losing battle with a bear. It gazed at him with its single eye and barked. Its token protest at his presence made, it gamboled along beside them as they resumed their walk.

Aidan did not waste time on small talk. It would be insensitive to a grieving woman to engage her in conversation about the weather or any other similarly trivial topic.

"Your brother was quite insistent, ma'am," he said, "that I promise to protect you. He did not have time to explain, but there was clearly some considerable urgency in his request. You will instruct me if you will on how I may serve you."

"You have already done so," she said. "You have fulfilled your obligation, Colonel, and I am deeply grateful. In particular I am happier than you can know to have learned that he did not suffer great pain."

It would be impertinent to probe further when she spoke so firmly and dismissively. He was, of course, a total stranger to her, as she was to him. But Morris had expended his final burst of energy on extracting a promise from a man he had known would not break it or even evade it if he could.

"Was Ringwood your brother's?" he asked.

"No." She spoke swiftly but quite unequivocally. "It is mine. My father left it to me. The property is unentailed, you see, and he and Percy had been estranged for a number of years before his death. My father wanted him to stay at Ringwood and learn to be what he called a committed member of the landed gentry. But Percy wanted a military career, and when he inherited some money from our great-uncle, he purchased a commission with it."

That perhaps explained Morris's apparent poverty. The problem was not, then, what Aidan had feared. It was not to be his task to help her leave her home, to escort her to another and help her settle to a new way of life. That was a relief at least.

"It looks," he said, wading deeper into impertinence, "like a prosperous property."

"It is." She stopped to take a stick from the dog's mouth and throw it for him to chase. She did not enlarge on her answer. "Percy is buried there? At Toulouse?"

"Yes," he said. "Alongside two other officers. Our regimental chaplain performed the burial rites. It was a formal and dignified and proper ceremony. I was there. The grave is clearly marked and will be tended. I saw to that."

"Thank you," she said.

There did not seem to be anything else to say. She did not appear to need anything material from him—or if she did, she was not going to admit it. She had her aunt to lean upon in her time of grief. There was also the young governess with the children—whomever they might belong to. She probably had friends and neighbors galore who would gather around to support her. She had no need of any further comfort from a stranger. He was no good at offering comfort anyway. He had been an officer for more than twelve years, since his eighteenth birthday. All the softer emotions that might at one time have been a part of his nature had long ago dried up from disuse.

But he had made that solemn promise, and it had encompassed those three particularly disturbing words—*no matter what*. Not being able to do anything for her except to bring her the news of her brother's death would always irk him, he knew.

"Do you have any family in England, Colonel?" she asked.

"The Duke of Bewcastle is my brother," he told her. "I have two other brothers and two sisters as well as other relatives."

"Do you have any nieces and nephews?" she asked.

He shook his head. "None of us are married." Freyja had come close—twice, with two brothers. One had let her down by dying, the other by marrying someone else. Freyja, according to Rannulf, who had written a long, witty letter about the latter debacle, had not been amused. That, interpreted, meant that she had been in a spitting fury.

"You must be longing to see them all," Miss Morris said, "and they to see you. Do you have a long leave?"

"Two months," he said.

"That is so brief a time," she said. "You must not waste any more of it on remaining here. I am truly grateful that you have given me two days."

It was graciously spoken, but it was a dismissal if ever he had heard one. His debt had been repaid very easily, then. Too easily. But there was nothing more he could do.

She turned back in the direction of the house after they had circled the lily pond. All had been said. She was expecting him to leave. Mostly, he supposed, he was glad. *Very* glad. But also uneasy.

If he hurried back to the Three Feathers after escorting her back to the house, there would be time to be well on his way home before dark. He was looking forward to being there, perhaps to seeing some of his family again, though they might well be in London for the Season. Bewcastle himself would undoubtedly be there since Parliament must be in session. But most of all he just wanted to be at home. It was three years since his last leave, and even that had been cut short.

"Good-bye, Colonel." She stopped when they reached the terrace before the house and held out a slim hand to him. "Have a safe journey home and enjoy your leave. I am sure you have earned every moment of it. Yesterday must not have been easy for you. Take my gratitude with you."

He took her hand and bowed over it. "Good-bye, ma'am," he said. "Captain Morris was a great hero. May you take comfort from that fact after the rawness of your grief is over."

She smiled with bloodless lips and sad eyes. The dog growled halfheartedly as their hands touched. Aidan turned and strode away down the driveway, past the children and their governess. At last he could begin to enjoy his leave.

But perhaps he would always have the niggling feeling that he had not quite fulfilled his vow. Captain Morris had been so very urgent in his request.

Promise me you will protect her. Promise me! No matter what!

He must surely have had *something* in mind.

William Andrews, Aidan's batman, had been with him for eight years. Through all the hardships and miseries of numerous campaigns, including the tedious advances and retreats that had made up the Peninsular Wars—rain and mud, snow and cold, sun and heat, flea-infested inns, insalubrious open-air bivouacs—through it all he had never been ill a day. Now, back in temperate England, back in the lap of luxury, so to speak, he had caught a head cold.

When Aidan returned to the Three Feathers and summoned him to pack his bags and make arrangements to have his horse ready for travel within the hour, Andrews appeared with a red beacon of a nose, drooping eyelids, watery eyes, a nasal voice that growled somewhere low in the bass register, dragging footsteps, and a martyr's air.

"What the devil ails you?" Aidan asked him.

"I have a slight cold in by dose, sir," he explained. He sniffed pathetically, then sneezed and apologized. "What bay I do for you, sir?"

Aidan scowled, swore eloquently, and sent his man off to bed, with strict orders that he was to dose himself with something to sweat the fever out of him and not get out of bed again before morning. Although Andrews looked at him with feeble reproach and opened his mouth to protest, he thought better of arguing and shuffled mournfully off, sneezing and apologizing again before he closed the door behind him.

And now what the devil was he supposed to do with himself? Aidan wondered. It was scarcely noon and the whole of the rest of the day yawned emptily before him. Sit in the taproom fraternizing with the locals? Explore the spacious metropolis of Heybridge? Take a brisk walk along the village street and back? That might kill ten minutes. Go for a long ride up one country lane and down another? Lie on his bed making pictures out of the stains on the ceiling?

He was hungry, he realized suddenly. It was five hours since he had had his breakfast, and he had refused the offer of refreshments at Ringwood Manor. The taproom and dining room were all one at the Three Feathers. There was no such thing as a private dining room. He went downstairs, ordered a steak-and-kidney pie with a tankard of ale, and struck up a conversation with the innkeeper and a group of his local patrons. Anything to pass an hour or three without expiring of boredom.

The main item of news with which the whole village was buzzing, not surprisingly, was the death of Percival Morris. They all knew that Aidan had brought the news and probed for more information without ever being impertinent enough to ask a direct question of such a grand gentleman. They had a curious way of asking the questions of one another or the empty air and then pausing for him to answer.

"I wonder exactly 'ow young Mr. Percival died," one of them asked of the pipe smoke above his head.

"I wonder what them big battles against the Froggies are like," another mused into the ale in his tankard.

"You all knew Captain Morris?" Aidan asked after he had satisfied their curiosity by providing a few suitably gory details of the Battle of Toulouse.

Ah, yes, indeed, they all had, though he had not been home for years.

"Broke his father's heart, he did, running off like that to take the king's shilling," one of them said, showing a woeful lack of understanding of how a man became a cavalry officer.

A spirited discussion followed as to whether old man Morris had had a heart to break.

"Look what 'e done to 'is own daughter, 'oo nursed 'im like a saint with one foot in 'eaven through all the years 'e was ill," someone else observed.

"Done?" Aidan repeated, his interest piqued. He did not bother to correct the man's grammar.

"Aye," the man said, shaking his head and sighing soulfully into his ale.

No further explanation was forthcoming. The conversation turned toward Miss Morris herself and her saintliness, which apparently extended beyond nursing an infirm father for four or five years before his death—a father who may or may not have possessed a heart. Among other things, it seemed, she had started and financed a village school, brought in a village midwife and paid her salary, taken in two orphans to live with her when no one else wanted them, and employed an assortment of undesirable types whom no one else would have touched with a ten-foot pole—or so one of them declared, and no one rushed to contradict him. Miss Morris, it would seem, took the Christian ideal of charity to an extreme. She also, Aidan concluded, must be very wealthy indeed.

"Too easily taken in she is, though," the landlord said, shaking his head and pulling out a chair to settle his large bulk at an empty table. "Too soft in the 'ead." He tapped his own with one finger to illustrate his point. "If you 'ad a penny to sell and a sorry enough tale to tell, she would give you a guinea for it as sure as I am sitting here."

"Aye." One of his listeners shook his head sadly.

"If you was to ask me," the landlord said, though no one had, "old man Morris done the right thing before 'e popped off. Women are too soft about th 'eart to 'ave the running of a grand place like Ringwood and to 'ave their fingers in such a deep purse as Morris's was."

"I was under the impression," Aidan said, reluctantly showing open curiosity, "that Mr. Morris left Ringwood to his daughter."

"Ah, 'e did," the landlord said. "But it was to go to Mr. Percival after one year. Now 'e 'as gone and got 'imself killed just before the year is up and Mr. Cecil Morris will get it all instead. I don't expect to see *him* in any deep mourning for 'is cousin."

Morris senior had left his property to his daughter for one year only? Now, since her brother was dead, it was to go to another relative? That would be unpleasant for her, Aidan thought, if she had had the running of the place since her father's demise. But at least the new owner *was* a relative. Doubtless she would soon adjust to the new way of things.

But still, she had lied to him to all intents and purposes. He felt annoyed. She might at least have told him she was about to lose ownership of her home. Except, he admitted with an inward sigh, that she did not owe him that knowledge. She owed him nothing. The debt was all on the other side.

Protection was the word Captain Morris had used. Aidan could remember the captain's hand plucking feebly at his sleeve with a dying man's last surge of energy.

Promise me you will protect her. Promise me! No matter what!

Damnation! Was there more to all this than was even now apparent?

The men about him had settled into a lengthy discussion of Mr. Cecil Morris, but Aidan had not been listening.

"What was Mr. Morris like?" he asked. He hated to pump strangers for information, but he felt the need to know more. "Captain Morris's father, I mean."

"Him?" one of the drinkers said. "He was no better nor any of us though he put on airs good enough for the King of England. He were a coal miner down in Wales before he married the mine owner's daughter and got rich. When the old man died, Morris sold the mine, got richer, bought the manor here, and set up as a gentleman. He had his son and daughter brought up as a gentleman and lady, but he was disappointed in them and serve him right too. Mr. Percival went off to the wars and Miss Morris wouldn't marry none of the nobs he trotted out for her inspection."

Ah, Aidan thought. The slight Welsh accent was explained. So was the very Welsh aunt.

"Ah, but it were the Earl of Luff what refused to let his son marry *her* when Morris suggested it," another man said after showing the innkeeper his empty tankard. "She weren't given no chance to refuse him."

"But she probably would 'ave," the innkeeper said, hoisting himself to his feet. "There never was any snobbery about Miss Morris."

Aidan got to his feet too, nodded genially to the innkeeper and the other occupants of the taproom, and went back to his room. He was going to go out for a long ride, he decided. He was going to have to decide what to do . . . if anything. It would be ill-mannered indeed to go back to Ringwood and start probing into Miss Morris's affairs again. But—very reluctantly—he no longer felt he could simply ride for home tomorrow morning.

CHAPTER III

Later that same afternoon, Eve walked into the village alone. Aunt Mari would have accompanied her if she had brought the carriage. But it was fresh air and exercise she needed more than company—except perhaps the chance to think and to plan.

What were they all going to do? Blank terror clawed at her. She had been trying hard ever since yesterday morning to concentrate upon the only fact that was of any real significance—Percy's death. She had loved him dearly. She wanted to be able to mourn him properly. But . . .

But he had died too soon.

Percy had left a will, and in that will he had left Ringwood to Eve. But Ringwood had never been his. It was still Eve's until the anniversary of her father's death. Now by an irony of fate it would go to her cousin Cecil on that anniversary. Percy's will was useless. He had died too soon. As if it would have been perfectly all right for him to die later, she thought bitterly.

In five days' time they would all be homeless. *All* of them. Her stomach churned with panic. If she could have focused merely upon her own predicament, she could have found a solution, employment being the most obvious. But she did not have the luxury of thinking only of herself.

She walked onto the humpbacked stone bridge that spanned the river between Ringwood and Heybridge and paused a moment to gaze down at the gently flowing water before entering the village and approaching the vicarage. There were five days during which to make plans. She could spare today to concentrate upon Percy. He deserved that much of her.

The Reverend Thomas Puddle was at home, Eve discovered when he answered her knock at the door himself. But his housekeeper was not, and he was a man who assiduously observed the proprieties. Instead of inviting Eve inside, he suggested that she stroll with him in the churchyard. A lanky, fresh-faced, auburn-haired young man, the vicar was always awkward and blushing with Eve—as he was with all his other young female parishioners, with many of whom he was a great favorite.

He had been about to set out for Ringwood, he told her now, having just returned home from two days away to learn the news of her brother's tragic demise. He spent some time commiserating with her before they discussed the memorial service she had come to ask him to perform.

"Tomorrow will suit me well enough," she assured him after learning that he must leave again on business the day after. "I can see to it that everyone is informed. I may leave all the details of the service to you, then?"

"You may indeed," he assured her. "Is there anyone who would be able to deliver a eulogy for your brother, Miss Morris? I never knew him personally and could talk about him only in very general terms."

She thought for a while as they came to a stop beneath the shade of a beech tree.

"I believe James Robson would be willing to do it," she said. "He and Percy were the same age and grew up together as neighbors and friends. I will write to him as soon as I return home."

But the hollow sound of hooves clopping over the bridge distracted them both at that moment. Eve was surprised to see that it was Colonel Bedwyn who was riding toward them, presumably on his way to the inn at the other end of the village. Why was he still in Heybridge? She would have expected him to be several hours along on his journey home by now.

He spotted them as his horse drew level with the

beech tree and touched his whip to his hat. He *did* look extremely powerful on horseback, as she had expected, even though he was not wearing his uniform. He was not a man she would want to cross, she thought. He looked dour and humorless. He looked like a man who never smiled. But she must not be unkind. He had called on her twice. He had offered to help her in any way he could.

He hesitated and then drew his horse to a halt. He turned back toward the vicarage, dismounted, looped the reins over the garden fence, and came striding into the churchyard. Eve felt both startled and dismayed. She wanted nothing more to do with him. She disliked him, though she was honest enough with herself to realize that her only reason for doing so was that he was the one who had brought her the devastating news.

She introduced the two gentlemen.

"It was Colonel Bedwyn," she explained to the vicar, "who brought word of Percy's death yesterday. He was Percy's commanding officer."

"A tragic business," the Reverend Puddle said. "His passing is a dreadful loss for Miss Morris and for the whole neighborhood. We have been planning a memorial service for tomorrow afternoon. Will you still be here, sir?"

"I have been delayed by the illness of my batman," the colonel explained. "He has contracted a head cold since our return to Britain. I do not know quite when we will be on our way."

The vicar murmured words of sympathy. Colonel Bedwyn looked at Eve and she felt the urge to take a step back. He had a piercing, very direct gaze. She pitied his men and was glad that Percy, although his subordinate, had at least been an officer.

"A memorial service?" he said.

She nodded. "Unfortunately," she said, "I do not have his body to bury. But he grew up here. Most of my neighbors and friends remember him well. He was my brother. There is a need for some ceremony, some official good-bye."

He nodded his understanding.

"We have been discussing whom to ask to give the eulogy," the vicar explained. "I came here after Captain Morris left and would not do a creditable job of it myself."

The colonel's black stare was still on Eve.

"Perhaps," he said, "it would be appropriate if I spoke a few words, ma'am. Your neighbors should know what a courageous cavalry officer the Percival Morris they remember turned into and how bravely he fought for his country."

"That is an extraordinarily generous offer, sir," the Reverend Puddle said.

"You would stay one more day?" Eve frowned. "You would do that for me, Colonel?"

He inclined his head. "I gave my solemn word, ma'am."

To protect her. It had broken her heart as she lay awake last night to realize that Percy had been plagued with very justifiable fears of what his death was going to mean to her. But what had he thought Colonel Bedwyn could do for her? He had been, she supposed, beyond rational thought.

"Thank you," she said. "That would be very good of you."

He nodded and finally looked away from her to take his leave of the Reverend Puddle. A moment later he was striding away to mount his horse again.

"A formidable gentleman," the vicar observed.

"Yes," Eve agreed. Also, very clearly, a man of his word. She realized that his offer to help her this morning and his offer now to stay an extra day in order to deliver a eulogy at Percy's memorial service tomorrow had nothing to do with simple kindness. His life had been saved and he felt himself in Percy's debt. He had given Percy his word that he would protect her, and in the absence of any other way of serving her, he would stay to say uplifting things about Percy for her comfort and her neighbors' edification.

She was grateful to him.

Aidan did not consider himself an eloquent man. Certainly he had never before delivered a eulogy. He had attended so many burial services for his men and fellow officers that it was depressing to think of, but the regimental chaplains had always said all that needed to be said.

"Captain Percival Morris once endangered his life and suffered severe wounds in order to save *my* life," he began when it came time for the eulogy, facing the impressively large congregation gathered in the pretty, typically English village church.

Miss Morris, dressed all in gray, sat in the front pew,

her black-clad and -veiled aunt beside her. The young blonde-haired woman who had been teaching the children on the lawn at Ringwood was there too, as was the housekeeper, who would have made an excellent sergeant if she had been of the other gender, Aidan had thought when he saw her march down the aisle behind her mistress. Most of the congregation was dressed respectfully in black. Perhaps some of them wondered why Miss Morris of all people was not.

"I was with Captain Morris when he died," he concluded after delivering his planned speech for a few minutes. "His last thoughts were of his sister. He asked me to bring her the news of his passing myself. And he asked me to beg her not to wear mourning for him. It is in honor of that plea that she wears gray today. We must all feel honored that we knew so courageous a man, one who gave of himself unstintingly in the service of his fellow countrymen and of the country itself. We must show our respect for him by directing it toward the sister whom he loved to the end. Ma'am?"

Aidan made her his stiffest, most formal military bow before returning to his seat. She sat straight-backed and dry-eyed and as pale as a ghost, he noticed. Mrs. Pritchard and several other members of the congregation were sniffling into their handkerchiefs.

He did not pay much attention to the rest of the service. The church bell tolled mournfully as the service ended.

He shook hands with the Reverend Puddle and congratulated him on a tasteful and dignified memorial service. He was wondering if this would be an appropriate time to have a word with Miss Morris or if he should more decently wait yet another day, but she took the decision from him by approaching him herself. She was holding out a gloved hand to him.

"Thank you, Colonel," she said. "I will always treasure the memory of all you said about Percy, most of which I did not know before. And I will always remember your kindness in staying another day for my sake."

"It was my pleasure, ma'am," he said, taking her slim, warm hand in his.

"How is your batman today?" she surprised him by asking.

"Much better, I thank you, ma'am," he said.

"I am pleased to hear it." She nodded. "A number of my friends and neighbors are coming back to the house for tea. Will you come too, please?"

It was everything he could have hoped for. The chances were that there would be little opportunity for a private word with her, but perhaps he could create the opportunity. He still did not know what he would say to her, though, what he would ask, how impertinently he would probe.

Before he could answer, someone else stepped forward, bowing and smiling and clad from head to toe in unrelieved black. Even the handkerchief dangling from one of the man's black-gloved hands was black.

"A speech of affecting sentiment indeed, my lord," he said to an astonished Aidan. "I could scarcely hold back my tears. My mama positively could not. What a comfort it must have been to poor Percival to have an officer of such illustrious lineage with him at his death—your father was the late Duke of Bewcastle, I understand, and your brother is the present holder of the title. I do thank you from the bottom of my heart, my lord, for condescending to honor us with your presence this afternoon."

"Sir?" Aidan said with distant hauteur.

"Colonel," Miss Morris said, her expression hard-eyed and tight-lipped, "will you permit me to present my cousin, Mr. Cecil Morris."

"This is a great honor indeed, my lord," the man said, bowing and scraping and simpering. "And if I might also present my mama? Where is she?" He turned his head to look among the groups of people gathered in the churchyard. "Now where did she go? Ah, there she is, conversing with Mrs. Philpot and Miss Drabble." He waved the handkerchief from one uplifted arm.

Aidan looked at him with considerably more attention. *This* was the man who was to inherit Ringwood? He was small and plump with a puffed-out chest and an important, bustling air. And obsequious to a fault. Miss Morris's cousin. He did not, Aidan noticed, speak with even a trace of a Welsh accent. Quite the contrary. His accent would make even Bewcastle sound provincial.

"Colonel Bedwyn can meet my aunt at Ringwood, Cecil," Miss Morris said. "He is coming for tea. At least, I believe he is." She looked inquiringly at Aidan.

"Oh, you simply must come, my lord," Cecil Morris added, abandoning his attempt to summon his mother. "I urge you to honor us with your company, as humble an abode as Ringwood Manor is compared to the ducal seat, I do not doubt. Lindsey Hall, I believe? Mama will be gratified beyond words."

"Thank you, ma'am." Aidan bowed to Miss Morris and ignored her cousin. "I will be there."

He strode off in the direction of the inn. He would have his horse saddled and ride over. Lord help the poor woman if she was going to have to live out her life in company with her cousin and his mother once the anniversary of her father's death had passed.

Was *this* what had so concerned Captain Morris?

Eve had been feeling kindly disposed toward Colonel Lord Aidan Bedwyn after church. By the time he left Ringwood after tea she despised him and was heartily glad she would never see him again.

Her neighbors were attentive. Almost all came back to the house and all spoke to her with kindly sensibility about the service and about Percy. Serena Robson, James's wife, sat beside Eve for almost an hour, holding her hand much of the time, chafing it, assuring her that this day was a dreadful ordeal for her but a necessary one, that once it was over she would feel better again.

"And you know," she said earnestly when there was no one else with them, "you are perfectly welcome to come and make your home with us, Eve. James agrees with me that nothing would suit us more."

Eve glanced across the room at James. Poor man, it was something he would surely hate. But she was touched by Serena's kindness. The two of them had been friends since Serena's marriage to James five years before. But friendship had its limits.

"I do not even want to think beyond today, Serena," Eve told her. "But thank you. You are most kind."

Truth to tell, she had been finding it hard all day to think rationally at all. Even the memorial service had been hard to concentrate on, much as she had tried. Only the colonel's eulogy had captured her undivided attention.

Time was running out.

She might have saved herself and everyone else under her care from this predicament if only she had married sometime during the past year. She had had several offers. But she had not considered any of them seriously. She had been waiting for John. Oh, foolish, foolish—she was no longer convinced that John was coming back at all. Even if he did, he would come too late to save her servants and friends.

She could scarcely believe that she was doubting John. Against all reason, perhaps, she had loved and trusted him through fifteen long, silent months.

No one knew about John, not even Aunt Mari. John, Viscount Denson, whose father, the Earl of Luff, had strictly forbidden the match when her father had proposed it to him, was with the diplomatic service and currently at the embassy in Russia—or perhaps by now he really was on his way back to England. He had promised to come straight home when he returned in March and finally make their secret betrothal public. By then, he had told her, he would be a respected diplomat, an important person in his own right, and his father would be powerless to stop him from marrying the woman of his choice. They would marry before the summer was out.

Eve smiled wanly as yet another of her neighbors bent over her to commiserate with her and comment on the beauty of the memorial service. Everyone was so very kind. How good it was to have friends who cared.

Where was John now, at this precise moment? She had no way of knowing. They had not written to each other even once during the fifteen months of his absence—it was not at all the thing, after all, for a man and woman to correspond when they were not married or at least officially engaged. At least, that was what she told herself during the first long months when she did not hear from him. She had been unable to write to him herself as he had given her no address. But surely, she had thought more recently, though she had tried to suppress the thought, he could have found some way of communicating with her without damaging her reputation. If only he would come, she thought. If only she could look up *now* to find him standing in the doorway, blond and handsome, with his usual air of ease and confidence. But all she saw when she looked up was Colonel Bedwyn standing listening to Cecil.

Surprisingly, the colonel made no apparent effort to get away from him. Eve had almost laughed at the snub he had dealt Cecil on the churchyard path and was disappointed that he would now bolster her cousin's sense of importance by giving him his undivided attention. Nevertheless, she was glad to be relieved of the duty of being sociable to the dour colonel herself. She would have still felt in charity with him if the afternoon had not ended as it did.

She had gone down to the terrace to see James and Serena Robson on their way. She waved to them as they drove away, feeling suddenly very weary and very lonely. She turned to go back into the house, but Cecil and Aunt Jemima were just stepping out. Cecil's coachman was bringing up his carriage to take them home. Colonel Bedwyn was with them. Apart from the nervous little smile Aunt Jemima darted her way, they completely ignored Eve just as if she were invisible.

"Now *this,*" Cecil said with an expansive gesture of one arm to indicate both the house and the park, "is quite inadequate as a gentleman's seat. It might even be called an undistinguished rural heap. A marble portico with Greek-style sculptures and pillars and steps is what I have in mind. That will impress the eye, would you not agree, my lord?"

Eve looked incredulously at the ivy-clad beauty of the front of the house. She waited for the colonel's cutting set-down of such a tactless comment in her hearing.

"Both the eye and the visitor," the colonel agreed, his voice languid with aristocratic hauteur. "Such an improvement to your property cannot fail to elevate you even further in the esteem of your peers, sir."

Cecil swiveled about. "And the driveway must be widened and paved," he said. "There is scarce room for two well-appointed carriages to pass each other along it. Some of the trees will have to go."

Her precious, ancient trees, Eve thought, aghast.

"An admirable idea," Colonel Bedwyn agreed. "They are only trees, after all. Of far less significance than a gentleman's carriage."

Cecil observed his surroundings with a self-satisfied air until his carriage obstructed his view by drawing up in front of him.

"It has indeed been a pleasure to make your acquaintance, my lord," he said. "And a pleasure and an honor for Mama, too. Perhaps you will visit us some other time when you are in Oxfordshire, after I have had a chance to make Ringwood into an estate worthy to entertain the son of a duke. Perhaps you will join me for a spot of shooting. Perhaps even the duke, your brother . . ." He allowed the preposterous suggestion to trail away.

The colonel inclined his head and offered his hand to Aunt Jemima, who was so flustered for a moment that she did not seem to realize that he was intending to hand her into the carriage. She clasped it and scurried up the steps when she did realize it.

"Eve?" Cecil finally deigned to take notice of her before climbing in to take his place in the carriage. "I shall return in four days' time to take up residence here. I trust you will not make any vulgar display of protest. You know how easily Mama's nerves become upset."

"Good day to you, Cecil," she said. "Good-bye, Aunt. Thank you for coming."

Her aunt raised a black handkerchief to her eyes after smiling with watery tenderness at her.

"How are Becky and Davy?" she had whispered soon after they had arrived at the house, with anxious glances to both sides. But she had chosen her moment poorly—Cecil had been bearing down upon them. Aunt

Jemima had smiled and nodded vaguely and remarked that she must get the recipe for the pound cake from Eve's cook.

When the carriage drove off, Eve was left standing on the terrace beside Colonel Lord Aidan Bedwyn.

"Ma'am," he began, "if I may—"

She did not wait for him to finish. Even the sound of his voice made her bristle with indignation. She turned and walked into the house without a backward glance.

CHAPTER IV

❧

"I ab buch better, sir," Andrews said. "I cad have us on our way by sud-up."

Aidan stood in his inn room, his back to his batman, and closed his eyes. Oh, the temptation! After a few moments he uttered—aloud—every ugly, filthy, obscene, blasphemous word in his considerable vocabulary.

Andrews sniffed.

"Blow your blasted nose," Aidan commanded him.

Andrews obeyed, sounding like a cracked trumpet as he did so.

"My civilian clothes," Aidan ordered, beginning to undo the buttons of his scarlet coat.

"Your riding clothes?" Andrews asked.

"No, not the riding clothes, blast it," Aidan said, shrugging out of the coat and tossing it over the back of a chair for his batman to deal with later. "Did I ask for riding clothes?"

"Do, sir," his batman conceded. "I thought perhaps you had decided to leave todight." The nose-blowing had obviously done nothing to clear his nasal passages.

"You thought wrongly," Aidan said curtly. "I will let you know when I plan to leave this infernal inn."

Less than half an hour later he was wearing civilian clothes again—white shirt and neckcloth, blue superfine form-fitting coat, cream waistcoat, buff-colored pantaloons, and white-topped Hessian boots. He was freshly shaved. He was still in as foul a mood as he had been half an hour earlier—fouler.

He still could not quite believe what he had learned from Cecil Morris, whom he had milked for information with consummate ease simply by flattering the man with his attention and his questions and his unqualified approval of every asinine answer. He would have been far happier throttling the little weasel.

Old man Morris must have been a pretty piece of work, Aidan thought contemptuously as he sat down to dinner in his own room—he was in no mood to put in an appearance in the taproom. When he had failed to persuade his daughter to marry any of the socially superior men he had presented her with, he had tried to exert some control beyond the grave.

According to the will he had written shortly before his death, Morris had indeed left everything to his daughter for one year only before it was to pass to her brother or, in the event of his prior demise, to her cousin. But he had also dangled a juicy carrot before her face. She could retain her inheritance for the rest of her life *if she married* during that year.

There were four days remaining until the first anniversary of Morris's death.

Cecil Morris was about to inherit. But though he had apparently peppered his cousin with marriage proposals when it had seemed in his interest to do so, he was no longer prepared to be bothered with her now that he did not need her. She was to be turned out of the house in four days' time. Cecil Morris neither knew nor cared what would become of her.

News of the death of her brother, then, had come as a double blow to Miss Morris two days ago. There was no doubt that his death had upset her in a thoroughly personal way. But the other implication of that death must at least have contributed to the gaunt look she had been wearing ever since. Apparently Captain Morris had left everything to her in his own will and had even signed papers legally relinquishing all claims on the Ringwood property to his sister during his lifetime. Unfortunately, his generosity had gone for naught. He had died before he had any claim on Ringwood and therefore any right to dispose of it as he wished.

In four days' time Miss Morris was to be homeless and, presumably, destitute. Her father had not even left her a dowry or a pittance on which to live.

Aidan dismissed Andrews after he had finished his meal and then entertained the empty room with a deliberate repetition of every nasty word he had uttered earlier in Andrews's hearing. But he felt no better for the venting of spleen.

Four days.

Captain Morris had been right to worry about her,

then. She did indeed need help and protection. And Aidan had solemnly sworn to provide both—*no matter what*. During his ride back to the inn from Ringwood he had pummeled his brain for ideas on what he could do for her. But even before arriving he had realized that there *was* only one answer. The trouble was, he did not like it at all—and that was surely the understatement of the century!

And there were only four days left.

Even though Miss Morris had pointedly snubbed him before he left Ringwood this afternoon—and who could blame her after that ridiculous scene with Cecil Morris she had witnessed?—he was going to have to persuade her to receive him again and listen to him and do what he suggested.

Those three words—*no matter what*—had just been hung about his neck like a millstone. They were about to deal him a life sentence just when he had begun to dream different dreams. There was only one way in which he could protect her.

Damn and blast, *there was only one way.*

He rammed his hat on his head and took up his cane.

After the last of the guests had left, Eve called her whole household together with the sole exceptions of the children and Nanny Johnson, who stayed with them in the nursery. Everyone else gathered in the drawing room, from which the tea things had been cleared.

There was no point in delaying this encounter any longer. Nothing was going to change now. Nothing could save any of them. The best Eve could do was give everyone a few days' notice—not that they would not all have given it to themselves by now. They all knew the truth.

"I doubt my cousin will keep any of you on," she said into the heavy silence that surrounded her. She had invited everyone to be seated but had remained standing herself. "Perhaps you, Sam, since you were once a groom at Didcote and Cecil is impressed by such things."

"I was dismissed for poaching, miss," Sam reminded her bluntly. "No one else would take a chance on me but you. I wouldn't work for *him* if he was to ask me."

"And you, Mrs. Rowe, have a reputation as the best cook in Oxfordshire." Eve smiled at her.

"But it got out that I was once cook for all the girls and their fancy gents in a London brothel, miss," the cook said. "And you was the only one who would give me a job. I am with Sam. If I was to cook for his nibs, I would poison his roast beef, I would."

"Ned." Eve turned to her one-armed steward. "I am so sorry. All our wonderful dreams and plans will have to be abandoned. You will not even have employment here."

They had been going to buy a piece of land adjacent to Ringwood—at least *Eve* had been going to buy it after the year was over, with Percy's approval, and Ned had been going to manage it. They had been going to set it up as a farm where destitute, permanently maimed soldiers could live and work and become self-sufficient in a sort of commune. Eventually the price of the land would be paid back and it would be truly Ned's, though

Eve had never planned to enforce that provision.

"That is all right, Miss Morris," he said. "I'll live. You are not to worry about me."

"Charlie. Dear Charlie." Eve looked kindly at him. "I am going to speak to Mr. Robson and see if he will offer you employment. I will do my best."

"Did I do something wrong, Miss Morris?" he asked, looking utterly forlorn.

Sam Patchett set a hand on his shoulder and promised to explain to him later.

"Thelma." But Eve could neither look at the girl nor say any more. She closed her eyes and pressed one hand over her mouth. There was a sharp ache in her throat and chest. Where would Thelma go? What would she do? Who would give her employment? How would she be able to feed and nurture Benjamin?

"Eve," Thelma said, "you are not responsible for me. Really you are not. You have been unbelievably kind to me. You have yourself to worry about now. I'll manage. I'll find something. I did before you took me in here."

Eve opened her eyes and gazed at her aunt. Her little cottage in Wales had been sold. The pension Papa had allotted her had not been mentioned in his will. Aunt Mari was old and worn out and half crippled. It had given Eve intense satisfaction to bring her to Ringwood and to pamper her with some of the luxuries she had never known before.

"You are not to worry about me, my love," Aunt Mari said firmly. "I'll go home where I belong and where I have friends to take me in. I'll make myself useful and earn my way. But what are *you* going to do? Your dada took you from your roots and brought you up as a lady, and now he has left you with nothing, the wicked man, all because he could not have his way. I'd tell him a thing or two if he was still alive to hear me. Believe me I would."

But Eve was not really listening. She was thinking about Davy and Becky. They were orphans. Their parents had died within days of each other of some virulent fever, and the children had been sent on an endless journey about England, passing from one to another of their surviving relatives, none of whom wanted them or were even willing to tolerate them. Last on the list had been their great-aunt, Mrs. Jemima Morris. Left to herself, Eve had always believed, Aunt Jemima would have opened both her home and her heart to the children, but Cecil had persuaded her that doing so would have shattered her nerves and ruined her health.

Unknown to Cecil, Aunt Jemima had come running to Ringwood, and Eve had taken the children in even though there was no blood relationship between her and them. Her father had recently died, Percy was off at the wars, the wait for John's return seemed interminable, she was lonely despite the presence of Aunt Mari in her home—and she had been unable to withstand Aunt Jemima's pitiful tears.

Mrs. Johnson, a widow from Heybridge who was known to have a way with children, had agreed to come and look after them, and Eve had set about the task of seeking a governess for them. A married friend of hers, now living thirty miles distant, had informed her of an unfortunate governess in her neighborhood who had been dismissed from her employment after it was discovered that she was increasing with her employer's child and had been grubbing out a meager existence ever since by taking in laundry. A week later Thelma Rice and her baby son had been established at Ringwood Manor.

What was to happen to Becky and Davy? Could Cecil be persuaded to allow them to stay now that he would have a larger home and a larger fortune to enable him to be generous? Would he let Nanny Johnson remain so that the transition would not be too terribly frightening for them? Would he let Thelma and Benjamin—but no! That at least was something she knew was out of the question.

"Agnes—" she began.

"You don't need to say no more to me, my lamb," her housekeeper said. "I did my time in jail more than once, I did, and I lived to tell the tale. I left London to look for a better life, and I got taken up for vagrancy. Then you took me in. I'll always remember that, and I'll bless you with my dying breath, but I'm not going to add one ounce to your burden. You are not my keeper, miss—I am. But if it's all the same to you, when you are forced to leave here, I'll stick with you for a while and be *your* keeper. It can be a cruel world out there."

"Oh, *Agnes*." Eve could no longer restrain her tears.

Agnes took charge of dismissing everyone, and they all tiptoed away—all except Aunt Mari—as if leaving the room of an invalid.

One of Eve's favorite times of day was after dinner in the evening, when she went up to the nursery and played with and read to the children while Thelma devoted herself to Benjamin and sang him lullabies when it was time for him to sleep. It was Nanny Johnson's time off.

This evening Eve was reading stories. Davy sat on one side of her, not quite touching her. He had learned during the months following his parents' death that the adult world was hostile and not to be trusted, and he was unlearning that cruel lesson with slow caution. Becky was curled up against Eve's other side. Placid and good-natured, she sometimes seemed to have been less deeply affected by her experiences than Davy. But she occasionally awoke in the night, Nanny reported, either crying helplessly or screaming.

Thelma was standing in the doorway to Benjamin's bedchamber beyond, listening to the story. The little boy must already be asleep. Muffin was curled up at Eve's feet, his chin on his paws, snoozing.

Everything seemed almost frighteningly normal.

Eve made every effort to concentrate her mind upon the adventures of two children who had escaped the clutches of an evil goblin in the dark forest only to find their way to safety barred by a ferocious lion with a thorn stuck in one paw. She tried desperately not to think about the future. She resisted every urge to set both arms about the children and hug them so tightly that she would convey her own fright to them. The little dinner she had eaten sat uneasily in her stomach.

Where was John? she kept wondering despite herself. Not that he could save everyone around her now even if he arrived tonight—it would be far too late to have the banns read in time. And it seemed selfish to think only of her own comfort and security. But where *was* he? It would be such an enormous relief just to see him, just to feel his arms about her again, just to be able to unburden herself of all her woes to him. Perhaps he would be able to think of something.

But there was *nothing*.

Her decision to wait for John had been a selfish one, she thought suddenly, as well as a foolish one. *He was not coming back.* He had not written even once either during the year he had expected to be away or during the months since he had expected to be back. She had been naive to trust his protestations of undying love. But her sudden loss of faith in him frightened her. She had clung to it for so long. And she loved him. With all her heart she loved him.

Was she the world's most gullible fool? If she had accepted one of her other suitors during the past year, she and all her friends and dependents would not be in this predicament now.

But how could she possibly have married a man who was not John?

A tap on the nursery door interrupted Eve's scattered thoughts. She looked up from the book as the door opened to reveal Agnes Fuller, looking even more sour than usual.

"It's that military gent," she said.

Eve merely stared.

"The one with the nose and the scowl and the long handle of a name," Agnes explained. "He has come calling. At *this* time of night."

"Tell him I have gone out. Tell him I have retired for the night," Eve said indignantly. How dared he! Colonel Lord Aidan Bedwyn was the last man she wanted to see—ever. His insensitivity to her and his words to Cecil on the terrace this afternoon had wiped out any sense of gratitude she had felt toward him.

"He said he wasn't going to believe no excuses," Agnes informed her. "He also wouldn't wait in the hall when I told him to. He went striding off into the parlor without a by-your-leave. I'll try chucking him out if you want, my lamb. I probably won't be able to budge him even though I can square up to most men, but I wouldn't mind a good scrap with him anyway for being so high-handed. There was no need to be, was there? I hadn't even *given* him any excuses yet."

"Well!" Eve got to her feet and handed the book to Thelma. Muffin scrambled to his feet with a woof. "We will see about *that*. But if anyone is to enjoy the pleasure of a good scrap with him, Agnes, it is going to be me. He had the *nerve* this afternoon to tell my cousin Cecil that all his ridiculous plans for improving Ringwood will make him a better-respected gentleman. He completely ignored me."

"Oh, how incredibly ill-mannered!" Thelma exclaimed.

"Right!" Agnes turned away, all belligerent ardor. "I'll give him what for, I will, that chest and them shoulders notwithstanding. I'll put another bend in that nose, I will."

"No, you will not." Eve sighed when her house-keeper stopped and looked back at her, a mulish expression on her face. "Finish reading to the children, will you, Thelma? I will see him, Agnes. Perhaps he wishes to go down on his knees and beg my pardon." She bent to kiss the children and bid them a good night. She instructed Muffin to stay, and he sat again, regarding her mournfully from his one eye.

"Shall I come right in there with you?" Agnes asked as they descended the stairs together. "Or would you rather I fetch Mrs. Pritchard?" Aunt Mari usually spent a quiet hour or two in her room after dinner before joining Eve for a cup of tea before bed.

"Neither. I'll see Colonel Bedwyn alone," Eve said. "But you may stay in the hall if you wish. I'll call if I need help."

She drew a deep breath as she opened the door to the visitors' parlor.

CHAPTER V
ی

He was standing in front of the fireplace, as he had been the first time she saw him, but he was not in uniform this time. He still looked almost as large and menacing, though. He had taken the liberty of lighting the candles in the branch on the mantel, it being almost dark outside.

"Colonel Bedwyn," Eve said briskly, closing the door behind her. She made no attempt to smile or be gracious. "What may I do for you?"

"You withheld the truth from me," he said, "in effect if not in strict fact. Your father *did* leave Ringwood to you, but only under conditions with which you have not complied. You are about to lose everything. In four days' time in fact."

For a moment she was so furious that all she could do was curl her hands into fists at her sides. Was this what aristocratic privilege did to a man? It made him believe it gave him the right to come where he had not been invited, to pry into her private business, to speak thus boldly and abruptly to her?

"*This* is what you have come for?" she asked. "To accuse me of lying? You are impertinent, Colonel Bedwyn. You may leave my house immediately. Good night." Her heart thumped uncomfortably as she stood away from the door. She was not one to lose her temper easily. She rarely spoke in anger.

"You might as well enjoy issuing such an order now," he said, not moving. "It will not be in your power to do so for much longer, will it?"

"Perhaps," she said, "when you come visiting next year or the year after to admire the *marble portico* and the *paved, treeless driveway,* you will say something equally impertinent to Cecil and *he* will have the satisfaction of ordering you off the property instead of me. But tonight I am still mistress here. Get out!" She felt rather like a mouse trying to impose her will on an elephant.

"He *is* a prize ass, is he not?" he said.

She was not quite certain she had heard him correctly. She looked into his dark eyes, but they had not changed expression.

"How else but by allowing him to fawn over me was I to learn the truth about you?" he asked.

She frowned. "The *truth* about me is none of your business," she said.

"I beg to disagree with you, ma'am," he told her. "Your safety and security and happiness were your brother's business. He passed that responsibility on to me at his death. That is what he meant, quite clearly, when he had me promise to protect you. He knew what his death would mean to you. By keeping the truth from me you refused him the peace he sought when he solicited my promise."

She had not considered his offers of help in that light before. She did not want to think of them that way now. He was a *stranger*. In addition to that he was a man from a different world, so far above her on the social scale that it was impossible to converse with him or deal with him as she would with any of her neighbors and friends. He was *Lord* Aidan Bedwyn, son of a duke. She approached the nearest chair and sat on it.

"You owe me nothing, Colonel," she said. "You do not even know me."

"I know," he said, "that I am responsible for you. I gave my word of honor. I have never broken my word once it has been given, and I will not start with you."

"I absolve you," she said.

"You do not have that power," he told her. "What do you intend to do? What are your plans?"

When she drew breath to speak, she found that she

could not draw in enough air. She felt as if she had been running hard. She shrugged.

"I will think of something," she said lamely.

"Do you have anyone to go to?" he asked.

She still resented the abrupt, probing questions into her private life. But she understood now that he must not be enjoying this any more than she was. How he must be wishing that he had not come upon Percy before he died. How he must be regretting the fact that his batman had caught a cold before he could leave as planned yesterday. She shook her head.

"Not really." She could not, of course, take up residence with James and Serena, even temporarily. Her only relatives were Cecil and Aunt Jemima, Aunt Mari, and her cousin Joshua, whom she would once have wed if her father had not forbidden the connection on the grounds that Joshua, though a wealthy shopkeeper, was neither a gentleman nor a landowner. He was now married to someone else and had three young children.

"You plan to take employment, then?"

"I suppose so." She smoothed her skirt over her knees. She had not changed since this afternoon, and she was feeling rumpled. "I am not without skills and I am not afraid of hard work. But it seems rather cruel and cowardly simply to go away and concern myself with my own survival. I have a few days, though, in which to try and arrange something. I should have thought ahead and planned for just this eventuality, should I not? Percy was always in danger of dying."

"Why *did* you not?" he asked her. "You knew the terms of your father's will. You knew, as you have just pointed out, that your brother lived in constant danger of dying."

"I suppose I did not like to admit that possibility," she said. "I suppose I chose to deny reality. He was my only brother. He was all I had left. As for marrying, it seemed calculating and distasteful to me to wed only in order to secure my inheritance. I always imagined that I would marry for love."

She did not mention John. Would she have married someone else this year if there had not been John? She was not at all sure of the answer.

"Percy told me he did not want the estate or the fortune and was determined to sign it all over to me as soon as it became his," she added. "Marrying someone this past year never seemed urgent to me. I would not have minded dreadfully even if he had changed his mind. He was as fond of me as I was of him. It was foolish of me to put all my trust in his surviving, was it not?"

He did not answer her but stared at her for a long, silent moment, his eyes hard, his features immobile.

"Why cruel?" he asked. "Why cowardly?"

"What?" She looked up at him blankly.

"To whom would your taking employment be cruel?" he asked. "It is the word you used a short while ago. To the pupils in the village school? To the mothers who need the services of your midwife?"

His eyes were looking very intently into her own, holding her gaze so that she found it impossible to look away. His was altogether an overpowering presence. She wished he would simply go away. But he was not going to release her until she had bared her soul to him.

"To them. To everyone," she said with a sigh. "Everyone at Ringwood Manor—I believe without exception—will be forced to leave here when Cecil moves in. It is not just me."

"Your aunt has no private means?" he asked, raising his eyebrows.

She shook her head. "Neither does Thelma, an unmarried gentlewoman who was turned out of her employment because she was bearing her married employer a bastard child after he had forced his attentions on her. Nor does her child. Or the other two children living here, orphans I have taken into my own personal care. Or Agnes Fuller, my housekeeper, an ex-convict. Or Charlie Handrich, who does odd jobs around here with great eagerness but whom no one else wants because they consider him a half-wit. Or Edith, my maid, or Nanny Johnson. None of them has independent means. And none of them has any great hope of finding employment elsewhere." She heard, appalled, the bitterness in her voice as she poured out the details, which were none of his business. "No hope at all, in fact."

"You have a bleeding heart," he said after a few moments of silence. She was not sure if it was an accusation or a simple statement of fact. "You have filled your home and neighborhood with lame ducks and now feel responsible for them."

"They are not lame ducks." She frowned up at him, her anger returning. "They are people to whom life has been cruel. They are precious persons of no less value in the sacred scheme of things than you or I. And there

67

is Muffin too, my dog, who was brutally abused by his former owner. Lives of infinite value, all of them. What am I supposed to do when I see suffering and have it in my power to alleviate it? Turn my back?"

He stared expressionlessly at her. "A rhetorical question, no doubt," he murmured.

"But now," she said, "it is no longer in my power to help them. Now that I have given them a home and hope and dignity and a life to be lived, they are to be turned out again. No one will give any of the children a home. They will end up in an orphanage—if they are so fortunate. And no one will employ any of the adults, not even my neighbors, though I will go to each of them in turn tomorrow and beg them to do just that. These precious friends of mine will become vagrants and beggars and perhaps worse, and society will declare that it expected that all along. It will pat itself on the back for being so much more perceptive than I."

He stared at her, still without expression. He was as granite-hearted as he looked, she suspected. Both his social rank and his military experience would have contributed to that. But what did it matter? He owed her nothing, not even sympathy, despite what he believed he owed Percy.

"I do beg your pardon," she said. "This is all sentimental drivel to you, no doubt. You will tell me, as others have before you, that I am *not* my brother's keeper—or my sister's either. Even *they* say it themselves. But I am, you see. My father was one of the poor until marrying my mother made him into a fabulously wealthy man. He was a coal miner and married

68

the owner's daughter. Did you know that, Colonel? I am not even close to being a lady by birth, you see, though I have been raised and educated as one. How can I not give back some of what I have done nothing to earn or deserve?"

"A thoroughly bourgeois attitude," he said, "though perhaps I do the bourgeoisie an injustice. Most of them spend their lives dissociating themselves from their past and cleaving to those higher on the social scale."

Which was exactly what Papa had done. Eve stared stonily at the colonel, and he stared back at her for so long that she grew uncomfortable.

"Go home to your family, Colonel," she said. "It is beyond your power to protect *me,* far less all those for whom I feel responsible. I will manage. I will survive. We all will."

He turned at last to stare into the unlit coals in the fireplace. He spoke brusquely. "There is a way of saving everything you hold dear," he said.

"No." She stared, frowning, at his back. "If there were, I would have thought of it, Colonel. I have considered *everything,* believe me."

"You have missed one possibility," he said, his voice cold and harsh.

"What?"

But he did not immediately proceed to tell her what it was. His clasped hands, she noticed, were tapping rhythmically against his back.

"You are going to have to marry me," he said.

"What?"

"If you are married before the anniversary of your

father's death," he said, "you will be able to keep your home and your fortune and the lame ducks too."

"Married?" She stared incredulously at his rigidly straight back. "Even if it were not the most preposterous idea I have ever heard, there are only four days left. Before the vicar had even finished calling the banns, Cecil would have his portico half built."

"There will be just time if we marry by special license," he said. "We will leave early tomorrow morning for London, marry the next day, and return the day after. You will be back here in time to thumb your nose at your cousin when he arrives to take possession. *That* at least will afford me some satisfaction."

He was serious, she realized. *He was serious.* And he spoke with all the confident assurance of a superior officer giving orders to his subordinates or his men. He was not asking her, he was *telling* her.

"But I have no wish to follow the drum," she said.

He looked at her over his shoulder, his expression grim. "I am thankful to hear it," he said. "You will not, of course, be doing so."

"You can have no wish to live *here*." The very idea was ludicrous.

"None whatsoever," he agreed curtly, turning to face her fully. "You are being obtuse, Miss Morris. It will be entirely a marriage of convenience. It would seem that you have no wish to marry. You are no young girl, and you must have had numerous chances to attach the affections of a man of your own choosing if you had so desired. Obviously you have not done so. Neither do I wish to marry. I have a long-term career in the cavalry.

70

It is a life hardly conducive to marriage and family. Neither of us will be greatly inconvenienced, then, by a marriage to each other. I will return to my regiment after spending the rest of my leave at Lindsey Hall. You will remain at Ringwood. We need never see each other again after I have escorted you home from London in three days' time."

"You are the son of a *duke*," she said.

"And you are a coal miner's daughter." He looked haughtily at her. "I do not believe the difference in our stations precludes our marrying, ma'am."

"Your brother, the Duke of Bewcastle, would be appalled," she told him.

"He need never know," he said without denying it. "Besides, I am thirty years old and have long been my own man, Miss Morris. The differences between us need never embarrass either of us. We will not be remaining together after our nuptials."

Why was she even arguing the point with him? There was still John, despite his failure to return to her. At their last meeting before he went to Russia, they had pledged themselves to each other. . . .

"I have never known anyone who married by special license," she said.

"Have you not?"

Was it really so easy?

What if John *was* on his way home? But could she afford at this precise moment to continue deluding herself? He was *not* coming. And even if he were, how could he help now? All was lost. Unless . . .

"Well?" Colonel Bedwyn sounded impatient.

She licked dry lips with a dry tongue. "There must be a million arguments," she said. "I cannot *think*. I need to think. I need time."

"Time," he said, "is something you do not have, Miss Morris. And sometimes it is best not to think but simply to do. Go upstairs and give your maid orders to pack a bag for you. We will leave early in the morning. Your aunt should accompany you for propriety's sake if she is able. Do you have a traveling carriage here? And horses?"

She nodded. There was the old carriage that had been such a symbol of wealth and status to her father.

"I will call in at the stables before I return to Heybridge, then," he said, "and give directions about the morning. I will not keep you any longer. Doubtless there will be much for you to do if you are to be away for three days."

He bowed with stiff formality and had stridden from the room before she could raise a hand to stop him. She heard him say something, presumably to Agnes, and then the front door opened and closed.

He was gone. She had not stopped him when she had the chance.

She had not said yes to his insane suggestion, had she?

But she had not said no either.

She should run after him and do it now—he had said he was going to the stables. She should tell him the full truth. But what was the truth? The stark truth was that Percy had died too soon and John had proved faithless. She had four days in which to take charge of a des-

72

perate situation—or not to.

She could not marry Colonel Bedwyn. *Marry Colonel Bedwyn?* She laughed suddenly, a convulsive, mirthless sound, then clapped both hands over her mouth lest Agnes hear her and conclude that she had run mad. She fought a silent battle with panic and hysteria.

She needed to think. She needed time. But she could not seem to do the former, and she did not have any of the latter, as he had so bluntly pointed out.

She got to her feet and began to pace back and forth across the room.

When Aidan rode up the driveway to Ringwood Manor early the following morning, William Andrews a discreet distance behind him, he could see that an ancient and hideously ornate traveling carriage was drawn up to the front doors. She had not countermanded his orders after he had left, then. She was going to go through with this.

If there was still any doubt left, it fled after he had ridden onto the terrace and could see around the carriage to the front doors. They stood open. His approach must have been noted. Miss Morris, dressed for travel, in gray as usual, was on her way down the steps, drawing on a pair of black gloves as she came. The scruffy dog bobbed along at her heels. She looked as pale as a ghost. Her aunt, assisted by a thin young maid, came down behind her.

In the doorway stood the housekeeper, her hands planted on her ample hips as if she were itching to quarrel with someone, and the young governess who had an illegitimate child.

They all looked as if they were about to attend another funeral today. Well, he thought grimly as he dismounted, he felt a little that way himself. A plump young lad loped up to hold his horse's head. Aidan guessed from his genial, rather vacant expression that he must be the servant whose mind did not move too swiftly.

"You are ready?" Aidan asked unnecessarily after nodding a curt good morning to the ladies. He had not admitted to himself until this moment how much he had hoped she would change her mind. Not that there would have been any changing of mind to do. She had given him no definite answer last evening.

"Yes." All she spoke was the single word.

"Allow me, ma'am." He held out a hand to help Mrs. Pritchard into the carriage.

"Don't you do it, my lamb," the housekeeper called out, fixing Aidan with the evil eye just as if he were about to abduct her mistress to have his wicked way with her. "Just don't do it. Not for us. We'll manage, the whole lot of us. You don't owe us nothing."

"Agnes," Mrs. Pritchard said after she had seated herself with a sigh, "you will only confuse Eve by keeping on saying that. Having said which, Eve, my love, I must say that now is the time to thank the colonel for his kind offer and send him on his way if you aren't quite, quite sure this is what you want for yourself."

Aidan tapped his riding crop impatiently against his

boot. One thing from which he cringed more than any-thing else was emotional drama, especially that of the female variety. The governess was looking stricken. The maid was sniffling.

"But of course it is what I want," Miss Morris said to them all, so falsely cheerful that she would have been booed off any stage. "Aunt Mari and I will be back the day after tomorrow and all will go on as before. Nothing will be any different except that Cecil will not be able to come here ever again to threaten our peace. Remember—not a word to anyone until we return. Muffin, stay." Aidan watched with disapproval as she bent to pat the dog's head instead of insisting upon instant obedience.

She climbed into the carriage then, placing her hand in Aidan's outstretched one but not looking into his face. Her own looked as if it had been carved of marble. Finally the maid scurried in after her, pre-tending not to notice Aidan's hand. If he said *boo* to her, he suspected, she would collapse in an insensible heap. He shut the door firmly, nodded to the coachman, mounted his horse again, tossed a coin to the lad, and followed the carriage down the driveway, over the bridge, and through the village, Andrews coming along behind.

London was a full day's journey away for such a monstrosity of a carriage, but fortunately the weather was fine and the road dry, and they made good time despite the fact that Aidan felt obliged to stop more fre-quently than the turnpikes necessitated. The carriage horses had to be changed at regular intervals, and the ladies had to stretch their legs and eat. Not that Miss Morris did much of the latter, he noticed, but Mrs. Pritchard seemed glad of the refreshments. She made an effort to be amiable toward Aidan, conversing with him cheerfully and rather loudly in her barely intelligible Welsh accent and preventing the awkward silences that would otherwise have descended upon them. He was very glad to be making the journey on horseback, not riding in the carriage.

Miss Morris looked like marble every time he set eyes on her, but he steeled himself against feeling sorry for her. What choice had he had but to talk her into doing what she was doing? Besides, who was there to feel sorry for him? His heart was not exactly dancing a jig over the prospect of tomorrow's business. Far from it. He was not a sentimental man. It would not have occurred to him to describe himself as a brokenhearted man today, but he felt a definite heavy sense of loss nonetheless. He had had other dreams than this.

By early evening they were entering the outskirts of town. Aidan and Andrews had been in the saddle all day, but that was nothing new to either of them. Aidan felt no great physical fatigue. He was, however, in the bleakest of moods. His life had been bought two years ago at a high cost indeed. Marriage to a stranger was to be the price of honor and an unpaid debt. A marriage of convenience—but a life sentence nevertheless, and to a woman who would indeed horrify Bewcastle if he ever heard about her. A coal miner's daughter, no less. Besides, he had not told the truth last evening. It was certainly true that until recently he had firmly believed a military career and marriage to be mutually exclusive ways of life. But what if, he had been asking himself for the past few months, there were a woman who had grown up knowing very little else but a military way of life herself? The daughter of a general who had always liked to have his family with him wherever he went, for example. It was not a hypothetical question. Aidan had met such a woman.

He was not betrothed to her. Not a word had passed his lips that could be construed as a commitment that bound him in honor to her. Not a word had passed her lips. But there had been a definite, unspoken understanding that soon words *would* be spoken on both sides. There had been an unspoken understanding that General Knapp would give his blessing when asked for it. Aidan had been feeling happy at the prospect of marrying after all and of being able to expect a tolerable life with the bride of his choice.

It was simply not to be. There was no point in brooding over what could not be helped. The words would never be spoken—not by any of them. No one's honor would be compromised. Any bruises to any hearts would be silently denied.

Aidan gave the coachman directions and rode ahead of the carriage to the Pulteney Hotel in Piccadilly, the best London had to offer. He reserved two rooms and a private sitting room for two nights and turned to take his leave of the ladies. It was only when he did so that he noticed how very out of place and uncomfortable they looked in such sumptuous surroundings. He should, he realized, have taken them to a more modest hotel, but it was too late now to change the arrangements.

"Someone will escort you up to your rooms," he assured them. "There is a private sitting room where you may dine and spend the evening. I will return in the morning, as soon as I have a license and have made the necessary arrangements. You will be ready?"

"Where are you going to stay?" Miss Morris asked. It seemed to him from the fixed way she looked at him that she was afraid to glance about her at all the splendor of the Pulteney's lobby.

"At the Clarendon, if there is a room to be had there," he said. "It would not be proper for me to stay here on the eve of our wedding."

She nodded. "We will be ready," she said.

Where, Aidan wondered as he strode from the hotel, was the best place in which to get thoroughly foxed? The possibilities were clearly legion. He was in London, after all.

But did he want to face tomorrow with a thick head?

Did he want to face tomorrow at all?

He just simply had no choice, had he?

Promise me you will protect her. Promise me! No matter what!

His solemn oath had rung a death knell over his dreams. He was to wed a stranger in a marriage of convenience instead of Miss Knapp in a marriage of mutual companionship and comfort.

CHAPTER VI

❧

"What do you think, my love?" There was a note of mingled mischief and triumph in Aunt Mari's voice when the door of her room at the Pulteney Hotel finally opened and she came into the private sitting room she shared with her niece, aided by her cane. She had been in there since breakfast, supposedly resting after the exertions of yesterday's long journey before getting ready for the wedding.

Eve had been waiting with some impatience for her to reappear. She had no idea exactly when to expect Colonel Bedwyn and so had long ago finished dressing. She felt smart, if somewhat dowdy, in her best gray walking dress. Edith, who was skilled with her hands, had brushed her hair into neat coils at the back of her head and coaxed a few waves to feather down over her neck and temples. Her black gloves lay on a table by the door, ready to be donned when it was time to leave. So did her bonnet—the second-best one she had worn yesterday since there was no sign of the best one she was *sure* she had seen Edith bring out of the house in its hatbox and hand to the coachman. Edith herself was tearfully insistent that she had *too* brought it and it must have tumbled off the carriage into the ditch for the birds to peck at and the foxes to pull at and some beggar to wear. Perhaps it had somehow been taken to Aunt Mari's room by mistake, Eve had suggested as much to soothe Edith as to convince herself.

"Ah," she said with relief when she saw it upraised on her aunt's free hand, "*there* is my bonnet."

Then she took a closer look. It was the same one she had worn to the memorial service at Heybridge two days ago, but it had been transformed almost beyond recognition. Wide lavender silk ribbon, cleverly pleated, lined the underside of the brim and had been fashioned into a cluster of bows at one side. Narrower, matching ribbons fluttered from each side.

"I had the ribbon in my box at home," Aunt Mari explained, chuckling like an excited child, "waiting for a special occasion. I decided that this was it, my love— your wedding. Lavender is a color for mourning, but it is much more cheery than gray."

"But it is not really a wedding." Eve crossed the room to take the bonnet from her aunt's hand.

"What would you call it, then?" her aunt asked. "It is a ceremony that will bind you to Colonel Bedwyn for the rest of your life. It is a wedding, all right. If I knew you were doing it just for me, I would argue like the fury against it even now. But it's not just for me, so what can I say?"

"Nothing." Eve drew on the bonnet carefully so as not to disturb her curls. "It is primarily for me, Aunt Mari. I cannot bear the thought of losing Ringwood and my fortune." She tried to keep her tone light, but not *too* light.

"That will be the day," Aunt Mari said tartly, "when you think only of yourself. You are the least selfish person I know, and you are doing this for everyone *except* yourself. But you may be rewarded yet. He is a good man, my love." Despite fingers that were somewhat gnarled with rheumatism, she brushed aside Eve's hands and tied the ribbons to suit herself, slightly to one side of her great-niece's chin. "Even though he seemed dark and humorless the first time I met him, the colonel was very kind yesterday. If he had been traveling alone, I suppose he would have ridden at a steady trot and arrived here hours earlier than he did with us in tow. But he didn't try to rush me in and out of the carriage—did you notice?—and he made an effort to talk whenever we stopped, though I suppose he is much more comfortable talking about horses and guns with men and other soldiers than conversing with ladies. Not that I am a lady by his standards. He should have seen me a few years ago when I was coming up from a shift down the mine. But the colonel is a gentleman—a true gentleman."

"Of course he is," Eve agreed. "Papa would approve—more than approve, in fact."

"I just wish you would not insist on ending your acquaintance with the colonel quite so soon," Aunt Mari said, standing back to note the angle of the bow before making a few adjustments. "I wish the two of you would spend a little time together just to see if there might not be a spark of something lasting between you. It wouldn't hurt to try, would it, since you are to be married anyway. He is on leave for two months. He told me so when I asked yesterday."

"You must absolutely not wish us upon each other for longer than a day, Aunt Mari," Eve said hastily. "It would be intolerable."

"But I so very much want you to be happy, my love," her aunt said. "You give yourself generously to everyone *except* yourself. I know this is no grand love story. I would have to be a fool to imagine it is. But who is to say it couldn't *become* a love match? It isn't as if you love any other man, is it, despite all my efforts at matchmaking during the past year."

Eve smiled as she moved toward the looking glass above the mantel, her legs feeling almost too leaden to carry her there.

"Oh, my!" she said. The newly trimmed bonnet seemed to add both flesh and color to her face. It made her look younger. After a whole year she had almost forgotten what it was like to wear colors. Her eyes looked larger, more blue than gray, more luminous. "You are *so* clever with your hands, Aunt Mari. Thank you, dear." She turned to hug her aunt, who looked inordinately pleased with herself.

She was a *bride,* Eve thought. These were her bride clothes and soon she would be on her way to her wedding. The thought caused a definite physical sensation, as if the bottom had fallen out of her stomach. She was about to marry a stranger for purely mercenary reasons and with no intention of keeping most of the marriage vows she would speak. She was going to marry a man who was not John. Until this moment she had been able to tell herself that somehow she would find a way out, that some miracle would surely happen to prevent this thing from happening. But she knew now at last that nothing was going to stop it.

Unless he failed to put in an appearance . . .

At that very moment there was a brisk knock on the sitting room door. Both Eve and her aunt turned to look at it as Edith came scurrying out of Eve's bedchamber, darted them a look of sheer fright, and opened the door.

Colonel Lord Aidan Bedwyn stepped into the room, diminishing it in size as he did so. He looked large and powerful and very masculine even though he was not dressed in his uniform, as Eve had expected he would be. He bowed to both ladies and bade them a good morning.

Eve curtsied. And then a strange, horrifying, totally unexpected thing happened before he could speak again. Looking at his elegant, immaculately clad person and thinking of him as her bridegroom, she felt a rush of pure physical awareness stab downward through her breasts and abdomen and along her inner thighs. She had never considered him a handsome man. But it would be naive anyway to believe that she was reacting just to his looks. It was his undeniable masculinity that was affecting her. This was their wedding day. Under other circumstances tonight would be their wedding night.

She tried desperately to bring an image of John to her mind, and then hastily pushed it away again even before it could form. It was too late for that. Soon—very soon—it would be disloyal even to think of him. For a moment she stared at the colonel in blind panic.

"Are you ready?" he asked, his eyes lingering on Eve's bonnet for a moment before moving to Aunt Mari.

Eve nodded and reached for her gloves.

"Perhaps you would fetch my hat from my room, Edith," Aunt Mari said, but she walked after the girl to stand in the doorway and point to the one she wanted.

Eve and the colonel, left virtually alone, locked glances. It was an extremely uncomfortable moment.

"I have the license," he said, speaking briskly, without any discernible emotion, "and I have made the arrangements. We are to be at the church in half an hour."

"Are you quite sure?" she asked softly.

"I never do anything I am not sure about, Miss Morris," he said. "And *you* are quite sure too, are you not? Remember the lame ducks."

With any other man she might have suspected an attempt at a joke. But there was no gleam of humor in his eyes or about his mouth. Aunt Mari came back across the room then, her hat in place on her head, and the tension lifted somewhat.

"Let us go." The colonel opened the door.

Purchasing a special license had been astonishingly easy, Aidan had discovered. Of course, it had probably helped that he had worn his uniform—the old, comfortable uniform, not the dress one—and all of London was deliriously, exuberantly in love with its military officers, even those, he suspected, who had never set so much as a single toe beyond the safe shores of England. The staff at the Clarendon, which had treated him with respectful courtesy last evening, had bowed and scraped and fawned over him this morning while other guests had stared admiringly and nodded approvingly and one of their number, a gentleman he had never before in his life clapped eyes upon, had insisted upon shaking his hand and congratulating him as if he were personally responsible for effecting the abdication of the Emperor Napoléon Bonaparte.

It was that very reaction that had persuaded him to change back into civilian clothes for his wedding, though he had fully intended to wear his dress uniform. He did not want to be noticed. More important, he hoped not to be recognized. This was something he wanted to accomplish swiftly and secretly. It would be altogether better for all concerned if Bewcastle never knew about his marriage. He hoped, more than anything, that he would not run into Bewcastle or any other member of his family today.

The license was in Aidan's pocket, and his bride and her aunt were seated opposite him in the smart carriage he had hired for the occasion. Andrews was following behind on horseback.

Miss Morris looked remarkably attractive this morning. It was the frivolity of the frills and bows on her bonnet that did it, he supposed, as well as the touches of color. And there were loose curls visible at her neck and temples. For the first time—and, he fervently hoped, the only time—he looked upon her with sexual curiosity. He was about to make mental comparisons with Miss Knapp, but he could no longer permit himself to think about her in any way at all.

Mrs. Pritchard kept up a running monologue, exclaiming loudly at the splendor of the buildings they passed, at the noise and bustle of the streets, at all the smart conveyances that passed them. She was trying, he realized, to set both her niece and him at their ease. He handed them down when they reached the church he had selected for the quietness of the neighborhood. The rector had assured him that they would not be kept waiting and that the ceremony would take a mere few minutes.

Miss Morris set a hand on his offered arm, and he led her inside the church. Her aunt came along behind them, aided by Andrews's steady arm. They were a wedding party of four, the bride and groom and two witnesses. For an unguarded moment Aidan pictured the sort of wedding Bewcastle would have insisted upon for him under different circumstances, the first of them to marry. It would have been a grand, glittering affair, full of pomp and splendor with half the *ton* in attendance.

The stone-flagged floor of the church echoed hollowly beneath his Hessian boots. The interior was dark in contrast to the bright daylight outside, and chilly. A little gloomy. The rector appeared through a doorway beside the altar and hurried toward them, a smile of welcome on his face. He was wearing his vestments and held a book tucked against one shoulder. He bowed and greeted them and led them forward, Mrs. Pritchard beside him. He instructed them on where they were to stand and beckoned a reluctant Andrews closer. All was cheerful, impersonal business.

And then suddenly it was happening. It had started. The nuptial service.

"Dearly beloved," the rector began, "we are gathered

together here in the sight of God . . ." He spoke with all the sonorous solemnity of a clergyman addressing hundreds.

Just a few minutes later, he was concluding in the same manner. ". . . I pronounce that they be man and wife together, in the name of the Father, and of the Son, and of the Holy Ghost. Amen." He made the solemn sign of the cross with his right hand.

It was all over before Aidan had quite composed his mind to pay full attention. He had spoken vows when instructed to do so without really listening to what he said. She had spoken vows, quietly and unwaveringly. He could not recall a single word of them. He had held her hand and placed on her finger the shiny gold ring he had purchased earlier, repeating certain words after the rector as he did so. He had done it as if in a dream. But the earth had moved during those few minutes. Something momentous, irrevocable, irreversible had happened.

They were married. Until death did them part.

The church for a moment seemed as dark and as chill as the grave.

And then Mrs. Pritchard, teary-eyed and smiling, was hugging her great-niece and—after a moment's hesitation—Aidan too. Andrews was shaking him by the hand—a rare occurrence indeed. The rector was smiling and nodding affably and offering his congratulations. And they were signing the register, without once having really looked at each other, his bride in a neat, sloping hand, he in his bold, no-nonsense style. Her aunt and Andrews witnessed their signatures, the aunt with an X, he was interested to note. Aidan offered his bride his arm and led her out onto the pavement, where the hired carriage waited to take them back to the Pulteney.

It was all over. All finished. His debt had been paid, her home secured. The shackle had clanged shut about his leg. The sun beamed its warm mockery down through a break in the clouds.

"What a lovely service," Mrs. Pritchard said after he had handed her carefully into the carriage. She made a show of spreading her skirts about her, he noticed, and propped her cane against her seat so that when her niece climbed in after her she was obliged to take the seat opposite. "It was short, but the minister spoke with great feeling. You chose him well, Colonel."

Aidan took his place beside his bride, who had moved as far along the seat toward the window as the space allowed. Her aunt beamed at them.

"What a handsome couple you make," she said.

"Aunt Mari!" Miss Morris said with quiet reproach.

Aidan realized with an unpleasant jolt of awareness that his bride was no longer Miss Morris. She had just taken his name.

"You are probably both ready for a meal," he said curtly. "I have given instructions for the carriage to return to the Pulteney. It is too late to start back for Ringwood today. I will show you both something of London this afternoon, if you wish." It was not something he had planned, but it had suddenly struck him that it would appear boorish to abandon them at the Pulteney for a whole afternoon and evening when they were both strangers to town. There was, of course, the chance that he would be seen and recognized and he would prefer that not to happen, but it did not matter quite as much as it had this morning. Besides, no one seeing them—unless he had the misfortune to come face to face with a brother or sister—need know that the younger of his two companions was his wife.

"That would be delightful if it would be no trouble to you," his bride said, sounding genuinely pleased. "I would love to see the Tower and St. James's Palace and Hyde Park or anywhere else you would recommend. Wouldn't you, Aunt Mari? We are in *London*."

"The weather is ideal for sightseeing," he said briskly.

"I must say I am quite worn out with all the excitement," Mrs. Pritchard said. "And there is another long journey to be faced tomorrow. I really must rest quietly at the hotel this afternoon—and such a splendid room and such a comfortable bed are not be wasted. But that mustn't stop the two of you from going out."

"Aunt Mari—" her niece began.

"After all," her aunt said, smiling placidly, "you no longer need me as a chaperone, my love, do you? You will be with your husband."

Was Mrs. Pritchard hoping to ignite some romance between them by choosing to leave them alone together for the whole of an afternoon? Aidan wondered. From the way in which his bride shrank farther into her corner of the carriage, he guessed that she was entertaining the same suspicion.

That was all he needed to complete his happiness

today—a damned matchmaker! The woman, like an old, wrinkled little sparrow, was regarding him with assessing, twinkling eyes.

Colonel Bedwyn returned punctually at half past one to the Pulteney to take Eve driving about London. She was surprised to find that she was looking forward to the outing despite the fact that she had not been able to prevail upon her aunt to change her mind about accompanying them. But it was just as well, she thought as she followed her new husband from the hotel. He had hired a curricle to replace this morning's carriage. Aunt Mari would never have hoisted herself up to the high, narrow seat.

"I have never ridden in a curricle," she admitted. "It seems alarmingly frail and high off the ground."

"Are you afraid?" he asked, handing her up.

Actually she was not. She was exhilarated. They would be able to see a great deal from up here, and they would be open to the warm, summery air. She had changed into a light gray, high-waisted muslin dress, but she still wore the lavender-trimmed bonnet, and at the last moment before she left Aunt Mari had produced another length of the wide lavender ribbon and tied it beneath her bosom in place of the gray sash she usually wore with this particular dress.

"I suppose you are an accomplished whip," she said.

He merely raised his eyebrows and came around the curricle to take his place beside her.

She did not understand why she felt so strangely light-hearted. She ought not when she remembered what had happened this morning and all that she had sacrificed. But Atlas-like, she felt as if an enormous load had been lifted off her shoulders. It was too late now to make a different choice. The deed was done. There was no point in regretting it or wishing it had not been necessary. In the meantime she was in London for the first and probably the only time in her life, the sun was shining, and she had a gentleman to escort her about and show her all the most famous sights. Life back at Ringwood was going to be a long and in many ways a lonely business. She was going to be facing terrible heartache there. But she might as well enjoy today. Secretly, although she had been horrified at the time, she was glad Aunt Mari had decided not to come with them.

"Shall we go to St. Paul's first?" the colonel suggested. "It is my favorite church in London."

"Everything is new to me," she said. "I am in your hands."

He looked closely at her before giving the horses the signal to start. "Lavender suits you," he surprised her by saying.

He really was expert with the ribbons, she noted with some admiration as they drove through the streets of London, even though both the vehicle and the horses were unfamiliar to him. It was hardly surprising, of course. He was a cavalry officer. He was also very large and solid. She could not prevent herself from swaying against him on occasion even though she kept a grip on the rail beside her. He smelled of leather and musk.

She was not surprised that St. Paul's Cathedral was

his favorite. The sight of it fairly robbed her of breath as they approached it. It was massive and beautiful. She had never seen anything to compare with the magnificence of the great dome.

"I cannot believe I am actually seeing such a famous building with my own eyes," she said. "I have always dreamed of visiting London."

"Do you like the pillared portico?" he asked, pointing at it with his whip. "I thought you might wish to build something similar onto the front of Ringwood Manor—without the flanking towers, perhaps. They might look a little pretentious on a manor that size."

She turned her head toward him, startled. His expression was as solemn as ever. But she could not be mistaken in his intent, surely. The man *did* have a sense of humor. She laughed.

"But I could not steal Cecil's idea," she said. "It would be unkind. Maybe I will build a dome instead."

He glanced at her sidelong, not even the suggestion of a smile softening his harsh features. Had she made a mistake? No, she did not believe so.

"Shall we go inside?" he suggested. He pointed upward. "It is possible to climb up to the highest gallery to inspect the dome from close to, both inside and out. But I must warn you that if memory serves me right there are five hundred and thirty-four steps, only the first two hundred and fifty or so of which are easy to climb."

"Oh, do let us go up by all means," she said gaily. "There must be a splendid view from up there."

There was, though for several minutes after they

stepped out onto the outer gallery, which circled the base of the dome, she was in no condition to enjoy it. She was severely winded and not a little alarmed by the difficulty and darkness of most of the climb. But she had refused to stop halfway up, as every instinct had screamed at her to do, and beg him to take her back down. She dared not think about the descent, always more frightening than going up.

"Oh, goodness me!" she exclaimed breathlessly. "We must be able to see for miles."

"For a minute," he said, "I was not sure you were going to survive."

As they moved slowly about the gallery, he proceeded to point out various landmarks to her, standing close beside her as he did so that she could look along his arm to where his finger pointed. The famous River Thames was below. He identified the various bridges that spanned it. All the boats and ships on its surface, representing the busy commerce of a nation, looked like so many toys. He indicated the Tower of London, Westminster Abbey, several other churches, their elegant spires almost dwarfed by the height of St. Paul's dome, and numerous other buildings of note. Beyond it all, on both sides of the river, she could see open countryside. The wind, no stronger than a breeze on the ground, whipped at them from the direction of the river. He lifted his free arm to hold his hat more firmly on his head.

"I have never felt more exhilarated in my life," she said and realized that she spoke the simple truth. This tall, powerful man beside her was her husband of a few hours. This was their wedding day. For a few moments she allowed herself to wonder how she would be feeling now if it were a real marriage, if they had wed each other for any of the more usual reasons. Again she felt that frisson of physical awareness.

"Have you not?" He looked at her in some surprise. "Has your life been so very quiet, then?"

"Really quite uneventful," she admitted ruefully. "I have always dreamed of coming to London, of seeing other faraway places, other people." She had hardly realized it until this moment. "Men are very fortunate. They have far more freedom than we do."

"Do we?" He looked long and hard at her before turning his head without comment to stare outward again.

This was a day she would always, always remember, she knew. Since it was all so irrevocable now, she was glad there had been more to it than just that awkward little ceremony this morning. She touched her wedding ring surreptitiously through her glove, though she did not really need to do so. She could *feel* it there on her finger, the symbol of the fact that she was bound for life to this man though she would not see him again after tomorrow. She wondered how long it would be before she could no longer remember clearly what he looked like. She turned her head to look at him now as if it were somehow important to remember, to memorize the harsh, angular face, the prominent nose, the rather thin lips, the dark hair and eyes.

He was looking back at her with narrowed gaze, as if he were doing the same thing as she. "Are you ready to tackle the steps again?" he asked.

She laughed uneasily. "I think I'll spend the rest of the day up here. Maybe the rest of the week. Perhaps the rest of my life."

"As bad as that, is it?" he said. "Hold my hand. I'll not let you fall. Word of honor." He held out his left hand and raised his right.

Even though she was wearing gloves, there seemed something very intimate about holding his hand—clinging to it actually—for such a long time. But until they were close to the bottom she would not for the life of her have relinquished his support. He was a very solid man to lean upon, she thought. Solid and dependable. For a long time she had prided herself upon her ability to stand alone, to depend upon no one but herself. Almost everyone who was closest to her now depended upon her.

He took her next to Westminster Abbey, which she did not like quite as well as St. Paul's, though she found the sense of history there almost overwhelming.

"Can you believe," she asked, standing in the middle of the nave and looking about her in some awe, "that every monarch since William the Conqueror has been crowned here?"

"Except for Edward V," he said. "And most of them are buried here too. I took ghoulish pleasure in that fact the first time I came here as a boy."

"Did you come to London often?" she asked.

"Not really." He led the way onward toward the altar. "Our parents always preferred to keep us at Lindsey Hall. We liked it better there too. We were a wild lot.

Still are, I suppose."

"Are you older or younger than your brothers and sisters?" she asked. She knew almost nothing about him, she realized. Yet he was her *husband*.

"I am second to Bewcastle," he explained. "Then there are Rannulf, Freyja, Alleyne, and Morgan. Our mother was a voracious reader, especially of history. She chose our rather outlandish names."

"Are you a close family?" she asked.

He shrugged. "I have not even been home for three years," he said. "I quarreled with Bewcastle on that occasion and left sooner than I had intended. But that was nothing new."

His manner was not encouraging and he offered no further information. Eve returned her attention to the abbey.

How odd, she thought, to be married to a stranger. And to a man who would remain forever a stranger.

He drove her past St. James's Palace and past Carlton House, where the Prince of Wales lived. He drove her through Hyde Park, which was far vaster than she had expected, far more like a piece of the countryside than a park in the middle of the largest city in the world. He kept to the quieter paths, avoiding the crowd of vehicles and horses she could see occasionally in the distance.

"We can go to the Tower of London if you wish," he said when they reached Hyde Park Corner. "There is a menagerie there that you may enjoy seeing since you seem to be fond of animals. Or we can go for ices."

"I am not sure I would like to see animals caged up,"

she said. "I would want to set them all free."

"The citizens of London would be thrilled at the prospect of encountering a lion or tiger around every corner," he said. "Your heart is bleeding again."

She laughed. "Ices?" she said, just realizing the other option he had offered. "I have heard about them but never thought to taste one. *May* we?"

And so he took her to Gunter's, where she enjoyed the indescribable luxury of eating her very first ice.

"Does London live up to your expectations?" he asked.

"Oh, yes," she assured him. "I wish I had a week here." She flushed and bit her lip when she realized how like an eager, naive child she must sound. "I am also longing to be home again, of course."

She had feared that they would spend the afternoon in near silence, awkward, even morose with each other. It had not been like that after all. He was not a talkative man or an obviously amiable one. But he had a gentleman's manners and did his part, as she did, in making sure that conversation flowed between them.

"Is it possible," she asked when they had finished their ices, "to find a shop where I may purchase gifts for the children? It would be so exciting for them to have something from London."

"For the orphans?" He raised his eyebrows and looked instantly haughty.

"For Becky and Davy," she said. "My children. And for Benjamin, Thelma's son."

She half expected him to say something like *for the illegitimate brat?* But he did not do so. He rose from his chair and drew hers back when she got to her feet.

"We will go to Oxford Street," he said. "You will find plenty to spend your money on there."

She found a brightly painted wooden spinning top for Benjamin and a porcelain doll that looked very like a real baby for Becky. The colonel, who had wandered away from Eve's side, in boredom, she supposed, came back with two cricket bats, a ball, and wickets.

"The boy will probably like these," he said, "if he does not already have them."

"No, he does not." She smiled at him. "Thank you. I had no idea what I would choose for him."

"All boys enjoy cricket," he said.

"Do they?" Had he? It was hard to picture him as a boy, playing, running, laughing, carefree.

She paid for her purchases, which included lace handkerchiefs for Thelma and Aunt Mari, and Colonel Bedwyn carried the parcels out of the shop and stowed them safely on the floor of the curricle before handing Eve up one last time. She was weary. Nevertheless, when the Pulteney Hotel finally came into sight and she realized that their afternoon out was over, she felt disappointment. So soon? she thought. Reality was going to set in soon enough, she knew, but she was not ready for it yet.

"Will you dine with us?" she asked.

"Thank you, but no," he said, offering no excuse. "I will return for you in the morning. We will make a timely start again."

He escorted her into the lobby after directing a servant to carry her purchases upstairs for her, and was about to take his leave when a distinguished-looking older gentleman in military uniform stopped abruptly beside them and raised a quizzing glass to his eye.

"Ah, Bedwyn," he said heartily. "I *thought* that was you. In England for the victory celebrations, are you?"

"General Naughton," the colonel said. "How do you do, sir?"

Eve took a step back, aware again that she was well out of her social milieu, but the general turned his quizzing glass on her and raised his eyebrows. Colonel Bedwyn cupped her elbow with his right hand and drew her forward.

"I have the honor of presenting my wife, sir," he said.

"Your wife? Bless my soul, I did not know you were married, Bedwyn," the general said. "How do you do, Lady Aidan? Enjoying a stay in London, are you?"

"Indeed yes," she said. "We have been sightseeing all afternoon."

"Splendid, splendid. I will see the two of you at some of the celebrations." He nodded genially and went on his way.

Eve was feeling rather stunned. *Lady Aidan.* Foolishly, that was one thing she had not thought about since agreeing to this hasty marriage. She was no longer Eve Morris. She was Lady Aidan Bedwyn.

"Until tomorrow morning, then," her husband said. And with a curt bow he was gone.

There was a terrible feeling of emptiness then. Like a child whose grand treat is over, she found herself gazing after him and into an endlessly gray future.

CHAPTER VII

Aidan was standing at a window of the drawing room in Ringwood Manor, gazing out at grayness. For the first time since his return to England the clouds were low and heavy and rain threatened. He hoped to be well on his way to Hampshire before darkness fell, but the final leg of the journey from London had been a long one and he had accepted the invitation to take some refreshments before resuming his journey. He lifted his teacup from its saucer and drained his tea.

The ladies were sitting in a group behind him—his wife, Mrs. Pritchard, and the governess, who had been introduced to him as Miss Rice. It had seemed strange to him that the governess should be invited to join them for tea, but several things had struck him as strange about this household—the fact, for example, that all the servants and children had been gathered on the terrace as the carriage approached earlier, not in neat lines of silent, respectful welcome but in a noisy cluster, all laughing and talking at once. And that infernal dog had barked its head off unrebuked. It was his wife's bourgeois background that gave her so little control over her underlings, he supposed—and that had impelled her into marrying a stranger for their sake.

Yet he had to admit that there was an undeniable warmth about the household that he had not encountered elsewhere. And what other woman would have abandoned everyone out on the terrace in order to take her children in person back to the nursery instead of turning them over to their nurse's care—and then spent all of fifteen minutes with them there while they unwrapped their gifts? Yet she was not even the mother of any of the children. He wondered suddenly if she had ever wanted children of her own. But it was too late to think of that now.

"Eve," Miss Rice was saying now into a short lull in the conversation, "and Colonel Bedwyn, I must say this." She spoke all in a rush as Aidan turned to look at her. "I must thank you both from the bottom of my heart. On behalf of the children, who have been frightened half out of their wits without quite understanding why, thank you. He came here again yesterday, you know—Mr. Morris, that is. Agnes told him you had gone out for the day with Mrs. Pritchard, Eve. He went into every room in the house and inspected every cupboard and drawer. He brought two servants with him to count all the silverware and china and crystal and linen so that all will be accounted for after your departure. And he had Agnes gather everyone in the hall before he left. He made us all stand in two lines, like soldiers at attention, and he told us that tomorrow we must all be gone from here or he will have us taken up for vagrancy and thrown in jail. He was looking very pleased with himself indeed."

Yes, he would have been, Aidan thought. He could just picture the scene.

"Oh, Thelma," his wife said in dismay. "Every room? How could he! Every cupboard and drawer?"

"Yes," Miss Rice said. "He said he will give us until

noon tomorrow. That is when he will be coming here."

"I will write to him without delay." His wife got to her feet and turned to look at Aidan. She looked paler today than she had yesterday, he noticed. She was all in gray again. The lavender-trimmed bonnet had not made its appearance for today's journey. "But I will see you on your way first, Colonel. I hope the rain will hold off for you."

"Write?" he said. "You are going to *write* instead of confronting him in person and seeing his expression when he learns the truth? You are either a coward, ma'am, or you lack a sense of drama."

She half smiled. "It *would* be delicious to behold, would it not?" she said. "I do not believe I can resist."

"Neither can I," he said. It had not occurred to him until this moment that he should see this thing through to the end. He strode farther into the room and set his cup and saucer down on the nearest table. "I do not believe I can deny myself the pleasure of witnessing the comeuppance of Mr. Cecil Morris and even partic-ipating in it."

"You are going to *stay?*" his wife asked, her eyes widening.

"Yes," he said with sudden decision. "Yes, I am going to stay—until a few minutes after noon tomorrow. I would be very surprised if the gentleman is late."

Lindsey Hall and freedom—relative freedom—could wait another day, he thought reluctantly. He owed her this much support. One day was not a great deal in the grand scheme of things.

"Wonderful, Colonel," Mrs. Pritchard said, getting

laboriously to her feet. "I will go and talk to Mrs. Rowe right away and tell her there will be one extra for dinner. I bet she will serve a wedding banquet suitable for royalty."

Behind him Aidan could hear rain begin to patter against the window.

Eve found the situation very awkward. Colonel Bedwyn was staying at the house, in the best guest chamber, a disturbing male presence. All was perfectly proper, of course—he was her *husband*. But there was all the strain of keeping a conversation going during a lengthy dinner, for which Mrs. Rowe had prepared far more dishes than usual, and in the drawing room afterward. Nevertheless, she was glad he had stayed.

Nothing and everything had changed in her life. Once he was gone, all would proceed as it ever had—forever and ever with no hope of any happy change. When John returned, he would discover the truth of her faithlessness and there would be an end of all their dreams and plans for the future. She needed time to adjust her mind to the new facts of her life. She needed to see the colonel for just a little while longer—just for one more day—so that she would know she had not simply dreamed it all.

Eve stitched at her embroidery in the drawing room after dinner, having snatched a briefer than usual time with the children—*how* she had missed them, and how *wonderful* it felt to be back home with them, knowing that they were safe and secure beyond any doubt. *Any* sacrifice would have been worth that assurance. Aunt

Mari, bless her heart, was keeping the conversation going by describing the park to the colonel. But Eve looked up reproachfully when she suggested that her niece show it to him in the morning, before noon. Even now, it seemed, Aunt Mari would not give up on her hope of convincing them to develop some sort of relationship.

"I daresay," Eve said, "the park will be too wet in the morning, Aunt Mari. The rain shows no sign of easing." Indeed it was drumming against the windows.

The colonel was sitting in a relaxed pose in a deep armchair, his elbows on the arms, his fingers steepled. Eve had the feeling he was watching her as she worked. It was a strange, very physical feeling as if there were some string stretched between them on which an invisible finger was pulling ever so gently. She was feeling slightly breathless. It was a relief to hear a tap on the door. Agnes opened it just wide enough to poke her head around it.

"You are needed in the nursery, my lamb," she said, glancing rather venomously at Aidan, who had reminded her before dinner that her mistress was now "my lady."

"I'll come immediately," Eve said, threading her needle through the cloth, folding it, and getting to her feet.

"The children do not have a nurse?" the colonel asked.

"They are usually sleeping by now," Eve explained. "There must be a problem."

"Eve spends a great deal of time with them," Aunt Mari was saying as she left the room. "She would be a wonderful mother to her own children."

Eve grimaced and hurried up the stairs. Neither Nanny Johnson nor Thelma would interrupt her while she was entertaining unless they felt they had no choice.

Sounds of sobbing greeted her as she opened the nursery door. Nanny Johnson was seated on a chair, Becky curled up on her lap. Davy was standing in the middle of the floor in his nightshirt. It was Becky who was sobbing, inconsolably by the sound of it. Thelma was in Benjamin's room, rocking him in her arms. He was making sleepy noises of protest, obviously disturbed from his sleep.

"She is finding it hard to believe that you will not be going away again," Nanny said, "and that Mr. Morris will not be coming back to make us all go away. He made the children stand in the servants' lines too, Miss Eve, when he gave us our notice."

Eve hurried across the room and scooped Becky up into her own arms. "Oh, my sweetheart," she said, her cheek against the top of the child's head, "I am not going anywhere. I went away only so that I could make all safe for you. And all *is* safe. Ringwood is mine, and this is where you will grow up, you and Davy. This is your home and always will be. And I will always love you. Always, no matter what. Come, let's sit down and I will show you something."

The child's sobs had quietened to hiccuped gasps by the time they settled in a chair. Although she was attached to both Nanny and Thelma, it was understandable that it was Eve she needed tonight. It had been brought home to her child's mind in the cruelest of manners yesterday that it was Eve who stood between her and the terror of abandonment again. Oh, how *dare* Cecil have so demeaned and so frightened children who were his own relatives!

"Look." Eve extended her left hand and spread her fingers. "Do you see my ring? It is a wedding ring. It means that I am married. And *that* means that I can stay at Ringwood all my life. It means that *you* can stay at Ringwood too."

"And Davy?" the child asked.

"And Davy." Eve kissed the top of her head. "You are both safe. You are my very own children. I love you both and will love you forever and ever." Though love was not always enough, she admitted to herself. Love would not have protected them if she had not married. She was *glad* she had married. She would endure all the consequences of having had to take such a drastic and painful course.

She looked up to smile reassuringly at Davy, but he was looking away from her toward the door, his bare feet braced apart, his hands clenched into fists, his whole body tensed as if to spring. The colonel was standing in the doorway.

"Easy, boy," he said quietly. "I am not your enemy. Or your sister's. You would defend her to the death, would you? Good lad. Men protect the women in their lives."

"Go away!" Davy's voice was trembling.

"Davy—" Eve began, but the colonel held up a staying hand without removing his eyes from the boy.

Nanny did not move.

"Miss Morris came to London with me two days ago," he said, "so that I could marry her yesterday. She is now Lady Aidan Bedwyn. I married her to give her my protection, so that she can stay here and so that you can have a home and be safe until you grow up and make your own way in the world. I married her because I am a man of honor and protect women whenever it is in my power to do so. I am a military officer and must return to my battalion soon. Lady Aidan is safe here— I have seen to that—but I will be easier in my mind knowing that she has another honorable man to look after her and the other women here. Or an honorable boy who will grow into a man, anyway. I believe you are he. Am I right?"

Eve watched the tension gradually drain from Davy's body.

"Yes," he said.

"Yes, sir," Aidan said quietly.

"Yes, sir."

"Good lad. Which is your bedchamber?"

"That one." Davy pointed. "I heard Becky crying. I thought that man had come to get her."

"You know now that that is not going to happen," Aidan said. "Ever. Why don't you go back to bed and let your nurse tuck you in? All is safe."

The thing was, Eve thought, rocking Becky in her arms, there was nothing soft in his manner. He had even forced Davy to call him *sir*. He had not smiled or looked anything short of ferocious. But she felt she was having a rare glimpse into a man whose depths of character she had not even begun to uncover. And she never would do so. Tomorrow he would be gone, this stranger, her husband.

His eyes met hers across the room and held her gaze. Neither spoke. They could not do so—Becky was falling asleep, Thelma was still rocking Benjamin, her back to the nursery, and Nanny was murmuring softly to Davy in his room.

It was a moment in which something passed between them, something intimate, almost tender, unexplainable, painful. Eve felt a soreness in her chest that felt very much like grief.

After a few moments he turned and left and Eve set her head back against the chair and closed her eyes. She had not known it would feel like this—as if something really had happened yesterday. Something that had deeply and irrevocably changed her life.

When Aidan got out of bed the next morning, woken by the sound of Andrews bringing his shaving water into his dressing room, it was to the discovery that the rain was still falling in a fine drizzle. He hoped the roads would not be too muddy for travel in the afternoon—not that he was unaccustomed to riding through mud.

He spent more than an hour after breakfast tramping alone in the outdoors. His wife had announced her intention of spending the morning in the nursery with the children. Mrs. Pritchard had taken the carriage into Heybridge. The park was very nicely planned indeed. There was a rose arbor to one side of the house with a wilderness walk beyond it, wooded and hilly and dotted with grottoes and rustic seats, from all of which there was a pleasant prospect—or would be on a fine day. A flourishing vegetable and flower garden stretched the length of the back of the house. The lily pond he had seen before was picturesque. The wooded valley behind it was blooming with azaleas and blue-bells and must be secluded and lovely on a sunny day. Well-kept lawns stretched before the house.

It was her home—narrowly, by the skin of her teeth, so to speak. Today she would be leaving here forever if Andrews had not caught a cold. Or if he had not come upon Captain Morris minutes before his death instead of minutes after. Or if the captain had not saved his life at Salamanca. How strange was the seemingly random pattern of events in one's life.

He made his way back to the house well before noon. He would not put it past Cecil Morris to arrive early, and he would not for worlds miss his visit.

His wife was in the drawing room, he discovered after changing into dry clothes, busy at her embroidery again, though he had the feeling that she had picked it up only when she heard him coming, to avoid the awkwardness of being tête-à-tête with him. He stood watching her for a few moments until he noticed that her cheeks had turned pink. He crossed to the window and stood looking out.

Cecil Morris's carriage drove into sight at precisely ten minutes to twelve.

"Here he comes," Aidan said.

"Agnes will show him up," she said.

"Yes." He turned and watched her thread her needle

through the cloth with steady hands and fold her work carefully before putting it away in a tapestry bag. He moved slightly to one side of the window, into the shadow cast by the draperies. They were both listening to the sound of hooves clopping and wheels crunching on the terrace below. A carriage door banged, and then the knocker rattled loudly against the front door. The housekeeper would not have opened it unbidden for this particular visitor, of course. For once Aidan felt in charity with her.

His wife turned her head to look at him before standing and moving closer to the drawing room door to greet her visitor. Moments later the door was flung open without even the courtesy of a knock and crashed against the round table behind it.

"Ah, Cecil," Eve said. "Good morning. A rather dreary day, is it not?"

Aidan was aware of the rumbling sound of other vehicles approaching up the driveway, but he did not turn his head to look. He did not move at all.

"I am amazed you are still here, Eve," her cousin said, taking off his hat and greatcoat, shaking droplets of water from both, and tossing them onto a nearby chair. "I expected that you would preserve some dignity by leaving before noon. You are not about to grovel and beg me to allow you to stay, are you? I would not hear of it, you know, and I abhor scenes."

"I hope Aunt Jemima is well?" she asked politely.

"I trust everyone else has already gone," he said, "and that that woman who calls herself a housekeeper and has so degraded the tone of the house for the past year or so is on her way." He drew out a pocket watch and consulted it. "They have two minutes of their allotted time left, the pack of them. You too, Eve. And then one hour's grace, which I will grant out of the kindness of my heart. At one o'clock I have men arriving, including the parish constable, who will haul the stragglers off to the magistrate. We cannot have vagrants as a financial burden on the parish, can we? Now, if you will excuse me." He paused to laugh at his own intended joke. "Or if you will *not* excuse me, as a matter of fact, cousin. I have wagons arriving and must go down to supervise their unloading."

"Cecil," Eve said, "I really must ask you to leave. Our midday meal is almost ready and I have not found you courteous enough to merit an invitation. I do not want anything of yours unloaded into my house. In fact, I expressly forbid it. Please go down immediately and see to it that it does not happen."

"Now see here, Eve," he said, his chest puffing out and his face turning a deep red, "I am not putting up with your antics, and don't think I will just because you are my own first cousin. I have never liked you, and today I don't mind telling you so. You are to leave the house right now, this minute. You have had your chance to take your personal belongings with you, but you have lost it. Now, are you going to go without any more fuss, or do I have to lay a whip about you?"

His accent had slipped into something quite distinctly Welsh, Aidan noticed. He cleared his throat, and Morris turned his head sharply to peer into the shadows by the window. His expression changed to

111

one of obsequious heartiness.

"My lord!" he exclaimed. "Have you come calling again? You ought to have told me so as soon as I arrived, Eve, and I would have given you an extra couple of hours to entertain your guest—might I even say, *our* guest? What are a few hours between close relatives, after all? You will perhaps understand, my lord, that my dear mother has lived in a cottage, though a very comfortable, spacious one, I must hasten to add, all her married life and is understandably impatient to move into her new home here. Left to myself, I would gladly have given Eve until the end of the week."

"Did someone mention whips?" Aidan stepped farther out into the light.

Morris laughed heartily. "A joke between cousins," he said.

"Ah." Aidan took a few more leisurely steps forward until he was close enough for the other man to be fully aware of the significant difference in height between six foot one and five foot four or five. "I have frequently been accused of lacking a sense of humor and now I know it has not been without reason. I believed you were serious."

Morris's laugh was a little more strained this time.

"I am something of a killjoy too," Aidan said. "Even in fun, I simply could not allow you to—ah, lay a *whip* about my wife."

There was a brief, heavy pause.

"Your wife." Morris had gone slack-jawed.

"My wife."

Morris laughed once more with arch jocularity. "You

are the dry one," he said with a broad wink. "You had me going there, my lord. No sense of humor, eh? It is the driest one I ever heard, I will give you that. And when were the banns called? Huh, huh? You forgot about those, did you?"

"Miss Eve Morris," Aidan said coldly, half expecting a conspiratorial dig in the ribs with an elbow at any moment, "did me the honor of marrying me by special license in London the day before yesterday. She is now Lady Aidan Bedwyn of Ringwood Manor. And I believe I heard her a minute or two ago telling you to take yourself off."

"Now see here—"

"You can leave under your own power," Aidan said, "or I can assist you—but *not* with a whip, you may be relieved to understand. Only a coward and a bully threatens those who are weaker than himself with whips or other weapons when he possesses two perfectly serviceable hands. Before you go, though—"

"Married! You have married Eve?" Morris's face had turned a dangerous shade of purple. Spittle had gathered in the corners of his mouth and sprayed out with his words. The truth was just beginning to dawn upon his mind, Aidan suspected.

"To a gentleman, Cecil," she said. "Therefore, I am the rightful owner of Ringwood Manor today, and you are not."

"No!" He whirled about and glared at her. "This cannot be. Whoever heard of a marriage by special license? It cannot be valid. And if you say it is, you are lying or using trickery and flummery and I will have

you exposed and punished for it. And if you ever expect mercy or charity from me—"

"Silence, man!" Almost unconsciously Aidan had adjusted both his tone and expression to those he used on men who were unwise enough to challenge his authority on the battlefield or parade ground. It did not involve raising his voice or making any menacing gestures, but it had its effect on Morris as it always did on others. He turned back to Aidan, bug-eyed, his face paling.

"Although you are my wife's cousin," Aidan said, taking one step closer so that Morris had to tip back his head to look up at him, "I have detected not the faintest trace of familial sentiment toward her in your words or your manner. You are no longer welcome here, sir. You will take your leave as soon as I have finished speaking, and you will never return. Never! Not even to the extent of setting one toe over the boundary of the park. Do I make myself understood?"

Cecil Morris stared mutely up at him.

Aidan lowered his voice. "Do I make myself understood?"

No sound came out and he cleared his throat. "Yes."

"I will be leaving my wife here when I return to my battalion in the near future," Aidan continued. "But I have long arms, Morris, and I have powerful friends in England, including my brother, the Duke of Bewcastle, with whom you were so impressed when I first met you. If I hear the merest whisper of a suggestion that you have been harassing or even slightly annoying Lady Aidan Bedwyn, those arms and those friends will

reach out and cause you bodily harm. Do you understand me?"

"Yes." The voice had become an ignominious
squeak.

"Good." Aidan, his hands clasped at his back, continued to look down at the man for several seconds
longer, having discovered prolonged silence to be an
effective weapon in further weakening jellylike knees
in even the most recalcitrant of soldiers. "You will
leave now."

Morris turned and glanced at Eve. He opened his
mouth but closed it again, leaving unsaid whatever he
itched to say. And wisely so. Aidan would have loved
an excuse to pick the man up by the scruff of his neck
and convey him down the stairs and out to his carriage
with his boot toes scraping ineffectually against the
floor. Morris stumbled toward the door, gathered up his
coat and hat with ungainly haste when he thought
Aidan was coming after him, and disappeared. Aidan
closed the door and turned to his wife, his eyebrows
raised.

Her eyes were alight with merriment. "Oh," she said,
"I am *so* glad you stayed. I would not have missed that
for worlds. It was priceless! *You* were priceless."

She came hurrying toward him as she spoke, both her
hands outstretched. He took them in his own and
squeezed them tightly.

"I confess," he said, "that I rather enjoyed it myself."

"Thank you!" she cried, returning the pressure of his
hands. "Thank you so very much for everything. You
will never know how grateful I am."

She was flushed and vivid and pretty again, as she had been in London two afternoons ago. She lifted her face to his—for what purpose he never afterward understood—and he bent toward her for no conceivable purpose at all. Somehow their mouths met and pressed together for a few timeless moments until they both jerked back and dropped each other's hands as if they had just scalded each other.

What the devil! It was surely one of the most excruciatingly embarrassing moments of Aidan's life—perhaps *the* most—especially as she stood there looking up at him, wide-eyed with dismay, color flooding her cheeks, and he could think of nothing to do but clasp his hands behind his back and clear his throat.

"I beg your pardon—"

"I do beg your pardon—"

They spoke simultaneously, just like a damned Greek chorus. Lord help him! He had just kissed his wife. Or she had kissed him. Whichever.

"I beg your pardon," he said again. "I'll go up and see if Andrews has finished packing my bags."

"Will you stay for luncheon?"

No. It was time to be gone. He was starting to wonder about her as a person. He had had a few tantalizing glimpses of a warmhearted, loyal, fun-loving woman, and it was not good for him to think of her as a person. Worse, he had caught himself more than once with lustful thoughts about her, most notably last night after he had gone to bed and realized that he was spending a night under the same roof as his bride for the first and only time in his life. It had been alarming and had felt disloyal. And then *that* thought had felt disloyal.

"I do not believe—" he began.

The drawing room door opened behind him, and he turned sharply, wondering if Morris had had the temerity to return. But it was Mrs. Pritchard, still dressed for the outdoors, her shoulders damp from the rain.

"Oh, good," she said, "you are both still here to tell me all about it. I had to get down from the carriage outside the stables and walk all the way to the house. Cecil and all his wagons are blocking the terrace. He would not even look at me though I called a very cheery good afternoon and asked him how he did. Now, *do* tell me everything."

Her eyes were sparkling with mischief, Aidan noticed. Both hands were resting on her cane.

"Oh, Aunt Mari," Eve said, her hands clasped to her bosom, "you ought to have heard Colonel Bedwyn. You really ought. He spoke with such quiet, refined menace that even I was quaking. I almost felt sorry for Cecil." She laughed—actually it sounded more like a girlish giggle. "Almost, but not quite."

"He made the mistake," Aidan said, "of threatening to remove my wife from the house with a whip."

"Oh, very stupid," the aunt said with a chuckle. "I wonder how he could have been so brave with you standing here, Colonel."

"That was the best part," his wife added. "He did not see Colonel Bedwyn in the shadows. You should have seen his face when he noticed."

Mrs. Pritchard laughed as she removed her hat and

shook the raindrops off it. "I'm glad I caught the two of you together," she said. "I paid a number of visits this morning. I thought it important that our neighbors know what has happened. All of them have been awfully worried about what was going to happen to Eve. Luckily, because of the rain I found everyone at home. I have wonderful news."

Aidan felt instant apprehension. The woman had that matchmaking gleam in her eye again.

"Everyone was so delighted," Mrs. Pritchard said, "to know that you are to remain mistress of Ringwood, Eve, my love, and that it is Colonel Bedwyn you have married that they all agreed that something ought to be done to celebrate. I explained that the colonel must go soon to return from his leave, but that was not going to stop anyone. Even as I speak all is being made ready for an assembly in the rooms above the inn this evening."

"Aunt Mari—" Eve began, sounding as aghast as Aidan felt.

"Surely," Mrs. Pritchard said, fixing pleading eyes on Aidan, "you can stay for one more night, Colonel. Surely—"

"Aunt Mari—"

Aidan held up one hand. Aghast he might feel, but there was perhaps some wisdom in the idea.

"I have just recalled," he said, "that Cecil Morris seemed not to believe in the validity of a marriage by special license. It is conceivable, I suppose, that more of the people in this neighborhood may share his ignorance. My leaving today might give rise to doubts and rumors that would cause unnecessary difficulties. A public appearance together, a wedding celebration, would certainly alleviate those doubts."

Mrs. Pritchard beamed her satisfaction.

"What do you think?" Aidan asked his wife.

"I think," she said, frowning, "that we are putting you to far more trouble than you expected, Colonel."

True enough. It had all seemed so very simple when he first thought of fulfilling his promise by marrying her.

"Besides," he said, "the rain is pouring down again."

They all turned as one to watch it stream down the windowpanes.

CHAPTER VIII

Eve looked through her wardrobe for a gown suitable for evening wear. Everything was woefully out of date. For the past year she had been in mourning, but even for a number of years before that she had spent most of her evenings at home with her father, whose failing health had kept him from the social life of the neighborhood by which he had set so much store. She briefly considered her choices and then settled for her gray, silver-shot silk. It seemed disrespectful to Percy's memory not to wear mourning at all for him despite his own express wish. Edith dressed her hair and suggested her silver chain and earrings to add a festive touch.

This was really too bad of Aunt Mari and Serena among others, Eve thought as she descended to the drawing room, feeling as nervous as a girl about to make her come-out. It was an obvious ploy to detain the colonel in the hope that the marriage would blossom into something more than it had ever been intended to be. It was embarrassing, to say the least. She had been amazed at his consenting to stay, but she guessed that his sense of honor had prompted his decision. She hoped he was not expecting the sort of elegant social event he must be accustomed to as the son of a duke.

He was awaiting her in the drawing room. Aunt Mari and Thelma had left early to help with some of the preparations at the assembly rooms—at least that had been Aunt Mari's explanation for leaving the two of them to travel and arrive at the Three Feathers together.

"I am so sorry about this," Eve said. "You cannot but be wishing you were well on your way home by now."

He bowed, and his eyes ran over her, though he made no comment on her choice of gown. He was wearing his dress uniform, but with dancing shoes rather than his cavalry boots.

"I could have refused to stay," he told her. "The point is, though, that I *can* leave tomorrow and resume my habitual way of life as if nothing had happened here. For you it will not be so easy. You must continue to live here with neighbors who know very well why you married and why you live alone, without your husband. I would not have them believe that there is no kindness, no . . . respect between us. I was taken aback when Mrs. Pritchard first divulged her scheme this afternoon, I must confess, but it did not take me more than a moment to realize that in fact it is just the thing that is needed."

His manner was stiffly formal as he spoke. Was it kindness or duty that motivated him? Eve wondered. She had had several teasing glimpses at possible kindness, even humor, but . . . *but he never smiled.* She nodded, and he took her shawl from her hands, set it about her shoulders, and offered his arm.

The rain had stopped an hour or so before, but the cobbles on the terrace were still damp and the air chill. Eve shivered as she climbed into the carriage. She wondered if the colonel would take the seat beside her or the one opposite. He took the one beside her. She could feel his body heat along her right arm and outer thigh.

"There will be dancing," she told him, "to music provided by local musicians. There will be card playing and conversation and refreshments. You will find it all very insipid, perhaps downright silly."

"You do not have to apologize for what will doubtless be perfectly civil, wholesome country entertainment," he said.

She could remember once telling John about an assembly she had recently attended and enjoyed vastly. He had shuddered theatrically and told her he would rather be hurled into a dungeon full of rats than be forced to attend such a vulgar affair. She had laughed at the time, and he had laughed too and changed the subject. Would *John* do what the colonel was doing now, just so that she would appear respectable—and not to be pitied—in her neighbors' eyes?

"I cannot forget," she said, "that you are the son and

brother of a duke, that you are *Lord* Aidan Bedwyn."

"And you are Lady Aidan Bedwyn," he reminded her as the old carriage jerked into motion.

"An impostor." She laughed.

"No." He turned his head to look at her. "My wife."

She shivered again. The reality of it had still not quite sunk home, she guessed. She was married yet not married. She had a husband yet no husband. By this time next week his very existence would seem like a dream. But she would be forever married to him—until death did them part.

"You still wear half mourning," he said. "Even though your father has been gone for longer than a year."

"Is it disrespectful to the occasion?" she asked him. "I cannot help remembering that just four days ago all my neighbors and friends were gathered for a memorial service in Percy's honor. Yet this evening they are coming out to celebrate my marriage."

"That is life," he said. "It goes on after even the most unspeakable of tragedies."

"I suppose," she said, looking at him with a slight frown, "you speak from a great deal of personal experience."

His dark, inscrutable eyes turned totally blank. It was worse than any emotion would have been. She felt chilled. For several moments there was silence between them.

"You mourn now for your brother?" he said. "Despite his wish that you not do so?"

"How can I not?" She sighed. "There were only the

two of us. We were always close, even after he had quarreled with Papa and went to live with my great-uncle. And then he . . . but I must not bore you." She turned her head to look out at the trees in the gathering dusk.

"Tell me," he said.

"My great-uncle was a wealthy shopkeeper and merchant," she said. "He was almost as rich as Papa, but he had no similar ambition to move up the social scale and break into the ranks of the landed gentry. He was happy with his life and achievements. When he died everything went to his son, except for a sum large enough to purchase Percy's dream—a commission in a cavalry regiment. Papa was furious, but there was nothing he could do to prevent it. He did change his will, however."

"The son did not object?" the colonel asked.

"Joshua? No." She shook her head. "He and Percy were good friends. He wanted to marry me." She probably ought not to have added that unnecessary detail.

"Joshua?" he said.

She turned to smile a little sheepishly at him. "I was nineteen," she said, "and he was eight and twenty. He was prosperous, confident, handsome, a relative, Percy's friend. I was lonely on my own here. I thought I might like to go back—closer to my roots, so to speak. To my own country, my own people—though my mother's family was English by birth."

"Your father would not allow the match?" he asked.

"Oh, by no means," she said. "Joshua was bourgeois. Determinedly so, even down to the thick accent. No,

Papa would not allow the marriage. I was heartbroken and forgot him within a month. He married six months after I refused him and now has three children. He is still prospering."

"But you do not wear the willow for him?"

"No." She laughed softly. "It was foolish to expect that I could go back and be happy. I had lived too long here to go back—most of my life, in fact. I know that now. I prefer my life as it is." Or as it was until a week ago, anyway, she amended silently.

"Where does Cecil Morris fit into the family picture?" he asked.

"His father and mine were brothers," she explained. "When Papa left Wales and bought Ringwood, my uncle came too and leased the largest tenant farm from him. He worked hard and it prospered and eventually he purchased it. But Cecil was always foolishly jealous of Percy and me. He wanted desperately to rise above his origins and be a gentleman—a rich, *idle* gentleman. They put a great deal of emphasis upon idleness as a mark of gentility, Papa and Cecil. I have often thought that he should have been Papa's son. Indeed, he very nearly did inherit. It is only thanks to you that he did not."

She had done too much talking, she thought as the carriage rumbled over the bridge and rolled along the main street of Heybridge in the direction of the Three Feathers. What interest could he possibly have in her family?

"I do not know if I ought to dance," she said. "I am, after all, still in mourning."

"But against your brother's express wishes," he reminded her. "Dancing is the principal form of entertainment at an assembly, I believe, and this assembly is in our honor. You would disappoint if you were to sit soberly in a corner with the chaperones. Is that your wish—to hurt your friends?"

He was quite right, of course. Aunt Mari would be disappointed. So would everyone else. And so would *she*. She was seized suddenly, as she had been in London two days ago, with a sudden rush of exuberance, with a need to grasp every moment of near happiness before she was alone to brood upon what she had quite deliberately given up.

"Can you dance?" she asked. It was hard to imagine.

"Ma'am," he said as the carriage swayed to a halt and they waited for the steps to be put down, "before a gentleman learns to recite his ABCs without stumbling, he has already mastered the graceful art of tripping the light fantastic."

Eve laughed. There it was again—that dry and elusive suggestion of humor.

She was, she admitted to herself finally, looking forward to the evening.

The assembly really was a rather undistinguished, even insipid event. Bewcastle would have called it vulgar. There was a large number of very young ladies, who could not possibly be "out," yet they danced and giggled and ogled the very young men, who blushed and tried to appear blasé and looked merely gauche. There were numerous older ladies, who gushed and laughed and talked too loudly, and older men, who conversed at great and tedious length on such topics as the wars, to please Aidan, and farming and hunting, to please themselves. There was an orchestra—two violins, a bass, and a flute—which scraped away with more enthusiasm than musical sense. There were tables almost buckling beneath fine, fattening delicacies and enough drink to intoxicate a hardened infantry battalion.

Aidan had never been much of a one for assemblies or social gatherings of even the most refined. But he had understood the importance of attending this one, and he recognized the good-heartedness behind all the merry-making. Her neighbors were fond of Eve—there was no doubt about that. They really *had* been concerned about her fate. It was obviously an enormous relief to them to know that she was safely married and could continue living among them as the mistress of Ringwood. But they wished her better than just that. They needed to see her with her bridegroom, to assure themselves that it really was a marriage, even if it had been conceived in haste and was not a love match—and even if circumstances dictated that he leave on the morrow.

He set himself to playing his part in giving them what they wanted.

He led off the opening set of country dances with his wife, standing at the head of the line of men while she stood at the head of the ladies' line, facing him. It was a vigorous set, which soon brought color to her cheeks and a sparkle to her eyes. She must not have danced for at least the past year, he realized, but she danced now with grace and energy and obvious enjoyment. She was smiling, even laughing before the set ended. He did not take his eyes off her. Partly it was deliberate, for the sake of her friends and neighbors, who were watching them with fond attention. Partly it was because she was good to look at—tall, slender, pretty whenever she was animated, as she was now. And partly because he knew that after tomorrow he would try to remember what she looked like and not always succeed. Yet she would always be his wife.

He danced three more sets with her in the course of the evening, this being a country assembly in which the rules of society etiquette did not strictly apply. Between sets he kept her hand on his arm while they conversed in turn with almost everyone present. Once or twice when she danced with other men he stood and watched her. A few times he danced with other women—with Mrs. Robson and Miss Rice among others. If Bewcastle could see him now, he thought wryly as he danced and conversed with the governess. Bewcastle would have an apoplexy—especially if he knew the history of the woman. Aidan almost grinned at the thought—but he sobered immediately at another quite unwilling thought. What if *Miss Knapp* could see him now?

In addition to all the refreshments with which they were tempted all evening, there was a sit-down supper in an adjoining room at half past eleven. How it could all have been accomplished with only half a day's notice, Aidan could not imagine. The meal was a veritable banquet. It was followed by speeches and toasts—one from James Robson, one from the Reverend Thomas Puddle. Aidan, to his intense embarrassment, was forced to make an impromptu reply.

"My wife and I both wish to thank you all for your generous kindness in organizing this assembly in our honor at such short notice," he began. There seemed to be nothing else to say. He looked down at Eve. She was studying the back of her hand, which lay flat on the tablecloth between them. "Captain Percival Morris was my friend," he continued, not quite truthfully. "His sister was therefore my friend too, even before I knew her in person. It was a distinct honor to be able to rescue her from some difficulty by marrying her. But it was only the haste of the marriage that was dictated by those circumstances. I daresay it would have taken place at some time in the future anyway, with more grandeur, perhaps, with larger numbers of our families and friends in attendance, but with no more precious memories to carry into the future with us than those provided by our very private nuptials in London."

There was hearty applause and one self-conscious attempt to raise a cheer. The fingers spread on the table-cloth curled into her palm.

"I must leave tomorrow," Aidan said. "I have business to attend to before returning to my battalion. I leave my bride with reluctance, but I leave her in the care of the aunt and the friends and neighbors who love her. Until my return."

There was more applause—a few of the ladies, including Mrs. Pritchard, were mopping at their eyes. Aidan reached down, took his wife's clenched hand in his own, slipping his fingers beneath hers, and raised it to his lips. She looked up at him, and their eyes met and held for a long moment. And the devil of it was, he thought, it did not *all* feel like a pack of lies. He had had no idea just four days ago that he was getting himself into something so deep.

"Join me, if you will," he invited the gathering, "in drinking a toast to Lady Aidan Bedwyn, my wife."

A number of the guests, including almost all the young people, crowded back into the other room soon after, and the music began again. The dull thudding of a few dozen feet on the wooden floor indicated that the dancing had resumed. Most people on their way out came to shake Aidan's hand and say a few words to Eve, but after a few minutes they sat with enough space all around them to permit some relaxation and private conversation.

"Thank you," she said. "You have done a great deal for my sake. I will never forget that. But how you must be looking forward to riding away from here tomorrow morning and finally going home to see your family. You will finally be free again."

He had a strong premonition that it was not going to be that easy, but he said nothing. It would have been ill-mannered to agree with her, anyway.

"If you did not wear the willow for your cousin longer than one month," he said, changing the subject, "what kept you from marrying anyone else until two days ago? I know that for the past year you felt honor-bound to wait out the term specified in your father's will. But what about the years previous to that? You are now—what? Four, five and twenty?"

"Five," she said. "Papa tried hard for a number of

years. He was very determined to marry me well. I cringed from the parade of genteel eligibles he brought to Ringwood for my inspection."

"You seem so fond of children," he said. "You never wanted children of your own?"

"I have children of my own," she said. "You do not understand, Colonel, do you? To you Becky and Davy are simply orphans I have taken in. To me they are— well, they are as precious as if they had come from my own womb." She blushed at her own words.

No, it *was* hard to understand. She was a woman who had so much love and tenderness to give away. Why not to a man? Why not to children she really had borne herself?

"It has struck me," he said, "that perhaps I made an error in assuming that you had no wish to marry in the future, to begin your own family."

"No!" she said so firmly that an elderly lady seated at the next table—Miss Drabble?—looked across at them for a moment. "No, I'll not have you do that to yourself. I *had* chosen the single state. I believe I always knew, especially after Joshua, that I would never marry unless I truly loved. I was fortunate enough to have the luxury of choice in the matter as so many women do not. At least, I *thought* I had that choice."

"But you never met the man you could truly love?" he asked.

"No!" Her answer was even firmer than before, though quieter. "Never. Perhaps that means there is no such thing as love, Colonel. Perhaps I have been chasing after the moon. What do you think?"

"About true love?" he said. "It depends upon your definition of the term. I do not believe in romantic love. It is a mere euphemism for sexual appetite with men and the desire for home and security with women. I do believe in loyalty and familial affection, though."

"So do I," she said. "And I have those things in abundance. I have my aunt and my friends and my beloved children. Why would I yearn for more? I have everything I could ever need. I am happy as I am. I have read somewhere that we often spend a lifetime searching for what we already have. I am one of the lucky ones—I know my good fortune. I know it because I almost lost it today. I will be eternally grateful to you for making my happiness possible."

He was reassured. Or perhaps he just chose to be reassured so that he would not have to worry about having destroyed all her hopes for future happiness in marriage. He suspected that she might have been too vehement in her denials. But what choice had he had? What choice had she had? None whatsoever. And so there was no point now in wishing that he might have done things differently to help her. There had been no other way.

"Should we dance again?" his wife asked.

He got to his feet and held out a hand for hers. "Yes, we should," he agreed. "One more time."

Her aunt, seated a short distance away with a couple of other elderly ladies, nodded happily at them.

One more time—there seemed such finality in the words.

It was drizzling again in the morning. Eve got up early despite a late night and went out to the stables to see Colonel Bedwyn on his way even though he had told her she would get wet and had suggested that she remain in the house. She was huddled inside a cloak, the wide hood pulled up over her head.

He was wearing his uniform, but not his formal dress uniform. This one looked worn, somewhat faded, slightly shabby. It molded itself to his frame and looked comfortable—and undeniably attractive. This, she realized, was how he must dress most of the time. He looked large and very masculine.

Sam Patchett led his great horse out into the stable yard. Charlie was hovering beside the batman's horse, eager to make himself useful.

Colonel Bedwyn turned to her. He was already wet, and she could feel dampness seeping through the shoulders of her cloak. They stared at each other, neither apparently knowing how to speak the simple words of farewell.

"This is the end then," he said stiffly. "I am honored to have been of some service to you, ma'am."

She forced a smile to her lips. "The honor has been all mine," she said.

They could hardly have been more formal with each other if they had tried.

He clicked his heels, bowed, and turned to take the reins from Sam's hand. But he turned back abruptly and held out his right hand. Eve set her own in it and they clasped hands tightly, almost painfully, for several wordless moments.

"Be happy," he said.

"You too." Her throat ached all the way down into her chest.

And then his hand was gone from hers and he mounted his horse in one fluid motion, looked to make sure that his batman was ready, and rode out of the stable yard, his horse's hooves clopping on the wet cobbles.

Eve raised a hand in farewell, but he did not look back. Soon the wall of the yard blocked her view of him and she hurried to the gateway to watch him ride down the driveway at a canter until he was lost to sight among the trees. Not once did he turn his head.

Some of the rain on her face felt hot. She swiped at the moisture and drew her hood lower. She could, if she allowed herself such an indulgence, cry and cry until she was weak and empty. For the loss of an honorable man she would never see again though he would forever remain her husband. For the loss of love and the man who had not come home in time. For her brother, whose death she had had no chance to mourn properly. For a future that appeared frighteningly bleak.

She counted backward on her fingers. Yesterday they had confronted Cecil and danced in the assembly rooms; the day before they had returned from London; the day before they had married; the day before they had gone to London; the day before there had been the memorial service for Percy; the day before he had offered to give the eulogy; the day before he had brought her the news from France. Seven days. Exactly one week. A week ago to the hour she had not even known Percy was dead. A week ago today she had never met Colonel Lord Aidan Bedwyn.

Now they were both gone. Forever.

She could no longer remember quite why it had to be forever with the colonel. But that had been their agreement from the start.

She could not bear to go back to the house just yet. Despite the rain and the wetness of the grass, she set off across the lawn toward the lily pond—the same direction she had taken with the colonel six days ago. Before she had gone very far, Muffin caught up to her, looking very much like an oversized half-drowned rat.

"Well, Muffin," she said, "perhaps *you* can explain. Why does one feel the need to weep when one does not even know for which of three men one mourns? Is it Percy? Or John? Or Colonel Bedwyn?"

Muffin, loping along on three legs and snuffling at the grass, had no answer to offer. In fact, he paid her no attention whatsoever, for which fact she was enormously grateful because she could no longer pretend that it was hot salt rain that was running down her cheeks.

CHAPTER IX

Inclement weather and muddy roads forced Aidan to spend one night at an inn. It was the afternoon of the following day before he finally rode up the long, straight, wide avenue, lined with elm trees standing at attention like soldiers on parade, that led to Lindsey Hall. Home at last!

He spurred his horse to a faster pace. He was not sure any of the family would be in residence. For all he knew they might all be in London for the Season, though they were not a family much given to the frivolity of *ton* entertainments. Certainly Bewcastle would be there, fulfilling his duties in the House of Lords. He hoped that one at least of his brothers and sisters was at home. He needed some distraction for his gloomy mood.

The house came into sight, and he felt the familiar rush of almost painful love for it. The massive stone mansion that was Lindsey Hall always succeeded in looking breathtakingly magnificent even though it displayed a mishmash of architectural styles. It had been in the family since it was built as a much smaller manor in the Middle Ages. Successive barons and then earls and then dukes had made additions to it without effecting any subtractions, and no effort had ever been made to blend the fashions of different ages.

The long avenue branched in two some distance from the house to circle a gloriously colorful flower garden with a marble fountain at its center—both courtesy of a Georgian great-grandfather. Water shot thirty feet into the air and sprayed downward in all directions, like rainbow-colored spokes of a giant parasol.

Aidan had barely moved onto the left-hand branch of the avenue before three riders came into view around the side of the stable block some distance away—two men and one woman. All of them drew rein at sight of him, and then Freyja shrieked and came galloping with reckless speed around the flower garden toward him.

"Aidan!" she cried when she was within earshot. "You fiend! You did not even let us know you were coming!"

He stopped as she rode up beside him and stretched out her right arm like a man. She was riding sidesaddle, which she had not always done. She wore her fair hair loose beneath a jaunty feathered riding hat. It reached almost to her waist in an unruly mass of curls. The same old Freyja!

"But this is what surprises are all about," he said, clasping her hand. "How are you, Free?"

She looked sun-bronzed and bright-eyed and healthy—and as unladylike as she had ever been during the years when a succession of governesses had despaired of her.

"All the better for seeing you," she said. "Does Wulf know you are in England? It would be just like him to neglect to inform the rest of us."

"I have not written to Bewcastle," he said.

And then two of his brothers rode up at a rather more sedate pace. Rannulf, the fair-haired giant, grinned and reached out a large hand.

"It is dashed good to see you, Aidan," he said. "How long do you have?"

Alleyne, younger, slimmer, darker, smiled cheerfully. "The warrior returns triumphant," he said. "The cavalry will not allow you pen or paper, Aidan?"

"Ralf? Alleyne?" Aidan shook hands with each of them in turn. "Two months, one week of which has already gone. I had some business to take care of." *Like getting married.* "And why use pen and ink when I could come in person? Is Morgan at home?"

"And Wulf too," Ralf told him as they all turned in the direction of the stables. "He came home a week ago for the Dowager Countess of Redfield's funeral and has not yet returned. He was going over some accounts when we left and Morgan was chafing in the schoolroom. Seventeen is a nasty, rebellious age, especially for a Bedwyn."

"Seventeen!" Aidan winced. "She must be quite the young lady by now."

"And a little spitfire," Alleyne said with a laugh. "She is going to be the worst—or the best—of the lot of us. One almost pities all the young bucks who are going to come courting next year after Wulf has dragged her off to London to make her curtsy to the queen."

"You have not arrived unobserved from the house, I see." Rannulf nodded in the direction of the front doors. "Here comes the master himself."

Aidan swung down from his horse and turned over the reins to Andrews. Bewcastle was coming toward him at a leisurely pace. It was characteristic of him that he never hurried and never raised his voice. Yet every servant was instantly obedient to his slightest command, and he had done an admirable job of curbing the wildest excesses of his siblings, most of whom were slightly afraid of him, though they would all have been broken on the rack rather than admit it. He was Wulfric, a name that suited him. There was something distinctly wolflike about him, including his silver eyes.

"Wulf?" Aidan walked toward him a little warily.

They had not been on the best of terms for years. The last time they had been together—three years before—they had almost come to blows and Aidan had cut short his leave.

"Aidan?" Bewcastle stopped well beyond hugging range or even hand-shaking range and spoke in his usual light, deceptively pleasant tones. "Dear me, I will have to have a word with the postal service. Your letter announcing your return to England has been delayed."

"Why write," Aidan said, "when I could get here as fast as a letter? How are you?"

"The better for seeing you in one piece and apparently healthy," Bewcastle said, raising his quizzing glass to his eye and looking his brother over from head to foot. "You cannot afford a new uniform, Aidan?"

Aidan shrugged. "One becomes curiously attached to comfort," he said, "when there is so little of it. I want to see Morgan. Has she fulfilled the promise of beauty she showed when I was home last? I hear she is the most headstrong of all of us."

"Is she?" The ducal eyebrows rose, adding an expression of arrogance to his lean, prominent-nosed, thin-lipped face. "It has escaped my notice. But I will concede that I am probably the last person on whom she would try the effects of a tantrum. Come up to the drawing room and we will all take tea." He glanced beyond Aidan to their brothers and sister, including them in the invitation, which was really, of course, a command. "I'll have Miss Cowper bring Morgan down."

It was definitely good to be home, Aidan thought as

he walked beside his brother toward the house, despite the fact that Wulf was there and that his welcome had been cool indeed in comparison to those of the others. Three years ago Wulf had refused to allow Freyja to marry the man of her choice, their neighbor and childhood friend, Kit Butler, because he was merely the second son of the Earl of Redfield. Bewcastle had forced her to accept the offer of the eldest son and there had been a dreadful scene when Kit had stormed over and fought Ralf out on the lawn until both of them were bloody. An officer on leave himself at the time, Kit had been sent back to the Peninsula in a hurry.

Aidan had arrived home a few days later and had taken Bewcastle to task over his tyranny. The trouble was, though, that one could never have a satisfactory row with Wulf. He had become frostier and quieter the more Aidan had fumed and had merely used his quizzing glass and his eyebrows when Aidan had suggested they have it out with fisticuffs. Aidan had left the day after that, a full week before he had intended to go.

The ironic thing was that Freyja's betrothed had died before the wedding, and Kit had become Redfield's heir after all. Last year, when he had sold out and come back to England, Redfield and Bewcastle had agreed upon a match between Kit and Freyja, and all had been set in motion for the betrothal celebrations when Kit came home for the summer. When he did arrive, though, he brought a fiancée with him. They were married now, apparently. Ralf had written Aidan about it. According to him, Freyja had had her heart broken all over again, though she had smashed her fist into Ralf's face when he had suggested as much to her. Good old Freyja.

They stepped into the meticulously preserved medieval hall with its oak-beamed ceiling, its intricately carved screen with a minstrel gallery above, its whitewashed walls decorated with arms and banners and weapons, and its massive oak dining table. As they did so, a tall, slender young girl came hurrying through the stairway arch, both arms held out in front of her. She was a dark-haired, dark-eyed beauty, the only one of them, it seemed, to have entirely escaped the family nose.

"Aidan!" she cried. "Aidan!"

She surprised him by rushing right into his arms, her own closing tightly around his neck. He wrapped his arms about her narrow waist, lifted her off her feet, and swung her about in a full circle.

"You have grown devilish pretty in my absence, Morgan," he said when he set her back down and loosened his hold on her so that he could have a good look at her.

"I have no memory," Bewcastle said softly, "of summoning you from your lessons, Morgan."

Miss Cowper, her long-suffering governess, fluttered apologetically in the background. For as long as Aidan had known her, she had always looked to him as if she expected Bewcastle at any moment to order the footmen to drag her away to the dungeons and chop off her head.

Aidan winked at his younger sister, his back to Bewcastle. He had not realized until that moment how desperately he had craved someone to hug.

It was only after returning home that Aidan realized how tired he was. After months and years of heavy campaigning, he was suddenly and utterly bone-weary. He went riding and walking and fishing with his brothers and sisters. He went with them to call on some of their neighbors. He even rode over to Alvesley, home of the Earl of Redfield, one afternoon with Ralf to express his sympathies at the passing of the dowager, and met Kit's new wife, who was as different from Freyja as it was possible to be. But what he seemed to do more than anything else was sleep.

It was on the excessive sleep that he blamed his deep depression. Delighted as he was to be at home with his family, he could not shake off his gloom. Nor could he stop himself from sleeping nine, ten, even eleven hours a night. He found himself dreaming of Eve by night and thinking of her by day, though in fact what had happened seemed like a dream. He even found himself wondering on occasion if it really *had* happened or if he had not imagined that whole bizarre week. He found himself too thinking of Miss Knapp, of the pleasant hope he had had of combining his career with marriage to a woman who could share his way of life, who could provide him with companionship and comfort and . . . yes, and with sex. Though he had occasionally kept mistresses, he had never particularly enjoyed casual and unequal relationships.

He spent little time with his elder brother. They had

not been close since their early boyhood, when they had been inseparable companions. But at the age of twelve Wulfric had changed totally when their father had decreed that it was time he was prepared for the responsibilities of his future—a future that had arrived early with their father's death when Wulf was just seventeen. He had been educated during the intervening years by a pair of tutors, while Aidan and his younger brothers had been sent to Eton. Aidan had often wondered if Bewcastle was a lonely person or if he had simply grown into a cold, emotionless man who enjoyed solitude.

It seemed that what remained of Aidan's leave was to be restful and peaceful at least. But that hope was shattered one morning a little over a week after his return home. He had been out for an exhilarating gallop across country with Alleyne. The two were breakfasting heartily afterward when the butler informed Aidan that his grace wished to see him in the library.

Aidan took a cup of coffee with him. He bade Bewcastle a good morning and settled himself in a deep leather chair on the opposite side of the hearth from him. He wondered what was up but would not ask the question. Wulf would get to it in his own time.

"The warm spell that persisted for a week or so after I landed seems to have deserted us for good," he said. "That wind makes it downright chilly this morning. Invigorating, though."

Wulf had never been one for small talk. "It would appear," he said, "that the Prince of Wales is determined to make a grand spectacle out of the allied victories. Half the sovereigns and princes and generals of Europe are expected to come and preen themselves as his guests, including the Czar of Russia, the King of Prussia, and Marshal von Blücher."

"I had heard rumors to that effect," Aidan said. "It seems that all England, London especially, is deliriously in love with anything on two legs and in uniform. One cannot expect Prinny not to want to bask in the glory of it all."

"Quite," his brother agreed. "This is not the first I have heard of it either. I must be returning soon to London and the House. The morning's post has brought a specific invitation to a state dinner for the foreign guests at Carlton House, though it is not until several weeks hence. There will be numerous other special celebratory events, though. Everyone will wish to outshine everyone else in hospitality."

Aidan grimaced. "I would rather you than me."

"Ah, but this particular invitation includes you by name." Wulf lifted a heavy embossed card off the top of a pile of letters in his lap and glanced at it. " 'The pleasure etcetera, etcetera.' Ah, here. Colonel Lord Aidan Bedwyn. Someone with Prinny's ear must know you are home on leave."

"I'll make some excuse," Aidan said hastily.

Bewcastle was looking down at the card again. He held his quizzing glass in his hand to enlarge the writing—a pure affectation, Aidan was sure. He doubted there was anything wrong with his brother's always keen eyesight.

"Someone else is named here too," he said before

looking up to meet Aidan's eyes. "Lady Aidan Bedwyn."

General Naughton! During that chance meeting in the lobby at the Pulteney, Aidan had introduced his bride to the general. It could be no one else. By happy chance he had seen no other acquaintance that day until, right at the end of it, he had run into General Naughton.

"Peculiar!" he said with studied nonchalance.

"I was amused when I first read it, I must confess," Bewcastle said. He was silent for a few moments while the word *first* hung in the air between them and Aidan pursed his lips. "*Is* there a Lady Aidan Bedwyn?" The question was softly asked.

"Yes."

"Ah." Bewcastle set the card down on the pile and regarded his brother steadily from his silver, wolfish eyes. "Might I inquire when I was to be informed?"

"You were not to be."

Bewcastle knew as well as Aidan did the unsettling effect of long silences. But Aidan did not squirm under his scrutiny during the one that followed. Bedamned to him. It was none of his business.

"Now that your secret is out," Wulf said at last, "perhaps you will satisfy my curiosity, Aidan?"

"I made a promise to one of my dying captains," Aidan explained, "to bring the news of his death in person to his sister and to give her my protection. The only way of doing the latter, as it turned out, was to marry her."

"Your marriage is of recent date, then?"

"Two weeks," Aidan said.

"By special license."

"Yes."

"Who?" Bewcastle asked.

"She was Miss Eve Morris," Aidan said, "owner of Ringwood Manor in Oxfordshire. She is the daughter of a wealthy coal miner."

"A coal miner."

"Yes, from South Wales. He married the owner's daughter and made his fortune that way."

"Deceased?"

"Yes."

They stared at each other for several silent moments.

"And you have now abandoned her?" Bewcastle asked. "Forever?"

"Forever, yes," Aidan admitted. "But it is not abandonment. She has a life at Ringwood she wished to preserve and dependents she wished to protect. Only by marrying in haste could she do either. Ours was a mutually agreed upon marriage of convenience. I make no apology for it, Wulf, or for keeping it from you. It was something none of my family needed to know about."

His brother gazed at him for long moments while Aidan realized that the coffee in his cup had turned cold.

"It will not do," Bewcastle said at last. "Appalling as it may be, this *Welsh coal miner's daughter* is now a Bedwyn. My sister-in-law. And her existence is known of in the Prince of Wales's intimate circle. It must be publicly acknowledged by her husband's family."

"No." Aidan spoke firmly. "It will not be, Wulf."

The ducal eyebrows rose. "Lady Aidan Bedwyn must be presented," he said. "It is safe to assume, I suppose, that she never has been? She must make a formal appearance at a queen's drawing room. Our Aunt Rochester will sponsor her. There must be a ball in her honor at Bedwyn House. The marriage has had a havey-cavey start, for which you will doubtless come up with an explanation to satisfy the gossiping tongues of the *ton*. But now all must proceed correctly. Your bride must be brought up to town and up to snuff, Aidan, difficult as the latter may prove to be."

"It is not going to happen," Aidan said. "Do you think I care the snap of my fingers what gossiping tongues wag about in London drawing rooms? They have to talk about something. Let them talk, then, about how I married beneath me and shamed my family and then cruelly abandoned my bourgeois wife—or perhaps even lower than bourgeois. Some new sensation will soon supersede this sorry one. Some heiress will run off with a handsome footman or some young chit will utter a naughty word in the hearing of a dowager, and drawing rooms will buzz with the new scandal."

"There will be no unsavory gossip about a Bedwyn," Bewcastle said. "Even one by marriage. This coal miner's daughter is now married to the heir to a dukedom. There must be no perception that she has been abandoned or hidden away, perhaps because we are ashamed of her vulgar origins. Bedwyns on average marry later in life than most people, but we do not abandon our spouses once we *do* marry, Aidan, or expose them to possible ridicule or pity."

"You will not budge me on this, Wulf," Aidan told him. "For one thing, my wife has exactly what she wanted of the marriage—independence and the freedom to live her life her way. For another, she has absolutely no connection with the world of the *ton* and therefore cannot be hurt by its gossip—she will not even know of it, if there is any, which I seriously doubt. Thirdly, my marriage is my business and I choose to leave my wife in peaceful obscurity in the country, where she belongs and where she wishes to be. I will come to London with you if I must and attend this infernal dinner and any of the other celebrations at which my presence is de rigueur. If anyone is impertinent enough to inquire about my marriage, I will answer in any way that seems appropriate to the occasion and the audience."

"You would dishonor both your bride and your family, then?" the duke asked softly. "You *are* ashamed of her, Aidan?"

Aidan swore viciously, causing his brother's eyebrows to arch upward in disdain.

"Lady Aidan has been invited to Carlton House," Bewcastle said. "It would be an unpardonable discourtesy, Aidan, to appear there without her—or not to appear at all. Your rank in the cavalry is such that you cannot fail to appear since it is known you are home on leave. Your wife must appear at your side. It will be something of a rush and a challenge for our aunt to bring her up to scratch, I do not doubt, but all things are possible to those who are determined to make them happen."

Aidan set his cup and saucer down and got to his feet. Even when they were both standing he was taller than his brother. He was also broader and heavier. It was to his credit, perhaps, that Bewcastle remained seated and put himself at a further physical disadvantage.

"My wife," Aidan said in his chilliest tones, "will not be appearing at any queen's drawing room or at any presentation ball or at any Carlton House dinner. She will not even be going to London. It is my wish and, if necessary, my command. Even you, Wulf, cannot step between a man and his wife. This is the end of our conversation."

Most men would at least have *looked* apprehensive at the cold menace in Aidan's face and voice. Bewcastle, of course, was not most men. He raised his quizzing glass to his eye and regarded Aidan thoughtfully through it.

"Quite so," he said in his soft, pleasant voice. "Close the door behind you when you leave."

And that was the end of that, Aidan thought as he made his way upstairs—he had promised to accompany Morgan on an outdoor sketching lesson, the condition under which Miss Cowper had agreed not to go herself.

"She *hovers,*" Morgan had complained to her brother. "She *breathes* on me. And she comments on *every* brushstroke, explaining what *she* would do if *she* were the one painting the picture. And then she apologizes for disturbing my concentration. But will she allow me to go out alone and paint in peace? No, she will not. She is afraid, no doubt, that I will bolt away from my easel and swim naked in the lake in full view of the gardeners or some other such shocking thing and Wulf will see me and have her chained to a damp, slimy wall in the dungeon as punishment. I would swear, Aidan, that she has never even noticed that there *are* no dungeons at Lindsey Hall."

Aidan was considerably shaken. The cat was out of the proverbial bag. He wondered how soon it would be before his other brothers and sisters found out. He wondered if he should take the offensive and tell them himself. He was not, as he had just assured Wulf, ashamed of what he had done—or of his wife. The very idea! But he did not want her bothered. He had promised her a marriage of convenience. He had taken himself out of her life and intended to keep out.

The news had severely rattled Bewcastle, though, he concluded when he returned to the house with Morgan early in the afternoon, having swum in the lake himself while she painted. The traveling carriage with its ducal crests emblazoned on both doors stood outside the carriage house looking as clean and shining as the day it had been purchased. There were no horses attached to it, but there were liveried footmen bustling about, looking as if they were making ready for a journey.

"Wulf must be going somewhere," Morgan said. "But he does not use that carriage for local visits."

"He has plans to return to London," Aidan told her. But so abruptly? He took a firmer grip on Morgan's awkwardly sized easel and lengthened his stride.

"Where is Bewcastle going, Fleming?" he asked the butler as they stepped into the hall.

"I am not in his grace's confidence, my lord," the butler said with a deferential inclination of the head.

"Then who the devil is?" Aidan asked. But Bewcastle himself wandered into the hall at that moment, dressed for travel. "Where are you off to, Wulf?"

His brother regarded him haughtily. "To London," he said. "I have already neglected my duties there by staying home for so long. You will follow tomorrow, Aidan, with Alleyne and Freyja. It is all arranged."

Yes, it would be. And he would go too, Aidan supposed. Being the son of a duke brought along with it inescapable duties once one was in England. And so ended his dream of a peaceful month and more of relaxation at Lindsey Hall.

"Do my eyes deceive me, Fleming?" Bewcastle asked pleasantly. "Or is my carriage really not awaiting me before the doors?"

CHAPTER X

"Perhaps you will get invited this year," Aunt Mari was saying hopefully, "now that you are out of mourning for your dada, my love, and now that you are Lady Aidan Bedwyn instead of just plain Miss Morris."

"I have no wish to go," Eve said. "Though I would if you were included in the invitation."

"You know," her aunt said reproachfully, "that it is not for myself that I want the invitation. I am already living in heaven. But it is time you were recognized for what you are—a perfect lady even if your dada and your old aunt *did* once earn an honest living down a coal mine. I thought maybe the prospect of a garden party might lift you out of the mopes."

They were riding home in the gig, having just paid an afternoon call upon Serena Robson. There had been other visitors there too, and conversation had turned upon the annual garden party at Didcote Park. Though the Earl and Countess of Luff regularly invited most people with any pretense to gentility in order to make up sufficient numbers, they had always pointedly excluded the Morrises. Serena had expressed the same hope as Aunt Mari, to the extent of declaring that she would not go herself this year if Eve was not invited.

"I am not in the mopes," Eve said, smiling determinedly. "Would you have me laughing all day long, Aunt Mari, merely to prove to you that I do not feel abandoned or slighted?"

She felt neither. She had made a bargain with Colonel Bedwyn, from which they had both benefited. She had kept Ringwood and—far more important—her children, while he had fulfilled his solemn promise to Percy. They were both now free to pursue their lives as they saw fit. What was so depressing about that?

But of course she *was* deeply depressed. Despite all that she had gained, despite all the rich blessings of home and family, she was filled with an emptiness so vast that it frightened her. There had been no word of or from John. And of course, there had been no word of the colonel either. Strangely, that latter fact contributed as much to her mood as the former. The realization that she would never hear anything more of the man who was her husband—except, perhaps, one day the news of his death—clutched at her with an inexplicable panic.

She was distracted from such gloomy thoughts by the sight of Thelma and the children topping the rise from the dell as the carriage drew level with the lily pond. With them, Benjamin astride his shoulders, Becky holding one of his hands, was the Reverend Thomas Puddle. Eve raised a hand to wave to them.

"Ah," Aunt Mari said knowingly, having noticed too.

The vicar had danced twice with Thelma at the wedding assembly. He had come a number of times during the past week and a half to call upon Eve and inquire after Mrs. Pritchard's health. Each time he had asked if it would be convenient for him to watch some of the children's lessons. It did not take an oversized brain to detect a budding romance between him and Thelma. It delighted Eve that he seemed not to hold her undeserved reputation as a fallen woman against her. A gentle soul himself, he attracted children without having to make any special effort to win their confidence.

"There perhaps is one happily ever after in the making," she said.

She was surprised a moment later that the first distraction to draw her attention on her approach home had not been the carriage standing before the doors of the house. It was not one she recognized. Indeed, it was far grander than any carriage she had seen before, including the Earl of Luff's. There was a coat of arms emblazoned on the door. She did not recognize it, but then she did not know a great deal about heraldry.

"We have a visitor," she said, nodding in the direction of the house. "I wonder who it can possibly be." She wondered, with a churning of her stomach, if it was John.

Agnes was awaiting them in the hall. She was beyond her usual sour self. She was fairly bristling with indignation.

"Who is it, Agnes?" Eve asked, her voice lowered since she could see that the parlor door stood open.

"I would of put him in there," Agnes said, jerking her thumb in the direction of the parlor, "but it wasn't good enough for his high and mightiness, was it? 'I will wait in the drawing room,' he said, all la-di-da, and made off for the stairs even before I could go and show the way. I don't know what the world is coming to, I don't, when people can invite themselves into other people's houses and act like they own them."

"Who?" Eve asked, frowning.

"Some duke," Agnes said.

For a moment Eve was afraid her knees were about to buckle under her. *Some duke?*

"Oh, Eve, my love," Aunt Mari said. "Can it be the colonel's brother, do you suppose? Is the colonel with him, Agnes?"

Eve turned without waiting for Agnes's reply and hurried up the stairs. What other duke could possibly be coming to visit her? But why? She flung open the drawing room doors and stepped inside.

He was standing across the room by the windows, facing the doors. He was immaculately and tastefully clad in a dark green superfine tailed coat and buff pan-

taloons and waistcoat with white linen and highly polished Hessian boots, a dark, forbidding-looking gentleman who bore such a resemblance to Colonel
Bedwyn that Eve's heart turned over. She closed the
door behind her back and gazed wide-eyed at him.

"Why have you come?" she asked him, her voice all
thin and trembling. "What has happened to him? Has
he met with some accident?" That mud—all that *mud*.

He inclined his head with slight courtesy, his long
fingers toying with the handle of a quizzing glass. "It is
a pleasure to make your acquaintance, Lady Aidan," he
said. "I am Bewcastle." He spoke in a light, soft voice,
not effeminate exactly—in fact, it was *definitely* not
that—but one that lacked the depth and force one
expected of a gentleman's utterance. Nevertheless, it
sent shivers crawling up Eve's spine and somehow
belied the words he had spoken.

Belatedly, she curtsied.

There were differences between the brothers, she
noticed. The Duke of Bewcastle was more slender and
not quite as tall, and his lean face with its prominent
nose and thin lips looked cold and arrogant and cynical
rather than harsh and grim. His eyes too were paler, a
lighter gray than Eve's own. Almost silver, in fact.

"You will be pleased to know," the duke said, "that I
left my brother in good health at Lindsey Hall yesterday, all his limbs intact."

"I am pleased to hear it," she said. *There was a duke
standing in her drawing room.* Why had he come?

"You will be wondering why I have come here," the
duke said, "since it is not to inform you that you are a

widow. I came to make the acquaintance of my sister-in-law."

Eve swallowed awkwardly. She was still dressed for the outdoors, complete with bonnet and gloves.

"You are welcome here, your grace," she said. *Was that the correct form of address for a duke?*

"I very much doubt that," he said coldly, raising his glass halfway to his eye and looking incredibly haughty. "But perhaps you can persuade that fierce housekeeper of yours to fetch a tea tray and we can discuss your future role as Lady Aidan Bedwyn over refreshments."

Her future role? "Yes, of course," she said, crossing to the bell rope and pulling on it. "Do have a seat, your grace."

They sat in unnerving silence until Agnes came. Eve handed her her gloves and bonnet and ordered a tea tray. *Where was Aunt Mari? And what must her hair look like? His eyes really were silver. They appeared to have the ability to look right through her.*

"My future role?" she said when the door closed behind Agnes and she could stand the silence no longer.

"I wonder, ma'am," Bewcastle said, "if you understand whom exactly you have married. I have not yet performed my duty to posterity. I have no wife, no child. Aidan is my heir presumptive. Only my fragile life stands between him and a dukedom—and between you and a duchess's title."

She could feel color flood her cheeks. "You think I married Colonel Bedwyn for that reason?" she asked. "You think me ambitious and conniving? How perfectly ridiculous!"

"Oh, quite so!" He still had his quizzing glass in his hand. For one moment Eve thought he was going to raise it all the way to his eye.

"Marrying into an aristocratic family brings with it certain responsibilities and expectations," the duke continued. "Marrying the heir brings even more. The wife of Lord Aidan Bedwyn, possibly a future Duchess of Bewcastle, must be introduced to society if it has not already happened. She must be presented to the queen. She must learn to move with ease in her husband's world."

Eve's eyes widened. "But I have no intention of moving in Colonel Bedwyn's world," she said. "He must surely have told you the nature of our marriage. It was agreed that we separate immediately after the nuptials and stay apart for the rest of our lives. I am sorry if you do not approve, but—"

"You are quite correct," the duke said in his deceptively quiet, courteous voice. "I do not approve, ma'am—and that is a marvelous understatement. I do not approve of my brother's choice of bride or of the clandestine haste of his marriage or of the nature of it. I can do little about the first two facts since you are and always will be the daughter of a Welsh coal miner and you are and always will be married to my brother. I *can* do something about the third fact. The nature of your marriage must change."

"There is a proverb, your grace," Eve said, clasping her hands very tightly in her lap in the hope of hanging onto her temper, "that sleeping dogs are best left lying.

There is no need to come here with threats. I have no intention whatsoever of shaming you by displaying my soot-blackened fingernails in public or murdering the ears of your acquaintance with my Welsh accent. I have no intention of traveling any farther than ten miles from Ringwood all of the rest of my life. You may safely forget about my existence. I will bid you a good afternoon." She got to her feet.

The duke looked bored. "Do spare me the theatrics, ma'am," he said, "and sit down. And do credit me with some degree of common sense. I would not have traveled all the way from Hampshire merely to instruct you to do what you are already doing. You misunderstand my purpose. Tomorrow you will travel to London with me."

Her eyes widened in shock as she sat again, but before she could say anything Agnes came back into the room with the tea tray, which she set down none too gently on a table at Eve's elbow. She gave the duke the evil eye and looked as if she were itching for an excuse to toss him down the stairs and out through the front doors without first opening them. He was looking bored again, as if he were unaware of the house-keeper's very existence. Agnes sniffed and left the room, banging the door behind her. Eve poured the tea with hands that were not quite steady.

"Aidan is not only the heir to a dukedom," the Duke of Bewcastle said as he took his cup and saucer from her hands. "He is also a high-ranking military officer, ma'am. In both capacities his presence in London is essential. There is to be a summer of victory celebrations in the nation's capital. Already there is one specific invitation to a state dinner at Carlton House with the Prince Regent and numerous other heads of state, an invitation that includes Aidan and . . . you, Lady Aidan Bedwyn. Your existence is already known of in the inner circles of the very highest society, you see, ma'am."

"*I* have been invited to *Carlton House?*" She laughed, thinking of Cinderella and glass slippers and pumpkins. "Then you may decline on my behalf, your grace. I might, you will understand, arrive there in a crumpled cotton dress with rags in my hair and proceed to tell vulgar stories and dance on the table after I have imbibed a few drinks." Her voice shook ignominiously.

He raised his glass three-quarters of the way to his eye. "Your scorn is misplaced, ma'am," he said, his voice very soft and sounding downright dangerous. "If you neglect to put in an appearance, you will embarrass my family. It will be whispered that there must be something wrong with you—or with us—if we have hidden you away in the country a mere few weeks after your secret nuptials. I cannot expect you, perhaps, to have great regard for most members of my family, of whose number you are now one, I must remind you, but I would expect even a coal miner's daughter to have some respect for the man who sacrificed his freedom for her."

She drew breath sharply. "Is *that* what he told you?" she asked.

"Is it untrue then?" He waited politely for her answer and then continued. "Use your sense, ma'am. My guess is that you possess your fair share. Aidan is thirty years old. If one uses the Bible as one's hourglass, he has approximately forty years of his three score and ten left, married to a woman he has pledged never to see again. Now clearly there is some sacrifice of freedom there."

She drew breath to answer and then discovered that there was nothing to say. How could she argue with the truth—except that she would further curb his freedom by appearing in his life again unbidden.

"Does Colonel Bedwyn know you are here?" she asked. "Does he want me to come to London?"

"Aidan will do his duty," he told her. "It is something he has always done. Always."

"Then why did he not come with you?" she asked. "Why did he not at least send a letter with you?"

"I believe," he said, "my brother feels honor-bound not to intrude upon your life any further. I feel no such compunction."

He *did* want her to go, then? It was just that he was too honorable a man to try to force her or even ask her himself?

"Aidan does *not* know I have come here," the duke said.

"He does not want me in his life," she said. "He would not want me coming to London with you. Is that where he is?"

"I do not have the power to interfere in the inner workings of the marriage even of my own brother," the Duke of Bewcastle said. "If you choose never to live together, never to consummate your marriage, never to have issue of it, then so be it. But I *am* head of my family, and I will do all in my power to prevent any form of disgrace being brought upon our name. Your failure to appear at your husband's side for the victory celebrations, Lady Aidan, will bring disgrace on my brother and therefore on the whole of the Bedwyn family."

Eve licked her dry lips. Was it true? She knew so little of aristocratic families and their sense of honor and propriety. But despising her origins as he clearly did, the duke would surely not have come all this way if her appearance in London was not of the most crucial importance. Was she really wavering, then? Was she really thinking of going? It was impossible. She laughed nervously.

"I would bring far more disgrace on you if I *did* go to London with you, your grace," she said. "I have been given a lady's upbringing and education, but nothing in my background or training or experience has prepared me to move in such elevated circles as those who frequent Carlton House and mingle with the Prince of Wales's set. You may make any excuse you choose—I am indisposed; I have other pressing responsibilities; I am the village idiot; whatever you like. I will not refute you."

"This," he said, "is how you would show your gratitude to my brother, ma'am?"

She stared at him tight-lipped.

"Soon," he said, "within the next couple of years at the latest, Aidan will be a general. He will reach the very pinnacle of his career and will without any doubt reap honors and glory for himself. He will, if he comports himself wisely and continues to distinguish himself as he has always done, be rewarded with titles and property of his own. Would you inhibit his steady rise to the top, Lady Aidan? Would you deprive him, if only in reputation, of what he had always valued more dearly than life? I refer to his honor."

The colonel had told her none of this. Perhaps because it was not true? Or perhaps because he was too honorable to burden her with the knowledge of how she had blighted his hopes? How could she know the truth? How could she know his real wishes in this matter?

"This is ridiculous," she said. "It is unthinkable. I could not possibly do what you ask without embarrassing myself horribly—and therefore embarrassing Colonel Bedwyn too."

"There will be just time," he said, "to bring you up to snuff, Lady Aidan. We must hope you are an apt pupil. My aunt is the Marchioness of Rochester. She will sponsor you in your presentation to the queen. She will help you in your choice of a suitable wardrobe for your various appearances, including your court dress. And she will instruct you in any aspects of polite behavior for which your education has not prepared you. There will be time for your presentation and for a ball at Bedwyn House to introduce you to the *ton* before the Carlton House dinner and all the other victory celebrations you will be called upon to attend with Aidan. Only one question remains—or rather, two. *Do* you feel gratitude even when your husband has not demanded it of you? And do you possess the necessary courage?"

There was a lengthy silence, which he showed no sign of breaking.

"If only I could know *his* wishes in this matter," she said.

The silence stretched again.

"Very well," she murmured at last. She licked her lips again and spoke more firmly. "I owe Colonel Bedwyn my home and my fortune and the security of many people who are dependent upon me. Most of all, I owe him my children, who mean more to me than life. If a few weeks in London will save him from the censure of his peers, then I will give him those few weeks. But I will do it for *him,* not for you. I will not be browbeaten every moment of every day and scolded whenever I fall. I will do my best—for Colonel Bedwyn's sake."

"That is all anyone can ask of you, ma'am," the duke said. "I suppose that inn I passed on the village street is the best accommodation the neighborhood has to offer?"

"It is," she said.

"As I suspected." He finished his tea, set down his cup and saucer, and got to his feet. "You will be ready to leave when I return in the morning, Lady Aidan."

It was a command, pure and simple. Eve wished heartily that the Three Feathers was renowned for its fleas and rats instead of only for its insipid fare.

When Aidan returned from an afternoon ride in Hyde Park with Freyja and Alleyne, he was feeling moderately cheerful. In the course of the day he had met a number of old acquaintances, including some military colleagues. All had conversed with him on a variety of topics. None had mentioned his marriage. So Wulf had been wrong. It was not general knowledge. There was not going to be any embarrassment and certainly no scandal. He was glad he had made the decision not to tell his other brothers and sisters.

He was feeling invigorated. His family had always been neck-or-nothing riders, including the girls. The three of them had galloped the length of Rotten Row several times without stopping instead of mincing along—Freyja's words—as most riders did, more intent on cutting a figure and impressing the pedestrians beyond the rails than in exercising their horses and themselves.

Fleming, Bewcastle's butler, was in the hall at Bedwyn House when they arrived, having come from Lindsey Hall the day before with several of the other servants and mountains of baggage.

"Has Bewcastle arrived yet?" Freyja asked him, pulling off her riding hat and shaking out her unruly curls. It had surprised all of them when they arrived yesterday to discover that Wulf was not yet in residence. Freyja had assumed out loud, quite unabashed, that he must have gone straight to his mistress's house upon his arrival in London.

"He has, my lady," Fleming replied with one of his peculiar stiff bows. "He has requested that Colonel Bedwyn attend him in the library immediately upon his return and that you and Lord Alleyne join him for tea in the drawing room one half hour from now."

"*Requested,*" Alleyne said with a chuckle. "*Immediately.* You are on the carpet over something, Aidan. At least Freyja and I have time to wash our hands before entering the august presence."

The butler led the way to the library, knocked lightly, opened the door, and stood to one side while Aidan strode in.

She was seated to one side of the hearth, clothed in gray, her hair dressed severely in a knot at the back of her neck. Her complexion was pale, almost pasty. When she rose to her feet he was given the impression that she had lost weight. She gazed at him with wide eyes and compressed lips, and he stared back. It was only when he caught movement with his peripheral vision that he realized they were not alone. Bewcastle had got up from a sofa. Aidan turned his eyes on his brother.

"What is this?" he demanded.

"*This?*" Wulf asked with faint hauteur. "Is Lady Aidan inanimate, Aidan? I have brought you your wife."

"That is where you have been?" Aidan asked, feeling cold fury gathering in his chest. "To Ringwood? Against my specific command?"

The ducal eyebrows went up. "Dear me," he said. "Since when have I taken my orders from a younger brother? I believe you mistake me for one of your enlisted men, Aidan."

"I *do* have the power to command my own wife," Aidan said, taking one menacing step closer to his brother. "I told you she was to be left at Ringwood. I told you I did not want her here. And I told you I was

164

not to be shaken in that resolve."

"You might be advised," Bewcastle said softly, "that neither Lady Aidan nor I am deaf, Aidan—at least, I assume that the lady is not. You will reserve that voice for the battlefield, if you please. I explained to you the necessity of your wife's being at your side during the coming weeks. I do not intend to repeat the explanation. The business of my family is my domain."

"You will have her conveyed back home," Aidan said icily. "Immediately. Better yet, I will do it myself." He turned on his heel to stalk from the room, angrier than he had been for a long time—perhaps since his last leave and his encounter then with Bewcastle's stubborn, autocratic will.

A flutter of movement caught his eye and he turned his head to see his wife sit back down on her chair, her back straight, her eyes on the floor in front of her, her face chalk-white and expressionless. Deuce take it, what had he just said in her hearing? He had been so furious . . . He stood still, looking at her.

"You have just recently arrived, ma'am?" he asked unnecessarily. "You made the whole journey today?"

She looked slowly up at him until their eyes met. Her own were flat and unreadable. "If you please," she said, her words crisp and quite icy, "one of you will find out the name and direction of the inn from which the next stagecoach to Oxfordshire departs. I will need a hackney coach to take me there. Perhaps you will be so good as to call me one immediately. One of you."

"Ma'am," Aidan said, "I beg your pardon. I did not—"

"Immediately." She got to her feet again.

Aidan glared at Bewcastle, but his brother had turned nonchalantly away as if he had not been the cause of all this.

"Perhaps," Aidan said, "we should—"

"Immediately."

"Perhaps we should cool down," he said, "and discuss this."

"If I were any cooler," she said, "I would turn into an iceberg. I am leaving. I am going upstairs to fetch my bag. When I come back down I will expect to find a hackney coach at the door. If I do not, I will simply walk away until I find one myself."

She crossed the room toward Aidan, made a wide detour around him, and went out through the door before shutting it behind her. Bewcastle turned and looked at the door.

"My carriage is available to you," he said.

"Blast you, Wulf," Aidan said viciously, "I would like nothing better than to ram all your teeth down your throat. She wants a damned hackney coach. That is what she will get."

He turned and strode from the room without waiting for a reply.

CHAPTER XI

❧

Eve did not go back downstairs immediately. She wanted to give them time to call a hackney coach for her. She did not want to have to wait in the hall until one came. She paced the sitting room of the sumptuous suite to which the housekeeper had shown her on her arrival earlier.

She was angry and humiliated. More angry than humiliated. Angry at *him*. Furious at herself.

I told you she was to be left at Ringwood.

As if she were some unwanted, discarded package.

I told you I did not want her here.

Brutal frankness, considering the fact that she had been there to hear him. But she had known that. There had never been any pretense between them that either wanted the other. Oh, she was so angry at herself.

I do have the power to command my own wife.

How could he! There had never been any question . . . How *incensed* she was with him.

And the Duke of Bewcastle. He had sat opposite her in the carriage all day—in retrospect it was surprising that he had not made *her* sit with her back to the horses—haughtily silent much of the time, talking about his family and its illustrious history when he *did* deign to converse with her, as if she were a particularly ignorant and uncouth pupil who needed educating in the important things of life. She would not be surprised to discover that if he were cut it would be ice water rather than blood that flowed from his veins. He was a shudderingly horrid man.

She could not *wait* to be back at Ringwood. Why had she left it in the first place? It had been agony to leave the children. Becky had clung wordlessly to her neck, unconsoled even by the promise of presents. Davy had gazed at her with silent reproach, as if to say that he had known all along she would prefer flitting off to the pleasures of London than staying with children who were not her own and whom no one else had wanted since the death of his parents.

Finally, when she considered that she had allowed enough time to elapse, she picked up her bag—the duke had instructed her to bring only a few changes of clothing—and went resolutely down the stairs. It was not an easy thing to do. She fully expected them to be standing shoulder to shoulder in the hall, dark and menacing and bad-tempered, to order her to do her duty. But only the stiff, stately butler was there with a couple of footmen, one of whom immediately relieved her of her bag.

"Is there a hackney coach awaiting me?" she asked.

"There is, my lady." The butler bowed and opened the front doors.

"And does the coachman know to which inn to take me?"

"He does, my lady."

She swept past him out the door and down the steps to the pavement, her chin up, thinking illogically that he could at least have come to bid her farewell. And then she saw that he *had* come, that he was standing at the carriage door, while the coachman was sitting up on the box. He opened the door as she approached and she climbed inside without either looking at him or availing herself of his offered hand. She was disappointed in him. Yes, indeed she was. She had begun to like him back at Ringwood. At the same time she felt guilty and humiliated—she had complicated his life by coming unbidden after he had thought himself free of her forever.

And then he climbed in after her, shut the door, and seated himself beside her. The seat was narrow. He pressed against her arm and her thigh, converting her anger from coldness to instant heat.

"If this is gallantry, Colonel Bedwyn," she said, "it is misplaced. I do not need your escort."

"Nevertheless," he said, "you have it, ma'am. I will see you safely settled at your inn."

She averted her head pointedly to gaze out at the busy streets of London, which had so enthralled her less than three weeks ago. Could it really be so short a time? It seemed like an age ago, a lifetime ago. Neither of them attempted any conversation.

She intended to dismiss him quite firmly as soon as they arrived at their destination, to tell him to remain in the coach and return to Bedwyn House. But The Green Man and Still was such a large inn and the cobbled yard so bustling with noise and activity that truth to tell she was bewildered by it all. She made no protest when the colonel, having descended first in order to take down her bag and hand her out, strode off in the direction of the door through which most of the human traffic seemed to be proceeding. The hackney coach drove away. He must have paid the fare in advance.

She went and stood inside the door while the colonel spoke to the man behind the counter. This inn was far more crowded and noisy than the Pulteney had been but just as daunting in its own way. She felt like a cowering country mouse.

"I have taken a room for you," the colonel said when he came back to her. "It is on the second floor facing the street. It should be a little quieter than one overlooking the yard."

"Did you pay for it?" she asked him.

"Of course," he said.

She opened her reticule. "How much?"

There was a slight pause. "There is no need for this," he said.

"On the contrary." She looked up at him. "There is every need. And thanks to you, I am not impoverished, am I?"

His jaw tightened. He looked more than usually grim. "I will take care of my wife's needs when I am in company with her, ma'am," he said.

"Does that include her need to be treated with respect?" she asked, snapping her reticule shut and stooping to pick up her bag. His hand closed about her wrist.

"Much more of this," he said, "and we will be attracting attention. If we must quarrel, at least let us do it in the privacy of your room."

"I am quite capable of finding my way there if you will tell me the room number," she said. "I will not keep you from the rest of your life one moment longer, Colonel Bedwyn."

But he had possessed himself of her bag again and was striding off with it in the direction of the wide wooden staircase. Eve went trotting after him, doing a far poorer job than he of avoiding bumping into hurrying guests and servants. They climbed to the second story and walked the length of a long gallery before stopping outside a door at the very end of it. He opened the door and she stepped into the room ahead of him.

It was not large or ornate or crowded with furniture—it was nothing to compare with the Pulteney. There were just a large bed, a chest of drawers, a washstand, and one chair. But at least everything looked clean. And some of the noise of the inn seemed to recede after he had come in behind her and closed the door.

There was no need for him to have come inside. Eve removed her bonnet and gloves and set them on the dresser, her back to him.

"Why did you come?" he asked. "Or does the question need to be asked? Bewcastle went to fetch you, and very few people can withstand Bewcastle's will when he has his mind set upon something. How did he persuade you?"

"It does not matter," she said. "Tomorrow I will be back at Ringwood and you will never see or hear from me again—or I you. You will be no worse for today except for the cost of an inn room and a hackney coach."

"The devil of it is," he said, "that I cannot remember exactly what I said to Wulf when I saw you there in the library and realized what he had done. Something about having told him to leave you where you were, I believe."

She went to stand by the window, as far away from him as she could get and set both hands on the windowsill. Below her a coach and four was slowing, about to make the turn out of the street into the inn yard.

"You said," she reminded him, "that you did not want me here. That is quite understandable. I do not want to be here either. It was part of our agreement that neither of us wished to spend any more time in the other's company than was strictly necessary."

She heard him set down her bag. She did not want to turn and look at him. He was wearing his uniform—the old, almost shabby one—and was looking altogether too formidable to be dealt with in such a restricted space.

"But the words were ill-chosen and ill-mannered," he said. "I did not mean them quite the way they sounded."

"And you said," she continued more deliberately, turning after all to glare accusingly at him, "that you *do* have the power to command your own wife. That was more than despicable, Colonel. We married for our mutual convenience. We parted with every intention of never communicating again. The question of your mastery and my subservience was never raised between us, the reason being that I am *not* your wife. Not in any way that matters."

He was angry too now. She could see it in the hardness of his jaw and the narrow set of his eyes. "Perhaps, ma'am," he said, "that is where we made our mistake."

"Mistake?"

"Agreeing to a marriage in name only," he said. "We should at least have made a real marriage of it even if we were to live the rest of our lives apart. Then there would be none of this ridiculous debate about whether you are really my wife or not, about whether I should

172

pay certain of your bills or not, about whether I have the right to command my brother to leave you in peace or not. Perhaps we ought to have carried our wedding day to its natural conclusion."

She stared at him, her cheeks hot. But during the precious seconds she should have used to find words with which to express her outrage, she instead paused to feel the physical effects of his words—a certain loss of breath, a tightening in her breasts, a pulsing ache between her thighs and up inside her, and a weakness about the knees.

"It would have been wrong," she said. "Neither of us wanted that."

"*Wrong?* We are man and woman," he said harshly, "and a few weeks ago we married. Men and women, especially married ones, go to bed together. They satisfy certain needs there. Have you never felt such needs?"

She licked her lips and swallowed. She wished the window were open. The room felt airless.

He made an impatient sound then and came striding across the room toward her, detouring about the foot of the bed. She set her back firmly against the windowsill and gripped it from behind with both hands. He stood before her, his legs braced apart, his large hands coming up to cup her face. She closed her eyes and his mouth descended on hers, closed, hard, pressing her lips rather painfully against her teeth. But almost immediately the pressure became lighter as he parted his lips over hers and licked at the seam with his tongue, coaxing a response and causing a sharp sensation there and a deeper throbbing between her legs.

When her lips parted, and then her teeth, he pressed his tongue deep into her mouth, exploring its surfaces with the tip. One of his hands was splayed against the back of her head, holding it close.

Her first conscious thought was that she was being disloyal, unfaithful. But unfaithful to whom? Colonel Bedwyn was her husband. She was *married* to him. If she did not do these things with him now, she would never do them with anyone. Ever. The thought brought with it a desperate yearning and she moved her hands to his shoulders. They were impossibly broad and hard-muscled, even allowing for his heavy military coat. She kissed him back, angling her head, opening her mouth wider, touching his tongue with her own. She allowed herself to acknowledge her own desire.

Heat flared between them in a rush of passion. His hands had moved away from her head. One arm was wrapped about her waist. The other hand was spread behind her hips. It drew her firmly against him so that she was breathlessly aware of heavy leather boots, hard, muscled thighs, and masculinity. Her arms clasped him about the neck while her body strained toward his, desperate to move closer, closer . . .

When he lifted his head and looked down at her, she was jolted for a moment by the realization of just what was happening and with whom. His hook-nosed face was as dark, as harsh as ever. She should have been a little frightened, perhaps a little repelled. Instead she felt only more deeply aroused, especially when she looked into his heavy-lidded eyes and saw an answering passion there.

"We are going to consummate this marriage of ours," he said, "on that bed behind me. If you do not want it, say so now. I am not issuing any commands."

It had not been a part of their bargain. Indeed, it had seemed very important at the time—to both of them—that they be married in name only, that they part as soon after the ceremony as they could. She could no longer remember their reasons. She would later when she was thinking more rationally. She would hate herself later if she continued now, if she gave in to sheer lust. But why would she? If there *was* a reason, she could not think what it could be. They were, after all, man and wife.

"I want it," she said, surprised by the low huskiness of her voice. But she held up a staying hand almost immediately. "There is something you must know first, though."

She almost lost her nerve. He raised his eyebrows.

"I am not a virgin."

He went very still and searched her eyes with his own while she listened to the echo of her words, appalled. She had never once dreamed that she would have to confess *that* to him.

"Ah," he said then, very softly. "Fair enough. Neither am I."

It was the last moment of rationality, of sanity, for a long while.

He turned with her and held her to him with one arm while stripping back the bedcovers with the other. He undid the buttons at the neck of her cloak and tossed it aside, tumbled her to the bed, pulled off her shoes and stockings, and lifted her dress up along her legs and over her hips while she raised them from the mattress. He sat down briefly on the side of the bed to drag off his boots. His coat came off inside out. He unbuttoned the flap of his breeches and came down on top of her, pushing her dress higher as he did so.

His weight was full on her. He was terribly heavy, robbing her of breath. His hands came beneath her, lifting her, tilting her, and then he was inside her in one firm, liquid rush. She caught what little breath was available to her. He was large and very hard. She was stretched and filled almost to the point of pain.

Almost.

She twined her arms tightly about him, and lifted her legs to wrap about his. She heard someone moan and thought it was probably her.

He braced some of his weight on his forearms and began to move almost immediately, withdrawing and pressing inward over and over again, setting up such a firm, fast-paced rhythm that it seemed perfectly natural to move with him, to flex and relax her inner muscles in a matching rhythm. Soon she could hear harsh, labored breathing—from both of them—and feel the wetness of their coupling. She could smell his cologne, his maleness, and something else that was raw and exciting and unidentifiable.

The ache of desire she had felt from the start became all focused there, where they worked their frenzied pleasure. Soon it became more than an ache. It became a yearning and a pain that did not quite hurt. It engulfed her from head to toe, moving outward in waves from her center—from *their* center. It threatened to become unbearable. It *was* unbearable. But even as she thought so, even as she cried out, everything shattered as if there had been some explosion deep inside. Instead of pain, though, there was only a deep, bone-melting peace.

He made a sound very like a growl, and his weight collapsed down on her again even as she felt a gush of liquid heat deep inside. He was hot and slick with sweat. So was she.

He rolled off her, though he did not take his arms from about her. They lay face to face, gazing at each other. He was Colonel Bedwyn, she reminded herself foolishly, and a vivid image came to mind of her first sight of him in the parlor at Ringwood, tall, powerful, dark, and forbidding. But she was too tired to digest just what had happened or to understand why it had been so very pleasurable. She was surely wearier than she had ever been before in her life. Her eyes drifted closed.

She wondered as she floated off to sleep if she would regret this when she woke up. Or if he would. Surely they would. But she would think about it later.

Coaches, both public and private, were incessantly coming and going at The Green Man and Still. Passengers, guests at the inn, and servants were constantly to-ing and fro-ing, with a great deal of noise and energy. Someone was forever calling out to someone else instead of moving close enough to be able to talk. There was all the cheerful bustle here that Aidan always associated with England and of which he thought with nostalgia when he was beyond its shores.

He was sitting in the dining room with his wife, eating dinner. There was enough privacy provided by the noise itself that it was unlikely their conversation would be overheard, but not as much privacy as he would have liked. They were behaving like polite strangers. They might appear like polite strangers to anyone who did not look too closely. He wondered if the slight flush in his wife's cheeks, the slight swelling of her lips, the slight heaviness of her eyelids would make it as obvious to a stranger as it was to him that they had recently risen from bed and a vigorous bout of sex.

He still could not quite believe it had happened—that either of them had *wanted* it to happen.

"How did the children react to your coming?" he asked. "Were you not afraid to leave?"

"Afraid, no," she said. "Reluctant, yes. I was expecting to be here for a few weeks. But they are safe and well cared for. I do not believe they will feel as insecure as they did last time. Aunt Mari likes to fuss over them—she is teaching Becky to knit. And Nanny Johnson and Thelma are good to them. The Reverend Puddle visits often and has won their affection."

He had been strangely touched by her attachment to two young orphans who were not her responsibility at all. But he had not realized fully until after he had married her that they were of central importance to her life, that without them she might have reacted differently to his suggestion.

"And your aunt is well?" he asked.

"Yes, thank you. She was delighted by my decision to come to London." She laughed. "Even after the duke had raised his quizzing glass all the way to his eye on hearing her Welsh accent when I introduced them."

"Why *did* you decide to come?" he asked once more. "I know Bewcastle can be very persuasive, but I do not see you as a woman of weak will."

She fingered a spoon she had not used. "He convinced me," she said, "that you would suffer from the censure of your peers if I did not come."

"I do not care the snap of two fingers about my peers," he said.

"Oh, but you do." She frowned. "You always do what you perceive to be right, even if it comes at the expense of personal sacrifice. Our marriage is proof of that. Duty is all to you, I believe. If your peers got the wrong idea about our living separately and believed that you were ashamed of me after marrying impulsively and so had callously abandoned me to a sort of country prison, you would be judged a dishonorable man. You would be hurt by such gossip, even though you would know there was not a grain of truth in it."

Perhaps she was right, he conceded. "And so you came to save me," he said. "You made me your newest lame duck."

She looked up at him, traces of her earlier anger in the slight hardening of her jaw.

"I came to do for you what you did for me," she said. "When you thought it important that my neighbors see us together, comfortable and amiable together and respectful of each other, you remained at Ringwood and endured all the tedium of a country assembly for my sake. You owed me nothing according to our agreement, yet you did it anyway. I came here so that I could do the same for you."

"But for you it would mean inconvenience for longer than a day," he said.

"For a few weeks, I expected," she said. "Perhaps even a month. I would have had to be carefully prepared—by your aunt, according to the duke."

"Aunt Rochester?"

"Yes." She was turning the spoon over and over on the table. "I am not a lady by birth, and only partially by education. I was brought up and have lived most of my life in the country among people who are gently born but by no means members of the *ton*. I know nothing of town fashions and manners. I know absolutely nothing at all about moving in high society or about what is expected of the wife of a duke's heir. I would have had to learn to be presented to the queen without disgracing myself and how to be presented at a ball in Bedwyn House without losing all my composure and committing some heinous social gaffe. And then I would have had to attend all the victory celebrations at your side, behaving as Lady Aidan Bedwyn ought."

It was hardly surprising that there was an edge of bitterness to her voice. Aidan dearly wished he could swear out loud.

"And all this Wulf said to you without mincing words, I suppose," he said.

"I do not like him," she said. "Indeed, I believe my feelings about him go beyond dislike. But at least I respect his honesty. He says what he believes. He does not say one thing and imply another."

"About what happened upstairs this afternoon—" he began.

She set her hand flat over the spoon, hiding it completely from his view and shook her head.

"It does not matter," she said. "Perhaps it is as you said. We needed to do that, to complete what we had started, so to speak. It does not matter. And I can hardly pretend, can I, that I did not enjoy it. I did. Let us leave it at that."

It was a long time since he had had a woman—before today, that was. The last time had been somewhere back in Spain before the winter crossing of the Pyrenees by Wellington's armies, back before his acquaintance with Miss Knapp had developed into something that had promised a future. But he could not pretend that he had taken his wife only to appease a rabid hunger for sex. It had been, as she had just said, a completion. And apparently an end too.

"Your coach leaves at seven o'clock in the morning," he said.

"Yes." She lifted her napkin off her lap and set it on the table beside her plate. "I should get to bed early. It has been a long day."

"Allow me to escort you home," he said. "I'll hire a private carriage. It will be far more comfortable than the stage."

"No. Thank you."

"I'll accompany you on the stage, then," he said.

She shook her head.

He stared at her, exasperated. How could he let her go alone? She had come for his sake, damn it all. And damn Bewcastle to hell and back.

"You would not have enjoyed it here, you know," he said. "Life at Bedwyn House, the Season and all that."

"I did not expect to enjoy it," she told him. "I did not come to be entertained."

"You would have found it impossible," he said. "Bewcastle, Aunt Rochester, even Freyja and Alleyne. You would never have coped with them or with all they would have expected of you."

"Impossible?" She looked up at him with a frown. "Never?"

"I apologize for the inconvenience you have been put to today," he told her, "and for the tedium of another day of travel tomorrow. But you will be altogether happier at home in Ringwood. You would never have been able to master every lesson here in time."

"Would I not?"

The quietness of her voice finally alerted him. "Not to Bewcastle's satisfaction, anyway," he said. "Or Aunt Rochester's. They are incredibly high in the instep."

"And you are not, Colonel?"

He leaned a little toward her. "I believe we have both long realized," he said, "that we are from different worlds. One is not necessarily superior to the other. They are just different. Bewcastle was wrong to persuade you to come here. You would have been miserable if you had stayed. What comes naturally to me, to

Bewcastle, to my sister, would not come naturally to you at all. That is not—"

But he had lost his audience. She pushed back her chair with her knees and got to her feet. He stood too, his eyebrows raised.

"Call a hackney coach, Colonel Bedwyn," she said. "I am returning to Bedwyn House—this evening. There is no time to waste. I have a presentation to the queen to prepare for and a ball and numerous other social activities, including a state dinner at Carlton House."

He stared at her for a few moments longer. Although she spoke quietly and looked perfectly composed so that she was attracting no unwelcome attention from any other guest in the dining room, he could see that she was furiously angry.

"I do not believe this is a wise choice, ma'am," he said.

"Then," she said with a stubborn, potentially dangerous lift of her chin, "you are going to have to use your husband's prerogative, Colonel, and order me back home. Please do it, and then I will have the pleasure of openly defying you. Will you call a hackney coach, or shall I?"

Devil take it, was this thing they had started three weeks ago never going to come to an end? Aidan strode away without another word while silently answering his own question. No, it was not. Not while they both lived.

He assumed that she had gone upstairs to fetch her bag while he called a carriage. He did not look back to see.

CHAPTER XII

One of the footmen on duty in the hall at Bedwyn House informed Colonel Bedwyn that the family was still at dinner. They would wait in the drawing room then, the colonel informed him, cupping Eve's elbow with one hand and turning her in the direction of the staircase. But the footman coughed discreetly.

"I believe his grace has plans to go out for the evening after dinner, my lord," the man said. "And Lady Freyja and Lord Alleyne will be attending the theater."

"Then we will interrupt their dinner," the colonel said, his voice hard and abrupt. "Have Fleming announce us."

The footman's eyebrows rose perhaps half an inch, the only sign he gave of holding an opinion on the matter. He turned and led the way. Eve, her elbow firmly in the colonel's grasp, tried to draw breaths that were both silent and steadying. The anger and bravado that had propelled her out of The Green Man and Still less than half an hour ago and into the waiting hackney coach and then inside Bedwyn House were rapidly deserting her—at least the bravado was. Until they set foot inside the hall and he spoke to the footman, Colonel Bedwyn had not uttered a single word. He had contented himself with looking thunderous.

The footman knocked on the door—presumably it was the dining room—murmured something to the butler when the latter opened it, and turned back in the direction of the hall. The butler's eyebrows rose perhaps three quarters of an inch.

"Lord and Lady Aidan, your grace," he announced, stepping to one side of the doorway.

The dining room was a long, high-ceilinged chamber with a table that took up much of its length. Eve was given an instant impression of grandeur and noticed the gold and crystal chandelier hanging from the painted, coved ceiling, and the fine china, crystalware, and silverware glittering on the table beneath the light of the candles. Truth to tell, though, most of her attention was taken by the three people seated at the table. The Duke of Bewcastle she knew. The young man at his left was obviously another brother, though he was more handsome than either the duke or the colonel. The lady on the duke's right had masses of wavy fair hair, eyebrows that were very dark in contrast, a dark-toned complexion, and the family nose. All three of them were dressed in formal evening wear and looked everything Eve had ever imagined of the aristocracy. If a single word could sum up those expectations, it would be *haughty*.

The two gentlemen rose from their places.

"Ah," the duke said with faint hauteur, his quizzing glass already in his hand.

"*Lady* Aidan?" the young man asked.

The lady merely stared with raised eyebrows.

"I have the honor," Colonel Bedwyn said, "of presenting Lady Aidan Bedwyn, my wife. Lady Freyja Bedwyn, the elder of my two sisters, ma'am, and Lord

Alleyne Bedwyn, my youngest brother."

Lady Freyja's eyebrows soared higher and her eyes swept over Eve from head to toe, making her horribly aware of her travel clothes, which were neat and clean but very far from being either in the finest of fabrics or in the first stare of fashion—or suitable for evening wear.

"You devil, you, Aidan!" Lord Alleyne exclaimed. He laughed, revealing himself to be even more handsome than Eve had first thought, and looked her over as frankly as his sister was doing, though with humor dancing in his eyes. "This happened today?"

"Almost three weeks ago, actually," the colonel said. "By special license."

Lord Alleyne strode down the long room toward them. "Before you even came to Lindsey Hall," he said, his eyes on Eve. "Yet you breathed not a word to any of us. I wonder why." He laughed again and favored Eve with an elegant, formal bow. "Your servant, Lady Aidan."

"Lord Alleyne," Eve murmured, curtsying.

"Oh, you must dispense with the *lord*," he told her. "I am Alleyne. What may we call you? You are not going to insist that we treat your wife with prim formality, are you, Aidan, when she is our sister-in-law?"

"I am Eve," she said.

"Eve." He grinned. "Did you offer the apple of temptation? Why did our brother keep your existence a secret from us? Are you going to tell?"

From close up, his smile was ambivalent. It was hard to know if it proceeded from pure good humor or from mischief. Was he being welcoming and brotherly—or was he mocking her? Certainly his questions were unanswerable.

"You are somewhat late for dinner, Aidan," the duke observed from his place at the head of the table.

"We have already dined," the colonel informed him brusquely.

"Ah," his grace said. "But you will join us for a glass of wine. Alleyne, seat Lady Aidan beside you."

He was not going to comment upon the fact that she had returned, then, Eve thought as Lord Alleyne offered his arm and she placed her hand on his sleeve. Neither was he going to take his cue from his brother and call her by name. She took her seat at the table and for a moment felt engulfed in panic. They were from different worlds, the colonel had said earlier. Different universes, more like.

"But this is no surprise to Wulf, it is to be noted," Lord Alleyne said as Eve seated herself and he pushed her chair closer to the table. "We have been slighted, Free. Kept in the dark. Kept from the most delicious family *on-dit* in a generation."

"Lady Aidan," Lady Freyja said with cold arrogance as the colonel seated himself beside her, "may one ask who exactly Aidan has married? I do not believe we have met before, have we? Are we acquainted with your family? Would we recognize the name if we were to hear it?"

"I am sure you would not," Eve said, looking into the disdainful eyes of her sister-in-law.

"My wife was Miss Morris of Ringwood Manor in

Oxfordshire," Colonel Bedwyn explained. "She has owned the property since the passing of her father a little over a year ago. Captain Morris, her brother, was my fellow officer in the Peninsula. I had the sad duty of bringing home the news of his death in battle."

"Ah, do accept my commiserations, Eve," Lord Alleyne said.

"And you fell head over ears for each other at first glance," his sister said, her eyes resting mockingly on Eve. "How unutterably romantic. But Morris? No, I am afraid I have never heard the name."

"It would be strange if you had." Eve smiled. "My father was a coal miner before he married the owner's daughter."

And so, she thought as her sister-in-law answered her smile without making any comment, the battle lines had been drawn. Well, she had been warned both by her own common sense and by Colonel Bedwyn. She had no one but herself to blame for this.

"A coal miner." Lord Alleyne chuckled. "It must certainly have been love, then. Aidan has always been the highest of sticklers, and he has no need of anyone's fortune—he has a vast one of his own. Did you know that, Eve? Now tell me, why is he pokering up at me?"

Eve was not sure she would like Alleyne. She did not know how to interpret his good humor, so different from the coldness of his siblings. She thought it wise to ignore his questions and wait for someone else to say something.

"Lady Aidan," the Duke of Bewcastle said as the butler poured red wine into the crystal glass beside her, "you will be ready after breakfast tomorrow morning to accompany Aidan and me when we call upon the Marchioness of Rochester."

It was not a question, but Eve answered it anyway. "I will, your grace," she said. She had made her decision. She would live by it.

"Aunt Rochester?" Lord Alleyne grimaced rather theatrically. "You are going to unleash the dragon on Eve, Wulf?"

"Is Aunt Rochester to be given the task of bringing you up to snuff, Lady Aidan?" Lady Freyja asked.

"I believe she is to be asked to sponsor me in my presentation to the queen," Eve replied, "and to give me some advice and direction on how I may move comfortably in Colonel Bedwyn's world for the next few weeks until I can return home to my own life."

"Aunt Rochester is up to most challenges," Lady Freyja said. "Even the most difficult."

"We must all agree with you on that, Free," Alleyne said, raising his glass in apparent toast to his sister. "She orchestrated *your* come-out, did she not? And the world kept turning."

She glared disdainfully at him.

"A hit, Freyja, you must admit," the duke said languidly. He rose to his feet, glass in hand. "We will drink a toast to the newest member of the Bedwyn family. To Lady Aidan Bedwyn."

There was no warmth in either his voice or his eyes. The others rose too and clinked glasses before drinking, but only Alleyne looked directly at Eve. Only Alleyne smiled—and quickly winked.

Colonel Bedwyn was stern and granite-faced. Unbidden, a memory of the afternoon came to Eve's mind—of the hour they had spent together in her bed at The Green Man and Still. Could it really have happened? It seemed like a strange, bizarre dream except that she could feel the physical effects of what had happened. Could *that* man possibly be *this* man? Her stomach performed an uncomfortable flip-flop.

The Marchioness of Rochester was at home the next morning, but she still had not emerged from her dressing room, her butler informed Bewcastle in a manner that showed all the proper deference for his rank while at the same time conveying unmistakable reproach. This particular hour of the morning was not, of course, the polite time for even so lofty a person as the Duke of Bewcastle to be paying a social call.

"If you would care to wait in the rose salon, your grace? My lord?" the butler asked, his tone implying that they might not care to do any such thing but to take themselves off until a more respectable hour. His eyes skimmed over Eve and apparently dismissed her.

Bewcastle was already moving toward the salon with firm strides. "Bring us refreshments," he commanded.

Aunt Rochester took her time about coming down. Aidan seated his wife on a settee and went to stand behind her. Wulf crossed to the window and stood staring out over the square. After perhaps ten minutes, during which they partook of refreshments without exchanging a word, the double doors of the rose salon opened with a flourish, the butler stepped to one side, and the marchioness swept into the room, dressed and coifed for a morning outing. She carried a long-handled lorgnette in her right hand, an affectation she had indulged in for as far back as Aidan could remember, though he suspected that, as with Wulf and his quizzing glass, she had perfect eyesight. She wore a jeweled ring on each finger.

"Bewcastle!" she exclaimed as she came. "Only you would have the effrontery to call at such an ungodly hour and expect to be received. But this is not well done of you. I have a meeting with one of my charitable committees, and you know how strict I am about punctuality. Well, bless my soul." She raised her lorgnette to her eyes. "You have brought Aidan with you. Where is your uniform, boy? You are going to have to wear it if you are to be seen about town with me. What is the point of having a colonel for a nephew if I cannot show him off in all his scarlet splendor at this of all times? I must say, though, that you are looking more and more distinguished with every passing year. How many years is it since I saw you last? Two? Three? Four? At my age time passes so quickly that a year seems no longer than a week. Who is the female?"

"Aunt?" Aidan bowed to her. "I have the pleasure of presenting my wife, Lady Aidan Bedwyn. My—" He was given no opportunity to complete the introduction.

"Bless my soul!" she exclaimed again, her lorgnette sweeping down over his wife. "Whose schoolroom did you steal her from? Whose governess was she?"

Eve was, of course, dressed in her habitual gray.

"She was Miss Morris of Ringwood Manor in Oxfordshire," he told her. "She is owner of the property, aunt."

"Where on earth did you find her?" she asked. Aunt Rochester was famous for her bluntness. What would have been deemed unpardonable rudeness in anyone else was dubbed eccentricity in the daughter of a duke and wife of a marquess.

"I brought the news to Ringwood Manor of the death in battle at Toulouse of Captain Morris, Miss Morris's brother," he explained.

"And she wept piteously all over that broad chest of yours, I suppose, and wailed soulfully about how all alone she now was," his aunt said scornfully. "She smelled a fortune as soon as it walked through her door with its feet in your boots and spotted a fool at the same moment."

"Aunt!" Aidan clasped his hands behind him and bent his sternest glare on her. If she were a man, by God, she would by now be lying prostrate on the Persian carpet, counting stars on the ceiling. "I really cannot allow you—"

But again he was interrupted.

"I am neither deaf nor dumb," his wife said quietly, getting to her feet. "Neither am I feebleminded. I do not appreciate being spoken of in the third person as if I were all three. And I have a strong aversion to being insulted. I will inform you that I am really quite wealthy, ma'am, if that knowledge will help quell some of your fears that your nephew has been duped by a fortune-hunter. My father worked hard as a coal miner, married the owner of the mine, inherited through her, and then worked hard to amass an even greater fortune. I was and am proud of him and of my heritage." She spoke in a more than usually lilting accent—deliberately so, Aidan suspected.

"You are Welsh!" his aunt said as if accusing Eve of some heinous crime.

"Aunt," Aidan said stiffly, "you owe my wife an apology."

She answered with a bark of laughter. "Impudent puppy!" she said.

"I did not bring her here to be insulted."

"Sit down," his aunt ordered suddenly. "Both of you. Sit! And you too, Bewcastle—and you may lower both those eyebrows and that quizzing glass. They do not intimidate me."

None of them moved.

"You have already kept me from my committee," Aunt Rochester said. "And I *never* neglect my duties to those less fortunate than myself. Now, *sit,* and tell me to what I owe this *honor*. I suspect that it would not have taken both my nephews to come here this morning merely to present Lady Aidan Bedwyn."

Eve sat again and Aidan moved around the settee to take the place beside her. Bewcastle remained standing close to the window.

"Lady Aidan must be presented at court and properly brought out," he said. "For better or worse she is Aidan's wife. Moreover, she has been included in an invitation to the state dinner for all the visiting European dignitaries at Carlton House. You will sponsor her, aunt."

"Will I, indeed?" she asked him haughtily. "You take much for granted, Wulfric."

"I do," he said. "You are a Bedwyn. Lady Aidan must be brought up to snuff. There is no one better qualified to accomplish that than you."

Aunt Rochester regarded him through her lorgnette.

"She will have to be taken to a fashionable dressmaker," Wulf continued. "She will need everything. In particular, she must set aside her mourning. Gray does not become her."

"Why is she not in black?" Aunt Rochester asked. "Her brother has just died, has he not?"

"He sent word with Aidan that she was not to wear mourning for him. But even if he had not done so, I would require her to set it aside for her appearance in society," Bewcastle said. "You will undertake this task, aunt?"

"It would appear," Aunt Rochester said with a sigh, "that I have no choice. It will be an interesting challenge. I have never before been called upon to sponsor a Welsh coal miner's daughter." The lorgnette was turned upon Eve, who sat quietly enough under the scrutiny, though Aidan expected that at any moment she would jump to her feet again and demand to be taken away. "At least she has a passably good figure and tolerable features. Something will have to be done about her hair, of course."

Bewcastle and Aunt Rochester proceeded to talk about her in the third person again—and rather as if she were inanimate. Aidan might have felt some pity for her if she had not brought this entirely upon herself. As

194

it was, it was just as well, perhaps, that she know fully this morning what yesterday's ruffled pride had led her into. And interestingly enough, he was rather curious to know where, if anywhere, that pride was going to lead her today and in the coming days. He had not really seen it in full force until yesterday—a strange reminder of how little he knew of the woman he had married. Would he be taking her back to The Green Man and Still this afternoon or tomorrow?

"If I approve of what is suggested, ma'am," she said after a minute or two, interrupting the conversation and drawing both his aunt's and Wulf's astonished attention to herself, "then I will allow the style of my hair to be changed. As for my clothes and my behavior, I would appreciate your help and advice, ma'am, before I decide for myself what is appropriate. Perhaps I should quell your worst fears, though, by assuring you that Colonel Bedwyn did not pluck me straight out of a coal mine. I have been given the upbringing and education of a lady."

"Bless my soul," his aunt said, "you have married a woman with claws, Aidan."

"Yes, aunt," he agreed.

"She had better keep them sheathed from *me*," she said. "And she needs to learn that the English language is designed to be spoken, not sung—except by those who are members of choirs. *Ladies* do not sing in choirs."

"It is her Welsh accent, aunt," he said. And damned attractive it was too, even if she *was* exaggerating it to provoke his relatives.

Bewcastle interrupted what might have developed into a quarrel. As usual, he spoke softly. "You are willing, then, Lady Aidan," he asked, "to put yourself in the hands of Lady Rochester? You can do no better, I do assure you."

"Thank you, your grace," she said coolly. "I am willing. Thank you, ma'am."

She glanced at Aidan, and he could see the stubborn set of her jaw that he had not really noticed until yesterday, though it must have been there from the start, he supposed, recalling her unwillingness to accept his assistance, desperately as she had needed it.

"If all this is going to be too much for you," he said, "say so now and I will take you home—to Ringwood. I will not coerce you into anything. It was no part of our bargain. And I will not have you coerced."

"I am not going anywhere," she said, looking steadily into his eyes.

"Oh, yes, you are, my girl," his aunt retorted, her lorgnette to her eye again. With it she was assessing Eve's appearance from head to foot. "You and I are going to pay a call on my modiste without another moment's delay. Wulfric, Aidan, you may leave. Go! Who is your dressmaker, girl? No, do not pain my ears by answering. Some rustic unknown, I suppose."

"Yes," Eve agreed. "My aunt and I, ma'am."

Aidan stood and looked at Bewcastle, who preceded him from the room after bowing distantly to both ladies.

The notion that Miss Benning, Lady Rochester's fashionable dressmaker, would cancel all her other appointments for the next few days merely because the marchioness was bringing her nephew's new bride to be outfitted for her court appearance and for what remained of the Season, had seemed to Eve to be a preposterous boast when the marchioness had mentioned it during the carriage ride to Bond Street. She had not really believed it.

Now she did.

The Marchioness of Rochester, she soon realized beyond any doubt, was a very important personage indeed. And today she had the full weight of the authority of the Duke of Bewcastle behind her—another extremely formidable figure. And Eve was the wife of his heir. She was also that rare client all dressmakers must dream of wistfully all their working lives—the one who needed simply everything. Not a single garment of those few she had packed and brought to London with her would do for Lady Aidan Bedwyn making her debut appearance in British high society. Miss Benning took one look at the carriage dress Eve was wearing and agreed with the marchioness.

They looked through fashion plate after fashion plate, the three of them, selecting designs for morning dresses, afternoon dresses, dinner gowns, ball gowns, carriage dresses, walking dresses, riding habits, cloaks, pelisses—the list went on and on despite Eve's intense dismay. She might be in town for only three or four weeks, the marchioness pointed out when Eve voiced a protest, but she simply could not be seen in the same thing wherever she went. Such stinginess would reflect badly upon Aidan.

And then there was the all-important matter of the court dress in which she would be presented to the queen. Eve soon learned that Queen Charlotte had some quite rigid rules about what was acceptable wear for ladies in her drawing room. The high-waisted, loose-flowing gowns currently in vogue were simply not allowed there. Court dresses must be wide-skirted and hooped and worn with a stomacher and hair plumes and lappets, in the fashion of a generation ago. And there had to be a heavy train too, exactly three yards long. Eve wondered if someone at court, some lowly footman perhaps, crawled from one lady to another with a measuring tape in his hands. And what fate lay in wait for the poor lady whose train was one inch too long or too short? Banishment from court and social ostracism for the rest of her life?

There were fabrics to select and colors and trimmings to choose among. There were measurements—interminable measurements of every inch of her body—to be taken.

It was all progressively bewildering and exciting and dizzying and tedious and draining. At every turn there was a protracted discussion. Fortunately Miss Benning agreed with Eve on the question of color. Soft pastel shades would put the focus on Lady Aidan Bedwyn's delicate complexion, fine eyes, and lustrous hair, she told Lady Rochester. But she agreed with the marchioness that the court dress must be of a far richer shade, the unspoken implication perhaps being that at court the gown was of far more significance than the person inside it. In most cases Eve won her point too about fabrics. She favored light, plain materials over velvets and bold patterns. She was overruled almost entirely, though, when it came to design. Anything that hugged her figure too tightly or showed too much bosom or too much ankle frankly alarmed her—she would feel half naked! But such styles were the very height of fashion, she was told, and she came to understand that to the beau monde fashion was a sort of deity that must be obeyed without question.

There were no prices on any of the patterns or fabrics. Eve could only guess what all this was going to cost—especially when all the accessories were added. She was very wealthy indeed, but she also had many people dependent upon her wealth. And Papa, despite his great desire to move up the social scale, had never favored extravagance. Neither had she. She had lived frugally all her life. Yet there was to be all this for a mere few weeks!

Had Percy had any idea, she wondered, of the consequences of his final words to his commanding officer? But the thought of Percy reminded her of her indignation against the Duke of Bewcastle, who had so arrogantly and heartlessly dismissed any need she might feel to wear muted colors out of respect for her brother's memory even if she followed his last wish and did not wear full mourning. Even if Percy had not made his request, the duke had told the marchioness, he would have required her to put off her mourning for the next few weeks. Percy, of course, was a mere nobody as far as he was concerned. So was she. She was merely someone to be ordered about like everyone else in the duke's sphere.

"For someone who is to have a whole roomful of Miss Benning's coveted garments, you are looking decidedly blue-deviled, Lady Aidan," the marchioness observed as she pulled on her gloves late in the afternoon. Her carriage had just returned, and a footman was jumping down from behind to come and open the shop door for her.

"I am weary, that is all, ma'am," Eve said. "I am not accustomed to all of this."

"You should have considered that before deciding to marry Bewcastle's heir," Lady Rochester said, sweeping out of the shop with the footman scurrying after her to assist her into the carriage.

It was the final straw. Eve, about to follow her, hesitated and then turned back resolutely to Miss Benning.

"About my court dress," she said.

Miss Benning was all ears.

CHAPTER XIII

❧

Eve was seated at the small escritoire in the sitting room of the gold suite they shared when Aidan went up there after dinner. She raised her head and explained that she was writing to her family at Ringwood. He assumed she included in that term the orphaned children as well as her aunt—probably the governess and her child too, and more than likely the ferocious housekeeper, the half-wit lad, and all the rest of the odd retainers with whom she had surrounded herself. He would not put it past her to be sending her affectionate regards even to that scruffy mutt.

He sat in a deep armchair and watched her while he considered and rejected the idea of going back downstairs to find a book to read. He was unaccustomed to idleness. Freyja had gone out to a dinner engagement. Eve had left him and his brothers to their port after dinner, but Alleyne had left soon after to call at White's Club to meet some of his friends before proceeding to a ball. Wulf was going out later to some unspecified destination—to visit his mistress, Aidan suspected. He could have gone out too. He could have gone to White's with Alleyne. He would doubtless have met a number of acquaintances there with whom to while away a congenial hour or two.

But he had a wife who had insisted upon remaining in London for his sake even though he did not want her here and she did not want to be here, and of course she could not go anywhere, except perhaps the theater, until she had been properly presented. Aidan drummed his fingers on the arms of his chair while she blotted and folded her letter, set it aside, crossed the room to a sofa, and took her embroidery from a bag beside her— all without looking at him.

"You make me nervous," she said after stitching for a minute or two.

"Do I?" He stopped drumming his fingers and frowned at the top of her head. "Why?"

"You are so silent," she said. "And you stare."

Silent? Just he? She had been writing a letter when he came into the room, her back to his chair. Had she expected him to chatter at her? And she had not spoken a word since finishing—until now.

"I beg your pardon," he said.

Now she was the one frowning as she looked up at him. "Do you ever smile?" she asked.

What the devil? Of course he smiled. But was he to be laughing and chuckling and chortling every moment without cause?

"I have never seen you do it," she said. "Not even once."

"There seems to be not a great deal to smile about," he told her.

"I am sorry about that," she said, bending to her work again.

The devil! She would be thinking now that he was referring to their marriage and her company. But he had stayed home with her, had he not? Both last evening and this?

"I am a killer," he said abruptly. "I kill for a living. There is nothing very amusing about that."

She looked up at him, her needle suspended above her work. He frowned. Now why the deuce had he said that? He had not consciously thought that way for years. He had never spoken such thoughts to anyone, least of all a woman.

"Is that how you see yourself?" she asked. "As a *killer?*"

He wanted to shock her then. He wanted to shake her out of the complacence most English people seemed to share, perhaps because the realities of war were very remote to them, safe as they were on their secure island.

"It is said that every woman is in love with a uniform," he said. "At present I believe everyone in England, man and woman alike, loves a uniform, provided it is British or Prussian or Russian. Everyone loves killers."

"But you have been fighting tyranny," she said. "You have been fighting to free countries and the countless people who inhabit them from the clutches of a ruthless tyrant. There has to be something noble and right about that, even if you do have to kill some enemy soldiers in the process."

"Next year," he said, "or the year after, it will perhaps be Russia that is the enemy, or Prussia or Austria or America—and France that is the ally. The British, of course, are always on the side of good and right. On the side of God. God speaks with a British accent—did you know that? A refined, upper-class English accent, to be precise."

She had lowered her needle to the cloth, but she continued to gaze at him.

"I am a killer," he said again. "The great advantage of being a soldier, of course, is that I will never be hanged for my crimes. I will be feted and adulated instead. The ladies will continue to fall in love with me, even though I am already married—and even though I do not smile."

What the devil was he babbling on about? He was feeling vicious—and alarmingly close to tears. He wished he could jump up and dash from the room without looking like an idiot, or that she would look down and get back to work. He could not remember when he had so lowered his guard before—perhaps it had not happened since he was a boy.

"I am so sorry," she said at last. "I had no idea. I assumed that because you look so . . . I did not understand. Is it deliberate, I wonder, that we block out the shocking reality of what happens when one army defends the freedom of a nation against another army? And that we forget that an army is made up of real men with real feelings and consciences? Did Percy feel this way too? He never said anything. But he would not, I suppose."

"I beg your pardon." He got to his feet and turned his back on her, staring down into the unlit coals in the fireplace. "I gave a foolish answer to the simple question of why I do not smile. I believe I do smile, ma'am. And if I do not, it is doubtless because I am a Bedwyn. Have you ever seen Bewcastle smile?"

But he used to, a long, long time ago. When they were boys, they had used to holler and shriek and laugh, the two of them, and look on the world about them as their wonderful and magical and everlasting playground. That was the time when they had been the best of friends and almost inseparable.

But she would not allow him to change the subject.

"Why did you join the military?" she asked him.

He drew a slow breath. "It is what second sons of the aristocracy do," he said. "Did you not know that? The eldest son as the heir, the second as the military officer, the third as the clergyman." Except that Ralf had evaded the fate of the third son.

"But you stayed all these years, feeling as you do," she said. "Why? Why have you not sold out? Apparently you are a very wealthy man and do not need the salary."

"There is such a thing as duty, ma'am," he told her. "Besides, you have misunderstood. I did not say I do not enjoy killing. I merely said that my life as a killer has prevented me from being a man who smiles at every empty frivolity."

He turned to look at her when she did not answer him. She was sewing again, though it appeared to him that her hand was not as steady as it had been before.

"Did you enjoy your fittings this afternoon?" he asked.

This time, to his relief, she allowed her mind to be diverted. "I have ordered so many things," she said. "It will be amazing if I wear each article of clothing even once during my brief stay in town. But Lady Rochester and Miss Benning both assured me that I have chosen only the bare minimum of necessary garments. It is all quite ridiculous. I dread to think what the bill is going to amount to, especially when all the accessories are added on—shoes, plumes, fans, bonnets, reticules, handkerchiefs, and so on and so on."

"You need not concern yourself about that," he said. "My pockets, as you just remarked, are deep."

Her eyebrows rose sharply. "I will be paying the bills," she said.

"I think not, ma'am." He addressed her with deliberate hauteur. "I will clothe you and cover all your other living expenses for as long as you are with me."

"No, you will not." She threaded her needle through the cloth and set it aside. There were two spots of color in her cheeks. "Absolutely not, Colonel. I am quite capable of paying my own way. I will not hear—"

"Ma'am," he said, narrowing his gaze on her, "the matter is not open for discussion. You are my *wife*."

"I am *not*." She stared at him wide-eyed. "You may speak to your men like that if you wish. You will not speak to *me* thus. I will not be bullied—not by you, not by the Duke of Bewcastle, not by the Marchioness of Rochester, not by anyone. I came to London of my own free will. I remained of my own free will—and against yours. I accepted Lady Rochester as a mentor of my own free will. I came and I remain, not as an inferior who must be whipped into shape in order not to shame the illustrious name of Bedwyn, but as an equal to return a favor you performed for me a few weeks ago. I will pay for my own clothes."

"You are *not* my wife?" He ignored everything else she had said. "There is a certain register in a certain church that would give you the lie on that, ma'am. You wear my wedding ring on your finger. You engaged in conjugal relations with me yesterday afternoon. Today our son or our daughter may be growing in your womb. Is it your claim that that child would be a bastard?"

She paled noticeably. Had she not considered the possibility of conception? Truth to tell, he had not either until assaulted with it as he had tried to fall asleep—alone—last night.

"It is very unlikely," she said.

"But possible." He had been a fool to give in to lust. If there were a child, they would be forever linked by something far deeper, far more compelling than the simple marriage bond. He would not allow any child of his to grow up without a relationship with its father.

She reached down to her lap for her embroidery, which of course was no longer there. She clasped her hands together instead, lacing her fingers. They turned white under his gaze.

"I ought not to have come," she said. "I ought to have resisted the duke's persuasions. It is not really true, is it, that the *ton* would condemn you if I were not here with you?"

He shrugged. "Who knows?" he said. "There are plenty of people who believe that callousness and even cruelty come naturally to the Bedwyns. Though anyone who knows anything of our history would know too that it has always been a matter of honor with Bedwyn men to treat their wives with respect and courtesy. It is why most of us marry late or not at all, I suppose."

"Would you have remained at home last evening and this if it were not for my being here?" she asked him.

"Probably not," he admitted.

"Undoubtedly not," she said, getting to her feet. "I am going to bed, Colonel. I am weary. You must go out if you wish. Go and find your brothers and sister or some colleagues and friends. You need not stay at home on my account."

"You are my wife," he said.

She laughed softly—a sound without humor—and

turned away.

"Eve," he said.

Her head jerked back his way.

"If we are to spend a few weeks in company with each other," he said, "I believe we must dispense with this awkward *ma'am* and *colonel* business. I am Aidan."

She nodded.

"And perhaps," he added before he could stop to consider the wisdom of his words, "we should live together as man and wife for these weeks. Yesterday afternoon was good. We will both have enough years in which to be celibate."

Her eyes dropped to the floor between them as she apparently thought over what he had suggested. All day it had been gnawing at him—the fact that they were married, that for the next few weeks they would inhabit this suite together, only the width of two connecting dressing rooms separating their bedchambers, that they had had each other once but apparently were not to have each other again. His sexual appetites were healthy enough, heaven knew. He did not know how he was going to deal with that other Bedwyn tradition— that its males, once they did marry, were scrupulously faithful to their wives. But in the meanwhile there were these few weeks.

"Of course," he felt forced to warn her, though doubtless it was the very fact she was thinking over, "your chances of conceiving would be considerably increased."

Her eyes came up to look into his, and he felt jolted

by their expression, though he could not put a name to it. Wistfulness, perhaps? "I believe I would like that to happen," she said. "Very well, then."

She *wanted* it to happen? She wanted a child? He had been mistaken, then, in the assumptions he had made before wedding her? She had still hoped to find a man to love and marry? She had wanted a normal married life with children? He wondered briefly about the lover or lovers from her past—it still amazed him to know there had been any—but he brushed his curiosity aside. If she had wanted to marry the man, she had had her chance. Whoever he was, he had not rushed to her rescue a few weeks ago when she had so desperately needed a husband.

"I will come to you tonight, then," he said. "In half an hour?"

"Yes." She nodded and turned away again.

She might be with child. The thought thrummed through her mind, like a refrain. She might be *with child*. Or if she was not now, then she very possibly would be before these weeks were over and she returned home alone to Ringwood. She had very deliberately relinquished her dream of a happily-ever-after when she had agreed to marry in haste three weeks ago instead of waiting for John to come home. Now perhaps she had found another dream to dream.

She had always passionately wanted children. It was perhaps one reason why, at the age of nineteen, she had been ready to accept Joshua's offer even though she had felt no romantic sentiment toward him. It was definitely one reason why, when she turned one and twenty, she had suggested that John openly admit their secret attachment to the earl and countess—already of one year's duration by that time—and risk their ire by marrying her. In the four years since then, culminating in this year of total separation while John was in Russia, she had fretted at the passing of her child-bearing years.

"No, leave it loose, Edith," she told her maid when the girl, having brushed out her hair, was preparing to braid it as usual for the night. "And I will not need my nightcap."

She met her maid's eyes in the dressing room mirror, and they both blushed. Edith turned away to hang up the gray silk evening gown Eve had just removed.

The advent of Becky and Davy into her life had been a blessing indeed, Eve thought as she moved into her bedchamber and closed the door behind her. She had taken them in only because she could not bear the thought of children being homeless and unwanted. But it had not taken many days before they had come to seem like her own children. They still did—they *were* her children. She had exasperated the marchioness after they had left Miss Benning's and gone to other shops to purchase various accessories by stopping to buy a pretty little bonnet for Becky and sturdy boots for Davy—and then, of course, she had had to buy a little sailor hat for Benjamin.

She missed them all dreadfully, she thought as she set a candle down on the table beside the bed. The days without them were already seeming to be endless. But perhaps these weeks would give her another child—a baby this time, child of her womb, to suckle at her breasts and cry every few hours for the comfort of her arms and the nourishment of her milk. It was too wonderful a thought to be dwelled upon. And of course there would be *only* these few weeks. She must guard against hoping too much.

There was a tap on the door and all thoughts of conception and babies fled as Aidan came into her bedchamber, wearing a royal blue brocaded dressing gown and slippers. He looked as large and grim and formidable as ever. He also looked overwhelmingly attractive, though she did not know why. He was certainly not a conventionally handsome man. And he was too broad and too large for a godlike physique. But she could hardly wait for him to touch her again, to be inside her again, to make love to her again.

Perhaps, she thought, it was because she had had yet another of those tantalizing glimpses behind the facade—this time at a man whose grimness hid suffering. He was a man who had devoted his adult life to duty—to family, to king, and to country—yet he saw himself as a killer. She felt a sudden and quite unexpected wave of tenderness for him.

"Don't let Aunt Rochester bully you into having it cut," he said, coming toward her and taking a lock of her hair between his middle and forefingers. "It is lovely as it is."

It was, too. It was a shade of midbrown that did not attract as immediately as blond or red or black might have done. But it was thick and shining, and now that it was loose he could see shades of honey and gold glinting in it. And it waved in ripples over her shoulders and partway down her back. She looked amazingly enticing in her prim white nightgown, her long, slim legs outlined against the fabric. He had wanted to think of her with no more personal interest than he would feel for a casual mistress, but he had been very aware, crossing from his own dressing room through hers and coming into her bedchamber, that she was his wife. That it was not just sex they were about to have but conjugal relations—the term he had used to her earlier.

He lowered his head and kissed her openmouthed. She smelled of roses and soap. But she set her hands on his shoulders and set a little distance between them before he could deepen the embrace.

"As I have told you before," she said, "I will allow no one to bully me, not about my hair or anything else. Not even you."

"We are not back to your clothing bills, are we?" he asked. It had not occurred to him that she would try to pay them herself. He was still incensed at the insult, which she probably did not even realize she had dealt.

She sighed and shook her head. "Not now," she said. "We will fight about those tomorrow."

"A good thing too," he said. "Tonight we will love. Tell me, Eve, are you one of those women who fear nakedness? Will you swoon quite away if I unclothe you? And if I remove my dressing gown before blowing out the candles?"

He was not wearing anything beneath it, but he would not force her to look at him if she preferred to perform in darkness and under cover. They had done neither yesterday, of course, but yesterday they had coupled with almost all their clothes on.

She shook her head.

He dispensed with her nightgown as soon as he had opened the buttons down the front of it. Although he had never been a great admirer of slender women, he found her very beautiful. She was slim and lithe and porcelain skinned. She was shapely in the right places. Her breasts were not large, but they were firm and uptilted, her nipples pink and puckering with the chill—or perhaps with embarrassment or desire.

He undid the silken sash of his dressing gown, shrugged out of the garment, and let it fall to the floor. Unlike her, he was far from beautiful. Though there was no excess fat on his body, he was large, he knew. He always had to be careful not to hurt his women. He bore the scars of numerous old wounds, and there were his large nose and his dark hair and eyes and complexion, all of which must repel some women. But she had admitted to having enjoyed what she had had yesterday. He would not hide from her now.

He cupped her shoulders with his hands and kissed her again, holding her slightly away from his body. She shivered. And then he lifted his head and watched as he slid his hands down from her shoulders to cover her breasts and then move beneath them—darkness against pale femininity.

"They are too small," she said, watching his face.

Ah. She was not confident of her sexual appeal, then.

"For what purpose?" he asked her. "For suckling babies? I doubt it. For pleasuring a man? No. They fit my hands perfectly, you see."

She looked down as he lifted them and set his thumbs over the hardened nipples and pulsed lightly against them. Then he lowered his head, took one nipple in his mouth, and sucked, rubbing his tongue over the peak. He felt himself tighten and harden into arousal.

"Oh!" she exclaimed, her hands tangling in his hair. She arched in against him.

"We had better lie down," he said, lifting his head. "Will you mind if the candles are left burning? I like to watch what is done. But I will extinguish them if you would prefer."

She hesitated, and he could tell from the look in her eyes that she would prefer darkness.

"Leave them burning," she said.

She lay down in the middle of the bed, but when he joined her there, he did not immediately top her as he had done yesterday when they had both been hot with passion. Neither did he lie beside her. Instead, he knelt on the mattress, spread her thighs wide with his hands, and then kneeled between them. She bit her lip and spread her hands, palm down, on the sheet on either side of her while he set his hands behind her knees, raised her legs, and spread his own wide beneath them.

He leaned over her then, his eyes devouring her, his hands exploring her slowly and thoroughly with all the expertise he had developed over the years, arousing her with feathering touches and light stroking, tickling, pulsing, scratching, pinching in erotic places he knew would heighten her desire. She lay still beneath him, her arms spread over the mattress, her eyes half closed, her lips parted, responding with heat and shortened breath and little moans of pleasure, but not participating. He played her with his mouth, his tongue, and his teeth as well as with his hands.

One thing was clear, at least. Her sexual experience was very limited indeed.

He slid his hands down over her slender, smooth legs, until they were behind him, finding and working the places on her feet that would arouse further need in her. And sure enough, when he moved his hands between her thighs, he found her hot and moist. He probed with the fingertips of one hand, stroking gently, parting folds, exploring between, sliding one finger up inside her, watching what he did and knowing that he could wait no longer than a few moments more before mounting her. He felt her muscles contract strongly about his finger and withdrew it.

"You are ready?" he asked, looking up into her eyes. He could read her body and knew the answer, but he would not penetrate before she had assented.

"Yes." The low huskiness of her voice caught at his breathing.

He slid his hands beneath her to cup her buttocks, tilted her, and entered her with one firm thrust. Heat, moisture, and tightening muscles enfolded him and he closed his eyes, drew a slow breath, and imposed control over himself. He wanted to cover her with his weight and release all his tension into her with a few powerful thrusts. But he had aroused her and must now satisfy her. He stayed on his knees between her thighs, kept his hands where they were, and watched as he withdrew and entered again and again, concentrating on giving her his full length and a strong, firm rhythm. He watched, detaching his bodily needs from what he saw, waiting for her body to respond.

She was beautiful, all woman—woman in the act of sex. He could hear the wet rhythm of what they did together and smell the rawness of sex mingled with soap and roses. She moved her arms to cup his knees with her palms.

Then finally came the moans and the tightening of her inner muscles and the hard straining up against him that were signs of imminent climax. He kept his rhythm steady, pressing hard through the narrow, tight, wet passage with each inward thrust. And then she relaxed and opened like a flower to the sun and he entered her one more time, pushing deep, holding still, and finally, when she was soft and fully opened and satiated, he gave her his seed.

She was half asleep when, a minute or so later, he disengaged from her, got up to extinguish the candles, and then lay down at her side, pulled the bedcovers up over their damp bodies, and slid one arm beneath her head. He had not intended spending the night in her bed—he never had literally slept with a woman—but she was sleeping and he was tired and he knew he would want her again before morning. They had only a few weeks together, after all. They might as well make the best of the time they had.

Just before he slept, she turned onto her side, burrowed her head against his shoulder, and sighed in her sleep.

Aidan was tying the sash of his dressing gown and looking down at Eve. She had woken when he had lifted her off his body, where apparently she had slept for the past hour or two after they had made love for the third time. She regretted his leaving the bed so early—surely it *was* early?

"What time is it?" she asked.

"About six," he told her. "I am always an early riser. I have promised to go riding in Hyde Park with Freyja and Alleyne. Go back to sleep."

Oh, riding! In the early morning! There was nothing lovelier. He was going with his brother and sister with no thought to the fact that she might wish to go too? But anyway, she had no riding habit with her.

"I thought of going to White's Club with Alleyne later this morning," he said, "and to Tattersall's afterward. He is looking at some horses to purchase. However, if you need me . . ."

"I do not," she said. "There are only four days to go before my presentation to the queen. Lady Rochester will be here soon after breakfast. In her opinion four days are by far too short a time to rid me of my rusticity and teach me how to curtsy correctly."

"Is a curtsy not a curtsy?" He frowned.

"Apparently not," she said. "And there are a thousand and one other things to learn. You may amuse yourself as you will during the days, Aidan, and not

217

feel that you must hover gallantly over me at every moment. And the evenings too—you must not feel obliged to sit with me as you did last evening."

He looked openly relieved. "Once you have been presented," he said, "you will be expected to appear everywhere. You *do* understand, do you not, that this is the Season, that your days will be filled with visits, shopping expeditions, garden parties, Venetian breakfasts, walks and rides and drives in the park, picnics, and numerous other activities? And that each evening will be crammed with parties and balls and routs and concerts and theater visits? Aunt Rochester will be able to give you more details."

"Yes," she agreed. "But you need not look so grim, Aidan. You will not be obliged to escort me everywhere—I already know that about *ton* marriages, you see. It will be enough that I will be seen and known as your bride. Soon enough we will both be released from this—this charade and will be able to return to our own lives."

He considered her words and then nodded briskly.

"Well," he said, "just follow my aunt's instructions and all is bound to go smoothly for you. And follow Wulf's directions too. Wear colors as soon as your new clothes begin to arrive. He is quite right—gray does not become you."

She turned onto her side, facing away from him, pulled the bedcovers up about her ears, and lay still. For a few moments there was only silence behind her, and then she heard the quiet opening and closing of her dressing room door.

Now why had she somehow expected that the night would make all the difference? What sort of foolish *female* notion was it that love changes everything? It was not even love they had shared last night. Women, Eve understood, often made the mistake of thinking that tender intimacy in bed must be a product of love. It had been *only* physical intimacy, utterly pleasurable for them both—she was well aware that all three times he had used considerable expertise to make sure that she enjoyed the act. He had succeeded very well indeed.

He was going riding with Alleyne and Lady Freyja instead of staying with her.

He was going to White's Club and then Tattersall's for the morning and probably the afternoon too.

When she had told him he might go out in the evenings, he had looked relieved.

He had told her to obey Lady Rochester.

He had told her to obey the Duke of Bewcastle.

She felt like weeping and weeping until the well of tears inside her was quite dry.

Instead, she picked up the pillow that still bore the imprint of his head and with both hands hurled it at the dressing room door.

CHAPTER XIV

The presentation at court was to be followed on the same day by a ball at Bedwyn House, at which Eve would be officially presented to society as Lady Aidan Bedwyn. It had been the Duke of Bewcastle's decision not to delay the ball. He had consulted no one on the subject, least of all Eve, but had sent out invitations, made the arrangements, and was confident and arrogant enough to expect everyone to come at such short notice, though there must be a dozen other important social events happening the same evening.

And the thing was, Eve thought, that everyone probably would come too.

She disliked the duke intensely. She was not fond of Lady Freyja either. Her sister-in-law was scarcely in company with her, and when she was, she treated her with a cool disdain that spoke volumes. Aidan was out most days and evenings, returning only to dine at home and to sleep with her at night. Eve almost despised herself for looking forward so eagerly to the nights and enjoying them so much. There should be more to a marriage than just that, though of course it was clearly understood that neither of them wanted more.

Alleyne seemed the only normal human being in the family. It was with Alleyne that she learned to waltz. The duke had hired a dancing master, presumably on the assumption that the country-bred daughter of a coal miner could not possibly know her left foot from her right. But Eve did appreciate the instructions in the minuet and the waltz, neither of which she had encountered before. Alleyne made himself available as a partner after she had mentioned the lessons to him at breakfast one morning, and he went through the steps with her with admirable patience and good humor. He was, she had come to believe, a genuinely amiable, if perhaps rather shallow, young man. Certainly he smiled enough to make up for his two elder brothers.

The Marchioness of Rochester was a hard taskmaster. Sometimes Eve resented her, as she did on the morning when the marchioness's own hair stylist arrived at Bedwyn House with instructions to cut Lady Aidan Bedwyn's hair short in the newest style. They did so love to give orders, this family into which she had married, instead of consulting her own wishes and contenting themselves with giving advice. Eve allowed the man to cut her hair in a style they both agreed would improve the look and condition of it without robbing her of all its length.

However, Eve had common sense enough to accept the fact that she needed instruction on matters that were outside her experience. A curtsy was *not* simply a curtsy, despite Aidan's opinion. There were different curtsies for different ranks of people and for different age groups. There was one specifically for the queen. It took Eve a long time to accomplish it to Lady Rochester's satisfaction. And then there was the matter of approaching the throne, and her demeanor once she arrived there. There was the extremely difficult task of getting herself out of the queen's presence again. Her three-yard-long train could not be looped over her arm, it seemed. Neither could she turn her back on Her Majesty. Walking backward with grace and dignity without treading and tripping all over one's train was not an easy matter. For a long time it seemed quite impossible. Eve went off into whoops of laughter several times when she landed ignominiously on her bottom during her early attempts. Aidan's aunt was not amused. She used her lorgnette to display her displeasure at such an unseemly display of levity.

There were people to learn about—the names and ranks of various people of the *ton* and who was more important than whom. There was a whole system of precedence to be memorized. There was the etiquette of a come-out ball to learn. There were the gentlemen with whom she might dance if they asked, and those with whom she might not. There were the invitations that must be honored once she had been properly presented, those that were optional depending upon her other commitments and her personal inclinations, and those that must be firmly refused. There were . . . oh, as she had told Aidan, there were a thousand things to be learned.

It was all very silly, Eve concluded before the day of her presentation, this world of the aristocracy with all its rules and expectations. It was also undeniably exciting and challenging. If Papa could see her now, she sometimes thought, he would feel that his life's dreams were complete.

But she missed home with a gnawing ache. She wrote every day to Thelma, the only adult in the house apart from herself and Ned Bateman who could read and write, but her letters were for everyone. Thelma, she knew, read them aloud, first to Aunt Mari, then to Nanny Johnson and the children, and then to everyone belowstairs. Her own letters contained messages from everyone, including a few sentences in the childish scrawl of Davy and the round infant hand of Becky that invariably brought tears to Eve's eyes. She was missed, it seemed, though Aunt Mari always had Thelma urge her to stay in London with Colonel Bedwyn as long as she wished as they could go on quite well without her under the circumstances. The Reverend Puddle's name appeared in many of the letters, and Eve guessed that he was a daily visitor at the house. Ned wrote about the farms and the laborers and the village school. Nowhere, in any of the letters, was there any mention of Didcote Park and John's arrival home from Russia. In many ways Eve hoped he would return while she was gone, learn of her faithlessness, and leave again, never to return. She hated the thought of facing him.

She looked forward to her presentation with excitement and trepidation—mostly the latter. Almost all her new clothes had arrived, though she had worn none of them yet. The court dress in particular had been whisked up to a wardrobe in her dressing room and kept carefully wrapped. She felt rather sick every time she thought of it.

Sick and defiant and rather proud of herself.

On the morning of the all-important court presentation, Aidan remained at home. He knew that Eve was nervous. She had not said as much, but she had tossed and turned more than usual in bed, and once he had woken to find her burrowing beneath his arm to curl against him, her teeth chattering. She had claimed to be chilly when she realized she had woken him, though she had not *felt* cold. He had kissed her until she was relaxed and then had turned onto her and made love to her. He had held her close until she fell asleep again.

He was going to miss their nights together, he thought sometimes. But he would not dwell on the matter. He would deal with it when the time came. He would, he supposed, *not* remain faithful to his wife, though he chose not to dwell upon that unpleasant prospect either. It went against his family honor, but how could he remain true to a marriage of convenience?

He paced their private sitting room while he waited for her to dress. She had been closeted with her maid—Edith, the timid one from Ringwood, one of her lame ducks—for almost two hours. Aidan was surprised to find himself a little nervous too. Ladies of his social class were brought up from the cradle for moments like this. Eve had had less than a week to prepare herself. It was all her fault, of course. She might have defied Wulf and stayed in the country. She certainly might have accepted *his* advice that day in The Green Man and Still and gone home as she had originally planned. But no. She was a stubborn woman, his wife. He had solved the clothing bill issue by visiting Miss Benning's shop in person and paying it in full, much to the woman's astonishment. He doubted that Eve knew yet.

Finally the door of her dressing room opened and Aidan stopped his pacing in order to take his first look at her.

Her shimmering satin petticoat and the shorter, lace petticoat worn over it were carefully draped over the hoops beneath them. Her stomacher, stiff and ornate, low at both bosom and shoulders, glistened with elaborate embroidery. The lined satin train, attached to the dress at the shoulders, billowed out behind her. Her hair had been combed back from her forehead, about which she wore a wide, jewel-studded bandeau. From the back of it flowed long lace lappets. A profusion of dyed ostrich feathers had been woven into the back of her piled hair and nodded over the top of her head to touch her forehead. She held the side of her train with one bare arm, encased in a long glove.

Her chin was high, her bearing regal. Her eyes beamed pure defiance.

She was dressed from nodding plumes to dainty slippers in unrelieved black.

"Well?" she asked as he stared at her.

"Ruby red?" Aidan raised his eyebrows. That was what Aunt Rochester had said of her court dress when Bewcastle had asked. "Have I turned suddenly color-blind?"

"No, you have not." She looped the train over her left wrist and advanced farther into the room.

"Does Aunt Rochester know?" He hardly needed to ask. Her expression was answer enough. "And Bewcastle?"

"I do not need their consent." Her eyes sparked as if she thought she had a quarrel on her hands—as she surely would when she showed herself downstairs. "But no, they do not. Perhaps your aunt will change her mind about sponsoring me and you will have your wish to be rid of me."

Aidan pursed his lips. Narrow rows of silk embroidery around the wide hem of the satin petticoat, and wider bands of embroidery all about the edges of the train gleamed in the sunlight shining through the window.

"What do *you* think?" she asked him.

"Does it matter?" He looked her over slowly again from head to toe. "Yes, I suppose it does. You have done this to anger us all, have you? To thumb your nose at us? To have your revenge for the high-handed treatment you have received? To remind us, perhaps, that your fortune comes from coal? Such defiance is all wasted on me. You might simply have gone home. I will take you even now if you wish. But it would be a shame to spoil your little demonstration. Will you take my arm?"

Actually, he thought, she looked more than a little magnificent. For the first time since he could not recall when, he wanted to laugh—with full-bellied merriment. It was, he confessed to himself, a splendid joke she had decided to play on them all. He would not spoil her moment by laughing at her.

She set her right arm along his without looking at him. She was too busy lofting her nose into the air.

They were all waiting in the hall downstairs, of course, to get their first view of her—Aunt Rochester looking formidable in purple, Bewcastle, Freyja, and Alleyne. All of them were loudly silent as Aidan led his wife downward.

His aunt was first to speak. It was a measure of her shock that she even forgot to use her lorgnette.

"What," she demanded, her purple-clad bosom swelling against her confining stomacher, *"is the meaning of this?"*

"Am I late?" Eve asked, sounding damnably cool. "I am so sorry, but I am ready now, ma'am."

"And *where*," his aunt persisted, "is the court dress we ordered from Miss Benning?"

"But this is it, ma'am," Eve said, all wide-eyed innocence. "If you will look more closely, you will see that it is almost exactly what we ordered."

Almost. Aidan was amazed to discover that he was enjoying himself. She had them all bested—a duke, a marchioness, and a lord. They had all underestimated their country mouse.

"It is black!" His aunt's voice was thunderous as she stated the obvious.

"Yes, ma'am," his wife agreed. "I gave Miss Benning instructions to change the color."

"Doubtless," Bewcastle said, his voice at its quietest and most pleasant and therefore at its most dangerous, "Lady Aidan is about to explain why she did so, aunt."

Eve removed her hand from Aidan's. She had rehearsed this moment, he realized. No wonder she had been tossing and turning last night!

"Captain Percival Morris, my brother," she said, her voice equally as quiet as Wulf's, though there was a detectable tremor in it now, "was every bit as precious to me as your brothers are to you, your grace. Perhaps more so—I *loved* him. He will not go unmourned merely because he requested that I not wear black for him and merely because *you* ordered me to wear colors because it would be more suited to the consequence of your family that I do so. For this occasion—and *only* for this occasion—I honor my brother's memory by wearing black during what you have repeatedly told me is the most important ceremony of my life. Today I am to meet the queen and make my marriage fully respectable in the eyes of the *ton* and the Bedwyn family. Today also I pay homage to my own family, the Morrises."

"Bravo!" Alleyne murmured, his eyes dancing with merriment.

Bewcastle raised his glass to his eye and looked Eve over with it from head to toe.

"It is to be hoped," he said eventually, "that your desire to deliver a speech, Lady Aidan, has not made you hopelessly late. Her Majesty does not take kindly to being kept waiting." He turned and walked in the direction of the library.

Aunt Rochester, rustling with dignified displeasure, led the way out without another word, and Aidan offered Eve his arm again.

It took some time to get her into the carriage without crushing either her hoops or her plumes or stepping on her train. By the time Aidan had seen the carriage on its way and stepped back inside the house, his family had dispersed. But the library doors had been left open, he noticed. Wulf was expecting him, then. Good! He crossed the hall with purposeful strides and shut the door firmly behind him when he was inside.

Bewcastle was seated behind his desk, his fingers stroking the feather of a quill pen, though he was not writing.

"See here, Wulf," Aidan said, "I will not have you taking Eve to task over this. She came here unwillingly because you convinced her that her presence was necessary for my reputation. She stayed because she would not give in to what she perceived as cowardice. She has suffered in silence through all the little ways we have as a family of demonstrating our superiority over the daughters of mere coal miners. She has worked hard to fill in the gaps of her education so that she can move comfortably in *ton*nish circles. And she has done it all at the expense of her own personal need to grieve for a brother she undoubtedly loved. What she is doing today is an expression of defiance, yes. It is also an expression of grief. I will allow it. I will not censure her, however disastrous her appearance at court turns out to be. And I will not have you censure her. I *will not,* Wulf."

Bewcastle did not move except to continue stroking the feather.

"Do I really not love any of you?" he asked at last, staring at the pen as if he had not heard a word of his brother's tirade.

"Eh?" Aidan frowned at him.

"She said her brother was every bit as precious to her as mine are to me," Bewcastle said. "Perhaps more so because she loved him. Do I not love any of you, then, Aidan?" He looked up at last, an uncharacteristic look of puzzlement in his eyes. "Or my sisters either?"

If Bewcastle had ever doubted himself before now, he had certainly never shown it—not from the age of twelve on, anyway.

"Did I love *you,*" Bewcastle asked, "when I insisted upon purchasing your commission when you were eighteen though you begged me not to? Did I love Freyja when I refused to allow her to betroth herself to Kit Butler when he was a mere second son? Do I love Morgan by insisting that she remain in the schoolroom until she is eighteen and that she come here for a come-out Season next year though she does not want it? What is love anyway? It is not something I can remember feeling. It is not something a man in my position can afford to feel."

Aidan felt intensely uncomfortable. Although they had been the closest of friends as boys, they had not been since. Bewcastle had no close friends, to Aidan's knowledge. Yet they were brothers.

"I believe you always do what you consider best for us," Aidan said. Unfortunately, it was not always what they considered best for themselves. Love? He did not know much about love himself either. Duty he could recognize. Wulf always did his duty.

"I hoped for a good marriage for you," Bewcastle said, sounding more like himself.

"This is not a bad marriage," Aidan said.

"Is it not?" His brother looked up at him. "Are you bedding her?"

Aidan held up one hand. "Not your business, Wulf."

"But it *is*," Bewcastle said. "You are my heir, Aidan, and since I have no plans to marry, I had hoped to pass on to you the responsibility of begetting future heirs."

"Even if Eve were to have a child," Aidan said, "and even if it were a son, he would be as much hers as mine, heir to Ringwood as well as second heir presumptive to the Bewcastle title. I truly believe she would consider the former of more importance. And she would have the raising of the child, not you."

"Or you either?" Wulf asked. But he made a dismissive motion with one hand before Aidan could answer. "I will say nothing about the black court dress. Truth to tell, the color becomes her far better than gray does. But she must not wear either tonight, Aidan. I trust you will see to the matter. You have married a stubborn woman."

Aidan chose not to comment.

Bewcastle got to his feet. "I have some matters to attend to in the ballroom," he said. "We will all gather in the drawing room when Lady Aidan returns."

And they would all be there in obedience to the ducal wishes, Aidan reflected, staring at the open door after his brother had left the room. It was strange how it was Eve who had found a chink in Bewcastle's armor and caused that rare slip into vulnerable humanity. Even Wulf, then, sometimes had doubts about his life and the choices he had made during the course of it?

When Eve returned from St. James's Palace, she felt so drained both physically and emotionally that she would have liked nothing better than to withdraw with all speed to her private suite—especially as there was a ball to attend in the evening. But alas, the Marchioness of Rochester descended from the carriage with her and there was no avoiding accompanying her to the drawing room, where the butler informed them tea awaited them.

Away from the unreal atmosphere of the palace,

where everyone had been dressed in a similar fashion, Eve felt yet again as if she were participating in some sort of masquerade. She looped her long train over her left arm and prepared to ascend the staircase. But Aidan was coming down it to meet them.

"You have both survived, then?" he said as he came, his eyes moving from one to the other of them. It was hard to tell if he was angry or not. One rarely could tell with Aidan. If she had not had a few glimpses of a real person, she might mistake the emotionless mask for the man. But she knew different now.

"And why would we not?" his aunt asked as he offered them both an arm.

They ascended slowly to the drawing room. Eve was very glad that the age of hooped skirts was past.

"Well, Bewcastle," Lady Rochester said as she swept into the drawing room, "*that* is done. There is nothing more tiresome on this earth than making a formal appearance at court. The crush was dreadful and the wait interminable. I am thankful there is only Morgan left to present. When she and Freyja marry, they can have their mamas-in-law perform the duty."

"It is possible, aunt," the duke said, looking at Eve with his quizzing glass halfway to his eye, "that Lady Aidan will save you the bother and present Morgan herself next year."

Aidan was helping Eve through the difficulty of sitting down with hoops and a train. Their eyes met, her own wide with astonishment. As usual, his were quite inscrutable.

"It would seem," Lady Freyja said, "that the queen

did not order you to be dragged off to the Tower to be beheaded for wearing black, Lady Aidan."

"Did anyone make a ghastly fuss, Eve?" Alleyne asked.

"No." They were all looking expectantly at her, Eve noticed. "No one."

"Well, girl," the marchioness said brusquely, "you might as well tell them the whole of it."

"We waited with all the other ladies in the long gallery for what seemed like forever," Eve said. "Then finally it was my turn and we were summoned. A lord-in-waiting straightened my train and another took my card and announced my name to Her Majesty, who was seated very grandly on her throne. I advanced, made my curtsy, kissed her hand, and then backed out, all without mishap."

It was already like a story taken straight from a book written to delight little girls. She, Eve Morris, daughter of a coal miner, had curtsied to the queen on her throne and kissed her hand! She could imagine Aunt Mari listening in rapture to the tale and wanting to hear it over and over again. It would surely become a family legend. Tomorrow she would certainly have plenty to write home about.

The Duke of Bewcastle was regarding her haughtily. Aidan was standing beside her chair, his hands clasped behind him, his face expressionless. Alleyne looked amused, Lady Freyja a little disappointed.

The Marchioness of Rochester clucked her tongue impatiently. "If *that* were all," she said, "I would not have urged you to speak, girl. Freyja has done as much.

So has every lady of the beau monde above the age of seventeen or eighteen. The queen almost *never* speaks to any lady being presented to her."

"She *spoke?*" Lady Freyja's eyebrows rose.

Eve had not realized it was so unusual. "Her Majesty leaned forward and asked me for whom I wore mourning," she explained, "and I told her it was for my brother, who fell in action at the Battle of Toulouse. She smiled very kindly at me and commended me for putting love of my family before any temptation to wear pretty clothes into her presence."

"She added," Lady Rochester said, "that the whole country went into mourning for *her* brother just a few months ago."

Alleyne chuckled. "A coup, by Jove," he said. "You will be the toast of the *ton,* Eve."

The duke spoke. "You have acquitted yourself well, it would seem, Lady Aidan," he said. "And you have done honor to Captain Morris. Now, do you intend to pour the tea, Freyja? Or is it to be allowed to cool in the pot?"

Eve looked up at Aidan, who was gazing back. He said nothing but turned away to fetch her tea. She wondered if he agreed with his brother's cold and surely grudging praise. Had she angered him? Humiliated him? Hurt him? And did she care?

Yes. Yes, perhaps she did.

She drank her tea while conversation flowed around her and then retired to her own rooms at the duke's suggestion to rest before the exertions of the evening. Aidan would have escorted her, but Lady Freyja spoke up first.

"I will walk up with you, Lady Aidan," she said.

Eve looked at her in surprise. While her sister-in-law had not ignored her during the past week, neither had she made any effort to spend time with her or converse with her. Eve curtsied to Lady Rochester before she left the room—a less deep curtsy than she had made to the queen, of course, but one suited to an older lady of elevated rank.

"Thank you, ma'am," she said, "for what you have done for me today."

The marchioness regarded her through her lorgnette. "I believe, Lady Aidan," she said, "it is time you addressed me as aunt."

"Thank you, Aunt Rochester." Eve smiled at her.

Lady Freyja held Eve's train for her as they ascended the staircase.

"These things are such an abomination," she said. "So is the whole silly ritual of making one's curtsy to a fossil of a queen, whose fashion sense is stuck in the last century."

An abomination? A silly ritual? A fossil? Oh, dear.

"But it will all make splendid telling when I return home," Eve said.

"It was a magnificent joke," Lady Freyja said. "Our first sight of you was priceless. Did you see Aunt Rochester's face? And Wulf's? I daresay even my chin dropped to my chest. And Aidan was even more poker-faced than usual. I will admit to a direct hit when one is given. I commend you."

"I did it for my brother," Eve said as they turned to

walk along the wide corridor to the gold suite and Lady Freyja dropped her train.

"Did you?" she asked. "But not just for that reason, I think. I believe an equally strong motive was to deal a set-down to the lot of us, Lady Aidan. You chose a particularly spectacular way of doing it and by a stroke of amazing good fortune you came away, not only unscathed, but vindicated too. You were very courageous. If the queen's brother had not died a few months ago, perhaps she would not have looked so kindly upon you."

Eve stopped outside the suite, her hand on the handle.

"I respect anyone who can stand up against us," Lady Freyja said. "I daresay it is not easy. I'll not come in. Wulf has ordained that you rest, and rest you must. I shall see you later. Shall I call you Eve?"

"Please do," Eve said.

"I am Freyja." Her sister-in-law held out her right hand and shook Eve's firmly before turning and walking back the way they had come—no, really she was striding. She was a small, shapely woman, but she moved and talked and sometimes behaved like a man.

An olive branch had just been extended, Eve realized as she stepped inside the magnificent cream and gold room that was the private sitting room she shared with Aidan. The duke had said she had acquitted herself well. The marchioness had given her leave to call her aunt.

Progress had been made indeed. All because she had defied them. Was that the key to survival with the Bedwyns?

But what about Aidan? *Had* she shamed him? Would

they all believe he could not control his wife and think the worse of him?

But all she could really think about at this particular moment, she decided, was getting out of these confining, ridiculous clothes and getting herself horizontal on her bed. However would she find the energy to attend a ball tonight? And her own presentation ball at that? The very thought of it caused her stomach to perform an uncomfortable flip-flop.

How she longed for Ringwood!

CHAPTER XV

She had pulled it off, by Jove! It was not until she had returned home and told her story—or rather until Aunt Rochester had told the significant part of it for her—that Aidan realized how much he had feared all week that something would go wrong and she would be horribly humiliated. He had stayed away from her all week, during the daytime and evenings anyway. He had sensed her concentration upon everything she needed to learn and practice and had not wanted to distract her. He had also, of course, been leaving her free to plan and execute her great rebellion.

He was glad she had not been cowed by the grandeur of his family. It was what he had feared most, perhaps, when she had insisted upon returning to Bedwyn House from The Green Man and Still instead of going home the next day on the stage. He had come to like her at Ringwood, even to admire her, strange as he found her attitude to orphans, vagrants, and other society undesirables.

But there was another test to be faced today, and perhaps it would be a more difficult one than the presentation to the queen. This evening she had to face the *ton,* mingle with them, converse with them, dance with some of them. And every single moment she would be watched and judged. Aidan felt little doubt that somehow word had spread of her humble origins.

He was wearing his dress uniform, with dancing shoes, as he had for the assembly at the Three Feathers a few weeks before—how long ago that seemed now! He was waiting to escort Eve down to the ballroom. She did not keep him waiting. Her dressing room door opened even as he glanced at the clock above the mantel to note that there were still a good fifteen minutes to go before Bewcastle would expect them to take their places in the receiving line.

She looked very different from usual and quite breathtakingly lovely. Gone was the drabness of the habitual gray and the magnificent severity of the unrelieved black. Her slim, high-waisted gown, artful and alluring in its simplicity, was a pale primrose in color. Embroidered primroses adorned the delicately scalloped hem and the short, puffed sleeves. Her slippers matched the gown while her fan and gloves were ivory. Ivory and primrose plumes nodded above her piled hair, which looked prettier than usual with curled tendrils feathering the back of her neck and her temples. Her bosom, above the low décolletage of the gown, was bare, he was pleased to see.

"I assume," she said, "that you are looking at me with greater approval than you did this morning. But one can never tell for sure. You always look grim."

That accusation was beginning to irritate him. However, he realized that she was nervous and therefore on the defensive. He said nothing but stepped forward and held out the long jeweler's box he had been holding in one hand since coming from his own dressing room.

"What is this?" she asked, looking down at it.

"A wedding gift," he said. "I did not give you one at the time."

She frowned. "But we are not—"

"Let us not have that nonsense repeated," he said. "We are married, Eve. Very much so. Take it."

She still hesitated, her frowning look now bent on his face. He clucked his tongue and opened the box himself. He gathered the gold chain in one hand, set down the box, stepped behind her, and placed the chain about her neck. She bent her head without a word while he secured the clasp. By the time he had finished, she was fingering the jewel that was pendant from the chain. It was a single diamond with no fancy setting. He had decided upon simplicity for her. The chain was just the right length, he noted. When she let go of the diamond—it was now clasped in her hand—it would nestle perfectly just above the valley between her breasts.

At first when he stepped away from her he was chilled and a little angry. She said nothing, but merely kept her head bowed. Then he heard her swallow and realized that she was fighting tears. What the devil? He clasped his hands at his back, feeling uncomfortable.

"Thank you," she said at last. "It is very beautiful and I will always treasure it. But I have nothing for you."

He made a dismissive sound.

"Aidan," she said, looking up at him, "all my new clothes have been delivered from Miss Benning's. But there has been no bill yet."

It was his turn to frown.

"Have you paid it?"

"Of course," he said brusquely.

Her lips pressed together and he thought he was going to have a battle on his hands again.

"It was not supposed to be like this," she said. "Not any of it. There was not supposed to be any—any *relationship*. I am so sorry."

"We had better go down," he said, offering his arm. "Wulf will not be amused if we are late."

"Is he ever amused?" she asked, laying her gloved arm along his sleeve. "Is he an unhappy man, Aidan? Or just a naturally cold one?"

"No one knows for sure," he said. "He never allows anyone close enough." Except that Wulf had allowed her to pierce his armor this morning. Perhaps there still was someone inside that armor.

Eve had been nervous during the morning. But somehow defiance against the disapproval of Aidan, the Duke of Bewcastle, the Marchioness of Rochester, and even, if necessary, the queen, had helped mask her fears. She had no such defense this evening. She only wondered that her legs would convey her along the corridor and down the stairs. She concentrated every effort upon not leaning too heavily on Aidan's arm.

How had she ever got herself into this predicament? Just yesterday, it seemed, she had been in the dell at Ringwood, surrounded by her nearest and dearest, picking bluebells. Yet now she was about to attend a *ton* ball at Bedwyn House in London, and *it was in her honor*.

And then they were downstairs and approaching the ballroom, and Eve could see the duke and Alleyne, both dressed immaculately in black tailed coats, the duke with gray knee breeches and silver waistcoat, Alleyne with fawn breeches and dull gold waistcoat, both with very white linen and copious amounts of lace at neck and wrists. Freyja stood a little beyond them, looking startlingly handsome in a gown and plumes of varying shades of forest green, sea green, and turquoise. All three looked the consummate aristocrats they were. And of course there was Aidan in his dress uniform.

And so Cinderella approaches the ball, she thought ruefully and smiled with private amusement.

"Charming," Alleyne said, making her an elegant bow. "I suppose Aidan has reserved the first set and the first waltz with you. May I have the second waltz?"

"Waltzes?" Aidan was frowning when Eve looked up at him. "There are to be waltzes tonight, Wulf?"

"Aunt Rochester has assured me they are quite de rigueur at every fashionable ball," the duke said, looking Eve over from head to toe, a jeweled quizzing glass half raised in one hand. "And of course Lady

Aidan, being a mature married lady, will be able to dance it even without the nod of approval of the patronesses of Almack's."

"Oh, pooh," Freyja said. "Who cares for those old tabbies anyway? Do you know the steps, Aidan? It would be too, too bad if you were to tread all over Eve's toes."

"I have waltzed in Spain," he said. "But does Eve know the steps? Do you?" He looked down at her.

"I learned them this week," she told them, "and performed them with Alleyne."

"Did you, indeed?" Aidan's frown turned to something resembling a scowl. "That was remarkably obliging of him."

"Yes." Eve smiled sunnily. Was it possible that he was *jealous?* Of his own brother? How delightful!

"Come and see," Freyja said, taking Eve's arm and drawing her in the direction of the ballroom doors.

Her first sight of the ballroom itself fairly took Eve's breath away. Hundreds of candles burned in the three crystal chandeliers overhead and in wall sconces along the length of the room, their light shivering over the gilded ceiling and walls. Wall holders and large gilded pots and vases held bouquet after bouquet of flowers, all in varying shades of yellow and white. Their perfume filled the air. The French windows leading to a balcony beyond were all thrown back to reveal colored lanterns placed along the balustrade. A full orchestra of formally dressed gentlemen was seated on the dais at one end of the room, tuning their instruments behind banks of flowers.

"Aunt Rochester whispered the color of your gown to Wulf," Freyja said. She laughed. "It is a good thing you did not change *that* as you did your court dress."

"I am overwhelmed," Eve admitted.

"You need not be," Freyja said. "Word of what happened this morning will have spread. There is no doubt of that. It will be known that you appeared before the queen in black and that she spoke to you with approval. There can be no higher recommendation. The admiring attention of the *ton* is yours before they even meet you. Wulf has raised his eyebrows. He expects you to come running."

Eve turned and hurried out of the ballroom to join the receiving line, her heart still hammering in her chest, but as much with excitement now as with trepidation. She calmed herself further by thinking of the letter she would be able to write home tomorrow.

Despite the short notice at a time of year that brought dozens of invitations to every fashionable household with every post, so many guests arrived at Bedwyn House within the next hour or so that Eve wondered if there would be enough room for them all in the ballroom. She stood between Aidan and the Duke of Bewcastle and curtsied surely hundreds of times before it was over. She had never held a smile for quite so long. Her face positively ached with it. How relaxing it must be to be the duke or Aidan, who simply looked haughtily well bred.

"We will go in and begin the dancing," the duke announced at last, during a lull in new arrivals. "I will greet latecomers as they appear."

Stepping inside the ballroom again was a nervous and thrilling moment for Eve. It looked twice as large and formidable when filled with guests. She appreciated Aidan's steadying hand on her elbow and smiled up at him. She was surprised by the rush of affection she felt for him.

The opening set was of country dances that Eve knew well, ones they had, in fact, danced at their wedding celebration in Heybridge. But it was one thing to kick up one's heels at a country assembly, and another altogether to be dancing in a London ballroom at the height of the Season.

"Oh goodness," she said as they took their places at the head of two long lines, one for the ladies, the other for the gentlemen. "Must we twirl all that way after the first figures?"

"We must," he said. "In full view of everyone present. I will try not to become dizzy and spin off through the ranks."

She flashed him a smile. *There* it was again, that poker-faced flash of dry humor. "Of course you will not," she said. "You are an accomplished dancer. We may dance together only twice this evening. It is one of the arbitrary rules the *ton* sets such store by. Your aunt made very certain that I was aware of that. *Are* you going to waltz with me?"

"I must," he said, "in order to discover how fine a teacher Alleyne has been."

"But it was the dancing master who taught me," she said. "Alleyne just had the infinite patience to partner me."

"Hmmm," he said.

It was just possible, Eve thought unexpectedly, that she was falling a tiny bit in love with her husband. But fortunately there was not time to explore that alarming possibility. The orchestra began to play a lively tune, and Eve, her heart hammering against her ribs, moved into her first steps at her first grand *ton* ball. The splendor of it all was almost overwhelming. Again she had that feeling of having stepped inside the pages of a child's storybook. But the sights and sounds and smells were very real, as was the feeling of utter exhilaration. When their turn came to twirl down the open space between the long lines in order to take their places at the bottom of the set, she laughed openly. It was strictly against the rules, of course. Lady Rochester had explained to her that ladies of superior breeding never displayed open enthusiasm in public, but rather affected an air of slight boredom. Eve did not care even though she knew that most eyes in the room must be upon her. She laughed.

And then a truly extraordinary thing happened. Her husband's face, dark and harsh as ever at first, gradually relaxed—oh, not exactly into a smile. His face did not smile. Neither did his mouth. But his eyes did. They softened and glowed with an expression she could only describe to herself as a smile.

And the whole world smiled.

Eve was caught up in her own exuberance. Her eyes were focused upon Aidan. But part of her was very aware of her surroundings, and aware too that she was no longer intimidated by them or by the dozens of people watching her. Let them watch. Let them censure her smiles. She did not care. Aidan was smiling at her. Yes, he was. She would swear he was.

She danced on, smiling, laughing, conversing with Aidan and sometimes with their closest neighbors in the lines, enjoying herself perhaps more than she had ever enjoyed herself before. Somewhere beyond that thought, she knew, there was reason and common sense. But tonight she did not want to face them. Tonight she was going to enjoy her Cinderella night at the ball.

While Eve danced the next two sets, first with Alleyne and then with Viscount Kimble, Aidan made himself agreeable to some of the chaperones, mothers and grandmothers who were doing duty by keeping watch over their young female charges even though many of them, he was sure, would be far happier in the card room. He moved from group to group, always standing in such a position that he could watch his wife.

It was altogether possible that Aunt Rochester would consider much of her week's efforts a failure. Wulf might think so too. Eve was certainly very different from any other lady present. She was openly enjoying herself—smiling, laughing, dancing with enthusiasm as well as grace. And she glowed. But no one seemed to be looking on her with disfavor. Quite the contrary.

"A pretty gel," the Dowager Lady Harvingdean said to him. "And sparkling as any happy bride ought. You must be doing something very right, Colonel."

He was undeniably enchanted with his wife. She was

like a promise of springtime bursting through the arid winter soil of his life. No, not a promise, perhaps. There was to be no future for them. But that was not a thought he cared to dwell upon tonight. Tonight he would simply enjoy watching her and look forward to waltzing with her later—and to having her all to himself when the ball was over. He was very much afraid that he was going to miss her dreadfully once she returned to Ringwood—but yet again he pushed aside any thought that might diminish his enjoyment of the evening.

The next set was a waltz, and at last he could lead Eve onto the floor again.

"Aidan," she asked him as the music began and he moved her into the lilting rhythm, "do you know any dance more divine?"

"None," he said firmly. "I believe the waltz is the dance the angels perform—on the clouds."

She laughed. "I like it when you do that," she said. "You look absolutely serious and then you say something absurd. Are you happy?"

"How could I not be?" he asked her. "I am at a *ton* ball, which will surely be pronounced the grandest squeeze of the Season, entirely at the whim of Bewcastle, the focus of all eyes, except those exclusively besotted with you. And I am here with a wife who keeps insisting that she is not married to me. Who in my situation would *not* be twirling with glee at every corner?" He took her into an exaggerated twirl about the corner that was approaching.

She laughed again, and then they fell silent. He had

always found the waltz rather tedious and even embarrassing. His partners had invariably been ladies with
whom he had danced out of courtesy. Being face to
face with a woman for half an hour when one did not
find her sexually appealing—or, worse, when she was
someone else's wife—was not his idea of a grand time.

This waltz was magical. Eve was tall and slender—
her head reached to his chin. She was light on her feet
and graceful. Her spine arched beneath his hand and
she anticipated his every move so that they waltzed in
perfect unison. The colors of gowns and plumes and
coats blurred into a glorious kaleidoscope of shades as
they twirled. Jewels sparkled in the candlelight. Aidan
found himself wishing that the dance would go on and
on. But of course it drew to an inevitable end.

"Ah, that was *wonderful!*" Eve said, her cheeks
flushed, her eyes glowing, her voice breathless. "You
are a superb dancer, Aidan. I *do* wish we were per-
mitted to dance again."

Duty was calling, he could see. He nodded in the
direction of Bewcastle, who was standing in the
doorway, looking inquiringly at him.

"More arrivals," he said, offering Eve his arm. "They
are very late indeed. We had better go and pay our
respects."

"If many more people come," she said, "some of us
will have to dance on the balcony. Have you ever seen
so many people gathered in one place? I certainly—"

She broke off midsentence, and when Aidan looked
down at her, it was to find that her smile was frozen on
her face and her gaze was riveted on the people they

were approaching in the doorway. For a moment her steps faltered.

"Ma'am," Bewcastle said, addressing her, "may I present Sir Charles Overly, who is with Britain's embassy in Russia, and Lady Overly? And Viscount Denson, also with the embassy? Lady Aidan Bedwyn and Colonel Bedwyn, my brother."

Eve curtsied as did Lady Overly. The gentlemen exchanged bows and greetings.

"You have returned to England for the victory celebrations?" Aidan asked Sir Charles.

"We have," the man replied. "Actually we returned two months ago as soon as the victory of the allied forces became imminent. But we are certainly looking forward to the Czar's arrival soon."

"May I congratulate you upon your marriage, Lady Aidan?" Lady Overly tittered and looked arch. "It is quite a coup. The Bedwyn men have been remarkably elusive in the marriage mart."

Eve smiled, but when Aidan looked down at her, it was to the discovery that her face had paled and her lips were bloodless. It was perfectly clear to him that she already knew one of the three arrivals—the blond, smiling, extremely good-looking Denson, at a guess. He was bowing to her.

"I see that sets are forming for the next dance," he said. "Will you honor me, Lady Aidan? With Colonel Bedwyn's permission, of course."

Aidan inclined his head and Eve, without a word or a glance, turned back into the ballroom.

They danced for a while, Denson with charming

smiles for everyone around them, Eve with her eyes lowered, her movements mechanical, all her sparkle gone. When the orchestra paused between tunes of the set, Denson lowered his head to say something to her, set a hand beneath her elbow, and stepped out onto the balcony with her.

Aidan watched them go, his fingers curling into his palms against his back.

"Is there somewhere more private we can go?" he asked.

There were two couples out on the balcony as well as a larger, noisier group at the far end.

"No," she said.

But he had seen the steps down into the garden and grasped her elbow again to lead her down. There were graveled walks down there and seats and an ornamental pond with a fountain. Lamps had been strung in the trees, and several guests were strolling there. It was a warm evening.

He had returned to England *two months ago*. A month before her marriage. Perhaps even before Percy's death. He had been in England all that time.

"Eve," he said when they had reached the bottom of the steps, "I had no idea it was you who had married Bewcastle's brother. Until I arrived here this evening, until you were almost upon us, I had no idea."

"You have been back in England for two months," she said.

"I have been busy," he told her. "There has been scarcely a moment to spare. I have been meaning every day to run down to Oxfordshire to see you. I cannot tell you how much I have missed you."

"Two months," she said. Two months for someone who had sworn he would rush home to her as soon as he set foot upon English soil again?

"How could you do it, Eve?" he asked her. "We had an agreement. We—"

"Percy died," she said. "He was killed at the Battle of Toulouse."

He led her toward one of the seats, which was set back slightly from the path and was shaded by the overhanging branches of a willow tree. She sank onto it and looked up at him. The light from a lamp in another tree illumined his perfect features. He looked more handsome than ever.

"I am sorry to hear that," he said. "But why did you do it, Eve, and so soon after? Why did you marry Bedwyn?"

"Papa died after you left," she said. "Perhaps you did not hear the terms of his will. Everything was to be mine only on condition that I married within a year of his death."

"You should have written to tell me so, then," he said. "I would have—"

"What?" she asked him. "Hurried home to me? But how could I have written even if it had not been improper to do so? I would not have known where to send the letter. I certainly would not have known your *London* address."

"Eve," he said, "you must understand. It is important for a man in my position to be seen during the Season, to entertain and be entertained. I would have come home in the summer. We would have married then."

"Would we?" She felt as if scales were falling from her eyes. Fifteen months ago, going to Russia had been more important than marrying her. This year entertaining and being entertained had been more important. "Percy would have turned over everything to me after the year was at an end or at least shared it with me if I had insisted. But he died too soon. Cecil would have inherited."

"You should have let me know." He leaned over her. "Damn it, Eve, you should have let me know."

"I had one week in which to comply with the terms of Papa's will," she said. "I had no idea you were back in England. You might have found a way of letting *me* know."

She knew suddenly beyond any doubt that he had had no intention of marrying her—ever. He had been fond enough of her, perhaps even in love with her, but he would not have married her. Had she not been so naive and so much in love herself, she would surely have realized that before now. This summer, if circumstances had remained the same, he would have found another excuse to delay speaking with the earl.

"Why Bedwyn?" he asked. "I would have thought him plump enough in the pocket not to need to snaffle up an heiress in such unseemly haste."

"He brought me the news of Percy's death," she said. "When he understood my predicament, he offered me marriage."

"And you forgot me so easily?" he asked, seating

himself beside her.

"How could I forget you? After all there had been between us?"

They had met when she was barely twenty. Her father had already been making overtures to the Earl of Luff in the hope of promoting a match between them. They had met in a country lane while they were both out riding. They had greeted each other and conversed politely for a minute or two, and then he had turned his horse to ride beside her. After that they had met often, by design, always in secret because the earl had firmly refused Papa's suggestion. John had been at university and then in London, beginning his career in the diplomatic service. But whenever he was at home, they had met. Their friendship had deepened inevitably into a romantic attachment. They would marry, John had promised, when he finished university and was of age. They would marry, he had promised later, when his career was established. And then had come the posting to Russia.

He had expected to be gone for a year. They would marry immediately upon his return, he had told her. She had desperately wanted them to marry before he left, or at least to announce their betrothal so that they could exchange letters while he was gone. She had wept in his arms, and he had held her tightly to him and shed a few tears of his own. And then . . . and then somehow they had moved beyond the brink of merely holding each other, kissing each other, and declaring eternal love for each other.

She had never been sorry—until now. She had

thought it was love. Perhaps in a way it had been—on both their parts. But it had been commitment only on hers. And even she had broken the commitment.

"How could I forget you?" she said again. "But, John, there was too much to lose. There were too many people dependent upon me, including children. You do not even know about the children. Colonel Bedwyn offered me a chance to save them. He has been very kind."

"Kind?" he said, possessing himself of her right hand and holding it to his heart. "Kindness is good enough for you, Eve, when you have known so much more?"

She was drawing back her hand when she looked up. Aidan was standing on the path a few feet away. She jumped to her feet.

"Supper follows this set," he said. "You would not want to be late for it, Eve. You will excuse my wife, Denson?"

Eve did not look back at John. He stayed where he was and said nothing in reply. She set her hand on Aidan's sleeve. All his muscles beneath it were rock hard.

"Perhaps," he said, "by the time we return to the ballroom you will have seen fit to recover your smiles."

"Aidan—" she began.

"Not now," he said softly. "This is neither the time nor the place, ma'am."

CHAPTER XVI

❧

She set down her fan on the back of the sofa in their private sitting room and drew off her gloves. Then she removed her plumes, dislodging some of the curls piled on top of her head as she did so. The animated smile she had worn all evening and half the night had been discarded outside the door. She looked worn and pale. She did not once look at him—or try to scurry away to the privacy of her dressing room.

"You were very nearly indiscreet," he said.

"Very nearly, perhaps," she agreed, her hand straying to the diamond at her bosom. "But not quite. It is unexceptionable to walk with a guest in a lamplit garden."

"And sit in a shady spot away from the path with him?" he asked. "And give him your hand to hold to his heart?"

How could I forget you? . . . He has been very kind. The words had rattled about in his brain since he had heard them three or four hours ago. He had not yet had a chance to explore exactly why he had been so shocked and so angered and so . . . hurt.

"I did not give him my hand," she said. "He took it and I was withdrawing it."

"Ah, pardon me." He stood before the hearth, his hands clasped behind him, regarding her bowed head. "All was coercion, I suppose—the dancing, the slipping out onto the balcony and down to the garden, the choosing of a secluded seat in the dark—as well as the

255

hand-holding."

"Aidan—" She looked up but then appeared to have nothing else to say. Her eyes were dark with misery.

"Who is he?" he asked. "I confess myself unfamiliar with either the man or the name."

"Viscount Denson is the son of the Earl of Luff," she said. "They live at Didcote Park, five miles from Ringwood."

"Ah," he said, realizing that he was behaving like the conventional jealous husband, yet unable to stop himself. He had been enchanted with her during the first hour of the ball. He had been . . . Yes, indeed, he had been falling a little in love with her. Perhaps it was as well that something had happened to jolt him back to reality. But he still felt angry and hurt.

She struggled to say more but then just shook her head and fingered one of the plumes lying on top of her gloves.

"You lied to me," he said. "You told me there was no one else. You told me you had no wish to marry anyone else."

"No," she said. "I allowed you to make that assumption without contradicting you."

"It was a lie of omission, then," he said, "rather than commission. But a lie nonetheless. You should have told me. I was cast firmly and unfairly in the role of villain in that affecting scene in the garden."

"Then you did not hear everything, or *anything,* I said." She took her hand away from the plume and clasped it about the diamond pendant. "I told him how you saved me and everyone who depends upon me. I told him how very kind you have been to me."

"Kind!" he said with very much the same tone and emphasis as Denson had used earlier. "I do not deal in kindness, ma'am. I have never been accused of being a kind man. I married you in order to repay a debt to a dying man."

"Then why," she asked, "are you so angry?"

It was an uncomfortable question, for which he had no answer.

"That private encounter will not be repeated," she said. "Is that what you are afraid of? That I will shame you and disgrace your family? It will not happen. I made a deliberate choice not to wait for Viscount Denson but to marry you instead. There was no deception involved, Aidan. Ours was never meant to be more than a marriage of convenience. We did not expect to spend more than two or three days together, did we? I accepted the consequences of what I was doing. I accept them now."

He knew that he should leave it at that. She was being reasonable and honest.

"I suppose," he said, "it is he who was your lover."

She shook her head slowly, though not in denial, he guessed. "Leave it, Aidan," she said. "That is all in the past. It is over. It is gone." There was a slight tremor in her voice, though what the emotion was that caused it he could only guess.

"Is it?" he asked. He hated the fact that he could now put a name and a face to her lover. "He is the son of your neighbor. I will be gone forever after I have returned you to Ringwood."

"Aidan." Her knuckles were white about the diamond. "Don't do this."

He gazed broodingly at her. He had not cared at all that she had not come to him a virgin—though he *had* been surprised. But he did care that she still loved the man, that the necessity of marrying *him* had destroyed all her hopes for future happiness. He felt like the villain of the piece even though he knew he was not and that Eve did not regard him that way. Damn him for a fool! Had he really let down his guard sufficiently to fall in love with her? Only to find that her heart was given elsewhere? And knowing full well that he was honor bound to leave her forever within a couple of weeks? Had he not learned years and years ago that tender feelings were best kept tightly leashed somewhere so deep in his heart that he could convince himself there were no such things? He had not come by his reputation for granite control without effort.

"You are right," he said. "Perfectly right. We will say no more on the matter. You will discourage Denson if he attempts another tête-à-tête with you, ma'am."

Her jaw tightened and her eyes hardened. "That was unnecessary, Aidan," she said. "I will not have you play autocratic husband with me. I had the choice of thinking only of my own happiness and waiting for love or of thinking of the happiness of other people and marrying you. I chose you. If I could go back and was faced with similar circumstances, I would do it again. I made my choice and will live faithfully with it. Not for the sake of the Bedwyns, but for my own self-respect."

He made her a curt bow. "We will say no more on this

matter, then," he said. "I will bid you a good night."

She was still staring at him, pale-faced and stubborn-jawed, when he turned and strode in the direction of his dressing room. Nothing had really changed. Nothing and everything. It was one thing to have married her when it had seemed that the marriage would make no difference to her except to allow her to keep her home and her fortune and her precious lame ducks. It was another to know that he had destroyed a dream of love that must have been all-consuming. Eve was not the sort of woman who would have given her virginity if she had not loved passionately and committed herself fully to a future marriage with her lover. He had been sleeping with her for a week, deeply satisfied with the sex, deeply satisfied with *her,* though the emotional component of their encounters had crept up unawares on him. He had not even realized until now, tonight, that it had not been just sex—not for him, anyway. She had been enjoying their nights too—he could not doubt that. But for her it had been all physical, as he had thought it was for him too. All the time her heart must have been yearning toward the lover who had not come back to her in time.

It was a disturbingly distasteful realization. It was humiliating. It was . . . It was damned painful.

He shut the door behind him and realized he was not alone.

"I thought I told you not to wait up," he said, his brows snapping together in an irritable frown. "I am perfectly capable of getting myself out of my garments and into my bed unassisted, Andrews."

"I know," his batman agreed. "But you will toss your clothes aside like so many discarded rags, sir, and then it will take me the devil of a time getting all the wrinkles shaken and steamed and ironed out of them. I would rather sacrifice three-quarters of a night of sleep."

"You have a damned impertinent tongue," Aidan said. "I don't know why I keep you. Don't just stand there looking like a long-suffering martyr, then. Help me out of this coat. Whoever designs military uniforms should be made to wear them and stand in the front lines in them during a battle. *That* would teach them a lesson if they lived long enough to learn it."

He would sleep in his own bed tonight, he decided— tonight and every night for the rest of his life. He would not go to her again. He could not. He could not bear to touch her again.

His spirits touched the depths of darkness.

Eve was in the morning room writing her daily letter home. There was so much to describe that she scarcely knew where to start. But instead of the buoyant mood in which she had expected to be writing this morning, she felt heavyhearted and on the verge of tears, though she had been unable to shed the latter all through what had remained of the night after she had gone to bed—alone.

John had been back in England for two months. Two months! Yet in all that time he had not found even a day to come into Oxfordshire to see her. He had been too busy with his social schedule. For over a year—and for years before that—she had loved and yearned for a man who had never had any intention of marrying her. She knew now that that was the truth. She did not know what effect the knowledge would have on her feelings. It was too soon to tell.

But recurring thoughts about John mingled with thoughts of Aidan. Why had he been so angry? Why had he behaved like a jealous, autocratic husband whom she had deceived? And why could she not feel simply angry with him? Why had it hurt to hear herself called *ma'am* again? Why had the bed felt so very empty without him? And why, if she loved John so unwaveringly, had she felt during the early part of the ball that she might be falling in love with Aidan? Was it possible to love two men?

Eve laughed as she mended her pen after writing one sentence of her letter, though she did not feel at all amused. She loved two men, one of whom had never intended marrying her, the other of whom had married her and intended leaving her forever—according to their agreement and her express wishes.

When she was one paragraph into her letter, making heavy work of describing her appearance at St. James's Palace yesterday, the door opened abruptly.

"Ah, here you are," Freyja said. "I thought you were probably still in bed. I cannot *believe* I overslept and missed the usual morning ride with Aidan and Alleyne. I do not suppose you ride?"

"How could I not?" Eve asked her. "I grew up in the country."

"But you have never come with us," Freyja said.

"I have never been asked," Eve told her.

"Oh, pooh," Freyja said walking closer. "If you wait to be asked when you are a Bedwyn, Eve, you will be left to fade into obscurity like a wilting violet. Which, by the way, I thought you probably were until yesterday morning. I have not been so diverted in a long while as when I saw you descend the staircase in your black court dress, your nose stuck in the air as if you were a duchess at the very least. And I admired your spirit last evening when I am quite sure Aunt Rochester instructed you not to grin like a bumpkin, but only to favor the occasional guest with a distant and gracious smile."

"Oh, dear," Eve said, "did I *grin?*"

"Aidan was clearly enchanted," Freyja said. "I daresay you will be the *on-dit* in every fashionable drawing room today, the two of you. A married couple who have the effrontery to gaze on each other in public as if they could devour each other. I am proud of you. We all knew, of course, that when Aidan fell, he would fall hard. I suppose the same holds true of all of us."

"Oh, but—" Eve began.

But her sister-in-law waved an impatient hand. "Go and change into your riding habit and we will take a turn in the park," she said. "I suppose you do have a riding habit?"

"Yes, a new one," Eve said. "But no horse."

"Wulf keeps a stable," Freyja said. "All prime goers. I'll have one brought around with mine. You are not going to need one that is lame in all four legs, I hope?"

"No." Eve laughed and cleaned her pen. She could finish her letter later. Perhaps some fresh air would blow away a few cobwebs.

"Good," Freyja said. "I despise women who shriek with terror every time a horse tries to move faster than a slow crawl and look about them frantically in search of a man who will gallop to their rescue."

Less than half an hour later they were in the saddle and trotting side by side through the streets of London in the direction of Hyde Park. It felt very good indeed to be on horseback again, Eve decided, especially when she had been supplied with such a splendid mount. It felt strange, though, and a little alarming to be maneuvering past carriages and wagons and pedestrians and crossing sweepers.

They turned heads as they proceeded. It was Freyja who caused that, of course. Clad in a forest green riding habit, a jaunty, feathered hat on hair that billowed loose and golden almost to her waist, she looked startlingly handsome even though no one could ever describe her as pretty. Eve felt very prim in contrast, dressed in her new sky blue riding habit and hat, her hair coiled neatly beneath it.

"Are you coming to Lindsey Hall for the summer?" Freyja asked. "I know Aidan has only a month of his leave remaining, but you could stay longer and meet Ralf—short for Rannulf, as you probably know—and Morgan. Or are you going to follow the drum?"

"Neither," Eve said. "I will be going home to Ringwood soon after the state dinner at Carlton House and remaining there. Perhaps neither Aidan nor the duke has explained to you the nature of our marriage."

"Oh, pooh, *that*," Freyja said. "You are not going to

keep to that foolish arrangement, are you? You will die of boredom within a year. If I were in your position, I would demand a place in my husband's life, and in that of his family too."

"But I do not——" Eve began.

"Aidan is my favorite brother," Freyja said. "His happiness is important to me. Not that I am not fond of all of them, even Wulf. But Aidan is . . . special."

Eve followed her sister-in-law's lead into the park and immediately remembered how she had felt when Aidan had driven her here the day of their wedding. It was like being instantly back in the country. But she was intrigued by what Freyja had just said.

"In what way?" she asked.

"Well, for one thing," Freyja said, "he was the only one who really stood up for me three years ago. Did he tell you about that?"

"No." But Eve remembered something. "He did tell me that he quarreled with the duke and cut short his leave three years ago. Was that about you?"

"I had just become betrothed to Viscount Ravensberg, our neighbor, eldest son of the Earl of Redfield," Freyja said. "There was a ghastly scene because I wanted to marry Kit, his younger brother, and when Kit heard about the betrothal he came galloping over to Lindsey Hall hell-bent for leather, breathing fire and brimstone, and banged on the doors until finally Ralf went out. They fought each other bloody out on the lawn in the darkness and then Kit rode back home and broke Ravensberg's nose—or perhaps it was the other way around. It really was a splendid commotion, quite worthy of the Bedwyns. Aidan arrived home on leave a few days later."

"And supported you?" Eve said. "How dreadful that no one else did. But how could the Duke of Bewcastle so ignore your feelings?"

"You obviously still do not know Wulf," Freyja said. "But I had consented to the betrothal. Ravensberg was, after all, the eldest son, and I know my duty."

They were not riding along one of the paths but across the grass. It was a cloudy day, but the air was warm and still. Birds were singing. Other walkers and riders were out.

"What happened?" Eve asked. "Are you still betrothed to him three years later?"

"He died," Freyja said with a shrug. "And Kit became the heir after all. A delicious irony, would you not agree? Wulf tried to match us up last year when Kit came home—he had been in the Peninsula fighting too, you see. But when he came, he brought a fiancée with him—a prim and proper, milk and water miss, I do assure you—and married her not long after. I wish him a long and tedious life with her. For me it was a welcome release from duty, of course. I would a thousand times rather be free than married to an old beau."

Eve looked closely at her. She doubted it very much—that Freyja did not care, that was. Her very hostility to the bride suggested that she had cared very much indeed—and perhaps still did.

"Why else is Aidan special?" she asked. She was hungry to know more about him.

Freyja pointed ahead with her whip. "There is Rotten

Row," she said. "We will be able to set our horses through their paces a little better once we arrive there. Aidan was always the most earnest of us, if that is the right word. He adored our father and was the most affected by his death. He used to follow him around when he visited all the farms and consulted his steward. Sometimes when he was missing and no one knew where he was, he would be found out in the fields working alongside the laborers. He was a happy, sunny-natured boy, always smiling and laughing."

"Aidan?"

"And then Father died suddenly and the terrible quarrels with Wulf started," Freyja said. "Not that they generally sounded like quarrels. Wulf will never argue with anyone when someone else is in the same room. He takes the quarreler apart into his library, and then one can hear a shouting voice alternating with silences. The silences are Wulf replying. He never raises his voice. He never has to." Freyja sighed. "He is *that* powerful."

"I do not like him," Eve said, and then could have bitten her tongue out for saying such a thing to his sister.

But Freyja merely laughed. "He was not always like that," she said. "They both changed. But Aidan remained good to the rest of us. I was at an age when I was not allowed to set my nose outdoors without a chaperone. Aidan was always willing to oblige, even when he was in the middle of doing something else. He would always go fishing or shooting with Alleyne or Ralf. He would always spend some time in the nursery with Morgan."

The tears Eve had been unable to shed the night before seemed to be lodged somewhere between her throat and her chest. They were very painful. It had been far more comfortable to know her husband only as a cold, morose man.

"Why did they quarrel all the time?" she asked.

"Who knows?" Freyja said. "Ah, Rotten Row at last. And not too crowded, thank heaven. Why do you not ask Aidan? You are married to him. Do you never talk with him?"

It was a rhetorical question, Eve was relieved to discover. She spurred her horse into a canter, and Eve did likewise. The Row was wide and long and straight and exclusively for the use of horses and their riders. Pedestrians strolled beyond the rails on either side.

"I'll race you to the far end," Freyja said, and with a whoop she was gone, bent low over the neck of her horse.

Eve chased after her. They were both laughing by the time they reached the Hyde Park Corner end of Rotten Row, almost neck and neck.

"I won," Freyja declared.

"Only by a hair," Eve protested, "and because you had a start of a whole length on me."

"Well, well, well," a male voice drawled. "Suddenly we have *two* hoydens in the family—three when Morgan joins us next year."

It was Alleyne, who must have just entered the park. With him was Aidan. It was a painful moment for Eve. She had not set eyes on him since he had disappeared inside his dressing room last night. She did not know if they had quarreled or not, if they were speaking this morning or not. He was regarding her with raised eyebrows.

"I did not know you rode," he said.

"You never asked me." She lifted her chin, her laughter all forgotten.

"Uh, oh," Alleyne said. "I sense a marital discussion about to proceed. Race me to the other end again, Free? Or are you exhausted after that narrow victory?"

Freyja's response was a derisive snort. She turned her horse and was off again, Alleyne in hot pursuit.

Aidan was wearing his old uniform. He looked perfectly at home in it and in the saddle of the same powerful mount he had ridden to London for their wedding. He was also looking grimmer even than usual.

"You might have asked to come," he said, "any morning when I got up from your bed and announced my intention of riding here with my brother and sister."

"I did not have a riding habit for the first few days," she told him.

"That situation could have been rectified," he said. "One word to Miss Benning and she would have had it finished and delivered within hours."

"Does your word carry as much weight as the duke's or your aunt's, then?" she asked.

"Of course," he said, sounding mildly surprised. "Let's ride."

They walked their horses side by side along Rotten Row, saying nothing for a while. They each nodded at other riders and a few pedestrians, several of whom

Eve recognized from the night before.

"Freyja has been telling me about what happened three years ago and last summer," she said.

"About Kit?" He acknowledged another rider. "She was badly hurt, according to Rannulf, but she would not admit as much even if you were to stretch her on the rack."

"She loved him, then?" she asked.

"One thing about the Bedwyns," he said, "is that they do not love easily but once they do they are in deep indeed. You would not guess it to know us, would you? Of course, none of us in this generation except Freyja have experienced it, so we do not know for sure. It will take her a long time to recover, I suspect. Perhaps she never will."

None of us . . . except Freyja have experienced it. The words were strangely hurtful. And they certainly gave the lie to what Freyja believed. Yet Freyja had said almost exactly the same thing about love and her family. How sad that she had lost the man she loved and that Aidan had been forced by honor into a loveless match. Last evening's exuberance seemed to belong to the dim distant past.

"You will ride with us each morning, starting tomorrow," he said curtly. "I will have your maid wake you in time."

He would not simply wake her himself? He was not going to return to her bed, then?

"Thank you," she said.

"And if there is anything else you wish to do," he said, "or any place you wish to visit, you will inform me and I will arrange to escort you."

It was a formal, chilly offer. The dutiful husband.

"Thank you," she said, "but I believe I will be able to entertain myself quite well without your assistance, Colonel. Your aunt has already accepted several invitations on my behalf and will accompany me. I need not trouble you."

"Damn you, Eve," he said softly and fiercely after a few tense, hostile moments of silence. "Damn you."

She was jolted with surprise. For what was she being censured? And why in such shockingly strong language? She turned her head away from him and then rode her horse over to the rail to exchange pleasantries with a young lady and her mother who had been ahead of her and Lady Rochester in the line at St. James's Palace yesterday.

CHAPTER XVII

During the following week, Aidan spent some time in his wife's company, most notably during the early morning rides in the park, which she always attended, and at two balls, one private concert, and one visit to the theater, where they sat in Bewcastle's box. But even on those occasions they usually contrived to avoid being alone together. Most of the time Aidan was with Alleyne or with military acquaintances, many of whom were in London for the celebrations. He spent mornings at White's or Tattersall's, afternoons at Jackson's Boxing Salon or the races, his spare evenings at one or other of the clubs after dinner at Bedwyn House. He spent the nights alone in his own bed.

As far as he knew, she had had no further meeting with Denson. Whenever she was not with him, she was almost invariably either at home or out somewhere with Aunt Rochester or Freyja or both. Not that she needed watchdogs. She had told him she would remain faithful to their marriage and he believed her. But he hated the thought of how she must long for just one more brief encounter with her lover. And he hated himself more for the jealousy he could not seem to quell.

He .was counting the days until all the European heads of state were expected to arrive in England and until the state dinner at Carlton House. After that, there would be other celebrations, but she would essentially be free to return home. He did not doubt that she would go on the earliest possible date. He fervently hoped so. He wanted her to be gone—gone from Bedwyn House, gone from his life. At the same time there was a certain feeling of panic in the thought.

How he *hated* all this emotional claptrap.

The day of the expected arrivals finally came. They were at the breakfast table, all of them—even Wulf, who was not at the House of Lords today.

"Have you ever seen the streets of London so crowded?" Freyja asked of no one in particular. "We could scarcely get through to the park, and coming back was even worse. Have you been out yet, Wulf?"

"Not yet," he said. "And quite possibly not at all. I would rather not be mauled by the populace of London. But it would seem that this time it is no mere rumor that the Allied visitors really have set foot on English soil. The Duke of Clarence brought some of them over on the *Impregnable*. They are expected in London today."

"So everyone in London seems to believe," Alleyne said. "And everyone and his dog is determined to see them come. I suppose the madness will begin in earnest after that. It is enough to make one head out for Lindsey Hall at a full gallop."

"But it is for the celebrations we came," Freyja reminded him with a sigh. "On Wulf's orders, of course. It is, I suppose, a great occasion, a historic moment—the celebration of the final defeat of Napoléon Bonaparte."

"Do you know," Eve asked, leaning forward slightly, "who exactly is coming today, your grace?"

"The Czar of Russia," Wulf said, "the King of Prussia, Prince Metternich of Austria, Field Marshal von Blücher, among others."

"Not the Duke of Wellington?" she asked.

"No, not Wellington."

"Ah, that is a disappointment," she said. "But how exciting it would be to see the others arrive. I do not blame everyone for crowding the streets."

Her cheeks were flushed with color, Aidan noticed, and her eyes were sparkling. She was looking remarkably pretty, but then it was some time since he had been able to see her any other way.

"You will see everyone tomorrow evening, ma'am," Bewcastle reminded her, "in the far more civilized atmosphere of Carlton House. You will see the Prince of Wales too—and the queen again."

"That will be wonderful," Eve admitted. "But today's excitement is a different kind of thing. It is something everyone can share, high and low alike. Happiness is bringing people of all types together, and people of all nations too. Did you not *feel* it this morning, Freyja? Did you not, Alleyne?"

Alleyne chuckled. "I suppose," he said, "you want to go back out there, Eve, and get bumped and jostled and have your eardrums pierced by the noise and your nose assaulted with the smells of the great unwashed."

"Oh, yes," she said, "I really do. Does no one else?"

"I daresay," Bewcastle said, leaning back in his chair and fingering his quizzing glass, "there are people of our class who cannot resist the novelty of a public spectacle, Lady Aidan, but there is a suggestion of vulgarity about participating in such a mass display of hysteria."

"Hysteria?" Eve said, frowning. "No, surely not that, your grace. I would call it euphoria."

Aidan set his napkin down on the table. "If you wish to go out there, Eve," he said, "I will escort you."

"Oh, *will* you?" She scarcely looked directly at him these days, and when she did, it was with a guarded look in her eyes. But now she was gazing at him with all the warmth and sparkle of an eager child about to be granted a begged-for treat. "Will you mind dreadfully, Aidan?"

He would. Becoming part of a jubilant mob in the streets of London was mildly repugnant to him. But Eve wanted to go, and she had made no demands on him in the week since her presentation ball.

"We will get down close to London Bridge," he said,

"and watch all of them come up from Dover."

"If you can get there," Alleyne said.

"We will get there," Aidan told him and Alleyne laughed.

"Oh, *thank* you," Eve said, getting to her feet. "I will go and get ready if you will all excuse me. Freyja, won't you come with us? And Alleyne?"

Aidan expected a contemptuous retort from his sister. Instead she shrugged and simply looked amused.

"You are a constant delight, Eve," she said. "You have confounded both Wulf and Aunt Rochester by becoming all the rage, yet you have steadily resisted all their attempts to mold you into a dignified duchess-in-waiting, expiring with ennui."

"I have learned a great many things from your aunt," Eve said gravely. "For all of which I am grateful."

Bewcastle raised his eyebrows. "Well, children," he said, "you had better all run along or you will miss the show."

There was, as it turned out, no show to miss except that of a capital city gone mad. Somehow their open carriage managed to maneuver close to London Bridge—perhaps because Aidan had chosen to wear his uniform and there were people enough in the crowd willing to cheer him, slap him on the shoulder, shake his hand if they could, and clear a path for his carriage. The route from the bridge to St. James's Palace was lined with carriages and pedestrians, all in a loudly festive mood. Every window of every building was crowded with heads. Hawkers of food and other wares were doing a brisk trade. So too, Aidan suspected, were the pickpockets. A score of times or more there was a stir of heightened excitement when a horse or vehicle was seen to approach from the south. But always it was a false alarm.

"I believe," Aidan said late in the morning, "we have been fed so many rumors that the truth is impossible to know. Perhaps all the dignitaries we are expecting at any moment are all taking their ease in their respective palaces in their respective countries."

But if they were, they had even royalty duped. The Prince Regent's distinctive gold and scarlet postilions were waiting at the bridge to escort the carriages when they arrived. The crowd was raucously teasing them since the crowd, it appeared, was planning to unhorse the carriages and pull them in triumph to the palace.

"May we wait just a little longer?" Eve set a hand on his sleeve and looked pleadingly at him.

How, God help him, was he to resist such a look and such a plea? He found himself wishing at every moment that something could be set right between them before they parted forever. He did not want her to remember him with hostility. He did not want to remember her with regret.

"Just a little longer," he said, setting a hand on top of hers as she smiled at him, and meeting Freyja's eyes across the carriage. There was a look there he did not often see from his sister—something assessing, wistful, almost sad.

Freyja had legions of admirers, some very eligible bachelors among them. She treated them all with a careless camaraderie that put an effective stop to any hope any of them might have had of courting her. He wondered how much she was hurting inside, how bright a torch she still carried for Kit Butler. There was no way of knowing. Freyja was like an impregnable fortress when it came to talking about herself.

Less than five minutes later a new rumor swept the street, from the opposite direction this time. The Czar had already arrived, people shouted urgently to one another. He was at the Pulteney Hotel with his sister, the Grand Duchess Catherine. He had come by a different route.

"Probably to avoid the rabble, wise man," Alleyne said as large numbers of the crowd began to hurry off in the direction of the hotel.

"*If* the rumor is true," Freyja said. "I am bored silly. Let us go somewhere else, somewhere quiet and civilized. How about the Royal Academy? Do you like looking at paintings, Eve?"

Aidan looked across at her. "What is your wish?" he asked.

"I suppose," she said, "we might sit here all day and later discover that *all* the guests have come by a different route."

"That is altogether possible, I am afraid," he said. "Are you dreadfully disappointed?"

"Not really." She smiled at him. "I have been a part of history anyway. I have experienced *this*. Today will surely be remembered. Perhaps even all this confusion."

"And you *will* see everyone tomorrow evening," he said.

"Yes." She set her hand on his arm again. "Thank you for bringing me, Aidan. I know this has been dreadfully tedious for you." She turned her head to look at Freyja. "The Academy would be lovely to visit. Is it far away?"

"Somerset House," Freyja said. "Not far."

Aidan did not resent the tedium of the morning. It had somehow restored some harmony with Eve.

They spent an hour at Somerset House inspecting the paintings displayed there. Eve was openly enchanted, and Freyja, who was usually restless when forced to remain too long in one place, especially over matters cultural, was content to stay at her side, gazing at each painting with her. Alleyne, who was something of a connoisseur of art, was at Eve's other side, pointing out noteworthy details.

After one turn about the room Aidan stood a little apart watching them. Eve had won their regard, he thought, in the only possible way—by not seeking it. Although she had paid attention to Aunt Rochester's instructions on matters she needed to know, she had made no attempt to ingratiate herself with anyone. *Here I am,* her presence seemed to say. *Take me or leave me.* She was, he thought, a lady, despite her origins. It was going to be very hard never to see her again after—

But his thoughts were interrupted by the appearance of a familiar face before him and the sound of a familiar voice—a round, florid, lined face topped with gray hair turning white, a gruff, hearty voice.

"Bedwyn," he said. "You are here, are you? Still on leave, are you? And caught up in all of today's madness? We have escaped it to come here, though admiring rows of pictures is not normally my cup of tea." He laughed heartily.

He was about the last person Aidan either expected or wanted to see at that particular moment.

"General Knapp," he said.

"But Lady Knapp and Louisa wanted to come," the general said with another of his hearty laughs, "and what was I to do? I was outnumbered. What is your excuse?"

Before Aidan could speak, those two ladies appeared one on either side of the general, both beaming at him.

"Colonel Bedwyn," Lady Knapp said, "this is a happy surprise."

"Ma'am." Aidan made his bow to both ladies. "Miss Knapp."

She was a dark-haired, large-boned young lady, strong and capable and sensible, not unpleasing to the eye though not exactly pretty. She was the ideal mate for an officer, having grown up to the life from infancy and not possessing a delicate bone in her body.

"I was so hoping we would see you here, Colonel Bedwyn," she said, curtsying.

"They dragged me back to England for the summer," the general said, laughing again. "Two against one. Not fair odds, eh, Bedwyn? And now they are dragging me about, filling my head with culture. It is enough to give me the migraines. Now what are you doing here?"

"He is looking at paintings, of course, Richard," Lady Knapp said, "and is to be highly commended for doing so. This is a timely meeting, Colonel Bedwyn. We arrived in London only two days ago and are giving a little dinner party tonight. But horror of horrors, we are one gentleman short. Will you oblige us on such short notice?"

"Please do, Colonel," Miss Knapp added.

It was at that moment that Aidan caught Eve's eye. She moved toward him and he realized with a sinking of the heart that the moment could not be avoided.

"I am afraid I will be unable to accept your kind invitation, ma'am," he said as Eve came up to them and looked inquiringly at the group. "May I have the honor of presenting my wife? General and Lady Knapp, Eve, and Miss Knapp."

She smiled and curtsied while the faces of all three Knapps registered surprise, even shock.

"Your wife, Colonel?" Lady Knapp asked.

"Well, this is a devilish thing," the general said. He coughed and appeared to recollect himself. "A devilish sudden thing. You did not breathe a word of your betrothal in the Peninsula, Bedwyn."

"I met and married Eve after returning," Aidan explained, taking her hand and setting it on his sleeve while wishing all the time that a large black hole would open at his feet and swallow him up.

"Well, Lady Aidan," Lady Knapp said, "I wish you well. I hope you are prepared for some hardships when you follow the drum."

"I will not be doing so, ma'am," Eve said. "I will be remaining at home while Aidan is away."

"Excuse me," Miss Knapp said. "I see someone I know just disappearing into the next room. I must go and pay my respects."

"I will come with you, Louisa," Lady Knapp said.

"An officer needs his wife with him when he is in the field," the general said with a stern look bent upon Aidan. "But if he chooses to marry someone who prefers to remain at home, I daresay society will applaud him. Good day to you, Bedwyn, Lady Aidan." He strode away in pursuit of his wife and daughter.

Eve stared at Aidan and he stared back.

"What," she asked him, "was that all about?"

"What?" he asked foolishly.

"They were severely discomposed by my appearance," she said. "Yet they surely do not know who I am. It was not snobbery, then. What was it, Aidan?"

"As the general explained," he said, "they are people who believe that officers should marry ladies who are willing to travel with them."

"Perhaps," she said softly, "women who are already traveling with the armies and know what to expect of the life."

"Perhaps," he agreed.

Her jaw tightened and her voice dropped in volume.

"Were you betrothed to her?"

"No, of course not," he said.

"There were expectations, though," she said. "An understanding, perhaps? Similar to, if different in detail from, the one I had with John—with Viscount Denson?"

"There was never an understanding," he said.

She continued to stare at him.

"Not a verbal one," he said. "Nothing had been spoken between us, Eve. And nothing had been spoken between the general and me. There was merely perhaps a . . . a—"

"An expectation," she said.

"Perhaps."

"And yet you dared accuse me of lying when I did not tell you about Viscount Denson?"

"I had not bedded Miss Knapp," he said.

She recoiled almost as if he had struck her. He had not meant it like that. He had merely meant to suggest that the secret she had kept from him had been of more significance than his secret because she had loved the man and committed her very body to him.

"Eve—" he said, but she had turned sharply away and was hurrying over to rejoin Freyja and Alleyne, who were in conversation with some chance-met acquaintances.

Lord! Aidan thought. Deuce take it, could there never be any lasting peace between them?

But did it matter when in a few days' time they would no longer be together?

It mattered, he thought unwillingly. It mattered.

Tomorrow, Eve decided on the following day, she was going to announce her intention of returning home. She had decided it after the dreadful realization at the Royal Academy that when he had persuaded her to marry him, Aidan had already been attached to another woman, so attached that her whole family had clearly expected a declaration at any moment. And the woman concerned was a general's daughter who had followed the drum with her mother. It surely would have been a perfect match for them both.

Eve had felt slightly nauseated ever since. She was missing everyone at home so much that it hurt. Her arms ached for her children. She was missing Ringwood itself. She was nervous about the state dinner. She was depressed by the discovery she had made four days ago that she was not with child and at the same time glad that there would not now be *that* complication in her life. She was weary of the endless round of social activities, which might have been exciting under other circumstances. She was tired of dodging John, whom she saw frequently and who was constantly trying to draw her away on her own with him.

Most of all she was horribly depressed at the unwilling knowledge that she was in love with Aidan. More than anything else she wanted to go home, the inevitable parting over and done with. She wanted to get her life back to normal, to begin to forget, to lick her wounds in private, to concentrate all her love on her children.

Tomorrow, the Carlton House dinner finally a thing of the past, she was going to tell Aidan and the duke that she was returning home. She would go by stage the following morning. The duke would argue, of course— or rather he would try to issue commands, but she would remain adamant. She was so terribly *weary*.

Besides, Aidan must be as desperate to be rid of her as she was to go.

"I will take my leave, then, Bewcastle," Aunt Rochester announced, getting to her feet. "It would be unpardonable to be late for the dinner at Carlton House."

They were at tea, all of them, in the drawing room at Bedwyn House. Aunt Rochester had returned there after accompanying Eve and Freyja on a brief shopping expedition to purchase some last-minute accessories for their evening finery—and Eve had bought a book each for the three children. The conversation all day had been about nothing except the coming evening. All the foreign dignitaries had indeed arrived yesterday. If they had waited by the bridge instead of going to Somerset House, they would have seen Field Marshal Blücher being mobbed by the crowd and his carriage de-horsed and dragged off to Carlton House, where he had been carried bodily inside.

"None of us will be late," the Duke of Bewcastle said, rising with the other gentlemen. "Freyja and Lady Aidan may wish to leave the room with you, aunt, in order to retire to their rooms for a rest."

Freyja uttered her peculiar derisive snort at the very thought, but Eve got gratefully to her feet.

"I believe I will do that," she said. Her stomach was still feeling queasy, but she rather thought it was with nervousness this time. In a few hours' time she was going to be entering Carlton House. She would see the queen and the Prince Regent and half the rulers and leading men of Europe. She would be sitting down to dinner with them all. How would she keep herself from collapsing into a quivering heap?

"Oh, Eve," Alleyne called as Aidan opened the door for her and his aunt. "I have just remembered that I have been carrying a letter of yours in my pocket for half the day. I took it from Fleming this morning, thinking I would be seeing you, but you had gone out already. Here it is."

"Thank you," she said, smiling at him and taking the letter. "I thought there was none today." She glanced down at Thelma's familiar writing.

She kicked off her shoes as soon as she reached the gold suite and withdrew all the pins from her hair. She shook her head and sighed. She was indeed going to have a sleep before getting dressed for the evening. She wished suddenly that she could just wave a magic wand and have it over with. But it would be a splendid story to tell at home. Was the Prince Regent as obese as he was reputed to be? Was the queen's conversation as tedious as Freyja said it was? Could any of the foreign dignitaries speak English well?

She sank onto the sofa to read her letter before retiring to her bedchamber. It was shorter than usual, she saw with some disappointment as she broke the seal. But no matter. In a few days' time she would be home with them. She began to read.

A few moments later she leapt to her feet, staring down in horror at the letter as if expecting to discover that she had deciphered the words all wrong. But with a welling of mindless panic she knew that she had not. She turned and stumbled toward the door, fumbled with the handle, and then dashed along the corridor and down the stairs and along to the drawing room without even realizing what she did or how she looked. She turned the handle before an attendant footman could get there ahead of her, and went hurtling into the room.

Solid safety was just a few feet away and even at that

moment getting to its feet. Except that as she rushed toward it, she knew there was no safety. No one could help.

"Aidan," she cried. "I have to go. I have to go."

His arms closed about her like iron bands, giving again for a moment the illusion of safety. But only for a moment. Panic was upon her.

"What is it?" he was asking over and over. "What is the matter? What has happened?"

"The ch-ch-ch—" Her teeth were chattering uncontrollably.

"Easy," he said. He kept one arm firmly about her. The forefinger and thumb of the other hand came beneath her jaw to lift it and hold it steady. He captured her gaze and held it with his own. "Easy, love. Tell me what has happened and I will set it right for you."

Foolish words. Ah, foolish words.

"He has taken them," she said, part of her brain recognizing that she was wailing. "He has taken them away and I cannot g-g-get them b-b-back."

"Who?" he asked her, his voice maddeningly calm. "Who has taken whom?"

"C-C-Cecil," she said. "He has taken the ch-ch-children and I cannot have them back. He is their r-r-relative and I am not. And I ab-b-b . . . I abandoned them. I have to go. I have to go and get them. They will be so f-f-frightened."

"So he has found a way of hitting back, has he?" he said. "We will see about that. You will have them returned. I warned him what to expect if he set foot on your property again."

"No, but you do not understand," she said, flourishing her letter, which was balled up in one of her fists. "He had them fetched. He went to the magistrate and had them declared his wards. He will not give them back. I know him. I have to go."

"Yes, I can see that," he said. "Take a few deep breaths. Panic never accomplishes anything."

"Might it be suggested," a cool, haughty voice asked, "that you take Lady Aidan to her room to rest, Aidan? She will need to recover her composure before this evening."

"But I have to go." Eve turned her head to stare at the duke, and struggled out of Aidan's arms. "Now. I have to go home to Ringwood without a moment's delay. The children will be frantic."

"It is out of the question," the duke said, "for you to absent yourself from the Carlton House dinner, Lady Aidan, after the invitation has been issued and accepted. Besides, setting out on a lengthy journey this late in the day is not a sensible thing to do. If you feel that your presence in Oxfordshire is going to change what you declare to be unchangeable, then Aidan will escort you there tomorrow in my carriage. I suggest that you rest now."

"No—" she began, but Aidan took her hand in his and drew it firmly through his arm, interrupting her as he did so.

"Eve wishes to return home now," he said. "And now is when she will go. I will take her."

"You will do as I say," the duke said.

"No." Aidan's voice was crisp. "Not on this, Wulf.

My wife's needs take precedence over either duty or family loyalty. You will make our excuses this evening if you feel it necessary."

No one spoke a word as he led Eve from the room.

Half an hour later they were on their way to Ringwood Manor in a hired carriage.

CHAPTER XVIII

They had been forced by a severe rain- and thunderstorm to put up at an inn for several hours, though they had not slept. Eve had paced their room, unwilling to lie down or to eat or even to talk. They arrived at Ringwood early on a chill, damp morning.

Everyone was already up, and in the manner of things at Ringwood, all came tumbling out of the house and stables to greet the new arrivals, all talking at once. The dog bobbed around, barking and unrebuked. But finally they were in the downstairs parlor, where a fire had been lit against the dampness and chill, and the hatchet-faced housekeeper carried in a tray of tea. She poured and handed the cups around and then took up her stand before the closed door, her hefty arms crossed over her chest. No one told her to leave.

Aidan left his tea on a table and crossed to the window. Mrs. Pritchard was weeping, Eve was trying to comfort her, and the governess was blaming herself for allowing the children to be taken despite the fact that the aunt, through her sobs, insisted that she had had no choice—none of them had. The dog had its chin in

Eve's lap, alternately panting and whining.

That weasel Cecil Morris had plotted his revenge well. A man of small stature and weak, self-indulged frame, he doubtless knew that he stood no chance of winning any sort of physical contest against Eve's male protectors or even against Eve and her housekeeper for that matter. And so he had devised another plan altogether and gone running to a magistrate to claim legal guardianship of the orphaned children, who were related to him in some way on the maternal side. Then he had sent the parish constable with four burly assistants to fetch the children from Ringwood.

"Agnes broke Will Perkins's nose with her fist," Miss Rice said. "There was blood everywhere, Eve. We would all have thought he was dead if he had not been bellowing so loudly. And Charlie head-butted Mr. Biddle in the stomach. But he had the papers, you see, signed by the Earl of Luff, and there was no arguing with those. Besides, it would have been more alarming for Becky and Davy if they had seen fighting. Mrs. Pritchard persuaded us all to quiet down before they were sent for. Mr. Biddle sent Will Perkins home."

"I mopped up the blood myself before the children were brought down," the housekeeper said, not waiting to be addressed before speaking up. "But I would as soon have broke *all* their noses, my lamb, and their heads too. The cowardly curs—five burly men to take away two little babies."

"You would have been arrested, Agnes," Mrs. Pritchard said, having blown her nose in her handkerchief and brought herself under control. "They would have dragged you off to jail."

"Well, that wouldn't have been anything new, mum," the housekeeper said, unabashed.

Aidan looked over his shoulder at the woman with reluctant approval. She really would have made a splendid and loyal sergeant had she not had the misfortune to be born a woman.

"How were they?" Eve's voice was shaking, though she was not weeping. She had not wept at all. After her near-hysteria in Wulf's drawing room, she had been withdrawn, tense, and uncommunicative. "How were they wh-wh-when they were taken away?"

"I told them they were going to spend a short holiday with their aunt, who was eager to see them," Miss Rice explained. "I told them it would be just while you were away, Eve. It would be fun, I said."

"But they knew," Mrs. Pritchard said mournfully in her singsong Welsh accent. "They weren't fooled for a moment. Davy was white about the mouth and Becky's eyes were huge enough to fill her face. And it was not just because Nanny Johnson had told them there were some bad men passing through the county and that was why Mr. Biddle and his men had come to escort them safely to their aunt's. Ah, my heart is sore with the memory of it."

"My children. Oh, my poor babies."

The pain in Eve's voice took away all sense of melodrama from her words. For perhaps the first time Aidan realized the full extent of her attachment to the orphans she had taken in. They were not just lame ducks to her. They were family. She could not have been more upset if they had been her own.

She leapt to her feet suddenly. "Why am I sitting here, sipping tea and warming myself by the fire?" she cried. "I have to go to them. I have to bring them home. They must be so frightened."

"I'll come with you, my lamb," the housekeeper offered. "I'll take that Morris fellow by the neck and tie a knot in it."

"Agnes, dear," Mrs. Pritchard said reprovingly.

Aidan turned to face the room and cleared his throat. He had everyone's attention instantly.

"The Earl of Luff is the magistrate here?" he asked. *Denson's father.*

"Yes, he is, Colonel," Mrs. Pritchard said.

"It is to him we must direct an appeal, then," he said. "There is no point in visiting your cousin, Eve, and appealing to his better nature. I strongly suspect that he does not have one. And there is no point in blustering and bullying. He has the law on his side. The law will uphold him even more firmly if you are seen to be belligerent—or if your servants are."

"See here—" the housekeeper began.

Aidan bent his coldest, haughtiest stare on her. "The ladies have finished with the tea tray," he said. "You may remove it and busy yourself with your usual morning activities."

She glared back at him, and for an interested moment he thought she was going to prove stronger than any man he had ever had under his command—he thought she was going to argue. Instead she strode forward, gathered up the cups with a great deal of clattering, picked up the tray, and left the room without another word.

"Poor Agnes," Eve said. "She wants to help."

"She *may* help," he said, "by doing her job and keeping the household running smoothly. You and I will call upon the Earl of Luff, Eve. Allow me to escort you to your room so that you may freshen up and change your clothes."

Mrs. Pritchard sighed. "Oh, I knew that if only you would come, Colonel, all would be well," she said.

He took Eve upstairs and stopped outside her room with her before proceeding to the guest room where he had stayed before.

"It is still early," he said. "Would you like to sleep for a few hours before we go out?"

She shook her head. "I could not sleep," she said. "I will not be able to rest until I have my children home. But Aidan, I cannot embroil you further in the sordid crises of my life. There is so little of your leave left, and you have not had the freedom to enjoy any of it properly yet. You must return to London or to Lindsey Hall. You must not worry about—"

He set a finger across her lips. "I will see this thing through to the end," he said. "When I leave you, I will leave you safe and secure and happy."

"Because of your vow to Percy?" she asked.

"Because you are my wife."

She drew breath to speak, and he thought she was going to argue the matter in her usual way. But she merely nodded and turned to let herself into her room.

When I leave you. It would be soon now, within a day or two, once the children were back home where they

291

belonged. He would return to London and enjoy what was left of his two months in England. He would be unencumbered at last, almost free again. He would recover the life that was long familiar to him. But first, he thought grimly, letting himself into the guest room and ringing for hot water for a wash and shave, there was Luff to tackle.

When I leave you . . .

Didcote Park, country seat of the Earl of Luff, was a property on which Eve had never before set foot, even though it was not far from Ringwood. Invitations to social events at the house were issued only to those families who were of indisputably gentle birth. Her father, with all his wealth, had never come close to qualifying.

The house was an elegant, perfectly proportioned Georgian mansion. It was where John had grown up—his home. But Eve had few thoughts to spare for him.

"What if the earl refuses to receive us?" she asked.

"Refuses?" Aidan looked at her with obvious surprise. "Why would he refuse?"

"I am," she reminded him, "the daughter of a Welsh coal miner."

"And the wife of a Bedwyn," he said.

How different their perceptions of reality were, she thought. As the son and brother of the Duke of Bewcastle, it would never occur to him that he might be refused admittance to even the grandest of stately homes. And of course he never would be.

"What if he will not listen to us?"

292

"Why would he not?" he asked. "It is his duty as a magistrate to listen."

How could she explain to him what it was like not to be of the privileged aristocratic class, not to have the power or influence to be confident of the outcome of a visit such as the one they were paying? The Earl of Luff knew her as the woman whose father had had the effrontery to suggest a marriage alliance between their families.

"What if he says no?" she asked. "What if he refuses to change his mind?"

"We will see to it," he said, "that that does not happen. If you expect the worst, Eve, the worst is what you usually get. Ah, here we are."

He helped her alight while Sam Patchett rattled the door knocker. Her knees felt weak, and her stomach was queasy even though she had eaten no breakfast and even though she had worn one of her smart new carriage dresses for confidence. Aidan was wearing his dress uniform.

"Colonel Bedwyn and Lady Aidan Bedwyn to see the Earl of Luff," he told the porter who answered Sam's knock. He cupped Eve's elbow and led her into the entrance hall, unbidden.

She had always coveted her independence. She might normally resent the confident manner in which he took charge. But this morning she was grateful for it. If she was doing this alone, she would probably be on her way back home by now, the door of Didcote firmly closed behind her. His confidence was obviously well founded. After a mere two or three minutes of waiting in the hall, they were escorted to a downstairs room that turned out to be a library, and were bowed inside.

The Earl of Luff was rising from behind a huge oak desk. He was an older version of John, his blond hair now gray and thinning on top, but he was still a distinguished looking man.

"Colonel Bedwyn?" he said. "Lady Aidan? This is an unexpected pleasure. Do have a seat. May I offer you something to drink? Or would you prefer tea, ma'am?" His eyes had swept over her with bland courtesy.

"Neither, thank you, my lord," Eve said.

"Ah," he said. "What about you, Bedwyn? Brandy? Claret? Something else?"

"Nothing." Aidan held up his hand. He indicated a seat to Eve, and they both sat. She felt almost dizzy with anxiety and exhaustion.

"Well, then." The earl seated himself in a leather armchair and crossed one leg over the other. "To what do I owe the pleasure?"

Surely he must know. They could have only one reason for being here.

"I want my children back," Eve said, hearing in dismay that her voice was thin and shaking. "You let Cecil Morris take them from me. But they are mine. They belong at Ringwood. They are happy there. I want them back."

He lifted his eyebrows in apparent surprise. "Are you referring to Morris's young cousins?" he asked. "The children your household would not allow to return home to him, ma'am, because you were not there to give your permission? It was a simple matter of dealing with your absence."

"Home?" she said. "They *were* home. They live with me. And my household was not consulted until Mr. Biddle and four other men came to take the children forcibly away. They belong at Ringwood."

"Pardon me, ma'am," he said, "but what is your relationship to the children in question?"

She felt the knife thrust of a deeper fear.

"None," she admitted, "except that I am Cecil's cousin on his father's side. But it is with me that they live."

"It is my understanding that they are orphans," the earl said, "and that they were sent to live with their relative, Mr. Cecil Morris. He explained to me that you kindly opened your home to them during an indisposition of Mrs. Morris, his mother, and that during that time you left them alone while you went to town to enjoy the pleasures of the Season with your new husband."

"I did not leave them alone!" she exclaimed. "I—"

"Perhaps, sir," Aidan said, "since there is some dispute over who has a claim to the charge of these orphans, you would reopen the case and listen to the arguments of both sides."

"But it would appear," the earl said, "that all the rights are on the side of Mr. Morris."

"They are *not!*" Eve cried. "He does not even *want* the children."

"Then he has a strange way of showing it, ma'am," he said, frowning.

"Will you at least listen to my wife's side of the

story?" Aidan asked, sounding infuriatingly calm, almost bored. "These children are important to her. She has cared for them for the better part of a year and thinks of them as her own."

"A year!" The earl's brows snapped together. "Mrs. Morris was indisposed that long?"

"She has not been ill *at all*," Eve said.

"I am asking you to grant us a hearing," Aidan said. "With both Morris and his mother present if they wish."

"Oh, *no!*"

He held up a staying hand.

"And any witnesses he may care to call. And any witnesses *my wife* chooses to call."

Eve could feel tension knot in her stomach. She wanted to plead with the earl *now*. She wanted to get him to see sense *now*. She wanted to go straight from Didcote Park to Cecil's to take her children home with her. She did not want a hearing at which Cecil could tell his lies again and force Aunt Jemima to tell lies for him.

The Earl of Luff sighed. "It seemed a perfectly straightforward matter," he said. "It still seems straightforward. I am not going to all the faradiddle of calling a formal hearing, Bedwyn, with clever counsel arguing the case around and around in ever more dizzying circles. But I will allow an *informal* hearing if I must. It will have to be today, though. I have plans for the rest of the week. Two o'clock in the assembly rooms at Heybridge. Take it or leave it. I'll have Morris informed."

Aidan got to his feet. "Thank you, sir," he said. "We

will be there."

"But," Eve protested, "I wanted this matter settled this morning. I cannot wait until this afternoon."

"Then, ma'am," the earl said curtly, "you must be happy with having it remain settled in Morris's favor. I will certainly be happy."

She got to her feet. "This afternoon it will be, then," she said.

A few minutes later they were back in the carriage and moving down the driveway away from the house. It was all very well to tell her not to expect the worst, Eve thought wearily, but how could she not do so? The law would seem to be clearly on Cecil's side. Love was going to be no argument.

"Eve," Aidan said, "we are going straight home and you are going to bed. You are going to sleep."

"I cannot sleep," she protested.

"But you will anyway." His voice was stern, his expression hard. "If you want those children back, you must sleep and make your mind more alert. I strongly advise that you allow me to do most of the talking, and that when you *do* talk, you not rely upon emotion alone."

"How can I *not* be emotional!" she cried.

"He will win if you are," he told her. "Take my word on it."

She stared into his cold, harsh face and felt suddenly so all alone that she could bear it no longer. She turned sharply away, buried her face in her hands, and wept. She rarely gave in to tears, but she could not control them now, try as she would. She had forgotten how physically painful it was to cry. Her throat ached. Her chest felt as if it had been pierced by a dozen knives. Her heart felt as if it would break.

For perhaps a minute she was alone indeed. Then a hand settled between her shoulder blades and rubbed lightly back and forth. When her sobs had finally been reduced to hiccups and convulsive heaves, a large handkerchief appeared in her hand. She dried her face with it and blew her nose.

She had never, she thought, been more tired in her life.

It was as if he had read her thoughts. He leaned over her, one arm coming about her shoulders, the other beneath her knees, and he lifted her bodily onto his lap. Before her mind could quite register the shock, he had braced his booted feet against the seat opposite and settled her against him in such a way that her head nestled comfortably on one of his shoulders. She did not know when her bonnet had been removed or who had removed it but it was gone anyway.

"It will get better, love," he murmured against her ear.

"Will it?" But it was a measure of her weariness that she did not need to hear his answer. At that moment she trusted him utterly. How wonderful it was sometimes to have the burdens of life lifted from one's shoulders.

"I promise it will," he said.

The next thing she was aware of was waking up outside Ringwood when the carriage rocked to a halt.

Cecil Morris was looking smug, his mother nervous.

Eve was pale and drawn, despite the fact that she had slept both in the carriage and in her bed after they returned home from Didcote Park. Mrs. Pritchard was visibly anxious, Miss Rice tense. The Reverend Puddle was seated between them and showing deep concern for both ladies. The parish constable and his four assistants—one of them sporting a swollen beacon of a nose and two purple eyes—stood about importantly as if they expected a brawl to break out at any moment. A rather large number of other interested persons were in attendance, though how they knew about the hearing Aidan had no idea.

The Earl of Luff was late, and when he did arrive, he appeared to be in a bad humor.

"Let us get this business settled without further ado," he said, seating himself behind a table that had been set up along one end of the largest of the assembly rooms and glaring about him as if he were the one who had been kept waiting.

Cecil Morris was called up first to take the chair beside the earl's table and repeat his reasons for believing that custody of the orphans, David and Rebecca Aislie, should be granted to him. He did so, after taking an oath of honesty on a large Bible, perjuring himself with every breath. According to his story, he was inordinately fond of his young cousins, as he had been of their poor dead parents, while his mother positively doted upon them. He had been prevailed upon, against his better judgment, to allow his cousin, then Miss Eve Morris, to offer hospitality to the children while his mother recovered from a lengthy indisposition, but he had been disturbed to learn that she had abandoned them in order to jaunter off to London to enjoy the Season.

Aidan set a staying hand on Eve's arm when she drew breath to say something.

He had sought and won legal custody, Morris explained, and had sent the constable to fetch the children because the last time he had gone to visit them and assure them that soon they would be at home with their dear aunt, his cousin's new husband had threatened him with violence. He had feared that the other members of the household, some of whom were convicted felons, would do him harm—or worse, harm the children—if he went in person to demand their return.

"And as you can see, my lord," he said, making a dramatic gesture toward the bulbous-nosed, purple-eyed constable's assistant, "my fears were not ill-founded."

Aidan, feeling Eve's continued agitation, reached beneath the table and squeezed her hand.

"Who did that?" the earl asked, frowning at the assistant.

"I did, your worship," Eve's housekeeper said from somewhere behind them. "And I would do it again to anyone who came inside my mistress's house without a by-your-leave, wanting to drag away poor innocent little babies just because *he*—that villain there—wants his revenge. I just wish it was his nose I had got at the end of my fist."

"Sit down, woman," the earl said sternly, grasping the bridge of his nose between his thumb and forefinger and looking weary.

"Well, you did ask," she said.

"I did," he agreed. "Now sit down. Lady Aidan, do you have any questions you wish to ask Mr. Morris?"

Aidan squeezed her hand again, but she ignored his silent plea to speak for her and got to her feet.

"Yes," she said. "Becky and Davy were brought by stagecoach to Heybridge on September 5 of last year. It will be very easy to verify that date with stage records. Will you tell the earl, please, Cecil, how long they were at your house before my aunt's alleged illness forced you to allow me to take them?"

"How am I to remember that?" he asked her. "A month, two months, maybe longer."

"My household records show," Eve said, "that I hired Mrs. Johnson as a nurse for the children on September 6. The same records will show a number of clothes and other supplies being bought for them within that same week. Mrs. Johnson will testify, if necessary."

"My dear mama was ill—" Morris began.

"And will you tell the earl about your visit to Ringwood two days before the anniversary of my father's death?" Eve asked him. "I will refresh your memory, if you wish. You thought at the time that you would be inheriting on that anniversary. In my absence, you had everyone in the house line up in the hall so that you could address them. Every one of my servants will attest to the fact that the children were included in that line. Will you tell us what you told them all?"

"I cannot remember," he said. "That was some time ago."

"Plenty of people can remember," she told him. "You

301

said that everyone—*everyone*—was to be gone by the time you came back to take up residence or you would have them all arrested for vagrancy."

"Eve!" His eyes widened in shock. "I did not mean my poor young cousins. They were in the hall because they were to come home with me. But *that woman*"—he pointed at the housekeeper—"threatened me with a carving knife, and for the sake of the children I withdrew."

There was a snort from somewhere behind. "If I had had a carving knife handy," the housekeeper remarked, "I would have sliced your ears off for you, you lying little rat, and improved your face."

"Woman," the earl said sternly, "hold your tongue or I will have you removed. Return to your place, Mr. Morris. We will hear from Lady Aidan. Step up here, ma'am, and take a seat. Tell me why I should grant custody of David and Rebecca Aislie to you when there is no blood relationship between you and them."

Aidan fixed his gaze on her as she seated herself and took the oath on the Bible, and willed her to stay calm, not to become distraught as she had so nearly become in Luff's library this morning.

She explained how on the death of their parents the children had been sent from one relative to another until they had arrived at Heybridge to be rejected yet again. There had been nothing left for them except an orphanage somewhere. But her aunt had come weeping to Eve, unknown to her son, begging her to take the children in. And so she had. She had hired a nurse and a governess for them and had spent as much time with them herself as she could until before long she had come to love them as her own. She explained how it had never occurred to her to seek legal custody of them since no one else wanted them.

"How do you explain Mr. Morris's actions of the past week if he does not care for them himself?" the earl asked. "He obviously felt deep concern over your absence and neglect of his young relatives. He went to some trouble to take them into his own home."

"Revenge," Eve said.

"I beg your pardon?" the earl asked.

She described how she had kept her inheritance by marrying before the anniversary of her father's death. She described again the threat Morris had made to everyone in her household two days before that date and his behavior on that morning until her husband had ordered him to leave Ringwood and never set foot on the property again.

"He threatened you with bodily harm?" The earl frowned.

"A joke, my lord," Cecil Morris protested, jumping to his feet. "Why would I threaten my own dear cousin. It was—"

"Sit down, Mr. Morris," the earl directed.

"He knows that I love the children," Eve said. "He was humiliated at being thwarted and at having Colonel Bedwyn witness his threat to me. He saw a way of getting revenge on me through the children."

"Mr. Morris," the earl said with a sigh he did nothing to hide, "do you have any questions to ask Lady Aidan?"

"I do," Morris said, jumping to his feet. "Where have you been for the past two weeks, Eve, while the children were languishing alone at Ringwood, abandoned by the woman who supposedly loves them so dearly?"

"I was in London at the invitation of the Duke of Bewcastle," Eve said, looking at the earl, "to be presented to the queen and to society as the bride of Colonel Lord Aidan Bedwyn. I was there to attend a state dinner at Carlton House last evening, though I missed that in order to hurry home when I heard what had happened here. I left the children in the care of my aunt, Mrs. Pritchard, and of their nurse and their governess. I wrote to them daily. I missed them dreadfully." She touched her heart with the fingertips of one hand. "I missed them here."

"Very affecting," Morris said with heavy sarcasm. "And tell me, Eve, what is Davy going to do for a father figure, so important to a growing boy? Your house is filled with women. Your *husband* is, I believe, about to leave you and never return. Everyone knows that you married him only so that you could hang onto Ringwood and your fortune."

There was a buzz of indignation from the gathered spectators.

Aidan rose to his feet. "I would like to answer that question if I may," he said.

Luff waved a weary hand in acquiescence. "Let us hear from you, then, by all means, Colonel Bedwyn," he said. "I have never in my life heard such a fuss over two orphans."

"For the last number of years I have fought my way

across the Peninsula and into the south of France with Wellington's forces," Aidan said, thankful that he had chosen to wear his dress uniform again, uncomfortable as it was, especially on what had turned into a warm, humid day. "And who knows that even now all the hostilities are finally over? Europe must be put together piece by piece again after years of warfare and pillage. My duty lies with the army. My home is Ringwood Manor. It is where my wife lives. It is where my heart will stay when I leave. It is where I will settle as soon as I am able. My wife's relatives and friends are mine, her servants mine, and her foster children my own. As far as I am able, even if only by letter for the next few years, I will be a father to young Davy—and to Becky."

Eve watched him, pale and wide-eyed. And the devil of it was, Aidan thought, he did not *feel* as if he were lying.

He sat down. So did Morris.

"And you, ma'am," the earl said, addressing Mrs. Morris. "What do you have to say in this matter? Do you want these children? Do you care for them? Do you love them?"

"Yes, my lord," she said in a voice that was little more than a whisper. "I love them dearly. But—"

They all waited politely for her to finish, except her son, who turned to glare at her.

"And so," the Earl of Luff said when it became clear that she had no more to say, "I have to weigh the claims of a man and his mother who have custody of the children and are related to them and claim to love them against those of a man who is presumably about to return to his battalion for an indefinite length of time and a woman who has no tie of blood and no legal claim to the children and who is perhaps unable to give them a balanced sense of family."

They were going to lose, Aidan thought in some astonishment.

"In that last matter, of course, you are quite wrong," a soft but quite distinct voice said from the back of the room.

Aidan looked sharply behind him. Wulf was standing just inside the door, dressed for travel but as immaculate as if he had just stepped out from under his valet's care, his quizzing glass halfway to his eye.

"Who in thunder—" the earl began. Then he peered more closely. "Oh, it is you, is it, Bewcastle?"

Eve, still beside the earl's table, grasped the arms of her chair.

"Quite so," Bewcastle said, strolling forward, looking as haughty and bored as he had ever looked. "Lady Aidan with no family to protect her and her foster children while Colonel Bedwyn is away serving his king and country? That is a patent absurdity, Luff. She has all the considerable support of the Bedwyn family behind her."

"You are willing to take these two waifs under the wing of the *Bedwyns?*" the earl asked.

Wulf's eyebrows arched upward. "Are they not already there?" he asked. "Are they not under my sister-in-law's wing, even if only figuratively speaking at the moment? And is not Lady Aidan a Bedwyn?"

The Earl of Luff gazed at him as if he might well

have two heads and then shook his head as if dismissing such absurdity. "Your sudden affection for these children *does* seem somewhat suspect, Mr. Morris," he said. "The relationship apart, your concern for them certainly appears to be motivated by spite. And with a single *but* Mrs. Morris has set in doubt her claim to love them. One wonders if they would not be considerably happier in Lady Aidan's household even if Colonel Bedwyn *is* to be gone for years. With the assurance that they will be under the Duke of Bewcastle's protection, I feel I must pronounce that it is for the greater good of David and Rebecca Aislie to be given into the legal custody of Lady Aidan Bedwyn, who gave them a home and affection when no one else wanted them. It is so ordered."

For a moment Aidan thought Eve was going to collapse. But she held herself erect, her knuckles white against the chair arms. And then her eyes sought his.

He smiled at her.

CHAPTER XIX

ॐ

Eve was wedged between Becky and Davy on the carriage seat, one arm about each of them. She could not bear the thought of letting them go—not yet. Becky was showing her a little lace handkerchief filled with treasures—a brooch with one of the paste diamonds missing, a silver earring whose partner was apparently lost, a bracelet with a broken clasp—all of which Aunt Jemima had given her. Davy was silent.

They appeared to have been well cared for. Aunt Jemima had apparently fussed over them and pressed food—especially cakes—on them in vast quantities. She had tucked Becky into bed each night and kissed her and sung lullabies to her.

"But I did miss your stories, Aunt Eve," she said. "And I missed *you*. And Benjamin. And Aunt Thelma and Aunt Mari. And Nanny."

"And everyone has missed the two of you," Eve said, hugging them both tightly. "I missed you dreadfully all the time I was away. I am not going away again, not without you. I am going to stay with my family. With my children. And no one is going to take you on a vacation again unless you are asked first if you wish to go and I am there to see that you are asked. It was rather thoughtless of Cousin Cecil to send Mr. Biddle to fetch you merely because someone imagined there were bad men in the area. He might have frightened you. But Aunt Jemima really did wish to see you."

"He said we were not to be allowed to go back to Ringwood," Davy said, speaking for the first time.

"He was mistaken," Eve said. "I daresay Aunt Jemima did not say that, did she? No less a person than the Earl of Luff, who is a magistrate in this part of the world, has just now stated that Ringwood is to be your permanent home and that I am to be your mama—or standing in place of your mama," she added carefully. She had always encouraged the children to remember their parents and talk of them.

Becky was gazing at Aidan, who was sitting on the

seat opposite, his knees occasionally brushing Eve's. "Are you our new papa?" she asked.

He did not answer immediately, and Eve raised her eyes unwillingly to his. He would surely be leaving tomorrow, especially now that his brother was here with a private carriage to convey him. There was no further reason for him to stay. She had been aware of it from the very moment of victory, which had brought knee-weakening relief and soaring happiness, echoed in the loud cheer with which the earl's verdict had been greeted. But it had been a bittersweet moment. He would be leaving tomorrow.

Yet he had smiled at her.

It had not been just the expression with the eyes she had interpreted as a smile during the ball at Bedwyn House. This had been a full-faced, radiant smile, curving his mouth, crinkling his eyes at the corners, brightening his whole face. All the dark, forbidding harshness had fled, to be replaced by a beauty full of light and warmth and potential laughter.

It had been somehow, strangely, more intimate than any of their couplings had been. Something deep within him, some joy brighter than the sun, had reached out to envelop her, to enfold her more closely than arms.

Or so it had seemed. It had been merely a smile.

He had smiled at her. For an eternity. For perhaps ten or fifteen seconds, until Cecil had stormed out of the room and Aunt Jemima, weeping piteously, had come hurrying forward to hug Eve and tell her that she loved the dear children, she did, she did, but she was too old and weary to cope with their day-to-day care. Eve had hugged her back and assured her that she could come and visit them—and visit *her*—whenever she chose. By the time she had returned her attention to Aidan, he had been at the back of the room in conversation with the Duke of Bewcastle and the Earl of Luff, looking remote and rather grim again in his uniform.

She had not tarried. She had just learned from Aunt Jemima that the children were below stairs in the taproom, being entertained by two of the Three Feathers' chambermaids. Eve had dashed down the stairs, taking them two at a time in grossly unladylike fashion, and had rushed into the taproom to scoop them up, one at a time, laughing and dancing them in circles. She could scarcely remember a happier moment in her life.

"I daresay," Aidan said now to Becky, "you remember your papa, do you? He will always be your papa even though he is unable to be with you any longer. I am here to stand in for him, to make sure that you are always safe and warm and that you have the care and the education to help you grow into a fine young lady and Davy into a fine young man."

"What will I call you?" Becky asked.

She had taken him by surprise, Eve could see. His eyebrows rose.

"Hmm," he said. "Let me see. My wife is Aunt Eve. I suppose that makes me Uncle Aidan."

It sounded absurd. So absurd that Eve laughed. Who would ever have thought it? Colonel Lord Aidan Bedwyn inviting two waifs to call him Uncle Aidan? How she *loved* him! But it was too painful a realization to cope with at the moment. She smiled down at Becky again.

Tomorrow he would be leaving.

The Duke of Bewcastle had accepted an invitation to stay for one night at Ringwood Manor. Anything was better, he had said in his habitual soft, haughty voice, than staying at the Three Feathers again, and judging from the look on the landlord's face when he had seen him enter the inn below the assembly rooms earlier, his grace had added, that worthy shared the sentiment.

It amazed and puzzled Eve that he had come, but she had not given much thought to his motive until she entered the drawing room just prior to dinner and found him there alone. There was no sign of Aidan.

She had always disliked the duke. She was also, she admitted at that moment, just like everyone else in his orbit, afraid of him. But it was a fear she had never allowed herself to succumb to. She resisted now the urge to make some excuse to disappear from the room again or to chat brightly about inconsequentials. She advanced deliberately across the room, both hands outstretched. He had no choice but to take them in his own, looking faintly surprised and perhaps also a touch uncomfortable.

"Thank you," she said. "From the bottom of my heart, thank you." She squeezed his hands before releasing them—more slender, longer-fingered, than Aidan's, a ring on each hand.

"I am unaware," he said, "of having done you any great service, Lady Aidan."

"I do not know how long you were standing there before you spoke," she said, "but you must have understood that the verdict stood very much in the balance, that the earl was just as likely to uphold his decision to grant custody to Cecil as he was to give the children back to me. It was what you said that swayed his decision. More even than that, though, it was your presence."

"I am glad to have been of some slight service, then," he said.

"Why did you come?" She wanted to retreat, to sit down and busy herself with something. His silver eyes with their very direct gaze were disconcerting at the best of times. But she stood where she was, a mere couple of feet from him. "It could not have been for the children's sake. You can feel nothing but indifference for the orphans of a shopkeeper. It could not have been for my sake. You tolerate me at best, despise me at worst, I believe, and I annoyed you considerably by insisting upon missing the dinner at Carlton House. It must have been for Aidan's sake, then."

"It is soothing," he said, "to discover someone who knows me so well that she can answer her own questions for me and thus save me the effort of forming them for myself."

She flushed at the haughty reproof. "Why *did* you come?" she asked.

"I came, ma'am," he said, "because I am head of the Bedwyn family and have always considered it my duty to concern myself with its members. You are now one of their number and will continue to be, no matter how

312

strongly you assert your independence, no matter how firmly you send Aidan away forever when his leave is over. It appeared that you might have need of my influence, which is, as you have witnessed, considerable. And so I came."

"You came for my sake, then?" She frowned. He seemed too cold a man to have acted out of kindness. But it had not been kindness. He had just said it himself—it had been duty. Just like Aidan, he was motivated by duty more than by anything else. They were so similar, the two brothers, in many ways. Yet they were not friends.

The duke slightly inclined his head.

"What is between you and Aidan?" she found herself asking. "Why are you not . . . close? You are similar in age and in temperament." That was not quite right, though. There was fire behind Aidan's reticence, ice behind the duke's. "You both place honor and duty above all else. Why are you not close?"

His eyebrows had gone up, his quizzing glass was in his hand, and his light eyes froze her. He had, she realized, retreated behind the thickest of his masks. She wondered suddenly if there was a real man behind even the thinnest of them.

"Do brothers have to be demonstrative in the Welsh manner, then, ma'am," he asked her, "clasped to each other's bosom, weeping sentimental tears with every parting and every quarrel and reconciliation, proclaiming the depths of their sentiment for each other in florid, impassioned language? Must there be something *between* them if they comport themselves with a more

313

English restraint?"

She had rattled him. He whipped her with cold words and open contempt for her compatriots. But she had rattled him.

"Do you love him, then?" she asked.

"You use women's words, Lady Aidan," he said. "*Love*. What is love but an abstract term that cannot even be defined except in terms of action? Aidan is a Bedwyn. He is my brother and—unless or until I produce a son of my own—my heir. His life is important to me as is his . . . happiness. I would die for him if such an extreme and dramatic gesture were called for. Is that love? You may decide for yourself."

The door opened before he had finished speaking and Aunt Mari came in, supporting herself on her cane. Thelma was with her—Eve had insisted that she dine with them, as she always did. Aunt Mari immediately began to talk with great enthusiasm about the trial, as she insisted upon calling this afternoon's hearing. The duke's expression became pained as he listened to the thick Welsh accent.

Five more minutes passed before Aidan put in an appearance, no longer in his uniform, but clad in elegant blue and gray evening wear with crisp white linen.

"Andrews arrived from London so late this afternoon that he had not got my shirt ironed," he said. "He would not hear of my wearing it unironed despite the fact that there was not a wrinkle visible to my unpracticed eye. I decided that being a little late was preferable to seeing him weep with mortification."

Turning toward him, Eve felt nothing but pain. He

had come all this way with her, braving his brother's wrath. He had fought for her today and for children who meant nothing to him. *He had smiled at her.*

And he was leaving tomorrow.

"But then you always were rather careless of your appearance, Aidan," the duke remarked.

"Dinner will be ready," Eve said. "Shall we go into the dining room?"

Belatedly, as Aidan offered Aunt Mari his arm and the Duke of Bewcastle stepped forward to offer her his, Eve thought that she should have had Agnes bring drinks into the drawing room. How gauche they would think her.

Even to dash down into the country for one day Bewcastle had brought a veritable cavalcade with him—his own crested carriage, a baggage coach to carry his belongings and his valet, two coachmen, two footmen for his own carriage, and six outriders, all dressed in glorious livery.

Aidan, standing on the terrace next morning with Eve to see him on his way, felt a strange pang of sadness. *This* was what Wulf had come to—that bright, energetic, mischievous boy of memory, now a cold, lonely aristocrat with so much power that he could exert it with the mere lifting of one long finger or the raising of one dark brow. Or with one softly spoken word. For a moment Aidan felt an unfamiliar tightness in his chest. He was not usually affected by farewells, especially when he expected to see the other again within the next few days.

Why had Wulf come? He had puzzled over the question ever since yesterday afternoon, yet could still not quite accept the obvious answer that his brother had come merely because a Bedwyn was in distress and his consequence might settle the matter. Why would Wulf care that Eve would suffer over the loss of two orphans, even if she was a Bedwyn? Was it possible that he had come—*was* it?—because he knew Aidan cared for Eve and *he* cared for Aidan? Cared, that was, not just out of ducal duty but out of brotherly . . . love? There had been no point in asking him. He would have looked back at Aidan with his silver eyes and raised eyebrows, quizzing glass in hand, looking as if he had never heard of the word.

The carriages disappeared down the driveway.

"I hope I am not inconveniencing you by staying an extra day," he said.

"No, not at all." But there was a slight frown of incomprehension between her brows.

She had, of course, expected him to leave with Wulf this morning. It was what he had said last evening that he would do. But he had lain in bed, unable to sleep again after awaking some time before dawn, the scene at the assembly rooms playing and replaying itself in his head.

My home is Ringwood Manor. It is where my wife lives. It is where my heart will stay when I leave.

When he had spoken the words they had not felt like a lie though he had assumed that they *were* essentially just that. Certainly they had been almost embarrassingly ostentatious. But he had been unable to get the words out of his head as he had tried to get back to sleep.

It is where my heart will stay when I leave.

. . . her foster children my own.

They were not his own. He could have no interest whatsoever in them except perhaps for a natural concern for young children who had been orphaned and left unwanted and unclaimed by all their relatives.

And then Cecil Morris's words had lodged in his brain and repeated and repeated themselves until finally Aidan had got up, dressed without summoning Andrews, and gone out to the stables to saddle a horse and take it out for a brisk ride into the sunrise.

. . . tell me, Eve, what is Davy going to do for a father figure, so important to a growing boy?

With the words had come images of the boy, thin and bewildered and bristling with menace in the nursery one evening, silent and passive in the carriage yesterday.

. . . what is Davy going to do for a father figure . . .

It is where my heart will stay when I leave.

They were her children. Eve's. And Eve was his wife. How foolish now seemed the memory of his decision to marry her, to take her to London for the ceremony, to bring her back home, and to leave her. Just like a neat little military maneuver, soon accomplished, soon forgotten. He might have taken into account that he was a Bedwyn, and that Bedwyns almost invariably loved their mates. It was a tradition he and his brothers had snickered and grimaced over when they were boys. And Bedwyns loved and nurtured their children, even if they were overscrupulous about instilling notions of duty and responsibility in them. Not that any Bedwyns to Aidan's knowledge had ever had foster children to deal with.

"It is a lovely day," he said. "I thought perhaps I would take the boy fishing." He felt intensely embarrassed as soon as the words were out.

"Davy?"

"I thought perhaps I would," he said. "I assured him after our wedding that he was safe, and I encouraged him to think of himself as the protector of his sister and the other women here. When it came to the point, of course, he was not safe at all, and he could do nothing to protect anyone, even himself. I should have realized that he is a child and that he needs adults to spend time with him and do all the protecting until he is old enough to do it for himself. I'll spend today with him at least."

Her frown deepened, and at first he thought he had made a mistake, staying, forcing his company on her for another day, seemingly questioning her ability to nurture the boy alone. But he had misunderstood the cause of the frown, he discovered when she spoke.

"You *are* kind," she said softly. "Sometimes I doubt it. You make it easy to doubt. I did not even realize until yesterday that both you and the Duke of Bewcastle hide behind almost impenetrable masks. But you *are* a kind man."

"Merely because I have decided upon a day of fishing?" Masks? He wore no mask, did he? Did Wulf? Yes, actually he did, and she had been perceptive enough to see that. But not himself, surely? "You do not know much about men, Eve, if you believe it is a great sacrifice on my part to stay for a day of pleasure."

"Davy's father was a shopkeeper," she said. "Not a particularly prosperous one. Yet *Colonel Lord Aidan Bedwyn* is making no sacrifice by giving up another day of his leave to take this man's son fishing?"

"It is a lovely day," he said abruptly. "You had better come too, Eve, and bring the girl. I daresay she and her brother would not feel comfortable being apart today especially as I am almost a stranger to them. We will take the gig and load a picnic basket up behind."

She had tipped her head to one side and was regarding him with eyes that were luminous and beautiful.

"Go and have their nurse get the children ready," he said, embarrassed, "and inform Miss Rice that she will not be teaching them today. Then you can go and give directions about the picnic basket while I see that the gig is made ready."

She smiled at him before catching up her skirt and running lightly up the steps to the house. He felt suddenly lighthearted, like a boy escaped from the schoolroom. He could not remember when he had last taken a day purely for pleasure. Was it to be a pleasure, then, spending a day with two young children, the offspring of a shopkeeper, as she had just reminded him? Teaching the boy to fish? Picnicking with them? And with Eve?

He wondered suddenly if he would have stayed were it not for the children. Would he now be seated in the carriage with Wulf, comfortably immersed in a conversation on politics or some such thing? Or would he have found some other excuse to remain?

He did not care to pursue the question. He strode off in the direction of the stables instead.

It is where my heart will stay when I leave.

There were a hundred and one important things to do since she had been away for two weeks. Eve had always been conscientious about her duties as a landowner. And she had always accepted her social obligations too—to call upon her neighbors, to be at home to their calls, to visit the sick. But she would not even feel guilty about taking this day for herself, she decided. After all, it was not just for herself, was it? It was for the children. *Her* children. If she had learned something from the experiences of the last few weeks it was that giving them her time and attention and love was the most important thing she could do with her life.

They found a quiet stretch of the river, on her land, but away from the house and well above the village. There, in a grassy meadow dotted with colorful wildflowers, blue sky and sunshine overhead, they set down the picnic basket they had carried from the gate where they had left the gig and went fishing. The horse had been let loose to graze in one corner of the meadow.

They all fished for a while, Aidan with Davy, Eve with Becky. She tried to remember the skills she had learned with Percy many years ago. Aidan came and helped them once in a while and held his hands over Becky's on the rod after it had been cast, showing her how to keep it steady without tiring her arms too quickly. Becky tipped her head right back and gazed up into his upside-down face, bent over her own, and smiled—a sunny, untroubled child's smile. Aidan looked down at her and winked.

It was a precious moment for Eve. How could she ever have expected that he would be gentle with children—that dour, powerful cavalry officer who had stood in the visitors' salon telling her of Percy's death in battle?

But Becky soon tired of the passive game of fishing, much to the delight of Muffin, who scrambled up from his perch on the bank and bobbed off ahead of them to chase flies. Eve waded through the meadow with Becky, identifying the various flowers, chasing butterflies but releasing the only one they caught after gazing with some awe at its colorings, chasing each other and Muffin—though it was too hot a day to play that game for very long—and sitting down beside the basket to make daisy chains. Eve made one long one to go about Becky's neck and a shorter one for her to wear as a coronet. The small one Becky made ended up about Eve's wrist.

All the time, while they played, while the child chattered on inconsequentially and sometimes sang softly to herself, Eve was aware of Aidan and Davy on the riverbank, engaged in the serious business of catching fish. Aidan explained quietly, she noticed, and patiently supervised while Davy did everything himself. Eventually they were both sitting side by side on the bank, both in their shirtsleeves, silent most of the time, talking occasionally. Davy, it seemed to Eve, was talking far more than he usually did. Neither of them laughed or even smiled, but they both looked relaxed and contented.

Almost like father and son.

Why had he stayed? She had lain awake most of the night, steeling herself for the parting facing her this morning. She had not even pretended to indifference. She did not want him to leave. It was as simple as that. She was not ready—she never would be. And then morning had come and she had discovered that she was to be granted a reprieve. There was to be another day to spend with him—and the same anguish to endure again tonight and tomorrow morning. She had been almost disappointed by his decision to stay. The worst of the agony would be over by now. Though perhaps not.

Undoubtedly not.

"Go and tell Davy and Uncle Aidan," she said at last to Becky, undoing the straps about the picnic basket, "that it is time to eat."

She watched Becky go and make her announcement. She watched Aidan turn and set an arm loosely about the child's waist and Becky wrap a chubby arm about his neck and lean into his broad shoulder. She watched Davy look up at her and draw her attention to the small fish he was reeling in.

Eve hugged her knees and very deliberately tried to impress the scene upon her memory. By tomorrow— But she would not think of tomorrow.

It was not time to eat, she soon discovered. In addition to the thick rounds of fresh bread and butter that

Mrs. Rowe had sent with generous slices of cheese, they were going to have freshly cooked fish.

"Why do you think Davy and I have been fishing all morning?" Aidan asked when Eve expressed her surprise. "We have been slaving and wearing our fingers to the proverbial bone in order that like real men we might feed our women. Have we not, Davy?"

There was no smile on his face, but it was unmistakably present in his voice. He sent Becky in search of some large, flat leaves while he and Davy went foraging for twigs and sticks with which to build a fire. He might have accomplished it all himself in half the time it actually took, Eve thought, tickling Muffin's stomach since her participation had not been invited, but he let the children do almost everything themselves, including building the fire and lighting it with the tinderbox he produced from the coat he had carried with him. He taught them how to clean and prepare the fish and watched them do it, and then he allowed them to set the fish out on the leaves and wrap them. He set the leaves in the fire himself.

Eve clasped her hands about her raised knees when her stomach rumbled with hunger, but she made no protest at the lateness of their meal. Both children were absorbed and enjoying themselves more than she had ever witnessed before.

"Papa built us a fire once," Davy said.

"Did he, Davy?" Becky looked up at him wide-eyed.

"And we roasted chestnuts," Davy said, "and Mama scolded him for letting us burn our fingers."

"Mama let me brush her hair," Becky said.

It was a brief exchange, but it brought tears to Eve's eyes and warmth to her heart. Although she had always encouraged them to remember, they had never before reminisced in her hearing.

"I believe," Aidan said, "the fish is ready. I'll take it off the fire and open the leaves, and Aunt Eve will judge when we may eat it. I am not going to risk having her accuse me of letting you burn either your fingers or your tongues."

They stuffed themselves with fish, which tasted slightly burned and delicious, and with bread and butter and cheese, jam tarts, and currant cakes. They refreshed themselves with lemonade. And then Aidan stretched out on the blanket with a sigh, one booted foot bent at the knee, one arm, its shirtsleeve rolled up to the elbow, draped over his eyes to shield them from the sun.

"This," he said, "is absolute bliss."

The children went off together with Muffin to explore the meadow. Eve packed the remains of their picnic back into the basket. Aidan slept, his breathing deep and even. Eve gazed at him, storing more memories. She would not lie down herself, sleepy as she felt. Someone had to keep an eye on the children. Besides, she did not want to miss a single moment of this day.

This is absolute bliss.

Yes, indeed it was. It was also a day of pure agony.

It was all so very like the family life she had always dreamed of—first with Joshua, then with John. And now she was having a brief glimpse at what such a life would be like—with someone else's children and a husband who was going to leave her tomorrow. Perhaps it did not matter. They *were* her children and he *was* her husband, and today they were together as a family. Perhaps today was all that mattered. Perhaps today was all anyone could expect. Perhaps tomorrow was always an illusion that never came.

"I suppose," he said, his voice breaking into her reverie, "that coming from an urban area of shops and businesses, Davy does not know a great deal about the country. Do you take him about the home farm, explaining things to him, letting him get his hands dirty, so to speak?"

"I never have," she said. "I have always wanted to keep them close to the comfort of home. They were so thin and pale and listless when they first came here, Aidan. It would have broken your heart to see them. But perhaps I should?"

"He will need to be prepared for some career," he said. "The land is a real possibility. He could learn to be a steward, perhaps even yours. Or perhaps be a farm worker, even a farmer."

"Perhaps a landowner," she said. "My property is unentailed."

He lifted his arm from his eyes and turned his head to look at her. "You may yet be with child," he said.

"No." She turned her head sharply away, alarmed to find the meadow blurring before her vision. No, she was not. There had been one week when she might have conceived, but she had not done so. She would never ever have a child of her own womb.

"Ah," he said softly after a few silent moments. "I am

sorry, Eve."

"You need not be," she said. "It would have complicated things hopelessly, would it not? You would have felt obliged to come here for a visit whenever you were in England on leave, and I would have felt obliged to let you come."

Another short silence.

"That would not have been desirable," he said.

"No."

There was one small cloud floating across the sky—only one. But it found the sun and covered it for a few moments. Eve shivered in the sudden coolness.

"I'll talk to Ned Bateman," she said when the cloud had moved off. "My steward. About Davy, I mean."

"Perhaps," he said, "I'll take Davy around the home farm tomorrow. I would like to see it myself. I know a thing or two about farming."

"Tomorrow?"

There was another of those brief silences that had punctuated their conversation.

"London at present is a place from which I would rather be absent," he said. "When Wulf described the dinner we missed at Carlton House, I shuddered. Did you not too? Everyone talking stubbornly in different languages, no one understanding anyone else, the grand duchess, the only person who could have interpreted fully, refraining from doing so out of contempt for the Prince of Wales and a desire for his entertainment to fall flat upon its face, the queen prosing on forever and then killing dead whatever still survived of the evening by forcing everyone to make their formal obeisance to her in the drawing room after dinner, the Czar of Russia flirting indiscriminately with all the ladies and pouting because he was no longer the center of attention. There will only be more of the same to be endured as soon as I return to London. I would rather be here."

Just for tomorrow? For a few more days? For the rest of his leave?

"Will you mind?" he asked.

"No." She was not at all sure whether she spoke the truth or lied. "No, not at all."

The children had come back—they had been squatting on the riverbank for some time. Muffin cuddled down beside Eve and nudged at her hand with his wet nose while Becky went to stand beside Aidan.

"Uncle Aidan," she said, "I brought you something."

He sat up, and she set a smooth pebble in his hand, still wet from the riverbed.

"For me?" he said, examining it closely before looking up at her. "I do believe it is the most precious gift I have ever been given. Thank you, sweetheart."

Eve was startled by the endearment. But Becky had skipped around the blanket to her side.

"And one for you, Aunt Eve," she said.

It was a gift, Eve realized as she hugged the child, that would live among her most precious treasures for the rest of her life as a reminder of today, one of the happiest of her life.

"I suppose," Aidan said, "we had better get that horse back to the stable before it bursts from consuming so much grass."

Becky yawned hugely, and he stooped to scoop her up in one arm while hoisting up the picnic basket with the other hand.

"You can bring the rods and everything else, lad," he said to Davy. "We'll let Aunt Eve play lady."

Becky nestled her head on his shoulder and promptly fell asleep.

CHAPTER XX

✍

Aidan had no idea how long he intended to stay. He deliberately did not ask himself the question. He only knew that he did not wish to spend the rest of his leave in London, where life would be as hectic and as much focused upon military matters as it was when he was with his battalion. And Lindsey Hall had lost some of its appeal. It would seem empty and bleak without most of his brothers and sisters there—even Ralf had gone to London, according to Wulf.

And without Eve.

He needed to relax. And England was experiencing a heat wave—day after day of blue skies and sunshine and a heat that soaked through the skin to soothe muscles and offer a warm balm to the soul.

It was difficult to understand his attachment to the children, who at first were his excuse for staying, but who soon became a large part of his reason. Perhaps it was because he knew they were the only children that either he or Eve would ever have. He could never come back once he left. She had made that very clear down at the river. If she had borne a child of theirs, she would have allowed him to visit during leaves, but she had not conceived during the week they had slept together.

The moment was all, then. These few days—as many as his conscience would allow him to steal—were all he would ever have with his wife and his children. Yes, strange thought indeed—his children. *Theirs.*

Eve declared a holiday from the schoolroom. Aidan took Davy about with him a few times, and soon the boy became his shadow wherever he went, even if it was just a visit to the stables or a stroll into the village.

They inspected the home farm, with Eve's steward the first time, alone together the next time, and Aidan pointed out to the boy all the different crops that were growing, taking him right into the fields, stooping on his haunches with him so that they could both touch the plants and see and feel the differences among them. They watched the animals grazing, cows in one field, sheep in another. They wandered about the barnyard, helping feed the pigs and chickens, looking inside the barn itself, still partly filled with last year's hay, one of the cows chewing contentedly there, its sickly calf beside it in the hay. He taught Davy how to milk the cow when it was explained to them that the calf was unable to feed without some help. They both tasted a mouthful of the warm, sweet liquid. They watched the smith at work. All the while Aidan breathed in the familiar smells of a working farm and felt the familiar pull of rural life.

The next time Eve and Becky went with them, the dog bobbing along with them on its three good legs, using the fourth as an occasional prop. They did not stay together the whole while. Eve and Becky stepped inside some of the cottages to visit the laborers' wives, and Aidan spotted Becky a short while later playing outside with a few other children. In the barnyard later she lost interest in the larger animals and sat in the grass and dust, playing with the most placid of the barnyard cats while the dog, which appeared to fear cats, pressed close to Eve's skirts.

Both children had grown sun-bronzed, Aidan noticed. So had Eve despite the floppy, shapeless straw hat she wore almost everywhere—the same hat she had worn on that very first day, if he remembered correctly, though now it was trimmed with pink ribbons instead of gray. She was wearing a pale pink muslin dress, which was neither new nor fashionable. She fit her country surroundings to perfection. Aunt Rochester would be horrified if she could see her now. She was purely pretty.

By the time they turned their footsteps homeward— they had walked instead of bringing the gig—they were all looking dusty and somewhat disheveled, especially the children. The day was particularly hot. Becky was up on Aidan's shoulders, clinging to his hair—he had not worn a hat. Another day was winding to its close, he thought regretfully. He could not delay his leaving much longer.

The river came into view to their right.

"Now *that*," he said, pointing, "used to be the answer to a hot day when I was a lad. We used to go swimming."

"Oh, did you?" Eve looked at him with bright eyes. "So did we. Percy and I. It was forbidden—our father had a fear of water. We used to go over there, where we were hidden by the trees from the eyes of anyone who might have reported us." She pointed a little farther along the river. "I used to have to sneak up to my room when we went home in order to hide my wet hair and then pretend to have washed it."

Aidan looked down at Davy. "Do you swim, lad?"

"No, sir." The boy shook his head.

"What?" Aidan frowned at him. "You cannot swim? Intolerable! We must set that matter right. And there is no time like the present." He turned in the direction of the river.

"Aidan!" Eve was laughing. "You cannot teach Davy to swim now. We have no towels."

"Why would we need towels in this weather?" he asked. "Becky, do we need towels?"

She grasped his hair a little more tightly. "No, Uncle Aidan."

"But I cannot, sir," Davy protested. "I would sink. I would drown."

"I'll teach you not to sink," Aidan told him. "I'll teach you not to drown."

Eve came along too, as well as the dog, which bounded along ahead of them to drink. She would not swim herself, Eve protested when they drew close. How could she when she had no suitable clothing with her? But she did take off her shoes and stockings and pulled off Becky's dress so that the child could splash about in the water in her shift. Aidan pulled off his boots, stockings, and shirt, but reluctantly left his pantaloons on. Davy stripped off to his drawers under Aidan's directions. He appeared not at all excited at the idea of learning to swim.

The water was deliciously cool, Aidan discovered when he stepped into it. It reached to his knees, though the river was wide at this point, and he guessed that it was quite a bit deeper farther toward the center. He reached up a hand for Eve.

"Your dress is going to get wet," he said, noting appreciatively the trimness of her ankles as she drew the fabric up above them. "You might as well take it off. I have seen you in less than your shift, after all."

She gave him a speaking glance as she tested the water gingerly with one toe and then lowered first one leg in and then the other. Her dress was bunched above her knees, but she must have realized the impossibility of keeping it dry and let go her hold on it. It floated about her on the water as he lifted Becky in and handed the child to her. Becky shrieked with the shock of the coldness. Davy did not, even though he shuddered and looked thin and white-bodied and miserable.

Eve played with a visibly and audibly happy Becky while Aidan set about the task of teaching the boy how to breathe, how not to fear the water, even when his face was fully submerged. Eve was holding Becky while she floated on her back. Aidan did the same with Davy, though the boy was extremely reluctant to lift his feet from the riverbed.

"It is a matter of trust, lad," Aidan said at last. "You have to trust me to hold you and not let you sink. Will you do that?"

"Yes, sir," the boy said solemnly.

After that, he floated, Aidan's hands firmly beneath him, feeling the boy gradually relax, gradually trust the water itself to hold him up. Aidan released his hold with one hand and merely kept the other splayed beneath the small of Davy's back for confidence. He looked back at Eve, who was spinning Becky in a slow circle, her dress totally wet and clinging to her slender curves. Even her hair was damp.

And then Davy gasped in horror and scrambled to his feet.

"My drawers, sir," he said. "They have come off."

And sure enough, the truant drawers were floating off with the current, already out of the boy's reach when he tried to grab them.

Becky had noticed. "Davy's drawers!" she shrieked.

Aidan waded after them. He could have reached them in a moment, but he slowed down when he realized that the boy was splashing after him and that he was laughing—giggling, rather, with a child's mingled embarrassment and hilarity.

Aidan grasped the drawers just before they would have swirled out to deeper water. He swung them over his head.

"Come and get them," he said.

Davy had come up to him, still convulsed with mirth, one hand covering his private parts beneath the water, the other reaching up in vain for his drawers.

"I cannot reach, sir," he said. "They will *see!*"

Aidan dangled them a few inches lower, laughing

back at the boy. "Maybe I should get you to swim for them," he said, threatening to throw them out into deeper water.

"N-n-no, sir. G-g-give them to me."

It was such a delight to see the boy actually laughing that Aidan was tempted to prolong the teasing. But he would not cause undue embarrassment. Still laughing, he dangled the drawers within reach, and then, when the boy grasped them, caught him in one arm and pulled him half under into the deeper water, mock-wrestling with him before finally setting him down safely on his feet in chest-deep water so that Davy could scramble into his drawers without exposing himself.

It was at that moment that Aidan, glancing back up the river, locked glances with Eve, who was standing quite still in the water, holding Becky in her arms. There was an arrested look on her face. It was only when he noted it that Aidan realized he was still laughing. Being totally undignified, in fact.

He gazed rather sheepishly at Eve, his laughter fading to a mere grin.

Davy was still giggling, safely ensconced in his drawers again.

"Well, lad," Aidan said, "are you ready for deeper waters? Will you come and swim with me if I promise not to let you go?"

"Yes, sir," the boy said. But it was not the usual passive obedience he was expressing this time. His eyes shone with eager, boyish excitement. He had forgotten his fears. He was enjoying himself. He was a young child out with an adult he trusted.

Aidan wrapped an arm about him and floated lazily on his back, propelling them along with his feet. He could feel the sun warm on his chest. Eve and Becky, he could see, were no longer in the water. They were in full sunlight on the bank, the dog settled beside them. Eve was pulling the child's dry dress on over her head, presumably having first removed the wet shift. She had no such comfort herself, foolish woman. Her dress clung wetly to her, looking rather like a second skin. She would have looked no less modest swimming in her shift.

Would this all seem like a dream when he was back with his battalion? he wondered. As painless and insubstantial as a dream? He quite fervently hoped so. But what dream would he dream for the rest of his life, to give him the hope all people needed in the future? His dream for the past several years had been a modest one—a home, a wife, a family after he had finally set his career behind him. Even the more recent dream had been hardly less modest—a continuation of his career, Miss Knapp as his wife, sharing his life. He had not loved her, had not expected ever to do so. All he had dreamed of was comfort and contentment. Would there ever be another dream? *Could* there ever be another?

Suddenly the sun felt a little less warm, the water a little colder.

The Reverend Thomas Puddle came to dinner that evening, invited by Aunt Mari, who had assured him that Eve would be delighted and would in fact be disappointed if he did not come.

Eve was indeed delighted. While she had been spending more time with Becky and Davy and Aidan, the vicar had been spending more with Thelma and Benjamin, and that very afternoon he had come to the point and offered Thelma marriage.

"I begged him to think again," Thelma told Eve, "to consider what it would mean to his position, his family, his parishioners, but he would take no for only one reason, he told me, and that was if I truly did not love him and wish to marry him. I could not lie to him, Eve. I adore him with all my heart. So does Benjamin."

Eve's only response was to hug her.

"But I have given him only a conditional acceptance." Thelma moved out of Eve's embrace, looking troubled. "You took me in, Eve, when everyone else treated me like some sort of leper. You gave me employment and a home. Becky and Davy still need my services. I would not—"

But Eve silenced her with one raised hand. "There are other governesses," she said. "I will find one. And if I lose *her* to a good man, I will find another. It will be a treat to visit the vicarage and not be forced to walk in the churchyard for the duration of my visit, no matter what the weather."

They both laughed.

"I wish *you* such happiness as I am feeling," Thelma began, but Eve held up her hand again.

"I *am* happy," she said. "I have my home and my family. I have my children. And I have friends and neighbors."

"And Colonel Bedwyn?" Thelma asked.

Eve shook her head. "I daresay he will be leaving within the next day or two. He will wish to see his family again before returning from leave."

It was a cheerful, festive dinner, with a smiling, blushing Thelma and a smiling, blushing Reverend Puddle, and Aunt Mari in fine form, happy for everyone and chattering away about the wedding that must be planned and the wedding assembly and a dozen other happy topics. She was as alert and tireless as any of them.

She was yawning profusely later when Eve went down to the drawing room after her usual hour of reading stories to the children and then tucking them into their beds and kissing them good night. Thelma had left after getting Benjamin to sleep, to walk the Reverend Puddle home—a sheer romantic absurdity, of course, since it must be perfectly plain even to an idiot that he was then going to have to walk *her* back home. Aunt Mari was alone with Aidan.

"The sun and heat today and all the excitement over Thelma and the vicar have quite done me in," she complained. "I'm off to bed early. So you needn't remain indoors to entertain me any longer, Colonel. Here is Eve come back from the nursery. Why don't the two of you go out for a walk on such a lovely evening?"

Ah, she was matchmaking to the end, Eve thought as Aidan got to his feet, helped Aunt Mari to hers, and handed her her cane.

"A good idea, ma'am," he said. "We will do it if Eve is not too tired."

Aunt Mari smiled merrily as she lifted her cheek for Eve's good night kiss.

Muffin, who had appeared to be fast asleep by the hearth just a moment before, scrambled to his feet and wagged his tail hopefully. Someone had mentioned the word *walk*.

They strolled toward the dell, crossing the lawn to the lily pond, pausing there for a while to look at the lilies and trail their hands in the cool water, and finally wound their way among the trees and down the steepening slope toward the brook. Muffin bobbed along with them, sometimes ahead, sometimes behind, sometimes coming to snuffle at Eve's skirt.

"What is the story of that dog?" Aidan asked when they were at the lily pond.

"He belonged to one of my tenants," she said, "a man whose lease I refused to renew because he was violent with his workers. He left Muffin behind, horribly, horribly maimed and abused. One can guess from the look of him now some of what he suffered—though he looks very much better than he did when I first saw him. Everyone thought it would be kindest to shoot him, but I would not allow that. I wanted him to have an experience of gentleness and love first, even if it became necessary to release him later from his pain. But he recovered as much as he ever can recover. Certainly he no longer cowers and whimpers whenever someone strange comes near him."

"One of your lame ducks," he said, seating himself on the low wall. There was no harshness in the accusation.

"Yes," she agreed. "One of my precious lame ducks." She bent to scratch Muffin's good ear.

She could not erase from her mind the sight of Aidan this afternoon laughing with Davy and teasing him. And of Davy himself, helpless with childish glee. The two somber men of her life, laughing and playing.

"And is Ned Bateman another?" he asked.

"Ned? Has he told you, then?" she asked.

"Yes," he said. "You are to buy land for him and an indeterminate number of maimed and wounded discharged soldiers so that they can set up their own farm and perhaps workshops too, and they are to pay you back in installments."

"Not lame ducks, then," she said. "They are going to pay me back. They are going to be independent. I only wish I could help more. There are going to be thousands of such men, are there not, now that the wars are over? Men without jobs? Men without their health and often without one or more limb?"

"Have you considered this thoroughly?" he asked. "Have you had a lawyer advise you? Are you having one handle the business and the details of the loan?"

"I trust Ned," she told him.

"I am sure you do," he said. "And it is certain he trusts you. But it would be better, and all concerned would be far happier if this thing were done properly and legally. Let me find a good lawyer for you."

"No—" She frowned.

"Let me get Wulf to find you one," he said. "Believe me, Eve, the men who will be part of this project will feel far more secure if there are papers, if they know exactly what is what."

"Will they?" she asked doubtfully.

"Believe me," he said. "Let me ask Wulf."

She nodded. She knew so little about good business practices. Perhaps it would not hurt to turn for advice to men who knew more, especially when they were her relatives, one her husband, one her brother-in-law.

"Eve," he said, "I have sometimes spoken with irritation and even contempt of your lame ducks. I am sorry about that. I honor your generosity and your love for all creatures, no matter their looks or their station in life or their history. Knowing you has been a humbling experience. I thank you for it."

She did not know what to say though she stood and stared at him for some time. When had he become so very dear to her? Was there a single moment? But she did not think so. It had crept up on her unawares, this love, this pain. She turned without a word and led the way to the dell.

"This is where I was that morning," she said when they were partway down the slope, "when Charlie came down from the house to tell me that I had a visitor—a *military* gentleman—and I thought it must be Percy. I was gathering bluebells with Thelma and the children while Aunt Mari guarded the picnic basket."

The bluebells were all long gone. So were the azaleas. But the dell was beautiful at any time of the day or year. It was lovely now, all deep green in the early twilight, the sky a deepening blue above the tree branches, the brook golden with the rays of the setting sun.

"And you came," he said, "not knowing what awaited you."

"No." She sat down almost on the spot where they had picnicked that day, and wrapped her arms about her knees. He sat beside her, and Muffin bobbed down to the brook and snuffled about among the stones.

"You are wonderful with the children," she said. "I have never heard Davy laugh until today. I think you must have had a happy childhood, Aidan. Did you?"

"Oh, yes, indeed," he said. "Our parents worshipped each other and loved us all unconditionally. We played and fought together with energy and abandon. We were hellions."

She still knew so very little about him. She was hungry for knowledge—now, before it was too late.

"The duke too?" she asked. "Did you play with him too?"

"With Wulf?" He draped one arm over his knee and gazed down the slope at the brook. "Yes, the two of us were very close as boys. Almost inseparable, in fact. I adored him. He was bold and daring and mischievous. I followed him happily into every conceivable scrape."

It was something she could not even imagine.

"What *happened?*" she asked him.

He shook his head slightly, as if coming out of some reverie. "Life happened," he said. "I said our father loved us unconditionally. That is not strictly true, I suppose. He was the Duke of Bewcastle and therefore bound by the duties and responsibilities of his position. Wulf was his heir, and he was having health problems. Wulf had to be trained from the age of twelve to take over those duties and responsibilities after his death. And so he was separated from the rest of us to all intents and purposes and put very much under the strict control of two tutors and our father himself. Poor Wulf." He had gone into his reverie again. "Poor Wulf."

"Why so?" she asked softly.

"He hated being heir," he said. "He hated the land and the thought of being bound to it and to the family as its head. He hated the idea of having no choices at all in his life. He wanted adventure and freedom. He wanted a military career. He pleaded and pleaded with our father—until he accepted reality."

This was the man she now knew as the Duke of Bewcastle? Could it possibly be true? But it must be.

"You both wanted military careers?" she asked.

"No." He was silent for a while. Eve could hear birds singing an evening chorus from their hidden perches among the trees. "No, that was the irony of our lives. I was the one born for the military—the second son—but I fought against my fate all through my childhood and boyhood. I abhorred violence. I loved the land. I loved Lindsey Hall. We used to plot together, Wulf and I, when we were very young lads, to dress up in each other's clothes, to exchange identities, to exchange lives. We looked enough alike, we thought, to fool everyone. We must have been *very* young at the time."

Eve suddenly remembered a moment from the morning, when they had approached a fallow field and Aidan had explained to Davy how and why it had been left uncultivated. He had stooped down and taken up a handful of freshly turned earth and shown it to Davy. *This is life, lad,* he had said. *This is the stuff from which all life comes.* And he had closed his hand about the earth, squeezed it hard, and closed his eyes tightly for a moment.

I loved the land.

"Did your father insist that you have a military career, then," she asked, "even though it was against your wishes?"

"I believe I was his favorite," he said. "I used to follow him around like a puppy, much as Davy has been doing with me. He was very involved with the workings of his farms. I learned from him and with him. I drank it all in. I wanted to spend my life doing what he did. I believe he was coming to realize that his choice of career for me was not in my best interests after all. But he died."

"Then what happened?" She frowned.

"I was fifteen when he died," he said. "Wulf was seventeen. I was still at school for a few years, but when I left and went home, I carried on where I had left off before our father died. I busied myself about farm business. I considered Wulf's steward unimaginative, even incompetent. I offered—" He stopped abruptly and Eve thought he would not continue. "Foolish boy that I was, I thought that if I explained everything to Wulf, everything that was wrong with the running of the farms, and offered to take the steward's place, he would be grateful. One week later he called me into his library and informed me that he had purchased a commission for me, as our father had always intended."

"Oh," Eve cried. "What unspeakable cruelty!"

"Cruelty?" he said. "I think not. It was Wulf's way of telling me what I needed to know, that there was not room for both of us at Lindsey Hall. Had I stayed, we would have been at daggers drawn for the rest of our lives. He was quite right, you see. There is room for only one master on any estate."

"But you did not want the commission," she said. "Why did you not refuse it?"

"I might have," he said. "But what was the alternative? I had to leave Lindsey Hall. *That* was clear. And I was a Bedwyn, you see. I had been brought up with a strong sense of duty. One of my duties at the age of eighteen was to be obedient to the will of the head of the family. Wulf was not just Wulf, you see. He was the Duke of Bewcastle."

"And so you went."

"And so I went."

All was suddenly very clear to her. Two brothers, very close as children, had been driven asunder by circumstances, leaving one with power over the other. Each of them had wanted the other's life, but circumstances had made it impossible for them to make the exchange. And so life—the realities of life—had driven an irrevocable wedge between them, destroying or at least submerging the love they had once felt for each other and making one of them cold and dutiful, the other harsh and dutiful.

If she had ever thought of the privileged life of the aristocracy as easy—and she probably had—she changed her mind at that moment. Aristocrats were perhaps less free than anyone else in England. It was a strange realization.

"But you became reconciled to your life?" she asked him.

He turned his head to look directly at her. The twilight was deepening, but she could still see the harsh angles of his face quite clearly.

"Oh, yes, of course," he said briskly. "It has been a good career. It still is and will be for years to come. I will end up a general, I daresay."

"Are you looking forward to going back?" she asked.

"Yes, of course," he said again. "It is always pleasant to take leave. I look forward to it—to the relaxation, to seeing England and my family. But I am always more than ready to go back. There is a restlessness that comes from being idle too long. Yes, it will be good to go back."

She felt deeply, horribly wounded. He was ready to go back. He was restless. It would be good to leave her and get his life back to normal. What had she expected? *What had she expected?*

She got to her feet and walked down to the brook, now more silver than gold. Muffin rushed around her for a few moments before going off on his own explorations again. Aidan came to stand beside her.

"This is a beautiful part of the park," he said.

"Yes." It seemed dark in the dell, but looking up she could see that the sky was still blue.

"What happens now, Eve?" he asked her. "After I leave, I mean? Will your life here satisfy you?"

She stooped to pat Muffin's head though he had not

demanded the attention.

"Oh, yes," she said. "I will be wonderfully happy. I have my children, and now they are officially mine. Ringwood and my fortune are indisputably mine. I have my aunt and my friends and neighbors. And you have made all this possible, Aidan. I will always remember you with deep gratitude."

She could no longer see his face as he looked back at her, tall and broad, with very upright military bearing.

"With gratitude," he said softly. "Well, then, I am amply rewarded."

His voice sounded very much as it had that first day and the days following it. She could not detect in it the voice of the man who had laughed with Davy and teased him this afternoon, or the voice that had called Becky sweetheart a few days ago.

She swallowed, her throat and chest suddenly sore with unshed tears. What if she were to blurt out the truth? she wondered. *I love you. Don't leave me. Come back to me. Have children with me. Live happily ever after with me.* She bit her lip lest she give in to the horrifying temptation.

"You have been more than kind," she said after drawing a steadying breath.

It felt final, like a farewell.

"You are chilly," he said as she shivered. "We had better get back to the house.

"Yes."

But a few moments passed before he offered her his arm. As if there were more to say when, of course, there was not.

CHAPTER XXI

❧

The following morning brought with it a special delivery in the form of an invitation to Colonel Bedwyn and Lady Aidan Bedwyn from the Countess of Luff to attend a garden party at Didcote Park two days hence.

"I have no wish to go," Eve said after reading it aloud to her aunt and Aidan at the breakfast table.

"Oh, but you must," her aunt said, clasping her hands to her bosom. "It is the first time you have been invited. Serena will be delighted—you know she has been vowing not to go herself unless you will be there too, my love."

Aidan looked at Eve and raised his eyebrows.

"It is an annual event," she explained. "Very exclusive. Only the best families get invited. The Morrises have never been among their number. Of course, now I am a Bedwyn and eminently respectable."

"And you have been presented to the queen," her aunt added.

"Yes, that too." Eve's eyes were twinkling with amusement. "Last year I was not good enough, but this year I am. I will not go."

"I beg your pardon," Aidan said. "Does the invitation not include me too? What if I wish to attend?"

She grimaced. "You could not possibly. Could you?"

"The thing is, Eve," he said, "that you will be living at Ringwood for the rest of your life. All your neighbors appear to be also your friends—with the exception of Luff and his countess until now. Why not be on good terms with them too if it is possible?"

"The invitation has arrived almost indecently late," she said. "The others were sent out a long time ago. Of course, you called at Didcote Park, and the Duke of Bewcastle himself put in an appearance at the assembly rooms. Suddenly I am a pariah no longer."

"Are you bitter?" he asked.

"No, of course not." She laughed at him.

"Then prove it," he told her. "Accept the invitation—for both of us."

Mrs. Pritchard still had her hands clasped to her bosom. "That's it, Colonel," she said. "You make her see sense. I want to hear all about it down to the smallest little detail when you come home. And a garden party is such a romantic thing, with all sorts of groves and arbors and grottoes for people to disappear into—in couples, of course."

"Why would we want to do that," Eve asked, though Aidan was interested to notice that she blushed, "when it is a social event we would be attending?"

"*Will be* attending," Aidan corrected.

He had promised Davy that they would take his cricket set outside this morning if the weather was still fine—and it was. They would set up the wickets on the lawn, he had said, and he would teach the boy enough of the rudiments of the game that they could play and enjoy themselves. Later he was going to give Davy a riding lesson in the paddock behind the stables, having discovered that he had not yet learned to ride. He excused himself from the breakfast table.

He had had a night of disturbed sleep. He had stayed too long. Oh, not in one way, perhaps. He had helped relax the children after the disturbing experience of being hauled away from their new home by the village constable. He had helped provide them with some pleasant summer experiences, some sense of family and stability. He had redeemed himself in Eve's eyes, he hoped, after his often high-handed behavior in London, so that she would perhaps have kinder memories of him than she would otherwise have had.

But he had stayed too long. He had fallen deeply in love with her and would suffer for a long time after leaving her, he knew. But just last evening, when they had walked down into the dell, she had told him that she would be happy after he had gone and that she would always remember him with gratitude.

Gratitude! The word had cut him as deeply as the ugliest curse would have done. At least there would be passion in a curse. She would always remember him with gratitude.

He was going to have to do the honorable thing and stop delaying his departure, he had decided while he tossed and turned in bed, trying to find some release in sleep. Yet now he had found a reason to stay three more days. But was it reason or excuse? It *was* important for Eve to be fully accepted socially in her neighborhood. But . . .

But there was a cricket game to organize.

He had told her that he would be leaving the morning

after the garden party.

Freyja had written to her, Eve. It was a witty letter, filled with perceptive and rather caustic observations on the people and events involved in the victory celebrations she had attended. But her letter also announced her intention of leaving town and returning to Lindsey Hall. She wondered if Eve would care to join her there for the summer. Eve was firmly determined to stay at home, but Aidan had decided to go and spend what remained of his leave with his two sisters.

"It is time for me to take myself out of your life, Eve," he had said.

"Yes."

"And return to *my* life."

"Yes."

She had been unable to form any other words, but had concentrated upon smiling at him with what she hoped was just the right degree of cheerful acceptance and polite regret. Yes, it *was* time. If he stayed much longer, she surely would not be able to let him go at all, but would disgrace herself by clinging to him and begging him not to leave her.

There were two days left, the first already well advanced after a vigorous game of cricket, in which Eve and Becky took part as well as the Reverend Puddle, who had come to Ringwood on some flimsy excuse and proved himself to be a very creditable bowler, especially when Aidan was in at bat. Thelma, Benjamin, and Aunt Mari formed an enthusiastic cheering section, applauding both sides indiscriminately. So when Aidan told Eve that he would be leaving, there were really just one and a half days left, to be followed by the garden party day. And then . . .

Eve concentrated upon enjoying to the full what time was left, cramming it with as many activities as she could dream up, trying desperately to live for the present moment and not look ahead to a time that would come soon enough anyway.

She and Becky watched Aidan give Davy a riding lesson in the paddock. When the boy looked reasonably confident, Eve suggested that they all go riding, and they did, Davy's pony on a leading-rein held by Aidan, who settled Becky up before him on the saddle, Eve riding her horse alongside. Later they went strolling through the wilderness walk and ended up playing a game of hide-and-seek among the trees and bushes, the children's shouts of laughter and merriment betraying their hiding places every time.

They played cricket and rode again on the second day and later took a picnic tea down into the dell with Aunt Mari, Thelma, the vicar, and Benjamin. Before tea all of them except Aunt Mari walked one behind the other along the middle of the brook, Benjamin astride the Reverend Puddle's shoulders, stepping from one stone to another, their arms out to the sides for balance— even Muffin ventured off the bank to search for fish. There was an occasional exclamation from one of them as a stone was missed and a shod foot was immersed in the water, and laughter from the others. After tea they sang—led by Eve and Aunt Mari, who added a rich contralto harmony to Eve's soprano. Aidan commented in apparent disgust that he might have known two

Welsh ladies would burst into song sooner or later—and then he joined in with a very creditable baritone harmony. The others added their voices with varying degrees of musicality.

On the morning of the garden party, they took Aunt Mari driving along country lanes and stopped to pick her so many wildflowers—Eve and the children did the picking—that she looked rather like a flower bush that had sprouted a head, according to Aidan. There was a great deal of chatter and laughter, a fair share of it coming from Davy, Eve was delighted to notice. He had blossomed into a little boy during the past week. How was Aidan's departure going to affect him? But she would not think of that today. Tomorrow would be soon enough. By this time tomorrow . . .

For a moment she felt as if the bottom were falling out of her stomach.

Despite herself Eve was rather excited to be attending the garden party at Didcote, about which she had heard so much in past years. And this year the weather was perfect for an outdoor entertainment. It was sunny and hot with just a slight breeze to provide some welcome coolness. Eve wore a pretty sprigged muslin dress with a flower-trimmed straw bonnet, both part of her newly acquired wardrobe, neither of which had been worn before. Aidan was dressed smartly, though not in his uniform.

The terrace before the house was decked with a profusion of brightly colored flowers in large pots. There were tables in the shade, covered with crisp white cloths and laden with large jugs of lemonade and stronger drinks and plates of small delicacies, both savory and sweet. Smart, liveried footmen waited behind the tables to assist guests with their choices. Huge pots of flowers had been set out on the newly cut lawns too, and a few smaller ones had been hung from tree branches. Tables and chairs had been set out, some beneath the shade of trees, some in the sunshine but with umbrellas to provide protection from the sun. Some colorful blankets had been spread on the grass for those who preferred to recline more at their ease.

There were already a number of guests present when Eve and Aidan arrived, some sitting, others strolling or standing in groups, conversing. A few of the more energetic were playing bowls on a flat side lawn. Two couples with racquets were hitting a ball back and forth across a net that had been set up beside the bowling green. The Earl and Countess of Luff were standing on the terrace, receiving newcomers.

So was John.

"Oh, no," Eve said involuntarily as she spotted him from the carriage window.

Aidan followed the line of her vision. "I suppose," he said, "that if you are to be in social contact with your neighbors at Didcote Park, you will inevitably be in contact too with Denson from time to time. It is not something you can avoid forever."

"It was your idea," she reminded him, "that I come here, Aidan. I would have preferred to stay at home."

"One cannot always run and hide from life," he said. "It is best never even to try, but simply to face what

353

must be faced."

There was no time to say more. The carriage drew to a halt, Sam Patchett jumped down from his place on the box to open the door and set down the steps, and the next moment Eve was smiling and curtsying and being presented by the Earl of Luff to the countess and his son.

"I am to congratulate you on your marriage, Lady Aidan," the countess said graciously, "and your connection with Bewcastle and the Bedwyns. You are on an extended leave from your military duties, Colonel Bedwyn?"

"A leave of two months, ma'am," he said, "rapidly coming to an end, I am afraid."

"I had the honor of attending Lady Aidan's presentation ball at Bedwyn House, Mother," John said, his smile directed fully at Eve. "One would have to say that during her short stay in town she became all the rage."

Serena Robson, having spotted Eve across the lawn, came hurrying up at that moment, both hands extended.

"You have arrived," she said, kissing Eve's cheek. "Do come and join James and me beneath that beech tree. You too, Colonel. I have hardly set eyes on either of you since your return from London. I want to hear all about it. Every juicy morsel."

They sat beneath the tree for half an hour, sipping cool drinks while Eve gave an account of her presentation to the queen and Aidan added with dry humor the details of the black gown and his family's reaction to it. After that the men wandered away to watch the bowling and Serena looked after them, sighing.

"He is not handsome, Eve, is he?" she said. "But he is undeniably distinguished looking and—oh, yes, indeed he is. He is a quite extraordinarily *attractive* man. James and I have been delighted that you have spent time together after all, both in town and here. He came back here to help you rescue those poor children, and rumor has it that he has been taking them about with him and even *playing* with them in the days since. Is there any hope—"

"He is leaving tomorrow," Eve said quickly. "He has so little time left in England. He needs to spend what remains with his sisters at Lindsey Hall."

Serena leaned across the table to set a hand over hers, but they were interrupted by a new arrival.

"May I join you ladies?" John asked.

"But of course," Serena said, indicating one of the empty chairs. "Please do."

"There is no place to compare with England in beauty, you know," he said, "especially the English countryside on a warm summer day. Sometimes it takes a year away in a foreign land, though, to make one fully appreciate that fact."

"You have been in Russia," Serena said. "You must tell us some of your experiences with polite society there. Is it elegant, refined, sophisticated?"

Eve listened to him as he talked, to his light, pleasant voice, and she looked at his handsome face with its perfect features and white teeth and the beginnings of laugh lines at the corners of his eyes. She watched his hands, slim, expressive, well manicured. He knew how to please and how to charm. She noticed how other ladies were aware of him and kept glancing at him, his blond hair bright and gleaming even beneath the shade of the tree.

Was it any wonder that, lonely and inexperienced as she had been, she had fallen in love with him? How much substance, though, had there been to her love? There could not have been much, surely, if she could so easily have fallen out of love with him and into love with Aidan. But perhaps that was unfair to herself. Love needed to be fed and nurtured if it was to flourish and grow. John had not been here for longer than a year to feed her love.

Neither would Aidan be here after tomorrow. Would she fall out of love with him too, then?

Mrs. Rutledge had joined them and was talking to Serena about some matter related to the church. John stood up.

"Lady Aidan," he said, "would you care for a stroll?"

Aidan, she saw at a glance, was in his shirtsleeves, wielding one of the racquets.

"Thank you," she said, getting to her feet. But she ignored his offered arm, and clasped her hands behind her back.

"Eve," he said as they set off across the lawn. "Eve, my dear, how is it that you look even more beautiful than ever?"

How did one answer such a question? She did not even try.

"I did not expect to see you here today," she said. "I thought you were busy with the victory celebrations."

He shrugged. "They grow stale," he said. "I wanted to see you. I thought Bedwyn might be gone by now. But he is leaving tomorrow? I overheard you say so to Mrs. Robson."

"Yes," she said.

"Poor Eve," he said softly, steering the way toward a long tree-lined avenue, at the end of which was an octagonal summer house. "Forced to make a marriage of convenience with a Bedwyn. They are a dour, humorless, emotionless lot, are they not? But no matter. He will be gone soon. I will be here for the rest of the summer to comfort you."

"There is no comfort you can offer me, John," she said.

"Ah, Eve," he said, looking down at her, "we were always friends, were we not?"

"Yes, we were," she agreed. She had always found him easy to talk to, easy to listen to. She had liked him long before she had loved him.

"We will be friends again, then," he said. "We will meet again as we have always met when I have been at home. We will be companions and friends through the summer."

"I think not, John," she said. "Even if we had not become more than friends I would think it impossible for us to continue such a friendship, clandestine as it was and clandestine as it would have to remain. But we *did* become more than friends."

They both smiled and nodded at a couple who passed them on their way back from the summer house to the main lawn. John exchanged a few pleasantries with them.

"You are a little upset now," he said when they resumed their walk, "because you were forced into your marriage and believe that therefore all is at an end between us. Nothing could be farther from the truth. We will be friends again—indeed, we have never stopped being friends, have we? And we will be lovers again, Eve."

She looked sharply at him. He was smiling warmly back at her.

"Tell me," she said. "I have wondered, though I believe I know the answer. Did you ever have any intention of marrying me?"

"Yes," he said without hesitation. "In my dreams I did, Eve. I love you dearly. Please believe that. Please never doubt it. My thoughts turn to you more often than is good for me. I believe I will always love you— always, even after I am married myself and have produced heirs satisfactory to my father. But no, in the realm of reality there could have been no marriage between us. You knew that as well as I did, even though you are the love of my life."

Had she known? Had her love for him made her suppress the truth, even from herself? No, No, she had not. How incredibly trusting and naive she had been. But the thing was, she realized, that John had not meant to deceive her. Not really. He had been playing a game of dreams and had assumed she knew the rules and played along with him. He was no villain. He was just not the man she had thought him, the man she had thought she loved. But then, she was not the woman he had thought her either.

It had been an illusion, all of it.

"A shallow love," she said. "You had been two months back in England before I knew of it, and then I discovered it quite by accident. You did not know who Aidan's bride was when you came to the ball at Bedwyn House."

"I paced the streets of London all that night after I *did* know," he told her. "I thought I would lose my mind, Eve."

But why?" she asked him. "You had no intention of marrying me anyway."

"I hate the thought of someone else touching you," he said. "*Has* he touched you, Eve? He is your husband, but it *is* a marriage of convenience. Please tell me—"

"John." Eve had stopped walking though they had not yet come up to the summer house. "My marriage is none of your concern. None whatsoever. Neither is my life. We were friends. We were lovers. Past tense. Even the friendship is past tense. There can be nothing between us ever again. Not ever."

"He is going away, Eve," he said, standing and gazing at her, a frown marring his perfect features. "He will forget you within a few days. You will probably never see him again. You will change your mind. You—"

"I will not change my mind," she told him. "I am married to him, John. For better, for worse, until death parts us. I choose to be loyal and faithful in every way."

"You will change your mind after a while," he said. "Eve, my dear, remember what has been between us for years now. Remember the last time we were together before I went to Russia. It was very, very good."

It had not been. Not physically. But that had nothing to do with anything at this moment.

"I am going back to the terrace for a drink," she said. "I would rather go alone. Good-bye, John. I wish you happy."

"I will be," he assured her, smiling again. "With you, Eve. I'll give you a week or two."

Fortunately he did not accompany her back up the long avenue. She did not go to the terrace for a drink after all. Aidan had finished his game, she could see, and was pulling his coat back on. She went to join him.

"Did you win?" she asked.

"I always win," he said, looking keenly at her. "We will get something to eat and sit down somewhere."

They sat side by side on a wrought iron bench beside a little fish pond rather than join a group.

"I went walking with Viscount Denson," she told him.

"I know."

She took a bite out of a lobster patty and then did not know quite how she was to turn it over in her mouth. He said no more.

"Do you not want to know," she asked him, "what we talked about?"

"It would seem," he said, "that you wish to tell me. But shall I make it easier for you? He wishes to continue the acquaintance. He wishes to resume your affair. He wants you to be his mistress. He has always loved you and always will."

It was all so uncannily accurate that she merely stared at him.

"I said no," she told him. "No to everything."

"That too I could have predicted," he said. "You are an honorable woman, Eve. You will not see me after tomorrow, but you will live a celibate life rather than be unfaithful to me, will you not?"

She wondered suddenly if there were any truth in that old romantic notion that a heart could break. "Would you care," she asked him, "if I did not?"

He turned his head to look at her. His eyes were almost black and totally unfathomable.

"I will not be here to care either way, Eve," he said. "You must live your life as you see fit. I will not be your conscience for you."

She set down her plate on the bench between them, knowing that she could eat no more. Her hands, she noticed, were not quite steady. She raised her eyes to his and realized when she could not see him clearly that she was very close to weeping. She had not demanded his love. All she had wanted was some small indication that he *cared* about her fidelity.

"Excuse me," she said, rising hastily and heading in the direction of one of the large pots of flowers, which she stood apparently examining until she was sure her eyes were clear enough to allow her to mingle with her neighbors.

You will not see me after tomorrow . . .

I will not be here to care either way . . .

Yes, surely hearts could break. After tomorrow surely hers would.

CHAPTER XXII

I always win.

It was what he had said to her after the game, but he had not been referring to the game. He was not even sure it was true. _Did_ he always win? He had always won the battle with his honor, he supposed. When he had realized his mistake at Lindsey Hall back when he was eighteen and had thought he could run the estate for Bewcastle, he had been ashamed of himself and the way he must have upset Wulf, who was new to his position and undoubtedly knew less at that time about estate management than Aidan did. He could have resisted Wulf's decision to purchase a commission for him. His brother could not have forced him into the military, especially as he was independently wealthy and did not rely for support upon his elder brother. But he had done the honorable thing and stepped into a career the very thought of which had horrified him.

Ever since then honor had been his guiding light— culminating in his marriage to Eve this very summer.

Yes, he had always won any conflict with honor.

But did that make him a winner? A winner of happiness?

Was there such a thing as happiness?

They stayed to the end of the garden party, mingling with the guests, never together after that encounter on the bench by the fish pond. Eve was smiling and animated and suddenly became as much the focus of admiring attention as she had been for that brief week in London. Perhaps she was simply enjoying herself, Aidan thought. Perhaps her spirits were buoyed by the fact that tomorrow he would be leaving, never to return.

But there had been those tear-filled eyes she had raised to him before rushing away to examine the flowers in the closest flower pot.

There were those tears.

Tomorrow he would win another battle by doing the honorable thing and leaving her.

But what would he win thereby?

Honor, of course.

But happiness?

What about *her* happiness? Was he so intent upon honor that he was ignoring what might just be staring him in the face? But what if he was mistaken? What had those tears meant?

They traveled home in silence, watching the passing scenery from opposite windows. Tomorrow he was to leave. Did she have nothing more to say to him? Did he have nothing more to say to her?

What was the meaning of your tears?

He thought for a moment that he had spoken the words aloud. But his lips were still closed and she made no response.

It was an enormous relief to Aidan when the carriage finally passed between the gateposts of Ringwood and made its way up the driveway to the house. Tomorrow would be a relief too, when he finally rode away and everything was finally over.

Did he dare risk his honor? he wondered. Did he dare grasp at happiness?

When Eve went up to the nursery after dinner, Aidan went with her. He sat with Becky on his lap, listening to the nightly stories, and then he told the children he would be leaving in the morning. He would write to them, he promised, and send them gifts from every new place he went. They must take care of Aunt Eve and learn their lessons well and grow up to be a fine lady and gentleman. He kissed them both. Becky clung to his neck and even shed a few tears. Davy was more his old quiet, contained self, but he allowed Aidan to tuck him into his bed and smooth a hand over his hair.

"I will not forget you, lad, just because I will not be here," he said. "I will always . . . love you."

"Nobody ever stays," the boy said softly, his voice devoid of expression.

"Aunt Eve is staying," Aidan said, "and Aunt Mari and Becky and Nanny. And you will be staying for them. I'll write, Davy. I promise."

The boy turned onto his side and covered his head with the blankets. Aidan left his room and the nursery—Eve was still busy in Becky's room. He went down to the drawing room, still wondering if he would grasp for the moon. The housekeeper was hovering outside the room, looking her usual sour self.

"I am to tell you," she said, "from Mrs. Pritchard that she has gone to her bed because she is tired and you are not to stay inside on her account."

Aidan folded his hands at his back and gazed broodingly at the housekeeper. "Agnes," he said, making a sudden decision, "fetch me some towels, will you? And a blanket?"

"Why?" She eyed him suspiciously.

There was not another servant of Aidan's acquaintance who would answer a direct order with the single word *why*.

"Not your business, Agnes," he said, keeping his voice stern, though his spirits were beginning to lift with a certain excitement now that it appeared he had taken the first step. "Fetch them. Preferably within the next few minutes."

She crossed her large arms over her chest.

"Don't you go breaking my lamb's heart any more than it is already broke," she said. "I am not afraid to take you on, I'm not, though I know I couldn't beat you even if I had a pistol in each hand and a dagger between my teeth."

Aidan smiled at her. "Agnes," he said, "I could hug you, but I doubt it would be a delightful experience for either of us. Her heart is broken, is it? By me? Fetch those towels and that blanket, woman, and let us have no more insubordination. I might have to have you court-martialed."

Her eyes squinted even more and her lips pursed. Then she nodded curtly, turned on her heel, and disappeared. She reappeared in the drawing room a mere couple of minutes later with the requested towels and two blankets.

"Even these nights can get coolish," she said, "once it gets past midnight. And I assume it *is* going to get past midnight?"

"I hope so, Agnes," he said as she set the pile down on the end of a sofa.

"You're not so bad looking when you smile," she astounded him by observing just as she was leaving the room. "But don't you waste no more of them on me. You give them to my lamb."

He grinned at the closed door and then sobered instantly. Why was he feeling so lighthearted? What if he was about to sacrifice his honor?

The door opened and Eve came inside, smiling, as pale as a ghost, looking about for her aunt.

"She has gone to bed," he said. "We are going out, you and I. We are going swimming."

"Swimming?" She looked blankly at him.

"In the river," he said. "And you will not have the excuse of no towel this time. There are a few." He nodded at the pile on the sofa.

"All those?" She frowned.

"Two of them are blankets," he said.

"Blankets?"

"One to lie on on the bank," he said. "Agnes assures me we may need the other for warmth if we are out after midnight. She may be right. We are going to swim, and then we are going to make love unless you can assure me that it is something you definitely do not want. And then . . ." But he had lost his nerve. "And then we will see."

"Aidan." For a moment color had tinged her cheek-bones, but now she was pale again. She drew breath to speak, but merely shook her head and was quiet.

He strode over to the sofa, scooped up the blankets

and towels, tucked them under one arm, and held out his free hand for hers.

"Come," he said.

For several moments he thought she was going to say no. She stood staring at his hand and then, at last, slowly raised her own to set in his.

"One last night?" she said.

"One last dream."

He had remembered the stretch of the river she had pointed out to him as the secluded place where she and Percy had sometimes swum in the summers. He led the way there unerringly in the darkness. Not that it was very dark. The moon was almost full, and it beamed down on them with a million bright stars. They did not talk on the way. She clung to his hand, memorizing the feel of it, the warmth and strength of it.

What had he meant—*one more dream?*

Her heart had been so constricted with the pain of unshed tears when she left the nursery that she had hardly known how to put on a cheerful face as she entered the drawing room.

"Here," he said when they were among the trees down by the river, in rather heavy darkness now, though the river gleamed in a wide silver band to their left. "This is the spot." He dropped her hand and his bundle, and then shook out one of the blankets and spread it on the ground.

They were going to swim—and then *they were going to make love.* Would she be insane enough not to protest?

"Come here," he said, reaching for her hand again and drawing her close.

He reached around her for the buttons at the back of her dress and undid them one by one. He drew her dress over her shoulders and down her arms, and let it fall in a pool at her feet—it was another of her new gowns, chosen carefully for this final evening, but not for abandonment on the riverbank. He was drawing her shift up her body.

"Lift your arms," he said.

"Aidan—" she protested in some shock.

"You told me yourself," he said, "that no one can see you here even in daytime. Swimming is not nearly as enjoyable an activity if it is not done naked."

What was it about his voice? It was unmistakably his even though there was not quite enough light beneath the trees to verify his identity with her eyes. But there was something about it. Something—boyish. Something one just did not associate with Colonel Lord Aidan Bedwyn.

Well, why not? she thought, lifting her arms. *Why not?* A few moments later she was naked and he was peeling off his own clothes and tossing them down beside the blanket in a manner to give his batman heart palpitations if he could see.

And then he caught her by the hand again and drew her in the direction of the river. He had no intention of stopping at the edge of the bank, she realized at the last moment. She drew and held a deep breath, closed her eyes, and jumped.

The shock of the cold water took her breath away so

that even after she surfaced Eve had to fight for breath as she trod water. The river was deeper here than it was farther up, where they had bathed with the children.

"I would rather have done that gradually," she said, spreading her arms along the water.

"Nonsense!" He laughed. "Agony by slow inches is far worse than agony by a swift yard. Look, Eve. Look at the water all awash with moonlight. And look at the stars. Feel the cool water—it is not at all cold once one is used to it, is it? And the warm air. Smell the trees and the wildflowers. Is it not good to be alive?"

"Yes." She looked around and breathed in deeply.

"And to have someone with whom to share one's exuberance?" he said.

"Yes."

She stopped questioning his mood. She accepted it. She began to swim a slow and leisurely crawl along the center of the river, and he kept pace beside her as the sounds of their breathing and lapping water and night birds calling or cooing among the trees soothed her spirits. After they had swum some distance he turned onto his back to return the way they had come, and she did likewise. They did not use their arms but merely kicked their feet to propel themselves slowly along.

"How many do you think there are?" he asked her.

"Stars?" she said. "Thousands? Millions? Where does it all end? I wonder. It must end somewhere, must it not? All things end."

"Perhaps," he said, "the universe does not. It is an idea the human mind cannot grasp. All things must end, as you have just said. But what if some things do not,

Eve? What if the universe does not? What if . . . what if other things do not? We would have proved the existence of the divine, would we not?"

How absurd, she thought suddenly. Here they were, two respectable adults, out swimming naked after dark, speculating about infinity and divinity. Trying to stretch their human minds so that they could conceive of something that had no end. Love, perhaps? Was that what he had been about to say? One could not imagine Aidan saying such things about love, but he was in a strange mood tonight.

They swam for more than an hour, sometimes with energy and speed, sometimes so lazily that they did little more than float. Once he dived unexpectedly beneath her and pulled her under so that she came up sputtering and had to get instant revenge by pounding her hands flat on the water and making it impossible for him to clear his eyes. They laughed with glee, just like carefree children. And then he caught her to him, imprisoning her arms to her sides, shook the water from his eyes, and kissed her.

"It is time to dry ourselves off before the wrinkles in our skin become permanent," he said. "And then it is time to make love. Unless you do not want it."

The moment of truth. But of course, there had never been any doubt in her mind from the start, only the conviction that there *ought* to be doubt, that she was going to increase tomorrow's pain beyond the point at which it could be borne. But she was already beyond that point, anyway.

"I want it," she said.

"Ah." He sighed and kissed her again—and then lifted her bodily out of the water and deposited her shivering on the bank.

"Brrr," she said and ran for the towels.

He came after her.

He had never made love before. Not *love*. He had had sex numerous times and with numerous women. He had even felt some affection for some of them. But he had never before made love.

He was terrified.

He had never given himself. Not *himself.* Not since childhood, anyway. Or perhaps not since that time when at the age of eighteen he had gone to Wulf, all eagerness and brotherly love, to outline his ideas for Lindsey Hall and all the other ducal estates and to offer to implement them in person. Since then he had performed his duty—always, scrupulously, honorably, and impersonally. In all the twelve years since he had become an officer, he had never given himself.

He was terrified.

What if it embarrassed her, even distressed her to be offered the free gift of himself and his love? It certainly had been no part of their original bargain. But neither had anything else that had happened since their wedding. This afternoon she had looked at him with tears in her eyes before hurrying away from him. He could remember exactly what words he had spoken to her just before she left.

I will not be here to care either way.

The words had upset her.

He lay down beside her on the blanket, wrapped his arms about her, and drew her against him. Her body was cool from the water, as was his own. Her mouth, when he found it and opened it with his own and penetrated it with his tongue, was hot. She splayed one hand against his chest, twined the other arm about his waist, and pressed herself against him. Heat flared between them almost instantly. She was, he realized, as hungry for him as he was for her, and every bit as ready. There was no need for foreplay.

"Come on top of me," he said against her mouth. "The ground is hard and I am heavy."

"No." She rolled onto her back, drawing him with her. "I want it this way. Please?"

Her legs parted as he came over her and twined tightly about his.

"Eve." He whispered against her lips, holding the bulk of his weight on his forearms, his hands cradling her face. "You are ready?"

"Yes. Come to me," she whispered back. "Come to me, Aidan. Please."

He thrust gratefully into her. She was hot and wet. Her inner muscles clenched about him, almost driving him over the brink of control.

"Easy," he murmured to her. "Let us hold off on the physical for a while. Let us love. Relax if you can."

Although his eyes had grown accustomed to the darkness, they were lying in the shade of the trees, and her face was further shadowed by his own. He could not see her, but he could feel her understanding and responding. Her inner muscles relaxed, and she untwined her legs from about his and set her feet flat on the ground on either side of him.

He moved in her.

He made love to her. Consciously, with every stroke giving her tenderness, giving her himself. Aware with every beat of the rhythm of sex that a deep, powerful, all-encompassing, unifying emotion could accompany and even surpass the familiar physical need and the knowledge that at any moment, whenever he wished, he could bring that to full pleasure and satiety.

He made love to her. Slowly, thoroughly, aware of *her,* of the silky feel of her skin, of the smell of her wet hair and of her very essence, of the inside of her body where she had invited and welcomed him, of her breathing and the low sounds she made occasionally deep in her throat. He could not see her, but she was Eve, she was his heart and soul, she was his love.

He was very aware of the moment when he took the final, ultimate risk, laying all before her—his honor, his emotions, his very self.

"Eve," he murmured, his mouth against hers again, "my love. My dearest love. I love you. For all time. For all eternity. It is my love I give you tonight."

"Mmm," she said, deep in her throat again.

But he lost his nerve. He feared that she would speak. He feared the words. He kissed her and deepened the kiss, pressing his tongue deep inside. And at the same moment he quickened and deepened and hardened his rhythm. He lifted his mouth away only when all her muscles clenched and he sensed her moving into climax. He tipped back his head, eyes closed, kept his weight on his arms, and released his seed in her. Even then he did not lose himself. Even then he was aware of her, moaning softly, shuddering with the spasms of her completion, gradually relaxing. Soft, warm, sweat-slick.

He slid free of her, lifted his weight off her, and moved to her side with one arm still about her, grasping the second blanket as he did so, and somehow spreading it one-handed over them both. She sighed and turned onto her side facing away from him, nestling her head against his arm and fitting her back and her bottom and her legs against him.

He gave them both a few minutes to recover. He thought that she might have drifted off to sleep for a few minutes. And then she whispered to him.

"Look at the stars," she said. "They are brighter than ever."

He looked and stroked his fingers through her drying hair.

"Eve," he said, "I am sorry about Denson. Deeply sorry. But—"

"You need not be," she said. "I did love him, Aidan. Or, rather, I was in love with him. But he is not the man I thought he was. Maybe I would never have discovered his essential weakness if we had married, but I believe I would have. He is not a man I could love for a lifetime."

He had not been allowed to deliver his carefully planned speech. He would have to go with the flow of conversation instead, then.

"What sort of man *could* you love for a lifetime?"

he asked her.

She was silent for a while. He guessed that she was considering her answer.

"A kind man," she said. "When we are young and foolish, we do not realize how essential a component of love kindness is. It is perhaps the most important quality. And an honorable man. Always doing the right thing no matter what."

His heart sank—on both counts.

"And a strong man," she said. "Strong enough to be vulnerable, to take risks, to be honest even when honesty might expose him to ridicule or rejection. And someone who would put himself at the center of my world even before knowing that I would be willing to do the same for him. A man foolish and brave enough to tell me that he loves me even when I have hidden all signs that I love him in return."

"Eve—" he said.

"He would have to be tall and broad and dark and hook-nosed," she said. "And frowning much of the time, pretending he is tough and impervious to all the finer emotions. And then smiling occasionally to light up my heart and my life."

Good God!

"He would have to be you," she said. "No one else would do. Which is just as well, considering the fact that I am married to you. You need never fear that I will be untrue to you, Aidan, even if you leave me tomorrow and never return."

He set his face against her shoulder, gulped, and swallowed.

"You meant what you said, did you not?" she asked. "It was not just the passion speaking. You meant it?"

"I meant it," he said against her ear.

"You are braver than I, then," she said, "my mighty, precious warrior. I dared not open myself to your scorn or your pity. But I love you with all my heart. I love you so much it hurts. Aidan, if it were not for the children I would follow the drum with you even if it were for all the rest of my life. But I cannot. I have to put them first. I will write to you every day, though. I will make a home for you to come back to every time you have leave. I—"

"Hush, love," he said. "I am going to sell out. It was part of the speech I started to deliver before you interrupted. I am going to sell out and live here with you."

"Oh, Aidan." She turned over all in a rush to face him, and one of her hands came up to cup his cheek. "I cannot ask that of you. You are going to be a general. There will be honors, titles—"

"You cannot bear to be married to a humble ex-colonel, then?" he asked her. "With only one title, which he has done nothing to earn?"

"Oh, Aidan." She brushed her lips against his.

"You need me here," he said. "You will need someone to manage your farms and estate after your steward has gone off to his new place on that madcap scheme the two of you have concocted. The children need me. They desperately need a father as well as a mother. Aunt Mari needs to have her hopes fulfilled, and Agnes needs someone to fight on a regular, daily basis. And Eve—ah, Eve, my love, I need you. All of you. But *you* most of all, my dearest love. *You.*" He kissed her hard.

"You are going to sell out?" she asked in wonder. "Now?"

"Not at this precise moment," he said. "Since Agnes sent us out here with an extra blanket, it seems to me only polite to make full use of it. I am going to make love to you all night long under the stars. But tomorrow, Eve, I'll go to London and take care of it. At the same time I'll have Wulf recommend a lawyer to deal with that land business. And then I am going to come home to stay."

"Home," she repeated softly.

"If you will have me," he said.

"If—"

She laughed then, and for no apparent reason he joined her. They laughed and hugged and kissed and murmured nonsense to each other.

"The Duke of Bewcastle is going to be furious," she said at last.

"I am not so sure of that," he said. "Not so sure at all. We Bedwyns have always taken marriage very seriously indeed, Eve. Anyone who marries any of us had better be prepared to be loved and cherished for a lifetime."

"I think I can prepare myself for that," she said.

They chuckled again before turning to the more serious business of living their night of love beneath the stars.

CHAPTER XXIII

༇

He was gone for a week. A whole interminable week. He left early on the morning following the garden party. Indeed, after they returned from their night at the river, he merely changed his clothes, saddled his own horse while his sleepy batman did the same for himself, kissed Eve, and rode on his way.

She had told no one that he planned to return even though Aunt Mari was mournful and the children often quiet and lethargic. She dared not tell. Confident as she was in his love and his determination to come back to her, she nevertheless could not shake the anxiety that something would happen to prevent his return. Better that no one knew except her.

She resumed all her activities with renewed energy. She spent more time with her aunt and with the children than she ever had. She threw herself into plans for a grand wedding for Thelma—the first banns were read two days after Aidan left for London. Serena, Aunt Mari, Miss Drabble, and Aunt Jemima—Eve had paid her a personal visit—formed a planning committee with her. Ned Bateman found the first two recruits for his new farm project, both of them men newly returned from the fighting in Europe, one of them with an eye and a hand missing, the other with a leg that had been amputated below the knee, both of them quite destitute.

With every breath she drew Eve lived and breathed Aidan. But she did it in secrecy, not daring to share her happiness lest somehow she kill it.

She had taken the children riding. Davy was determined to master the skill, and of course it was desirable, even necessary that he do so. Sam had given him a few lessons in the paddock, cheered on by Charlie, who had assumed the personal care of Davy's pony, fussing over it, Sam had reported, just as if it were the most prized racing horse in the country.

Eve had taken the children riding, Davy without a leading-rein for the first time, Becky up before Eve's saddle, though the day was not far distant when she too must have a pony and learn to ride.

It was the middle of the afternoon when they rode back into the stableyard and Sam lifted Becky down while Davy dismounted on his own and Charlie checked the pony anxiously for damage. Eve slid down from the saddle and looked up at the sky after scratching the head of Muffin, who had come bobbing to meet her. There were clouds, suggesting that the long hot spell might finally be coming to an end. But they were high and unthreatening for the moment. The somewhat cooler day was actually quite welcome.

"Horses approaching, my lady," Sam said suddenly, cocking his head in a listening attitude.

Aidan! Eve tried not to expect that it really was he, but she hurried to the gateway with the children and saw the two riders approaching with another coming a short distance behind them.

"Uncle Aidan!" The words burst from Davy's lips at the same moment as he started running.

One of the horsemen took a shortcut across the lawn,

and when he was close, he dismounted, laughing, and held out his arms to sweep Davy up in the air.

"Uncle Aidan!" Davy cried again. "You came back. You came back."

Eve clutched Becky's hand and hurried toward them, her heart welling with such happiness that it felt rather as if it would burst.

"I did, lad," Aidan said, hugging Davy tightly before setting him on his feet. "How could I keep away? I am home to stay."

"Papa," Becky whispered. And then she broke away from Eve's grasp and went skipping joyfully toward Aidan, holding out her arms as she went. He picked her up and held her tightly to him, his eyes clenching shut for a moment. "Papa, I have a loose tooth. Look."

Papa.

He looked, giving the child his whole frowning attention while she wiggled the tooth with one finger.

"Indeed you do," he said. "Is my little girl losing her baby teeth already? You are going to be all grown up before we know it. Do you have a kiss for me?"

She puckered her little mouth and offered it to him. He kissed her and then glanced up and held out one arm to Eve. The look on his face made her heart turn over.

"Eve," he said as his arm came about her and she felt the warm solidity of his chest with her hand and then her bosom. "Eve, my dearest love, I am home."

"Yes," she said, and she lifted her face, smiling, while Muffin woofed at her side. Aidan kissed her full on the lips for all to see.

It was only at that moment that she remembered what she had seen from the gateway of the stableyard— Aidan with his batman behind him. *And another rider.* She took a step back, biting her lip and feeling herself flush while Aidan laughed and set Becky down.

"I have my brother with me," he said. "The one you have not met before. Ralf, come and meet Eve." He set an arm about her waist and drew her to his side. "Rannulf is his official name, but he is known as Ralf."

Lord Rannulf Bedwyn had dismounted and had come walking across the lawn. He was almost as tall as Aidan and just as large. He had the family nose. But he was fair like Freyja. When he removed his hat, Eve could see that as with Freyja, his hair was wavy—he wore it unfashionably long. She found herself thinking of Norse warriors.

"Eve," he said, holding out a hand for hers. "I am delighted to make your acquaintance."

He had a powerful grip.

"And I yours," she said.

"These are our children," Aidan said. "Becky and Davy, another uncle for you. Uncle Ralf. And I see Aunt Mari coming down the steps to the terrace. She must have seen me come. Excuse me a moment."

He released his hold on Eve and went striding off in the direction of the terrace. Soon he had Aunt Mari enfolded in his arms while her cane clattered to the cobbles.

"I thought," Lord Rannulf said, "that he would wear out the floors of Bedwyn House during the past week from pacing them so impatiently. Everything proceeded altogether too slowly for Aidan."

"And for me too," Eve admitted, smiling at him. "I am glad you came with him. I'll have a room made ready for you."

"Oh, only for one night," he said as they watched the children follow Aidan onto the terrace. "I am on my way north but could not resist making a stop here to see my new sister-in-law. I have been summoned by our maternal grandmother. She has found just the right bride for me—again. This is the fourth or fifth time, I believe. I will not succumb this time any more than I did the other four or five, since my freedom and perhaps my very sanity are at stake, but I cannot simply ignore the summons. She has made me her heir, you see, and annoying as she can be, I . . . well, I am fond of her. So I will go, Eve, and put my freedom in dire peril once more."

He grinned at her, revealing strong white teeth and blue eyes that danced with merriment and roguery.

"Perhaps," Eve said, "she has chosen wisely for you this time."

"There is, of course, always that possibility," he agreed. "But I have a curious aversion to having my future wife chosen for me—or even to choosing her myself within the next five or six years."

"You must be ready for refreshments," Eve said, leading the way to the house, "and for a rest."

"I will not deny it," her brother-in-law said, falling into step beside her. "If there is something more uncomfortable than riding with a cavalry officer who has lived in the saddle for the past twelve years, it would have to be riding with a man who is on his way to a reunion with his beloved. I sincerely hope no one asks it of me ever again."

Eve laughed.

And then Aidan turned from his conversation with Aunt Mari to watch her come, his eyes alight again with admiration and love. He held out his hand to her when she was close, and she set her own in it and felt his fingers close strongly about it.

"Aunt Mari," he said, "meet my brother, Lord Rannulf Bedwyn. Mrs. Pritchard, Ralf. You may think she is singing when she first speaks. She is Welsh, you know."

"And proud of it too," Aunt Mari said. "You may give me one of those strong arms, young man, and help me inside since Agnes has gone off with my cane. Come along, children."

A few moments later Eve and Aidan were alone on the terrace. He grinned at her.

"I asked her to do that," he said. "It has occurred to me that I never did carry you over any threshold after we were married. What better threshold than our own, and what better time than now, the beginning of our happily ever after?"

"None," she said. "But is there such a thing, Aidan? Happily ever after, I mean?"

"No," he said, his smile softening to tenderness. "There is something infinitely better than happily ever after. There is happiness. Happiness is a living, dynamic thing, Eve, and has to be worked on every moment for the rest of our lives. It is a far more exciting prospect than that silly static idea of a happily ever after. Would you not agree?"

"I would," she said, and then she half shrieked, half laughed, and wrapped her arms tightly about his neck as he scooped her up and twirled her once about before carrying her up the steps and into their house.

Into their home.

Into another dream. No, better than a dream. Into the dynamic, exciting, happy reality they would work on together every day for as long as they both lived.

Center Point Publishing
600 Brooks Road • PO Box 1
Thorndike ME 04986-0001 USA

(207) 568-3717

US & Canada:
1 800 929-9108